Feather
Crowns

Feather Crowns

A NOVEL BY

BOBBIE ANN MASON

HarperCollins*Publishers*

HarperCollins books may be purchased for educational, business, or sales promotional use. For information please write: Special Markets Department, HarperCollins Publishers, Inc., 10 East 53rd Street, New York, NY 10022.

FIRST EDITION

Designed by Alma Hochhauser Orenstein

Library of Congress Cataloging-in-Publication Data

Mason, Bobbie Ann.
    Feather crowns / by Bobbie Ann Mason. —1st ed.
        p.   cm.
    ISBN 0-06-016780-7
    1. Quintuplets—Kentucky—Fiction. 2. Farm life—Kentucky—Fiction.
    3. Family—Kentucky—Fiction. I. Title.
PS3563.A7877F4   1993   92-56227
813'.54—dc20

93 94 95 96 97 ❖/RRD 10 9 8 7 6 5 4 3 2 1

Acknowledgments

I am grateful to the Pennsylvania State Arts Council for support during the writing of this novel. I wish to express my appreciation for helpful advice and source materials to Lon Carter Barton, historian of Western Kentucky, and to Thomas D. Clark, historian laureate of Kentucky. I am grateful for the encouragement and enthusiasm of my agent, Amanda Urban; my editors at HarperCollins, Susan Moldow and Ted Solotaroff; and my editor at *The New Yorker,* Roger Angell. As always, I am especially thankful to my husband, Roger Rawlings, for his moral support and confidence in my writing. And I am forever indebted to my mother, Christianna Lee Mason, for her wisdom and language and love.

In memory of my father,
Wilburn Arnett Mason
(1916–1990)

Contents

I

Birth

February 26, 1900

1

CHRISTIANNA WHEELER, BIG AS A WASHTUB AND CONFINED TO BED all winter with the heaviness of her unusual pregnancy, heard the midnight train whistling up from Memphis. James was out there somewhere. He would have to halt the horse and wait in the darkness for the hazy lights of the passenger cars to jerk past, before he could fly across the track and up the road toward town. He was riding his Uncle Wad's saddle horse, Dark-Fire.

The train roared closer, until it was just beyond the bare tobacco patch. Its deafening clatter slammed along the track like a deadly twister. Christie felt her belly clench. She counted to eight. The pain released. The noise of the train faded. Then the whistle sounded again as the train slowed down near town, a mile away. The contractions were close together now. The creature inside her was arriving faster than she had expected. The first pain had been light, and it awakened her only slightly. She was so tired. She dreamed along, thinking it might be no more than the stir and rumble she had felt for months—or perhaps indigestion from the supper James's Aunt Alma had brought her.

"You have to eat," Alma had told her. "That baby'll starve, though by the looks of you I reckon he could last a right smart while. You've got fat to spare."

"I can't eat butter beans," Christie said. "They're too big."

Alma hooted. "The beans is too big? You keep on with them crazy idies and we'll have to carry you off to the asylum."

"Good," said Christie, making a witch face.

In late December, when the doctor advised Christie to stay in bed, they talked about moving her back up to Alma's house, where the women could take care of her more easily, but Christie wouldn't go.

She had had enough of that place—too many people under one roof. She said she didn't want her children to be in their way. And she didn't want to be waited on like James's Uncle Boone, who wheezed and didn't work. He believed he had TB.

She tried to turn, expecting the pain to come back, but her stomach felt calmer now. Dr. Foote probably wouldn't want to come out this late, she thought, when the clock began to strike midnight.

Alma burst through the back door a few moments later. She hurried through the kitchen into the front room where Christie lay.

"Lands, here I am again." Alma wore enormous shapeless shoes and a big bonnet with a tiny gray-leaf figure that resembled mold seen up close. A woman in a blue bonnet followed her into the room. "Hattie Hurt's here," Alma said. She grunted—her laugh. "It's just like James to run off after the doctor when Hattie was right near. Why, Hattie can dress that baby."

"Babies like to meddle with our sleep right off," said Hattie cheerily. "They don't want to come in the middle of the morning like civilized company." She dropped her leather satchel on a chair and hurled off her coat all in one motion. Then she unbuckled the satchel. "Where's Mrs. Willy?" she asked. "She always beats me to a birthing."

"She went to Maple Grove to see her daughter and grandchillern and didn't say when she'd be back," Alma said.

"Mrs. Willy told me to take calomel when the pains commenced, but I didn't," Christie said.

"You'll feel better when you get this baby out, Christie," said Hattie soothingly.

"It's not a baby."

"She's talking foolishness again," said Alma.

Christie tried to sit up. She was in her front room, or Sunday room. The bed, directly across from the fireplace, was sheltered from the front door by the closed-in stairway to her right. To her left was the kitchen. The door was swung back all the way against the kitchen wall so that the two rooms joined into one. Christie leaned over to the bedside table for a rag, and Alma ran over to help her. Alma was rarely this attentive. Christie didn't want to depend on her, but she was helpless. She had been helpless for weeks, and the condition had made her angry and addled. The children seemed scared of her lately.

"Alma, reach me a drop of water. My lips is parched."

"You done flooded the bed," Alma mumbled. She brought Christie a cup of water and a wet rag, then turned to the kitchen stove to tend the fire. "This water's going to take awhile to boil," Alma said.

"We've got time," said Hattie, busy with her jars and tools. Her apron was freshly starched. It gleamed white as new teeth.

Christie's belly was tight. It needed to loosen up. She tried to knead it, to make it pliable. She thought it might explode. She ran her hands around the expanse—the globe of the world, James had joked. She hadn't needed a doctor for her other babies. It seemed that each time she had a baby her belly stretched and could accommodate a larger one. The second boy had been a pound heavier than the first, and then Nannie was so big she caused a sore that didn't heal for weeks. But what Christie had in her now was more than twice as large as any of the others. She had a thing inside her that couldn't be a baby—it was too wild and violent.

Hattie Hurt had visited several times during the winter, even though they hadn't been able to give her anything more than a ham and some green beans Christie had put up in jars. Dr. Foote was sure to charge more money than they could pay, but James said he'd sell a hog.

"Let me take a look at what's going on down there," said Hattie. "Can you get them drawers off?"

Christie's stomach was quiet now. She loosened her clothes and pushed down her step-ins, one of three enormous pairs she had sewed this winter. James had joked about those too, but she thought he was trying to hide his concern.

Hattie Hurt had strong hands and a gentle, reassuring voice. Her voice reminded Christie of her grade-school teacher, Mrs. Wilkins. Christie still remembered the teacher leading a recitation of short *a*'s: march, parch, starch, harsh, marsh, charm, snarl, spark. She remembered how Mrs. Wilkins moved her jaws in a chewing motion to stress the sound.

Hattie poked around, feeling Christie's abdomen. She examined the place between Christie's legs. "You're pooching out some," she said. "Now just lay back and wait real easy. We don't want to force it too soon."

While Alma worked at the stove, the children still slept. Christie could see Clint and Jewell in the loft, above the kitchen, on a feather bed. She heard them stirring. Nannie was sleeping on a pallet in the corner between the fireplace and the kitchen wall. This winter, because of her pregnancy, Christie and James had shut off their north bedroom and slept close to the brick fireplace in the front room. Ordinarily, the children weren't supposed to enter the front room except on Sundays, but this winter they had all moved in. The front room contained Christie's best furniture, the almost-new cabbage-rose carpet, and her good Utopian dishes in an oak china-safe. James had made their furniture when they started out together in Dundee. When they moved to Hopewell, they stored it in Christie's parents' stable in Dundee until their own house was ready. When the furniture finally arrived, it had some mouse stains, but Christie had never seen anything so lovely. She sanded it down and oiled it. Now her weight had broken two of the slats in the bed, and the corn-shuck mattress beneath the feather bed sagged through the hole in the slats. It almost reached the floor, until James put a hassock under the bed for support.

"Is it time for breakfast?" Nannie asked. She was standing beside the bed, twisting the hem of her muslin nightdress across her face.

Christie pulled the dress away and patted her child. "No, hon. Go back to sleep."

"I want to get in with you. Where's Papper?"

"He's outside." She started to make room for Nannie in the bed, but her belly contracted then and she cried out involuntarily.

"You hurt me," said Nannie. "You hurt my fingers."

Christie released her. Alma came over from the stove and steered her back across the soft carpet to her pallet. "Go look for your dreams, child," she said. "They'll get away from you." Turning back to the kitchen, she said to Christie, "I told Mandy to get on down here and carry the chillern up yonder to the house, but where is she?" Alma cupped her ear to listen. "The moon's shining big as a Sunday communion plate, so I don't know what she'd be scared of."

"Hoboes from the train," said Christie. "And devils behind bushes."

"She ain't got the sense God give a tomcat."

Amanda was Alma's sister-in-law, married to Alma's brother, Wad Wheeler. Alma bossed everybody in the household, but she bossed Amanda the most. She believed Amanda thought herself too good for ordinary work.

"I wonder if Mrs. Willy's back yet," said Christie.

"Oh, I don't think she knows a woman's behind from a jackass, to tell you the truth," Alma said, scowling till Christie imagined Alma's loose-jawed face drooping all the way down to her apron.

Christie couldn't help laughing, although it jiggled her stomach uncomfortably. During the winter, she had grown so fat she had to enter the narrow door of the springhouse sideways. Her ankles swelled and her feet ached. She made clumsy padded house-shoes out of double thicknesses of burlap, folded and stitched on top and gathered around and tied with twine at the ankles. She shuffled through the house, skirting the ashy hearth. For several weeks, she thought she must have miscalculated her time. She kept thinking the baby was due any moment. But the storm inside her kept up, at an ever more frantic pace. And now her time *had* come, the full time since the heat of last June when she and James had lain in the steamy night without cover, their bodies slippery as foaming horses, while the children slept out on the porch. She recalled that the midnight train had gone by then, too, and that she had imagined they were on the train, riding the locomotive, charging wildly into the night.

Christie screamed and grabbed Hattie's arm. A sharp pain charged through her like the train. Hattie held Christie's hand throughout the agony, while the thing inside tore loose a little more.

Alma said, "The water's about to boil and Mandy ain't here. I've a good mind to go up there and give her what-for."

The hurting passed. Christie sank into her feather bolster and pulled the cover up to her neck. Hattie wiped Christie's face.

"Bring me that likeness of my mama, please, Hattie," said Christie.

Hattie handed her the silver-framed photograph from the mantel. In the small portrait, Mama had a large smile, as though she had been caught by surprise.

"She looks right young," said Hattie.

"Yes, but she'd look old if I was to see her again. It's been two years since I was home." Christie touched the bleached-out image, wishing it would come to life under her fingertip. "I never oughter left Dundee," she said.

"You need your mama," said Hattie soothingly. "A woman always needs her mama at a time like this. But we'll do the best we can, Christie."

On the very day Christie and James married, her Aunt Sophie told her, "It's nine months from the marriage bed to the deathbed." At the time, Christie had dismissed the words as the careless remark of an old maid—Aunt Sophie had been to a female seminary and was thoughtlessly outspoken—but lately Christie had dwelt on the thought. She hadn't mentioned it to James, not wanting to worry him. But she was afraid she would die. No woman could pass a child this big. The commotion inside her felt like a churn dasher, churning up crickets and grasshoppers. Christie had thought she might be carrying twins, but the doctor hadn't encouraged that idea. Christie never felt sorry for herself, but this pregnancy had been different—hard and spiteful, as if something foreign had entered her body and set up a business of a violent and noisy nature. Almost from the beginning, it seemed she could feel the thing growing oddly inside her. At first, the sensation was only a twinge, like a June bug caught on a screen door. Then it grew into a wiggly worm, then a fluttering bird. Sometimes it was just kittens, then it would be like snakes. It kept changing, until the commotion inside her was almost constant, and terrifying. One day a clerk at the grocery where they traded showed her some jumping beans from Mexico. The beans were somehow electrified, jerking as though taken by fits. She had something like that in her. She imagined there were devils in her, warring over her soul. And even at calm, peaceful moments, she knew something was not right. The baby drained her strength, and now she could barely eat. Even though her breasts had grown huge and firm, she was afraid her milk wouldn't make.

"I know you want your mama," said Hattie. "Believe me, I know how it is."

Hattie worked busily, clipping Christie's hairs and washing her with a clear, sweet-smelling liquid. She laid out the contents of her bag on the small bedside table—shiny scissors, a slender knife, cotton wool, tubing, twine, soap, a device for expelling milk, bandages, small cotton cloths, blue bottles of liniment and alcohol and calomel, a variety of ointments in tiny round tins. As she worked, Hattie repeated a story Christie had heard before, how her husband had had his teeth pulled one day and the next day was kicked in the face by a mule. He said he regretted having paid the dentist to do what the mule would have done for free.

Steps sounded on the back porch, and Alma's brother Wad entered the kitchen. He never knocked on a door. Behind him was his wife, Amanda, Christie's only real friend on the place. Amanda was pretty, with soft gray eyes and a warm smile. Even though it was the middle of the night, she had put on a clean dress and had pinned her hair up under her fascinator just as though she were going someplace important.

"Well, fine time you picked," yelled Wad across the kitchen to Christie.

"Don't let Wad in here," Alma said to Amanda. "And shut that door. You're letting the cold night air in."

Amanda pushed her husband out and closed the door. Christie could hear him out on the back porch stomping his boots in the cold. He was many years older than Amanda—his second wife.

Amanda crossed the kitchen to Christie's bedside. She said, "Wad sent Joseph to get Mrs. Willy. That's how come we didn't get here so quick."

Joseph, one of Wad's grown sons by his first marriage, lived down the road a short piece.

"I thought Mrs. Willy was gone to Maple Grove," Alma said.

"Joseph said he saw her driving her buggy uptown yesterday evening peddling eggs," said Amanda, pausing over Nannie, who had gone back to sleep on her pallet. "I'll gather up the younguns and take 'em up to our house to get them out of the way. Come on, precious."

Clint and Jewell were awake now, their puzzled faces peering down from the loft. Clint, the older boy, had been suspicious for some time about his mother's condition, but Christie didn't want James to tell him where babies came from yet. Clint was still too young, and he should see it in cows and horses first.

"Where are we going?" said Jewell, scrambling sleepily down the stairway.

Christie heard Amanda cooing to the children, saying that their papa had gone to get a surprise for them. "It's like Christmas and we have to go away and close our eyes for the rest of the night so in the morning we can see the surprise—if we're real good." Amanda always took time to talk to the children. She turned even everyday events into stories. She had a way with all the children on the place, maybe because she seemed like such a child herself, although she was three years older than Christie and had two daughters.

Amanda was hurriedly wrapping the children in their coats.

"Get your caps, boys," she said. "Tie your shoes, Clint."

"It's a baby," said Clint.

"Papper's gone to get a baby," said Jewell. He reached out and pulled Nannie's nightdress, and she jerked it away from him. "You're a baby," he said. "Nannie's a baby."

"Stop that," said Alma, slapping Jewell. "This ain't no time for such foolishness. Get on out of here."

"Wait," said Christie. "Come here and give me a kiss."

She hugged each one of her children till they squirmed. Then, as Amanda whirled them away, the pain came again—a wave like the long, growling thunder that sometimes rolled through a summer sky from end to end. She was washed with pain, but she didn't feel how deep it went because she was seeing her children's faces go out the back door, one by one.

2

IT HAD BEEN A HARD WINTER, THE COLDEST IN CHRISTIE'S MEMORY. It was too cold for the roosters to crow. Alma beat icicles off the bushes, and the children collected the large ones for the springhouse. When the men stripped tobacco out in the barn, their hands were nearly frost-bitten. The winter wheat was frosted like lace, and the ponds and the creek were frozen solid. Some of the children went sliding across the pond on chairs. Christie couldn't see their fun from the house, but she recalled chair-sliding when she and James were courting back in Dundee and her father's pond froze over. James pushed her hard and fast, and she flew freely across to the other side, laughing loud and wild. That was the only time in her life the pond had frozen solid enough to slide on, but this winter James reported that six cows were standing on Wad's pond.

Amanda had told everybody it would be a hard winter. The persimmons said so, she believed. She broke open persimmon seeds for the children. Inside each one was a little white thing, the germ of the seed. Amanda said, "Look at that little tiny fork. That means a hard, hard winter's a-coming! If it was drawn like a spoon, it would be a sign of mild weather; and if it was a knife, it would mean a lot of frost, but not too thick for the knife to cut. But the fork is the worst."

When James and the boys stripped tobacco, Alma had to wash their smoke-saturated clothes. Christie gazed outside helplessly at the bare black trees, the occasional birds huddling inside their fluffed feathers, and the cows chomping hay beside Wad's barn, making a picture of color against the dusting of snow that had come overnight. Wad's mercury had gone down to naught on ten different nights that January and February. A snow in early January, after the ice storm, lasted till the end of the month. None of the farmers around had ever seen such weather—but then they always said that, Christie noticed. They'd never seen it so warm, or so cold, or so changeable, or so much rain to follow a cold spell. This year, everybody said the cold winter had something to do with the earthquake that had been predicted for New Year's.

Livestock froze: a cow who freshened too early; then her calf, stranded across the creek; then another cow who was old and stayed out in the storm. Wad and James worked to repair the barn so they could keep the cows in at night. They spread hay for insulation, piling bales in front of some of the largest cracks in the walls. The breath of the cows warmed the barn like woodstoves. Christie felt like a cow inside her tent dress and under the layers of cover on the bed. Her bulk heated up the bed so much that many nights James thrashed himself awake. They couldn't let the fireplace go cold—the children needed its warmth—but Christie felt as if she were carrying a bucket of hot coals inside her. In the past, she had been comfortable with pregnancy because of the privacy of it. It was her secret even after everyone knew. They didn't really know the feeling—a delicious, private, tingly joy. The changes inside her body were hers alone. But this time the sloshing, the twinges, the sensation of blood rushing, the bloating, the veins in her legs popping out—all were so intense it was as if her body were turning into someone else's. Walking from the stove to the dishpan—barely four steps—was a labored journey, her legs heavy like fence posts.

As she grew larger, she felt as though she were trying to hide a barrel of molasses under her dress. She was used to sleeping on her back, but when she gained weight, lying like that seemed to exert enough pressure to cut off the flow of blood to the baby. When she sat, she couldn't cross her legs. Her hip joint seemed loose, and it was painful to bend or stoop or turn her foot a certain way. The right leg seemed longer, and she walked in a side-to-side motion. She learned to minimize the painful motion, and her right leg grew stiff.

At night, James stroked her belly so sensuously she feared the baby might be born with unwholesome thoughts. As the season wore on and she grew still heavier, she retreated from James and wouldn't let him see her belly. She didn't want him to see the deep-wrinkled, blind hollow of her navel turning inside out. It made her think of the apron strings she made by pushing a safety pin through a tunnel of material and reversing it so the seam was inside. He seemed proud and happy about the baby, but she didn't think he would care to know that the baby was kicking—flutters and jabs inside. Men were afraid of babies. There was so much you didn't tell a man; it was better to keep things a mystery. One night as she was falling asleep, she felt a sharp jolt, unmistakably a foot jamming the elastic of her womb. The kick was violent, as though the little half-formed being had just discovered it had feet and was trying to kick its way out.

Sometimes a small event would soar through her heart on angel wings: the train going by, the frost flowers forming on the window light, flour sifting down onto the biscuit board, a blackbird sailing past the window in a line parallel to the train. For a moment, then, she thought she was the blackbird, or that she had painted the frost flowers herself, or that she was setting out carefree and young aboard the train. One day she heard a flock of geese and went outside bare-headed to watch them tack across the sky. The lead goose would go one way and the others would fall out of pattern, and then he would sway the other way and they would all follow, honking. The stragglers seemed to be the ones yelling the loudest. She felt like one of those stragglers, trying to keep up but finding the wayward directions irresistible. It wasn't just her condition. She had always felt like that. She was hungry at odd times, and she would fix herself a biscuit—cold, with sorghum and a slice of onion. In the henhouse one day, gathering eggs, she leaned against the door facing, breathing in the deep, warm fumes. She cracked an egg against the door and slid the contents down her throat. Then she laughed, like somebody drunk. Several boys had been drunk and torn up some hitching posts on the main street in town not long ago, she had heard. She wondered what it was like to be drunk. It would probably mean laughing at the wrong times, which she did anyway.

Back before she took to her bed, James had a spell of sleeplessness that made him drag for several days. A farmer couldn't afford to lose sleep, and she blamed herself for waking him up when she got up in the night to use the pot. One Saturday just before Christmas, he had hardly slept all night. He made his weekly trip to town as usual, but he didn't stay long. He came home and slept the rest of the morning. He had never done that in his life, he said, annoyed with himself.

That was the day Mrs. Willy came visiting. Mrs. Willy, who lived by herself in a little white house, lost her husband in a buggy wreck soon after they married. She raised a daughter alone. Now she helped out women and sewed.

"Come in, Mrs. Willy," Christie called. "Clint, get Mrs. Willy a chair. Get her that mule-eared setting chair." But she was in no frame of mind for company. She had ironing to do.

Mrs. Willy stepped across the floor as tenderly as if she feared her weight would break a board, although she was slender and pigeon-boned. Alma had remarked that Mrs. Willy hung around pregnant women like a starved dog around the kitchen door.

She settled down in the chair Clint had pulled out from the back porch.

"Go on out and see if you can help Papper," Christie said to Clint. The other children were gathering hickory nuts with Amanda. James was in the barn rubbing down horse leather.

"I've got a splinter," Clint said, holding up his thumb.

Christie felt her apron bib for a needle she kept there. Holding the boy by the daylight through the window, she picked at the splinter until it shot out. She kissed the dirty little finger.

"I didn't cry," he said proudly.

"Now go on. Papper needs you."

Clint slipped out the back door. Christie had been heating an iron on the stove. She spit on it now to test it. It hissed. She started ironing a shirt.

"I need to do my arning," Mrs. Willy said. She leaned toward Christie with hungry eyes. "What's that baby up to in there today?"

"Growing." Christie didn't want to talk about her pregnancy. She didn't want to satisfy the woman's curiosity.

"And how's your man holding up?"

"He don't sleep good," said Christie, aiming her iron down a sleeve.

"Witches might be bothering him."

"Witches?"

"Here's what you do," said Mrs. Willy, untying the strings of her splint bonnet. "Make him sleep with a meal sifter over his face. When the witches come along they'll have to pass back and forth through ever hole in that sifter, and by the time they get done he'll have had enough sleep."

Christie laughed until she had to catch hold of her side.

"Don't you believe that?" asked Mrs. Willy. She was unsmiling, her face like a cut cabbage.

"I can't see James sleeping with a meal sifter on his face," Christie said through her laughter. "Anyway, I wouldn't want witches working in and out of a meal sifter so close to *my* face while I was sleeping. I'd rather be wide awake."

Christie felt her laughter shrink like a spring flower wilting, as Mrs. Willy retied her bonnet strings.

"You've got to get used to waking up through the night," Mrs. Willy said. "That's the Lord's way of getting you used to being up with the baby in the night."

"Does the Lord carry a meal sifter?" Christie asked.

"Why, what do you mean?"

"Oh, sometimes I can't tell witches from devils," Christie said. "Reckon it was witches that made our mule go crazy last summer? And what about that swarm of bees that got after Wad one spring?" Christie paused to tighten a hairpin. She cast a glance at the ceiling. "And that he-cow that busted out of his stall last week? Witches?"

"Christianna Wheeler!" said Mrs. Willy disapprovingly, realizing she was being mocked. "If you act ill towards people, that baby will have a ill disposition."

"I can handle any witches that get in my house," said Christie, pushing her iron forcibly up the back of the shirt.

"Well, Christie, when you went to camp meeting down yonder at Reelfoot, Alma said you got enough religion to get you through to your time. I hope so."

Christie didn't want to think about Reelfoot. There was a lull, while the fire in their voices died down into embarrassment. Christie finished the shirt and lifted a sheet from the wash basket.

Mrs. Willy said, "You need some new domestic. That sheet's plumb full of holes."

"This sheet's old. I'm aiming to tear it up into diapers."

Christie was glad when the woman left. She made Christie nervous, watching her iron and waiting for a crumb of personal detail. Christie wouldn't tell Mrs. Willy about the particular sensations—the way the blood flowed, the way all those creatures turned somersets in her stomach, the way she jolted awake. One night she had awakened after dreaming that her little sister Susan was alive again. In the dream, Nannie had been tugging on her nipple, but Nannie was Susan. The rhythm of the sucking had words, like words to a song. One of Susan's first words was moo-moo, her word for milk. Awake, Christie remembered the time her mother made a pinafore for Susan, starching the ruffles and working the fine lace. But the dogs tore it off of Susan, chewing it to tatters. Mama had worked on that pinafore for most of one winter.

A few days after Mrs. Willy's visit, James came in unexpectedly from the barn, slamming the kitchen door. He said, "I heard you was nasty to Mrs. Willy."

Christie was standing at the stove, stirring cream corn. "Mrs. Willy?" She turned away from James and reached for a bowl on the shelf. Her heart pounded.

James said, "Her sister's telling how you laughed at her and hurt her feelings."

Christie set the bowl on the table and dumped the corn in it. She said, "Some people like to talk."

For a second James's face looked as hard as clay dirt baked in the sun. "We have to live with all kinds," he said. "You can't just laugh to a person's face, Chrissie."

Christie bent her head down. She was conscious of her swollen breasts, her own, not his or anyone else's. James had never talked to her like this.

"When we moved here, we promised we was going to get along with everybody," he said. "You remember that."

Christie nodded. She was tired. She put her hands on her stomach, and she felt it move. James rarely got upset with her. He usually turned everything into a joke, he was so easy.

"Since you and Mandy went down to Reelfoot, it's like you come back a different woman," James said. "I don't know what's got into you, Christie. You're making my heart ache."

She turned, and her skirt tugged against her middle.

James's face softened a little then. "That baby's coming sooner than we thought," he said, touching her stomach. He seemed shocked to realize her girth.

In bed that night, Christie couldn't get comfortable. She felt monstrously heavy, as if with the weight of opinion. When she got up to relieve herself, she took the pot into the kitchen and tried to hit the side to muffle the sound. Afterward, she reached inside the warming box of the stove for a chicken wing. She gnawed the chicken, then searched for a piece of liver, the grease congealed with the crust. In the dark, she nibbled like a mouse, as quietly as possible, chewing breathlessly. She felt better. She heard Nannie stir on the pallet.

But the pregnancy dragged on, like the winter. Her mother couldn't come from Dundee on account of her bronchitis. And Mama was afraid of the earthquake. Christie had to be helped back to her feet when she sat in her rocking chair. She was afraid of falling. She had to struggle up the steps to the porch. On New Year's Day, she managed to cook field peas and turnip-greens-with-hog-jaws for good luck, but the cornbread burned. She hated being fat. She remembered an old woman in Dundee who told Christie's mother, "I had a fat place to come on my leg, just like a tit." The woman said,

"The doctor mashed it up real good and then drawed that fat out through a little hole."

Christie fell asleep early at night, curving away from James. She couldn't sleep comfortably in any position except on her side, with a knee pulled up to support her belly. She curled her body around the baby, holding it as closely as possible—hooked to it from heartbeat to heartbeat, her blood flowing into her child.

3

THE CONTRACTIONS WERE MORE FREQUENT. CHRISTIE LOST TRACK of who was there. James still hadn't come with the doctor. Amanda had returned with an ax, which she had placed under the bed to cut the pain.

"I had five younguns and didn't need no ax," said Alma.

"We might need it," said Christie. "To get the devils." To distract herself from the pain, she was pulling at a sheet tied by one corner to the bedpost.

"Why, Christie, you do have an imagination," Hattie said, all smiles. Her wavy, gray hair framed her broad, gentle face.

"Here, Mandy, take this rag and wash out that bucket," Alma said to Amanda. "I'm going to scald it."

"James oughter be back by now," Amanda said, holding the rag like a flower.

"If you ask me, we can do without that doctor," said Alma. "Doctors just want to get their eyes full."

"It's going to be a mighty big baby, but we've got plenty of time," said Hattie calmly. Her apron was so white it seemed to shout.

"Chris, you better get up and walk some," said Alma. "That baby ain't gonna get out of there with you a-laying like that."

The talk went on around Christie, the sounds rising and falling senselessly, like the confusing messages of those preachers at Reelfoot. She wondered what would have happened if she hadn't gone to Reelfoot Lake that day back in the fall. Amanda had talked her into going to the brush-arbor meeting there. Afterward, Amanda had told her not to feel ashamed, to take it easy and let the easiness transfer to the baby. That was the sort of idea Amanda believed in.

Amanda wouldn't let a post or tree come between two people walk-ing along together. She took black cats seriously. She believed every tale she had ever heard about snakes. She had believed intensely in the earthquake that had been predicted, and she still feared it might happen. When she and Christie came home from Reelfoot, Amanda had told her husband that they had been possessed by the spirit. "But in a good way," she said. "It wasn't the Devil—more like the Holy Ghost."

"What do you know about the Holy Ghost?" Wad had asked sus-piciously.

"I know he's welcome in our house," said Amanda. "That's enough for me to know."

"You better leave the Holy Ghost where he belongs—at church," said Wad.

Now, opening her eyes a crack, Christie glimpsed Amanda's vacant stare. Wispy hair stuck out in little feathers all around Amanda's face.

Christie pushed down on the bed with her elbows, trying to rise, but she was too heavy and she fell back against the bolster. She heard the pot of water boiling. She felt warm, wet rags between her legs. The clock pendulum swung insistently, loudly. She felt as though the rhythms inside her were trying to catch up to the clock's. She saw a lantern light through the front window. James appeared, conferring with the women in low voices Christie couldn't hear. Then he was standing over her, touching her steaming forehead. Was this the same man she had bounced around with long ago at a play-party in Dundee? The man who proposed marriage to her at another play-party, a year later?

"The doctor's on his way," he said. His palm was sweaty.

"I don't want him to touch me again," said Christie, pulling her hand out of James's.

"He can give you something to stop it from hurting so much."

The pain made her scream then, and James, looking frightened, backed away.

"It's supposed to hurt," Alma said sharply to James. "Why, Hattie here can catch this baby. She's delivered half the people on this road."

"Now, hush, Aunt Alma," James said, frowning. "This is a special case."

"I ain't going to stand in nobody's way," said Hattie.

Christie cried, "Please, God!" She wanted it to be over and all the people gone. Clutching the sheet tied to the bedpost, she focused her eyes on a spiderweb in the window to the left of the fireplace—just a little thing, so frail and light, but capable of holding life.

"I'm going down the road to meet the doctor," James said, backing away.

After he left, it was quiet for a while. The women waited and walked the floor. Their soft laughter and the burble of their talk were constant, like jelly simmering. Christie wished she could go to sleep and wake up delivered. She stared at bouquets of roses in the wallpaper. Through the doorway, she could see the Black Draught calendar on the kitchen wall, where she had recorded her due time with a penciled X—Saturday, the date of the full moon.

"Hold on to me, Christie," said Amanda, grasping Christie's wrist. Amanda's hand was so light it felt like chicken bones.

"Let me look again," said Hattie, raising the sheet and spreading Christie's legs. "It's coming along. You're pooching out more. That's what we like to see." She prodded Christie's abdomen with something soft. "How does it feel now, hon? A little tight?"

When Christie went to the doctor in town, he examined her privately while James waited in another room. James was reluctant to allow the doctor to touch her, but her condition was so alarming they knew it had to be done. And they agreed that when the time came for the birth, the doctor ought to be called. But now Christie dreaded seeing him again. Her mother had known a woman who died after a doctor pulled the baby out by its head with metal tools. The baby died too, it was so squashed and bruised.

Although she was deeply embarrassed to go out in public in her condition, James had taken her to town in the wagon. She was too big to climb up into the buggy, and Wad was afraid her weight would break a rod. She rode to town, half reclining in the wagon on a feather bed, her shoulders cushioned by pillows. She hugged her pumpkin body to herself under a quilt, hoping no one would see her. It was a muddy day, before the freezes began, and the wagon wheels ground through ruts, the mules heaving and jerking. She felt she would lose the baby if the trip went on much longer.

Dr. Foote's office was above the drugstore, up a dark stairway that took her breath. He gave her a thin towel to put over her face, then instructed her to loosen her underclothes. She lay on a long table, listening to murmuring voices coming through the wall. He raised her dress and fastened it with clothes-pins onto some poles so that it made a barrier that kept them from seeing each other's faces. His thick hands traveled the mound of her stomach, with her drawers still in place—a sensation that tickled and tingled. When James did that, it was more exciting than when the clothing was removed. It was anticipation that electrified her. The doctor did not seem to realize the effects of his explorations, and she held herself rigid, trying not to squirm away from the tickling. He ran his fingers over the curvature of her body. She had so much fat on her she did not know how he could feel the baby. He listened to her belly through a slim metal device that was cupped on each end. Then the worst occurred. He told her to part her legs. As she did, he pulled the drawers down and thrust his hand between her legs. The table was hard. Outside, a driver was running mules through town and there were loud shouts.

Slowly, the doctor worked his cold, thick finger up into her, while his other hand crawled over her belly.

When he finished, he disappeared into another room, allowing her to collect herself and rearrange her clothes. She kept thinking, if only she had not had her clothes on it would have been more bearable.

He reappeared, still not meeting her eyes, and spoke to her of fibroids growing inside her womb. He handed her a note for a preparation to shrink them. He said she should keep quiet and not jar herself during the last three months. There was the danger of hemorrhaging, he said. Fibroids sounded evil, she thought. The pharmacist downstairs said the preparation was the same thing as Lydia Pinkham's Vegetable Compound, which was cheaper. They went home with a bottle of that instead. It tasted like Wad's whiskey, which he claimed he kept for medicinal use.

If there were fibroids in her, they had not gone away.

Now Alma pushed several folded sheets underneath Christie. Each one could be removed as it got stained. Alma had also brought a stack of newspapers, for the same purpose. The room was warm, but Alma and Amanda rigged up a sheet overhead, tying a corner to each bedpost. The sheet made a tent to hold in the warmth. The light flickering through the sheet was peaceful. It made Christie think of the canopy of tobacco plants hanging from the rafters of the barn.

Her belly seized and cramped again, and she began to double up. Hattie persuaded her to open her legs and let her wash down there again with a scalding rag, and then she applied some slippery jelly.

"The hardest thing is when they get hung," said Hattie. "Sometimes it takes a long time to work them out."

"Wad had a cow once with a calf to get hung," said Alma. "He had to work that calf out like threading elastic through bloomer hems."

"Don't make me laugh," said Christie. "It hurts."

Alma swished the rag into the bucket of hot water and squeezed it dry as she spoke. "He needed one of them contraptions doctors use— like a post-hole digger with two or three pair of scissors opening out the sides."

"You just relax, Christie," said Hattie kindly. "Nobody's going to use any sech thing on you."

Alma's bluntness didn't bother Christie. She had been with the Wheelers long enough now to know their crude ways. They were hard-skinned people. Christie's children got teased by everyone in the family, and they always came bawling to her. James said they'd learn to take it, that it would make them tough. James was a Wheeler, after all. She hadn't known what that meant until they moved here. The Wheeler clan had been a surprise to her, as if she'd gone out to the garden to pick English peas and found it full of goats.

Christie took Amanda's hand when she passed near and signaled for her to bend down. Alma and Hattie were out in the kitchen. Christie whispered, "I'm scared, Mandy."

"Don't you be scared. We're right here with you, and we won't let that doctor do nothing to hurt you. We'll hold on to them knees."

"If I live through this, I don't want you to show me what I've got in here."

"Now, Christie, don't talk crazy."

Christie heard Alma sloshing rags in boiling water. Christie lowered her voice and said to Amanda, "We never should have gone to Reelfoot."

"No! Don't think that. And don't you say it."

"I keep thinking about it."

"No. Nothing happened. If you say it did, I'll contradict you." Amanda squeezed Christie's hand. "Don't worry, Christie."

Mrs. Willy came in then, carrying a satchel. "I seen the light and knowed I'd better get in there!" she said. She had a high voice like a little dog.

"Get over here by the fire, Imogene," said Alma.

"I brung some gunpowder to make the pain easy."

"Howdy, Mrs. Willy," said Amanda. "I thought you were at Maple Grove."

"I was but I done got back. Joseph come riding up and yelled through the winder that Christie was a-fixing to have that baby any minute. He woke me up clean out of a dream. So I threw on my everyday clothes and didn't even take time to find a clean apron." Mrs. Willy was tall, despite her humped back—like a tree that had lost one of its twin trunks and the stump had smoothed over with time.

Christie closed her eyes and let the women go about their business. She heard a screech owl outside, its mournful whinny like a lonesome horse. She enjoyed hearing the cry of a screech owl. She had always liked to imagine the freedom of being able to flutter over the land.

When she was a child, her mother told her a story about a screech owl who had lost her husband in a barn fire. The owl went traveling through the night, telling her mournful story to all the night creatures who would listen. But her husband had not perished, after all; he had flown away to safety, carrying some mice and barn swallows with him. *He* thought *she* had burned up in the fire. Their pitiful whinnies crossed each other in the night until finally they found each other again. Christie had told her own children that story, but she was not as good at making the owl's cry as her mother had been. The screech owl was scary, but the hoot owl brought good news. The hoot owl brought babies. For several days now, Nannie and Clint and Jewell had been listening for the hoot owl.

Waiting for James to come in with the doctor, Christie tried to endure the continuing contractions by naming every item she had seen in the drugstore: Lydia Pinkham's Vegetable Compound, the Wine of Cardui, the cotton and gauze and bluing. She visualized the shining oak counters and the tall, glass-fronted cabinets, filled with hair tonics, worm medications, liver pills, syrups and salves and potions. She kept listening for the doctor's horse. She thought about a time back in Dundee when she and James were newly married. One evening he came home from court day, riding up proudly on a chestnut horse, carrying two glass cake-stands just alike, with designs of grapevines entwining the pedestals and grapes clustered on the covers. The cake-stands were so beautiful they made her cry.

It was past two o'clock, and James was still outdoors. The doctor hadn't come. During a lull in the labor, Christie was trying to name as many countries as she could think of, when the pain grabbed her and she squeezed so tightly and pushed so violently that the baby popped out. Hattie had gone to the back porch for something, and Alma was working with the fireplace, and Mrs. Willy was watching out the window for James and the doctor. Amanda was in a rocking chair sewing a button on her dress.

"It's here," said Christie, falling back, drained.

"Well, I'll be," cried Alma, bumping into Mrs. Willy in their rush to catch the baby. "Why, it's little! It's the least little baby I ever did see!"

4

CHRISTIE DIDN'T FEEL THE SCISSORS CLIP THE BABY FROM THE CORD or the twine being jerked in a knot, but she could feel the baby being taken away. Hearing his cries and muffled whimpers, she struggled to lift her head just as Hattie thrust the baby at her. Hattie had wrapped him loosely in warm outing flannel and rubbed drops of olive oil on his face. He cried louder, his face scrunching up like a shriveled apple. The little bundle rested against her cheek and shoulder. She moved her head to cradle him against her. He was tiny, no bigger than a screech owl. The owl's cry echoed in her mind. Her belly seized again then, and the pain clutched her for a full minute before releasing. She held on to the bedpost with one hand, and with the other she touched the little body beside her. He was squirming and moving his head from side to side. His lips were narrow and parted, the forehead sharp and angled, the head coming to a slight point in a cap of wet, black down. Mrs. Willy wiped a red streak from his neck. Christie pulled at the blanket around him and gently curved her hand beneath him. The baby was hers, her creation. Yet he wasn't at all what she expected. Mrs. Willy moved back, giving off a sour wintertime odor of sweat and dirty clothes and onions, overlaid with a sweet perfume. Christie had washed herself all over earlier in the evening when the pains began. She had put on clean clothes. Alma always smelled like food; layers of bacon grease and fried meat odors permeated her clothing. James smelled like hay and manure and fresh grass. The baby had no separate smell—just Christie's own body, radiating warmth, the hot smell of blood from between her legs.

"Let me have him again," said Hattie. "I'll wash him some more and stir his circulation."

"Don't get him cold," Alma warned. She stood by the back door across the kitchen while Hattie washed him, so that nobody would open it while the baby was exposed. The baby gave out a loud squall when the wet rag touched him.

"He's a Wheeler, all right," said Alma.

"He's got the teeniest fingers," Mrs. Willy said, touching the baby's hand. "I believe he's the little-bittiest baby that ever was. No wonder you had him that quick a-laying down."

"Where's Mandy?" said Christie, turning her head.

"Right here, hon," said Amanda, moving into view. "He's so little I'm afraid to touch him. You sure surprised me, Christie! I've been standing here like a goose."

"That belly's still a punkin under there," said Hattie. She wrapped the baby in outing and set him beside Christie's breast. Then she pulled the quilt up protectively.

"He wants to suck," said Christie, watching the little mouth making blind motions, gaping like a baby bird.

"Tell him to go right ahead. I'm going to check down there again," said Hattie. She moved the sheet and parted Christie's legs. "You're still wide open," she said, wiping around with a fresh rag. "And that belly ain't gone down any. We might have a time a-getting that afterbirth out."

"It's them fibroids," Amanda said. "They just squeezed in on this little baby and about smothered him!"

"It's not really fibroids," said Christie. "There's something else in there, a-growing."

"Hush," said Amanda, bringing her finger to her lips. "Dr. Foote said it was fibroids, now, didn't he, Christie?"

Amanda helped her open her shift and scoot the baby in place. He was so light he could be held in a hand. Christie felt him begin to draw, but the milk didn't come. The baby swigged and lost his hold. He sucked at air. She tried to feed the nipple back into his mouth. He caught it for a moment, then turned aside, a bubble of yellow between his lips.

"It's there," she said, easing back against her bolster. "It's there."

The baby had thick, black hair and hands tiny as baby bird wings. His fingers worked, grasping easily, as if they were destined for some handiwork, like carpentry. The little hands flexed as she guided the nipple into his gaping mouth again and he took hold. His features had that early misshapen look—the eyebrows and forehead lumpy, the forehead pushed back. The skin was red and healthy, and soft as the inside of her cheek. Mrs. Willy and Alma were talking, but Christie couldn't make out the words. Hattie was still washing her. She removed one of the folded sheets, and when the whisk of air from the flapping sheet hit the cooling water of the cloth Christie almost sneezed. She felt full and heavy and not much relieved by the birth. The baby seemed so normal, with his perfect little fingers and their little nails like fish scales. She unwound the outing to see the rest of him, taking care to keep the quilt hooded around him so he wouldn't catch the draft. The delicate toes, the scrawny legs, the little worm between them—all normal, but so small.

"She ain't through yet," Hattie was saying. She was massaging the upper part of Christie's belly.

"It's like this when a cow's putting out twins," Alma said. "She rests in between, like it's all over, but it ain't."

Christie said, "That's not a baby in there. The baby's out here."

"We got this far without that doctor," said Amanda happily. "You're doing good, Christie. Don't you worry none."

"You just lay back and relax and don't bear down any till you need to," Hattie said.

"Are you sure you won't take some of this gunpowder?" asked Mrs. Willy.

"She don't need that," said Hattie impatiently. "Nobody uses that anymore."

"She looks like she might explode as it is," said Amanda, laughing.

Christie tried to think. What to name the child, now that he was real? James wanted the baby named after him if it was a boy. Somehow they hadn't named Clint and Jewell after anyone in either family, although so many men on her father's side had strong, good names. Her father was Lake Wilburn, and his brothers were Forrest, Clark, and Reuben. Her mother's brothers all had old-fashioned names: Willis, Zeb, Zollicoffer, Quigley. Except for Uncle John. John was all right. Maybe James would settle for James John. Or John James. Which sounded better? But she thought of her papa. She wanted the name Lake. James Lake.

"Is that baby getting his titty?" cooed Amanda, as Hattie removed the soiled sheet beneath Christie.

"He's going at it like a Wheeler," said Alma, who never used baby talk. "But I can't get over how little that thing is. You could carry him in a pocket."

The baby let go of Christie's breast and squirmed, then whimpered. Mrs. Willy scooped him up against her shoulder and patted his back. For all Mrs. Willy's faults, she had a gentle touch and seemed used to handling babies, Christie thought. The woman had on a dark bonnet with no trimming, as if she were still in mourning. She had hovered beside Hattie's elbow all night, like a shadow.

"The baby's all in one piece and I didn't die," said Christie.

"You're talking nonsense," said Alma.

Hattie shook her head worriedly. "You're still as big as a barn and that-there's the littlest baby in the Jackson Purchase, so something's going on here."

"It must be the devil's nest," Christie said calmly. "He's still stirring around in there."

"We'll see," said Hattie, feeling around on Christie's stomach. "I believe there's more'n one baby in there. I've believed it all along, but I didn't want to say."

"It feels like the devil, with his pitchfork, pitching hay," said Christie, who had been paying little attention. Her insides were moving again. She felt waves inside fluttering, like a hog trough when the slop is poured in and the hogs start it sloshing. She grabbed the sheet and tried to push down.

She caught sight of the moon, shining through a crack between the curtain and window facing. She heard a horse galloping up the lane, a horseshoe hitting a rock, the slobbering sound of the horse as he was brought to a halt by the door.

"The doctor's coming," said James, bursting through the front door.

"It's a baby," Christie said as James rounded the staircase. A grin spread over his face when he saw the baby on the pillow beside her. He rushed to the bed then, his grin turning to beaming pride when the women told him he had a baby boy. Embarrassed, he stroked the baby. He didn't seem to realize how unusually small this baby was. To him, every newborn must be frighteningly small, Christie thought.

"How's the little mama?" he said, patting her face. But he wouldn't kiss her in front of the women.

He ignored the doubts and fears she thought must show on her face. He disregarded her enormous size, still like a burial mound under the quilt. When he lifted the baby, she remembered him calling at her parents' house on Sundays, bearing presents—a fresh-killed hen, a precious salt-cured ham, a clutch of quail eggs nestled in his cap, and, once, a hairbrush, a present that Mama declared was too intimate.

The moon was glowing bright from the top of the sky when Dr. Herman Foote came through the door. The sound of his horse's reins thwapping against the front-porch post carried through the house in a comforting background rhythm, along with the sounds of the clock, the boiling water, the stir of the women.

"How are we doing, Mrs. Wheeler?" Dr. Foote asked in a gruff voice. He stood by the stairs for a moment, surveying the room, like a traveler who had arrived at an unexpected destination. "Nobody wants me to sleep tonight," he said, laying down his bag. "I've been out prowling all over the country dragging babies into the world." He cast a skeptical look at the contents of Hattie's satchel. Hattie started gathering up her things without a word.

"I'm weak," said Christie. "But I didn't have much trouble."

"It ain't over with yet," said Alma.

"I'm still big," said Christie.

Dr. Foote examined the baby, repeating the tests the women had done. The baby, who had been sleeping peacefully, yelled out.

"Going to scream at me, are you?" the doctor asked the baby. "You look all there to me. Now let's see where you came from."

"Fooling with him like that will make him dizzy," said Hattie.

"I'll go see to your horse," said James, going to the front door.

"We're right here with you, Christie," said Amanda.

"Shut the door," Alma said to James. "We can't have this cold coming in."

When the doctor rolled up his sleeves, Christie had to smile. It seemed like such a typical thing for a man to do when he got down to work, even in winter. She felt warm, and she had her legs still propped up, her knees bent. People swirled around her. She could see Amanda and Hattie whispering. Hattie glared at the doctor. Amanda lifted the baby and rocked him in her arms.

"A little baby boy," she said in a voice of surprise, as if they had expected maybe a mouse. Or an owl.

"He's all there, but my lands, what a little baby," said Dr. Foote.

"You said there was fibroids," Christie said.

"Well, fibroids can make a baby lose weight. But this baby's skin's tight. I don't think he's lost any weight."

Christie almost doubled up with another contraction.

"She needs to set up," said Hattie.

"No, I want her to lay back," said the doctor. "Now, Mrs. Hurt, you're just as well's to go home and let me handle this."

"Ain't this women's work, Dr. Foote?" Alma asked.

"I guess women are new at this," said Hattie sarcastically.

Dr. Foote laughed. "Oh, you ladies."

He had a bald head and a loose-skinned face and a manner that was slightly confused but kindly.

"Lay on your side, Mrs. Wheeler," he said. "That's right. Now draw your knees up."

Hattie and Alma fastened a quilt up against the side of the bed nearest the kitchen, making a side to Christie's tent. They twisted the ends around the bedposts and tied them with some strips of muslin. Christie couldn't see the women from behind the partition. Her position was awkward, pressing painfully on her insides. She recognized the sensation of the doctor's fingers. His broad, thick hands searched her body. Then he inserted a slippery finger and mashed down from the outside with his other hand. He removed his finger and reached for something from his bag. She could feel his fingers again, pushing into her, widening her opening.

"You're a big gal," said Dr. Foote. "I wouldn't have thought you'd gain this much. When I saw you back in December you looked ready to deliver right then."

"You told me to go to bed the rest of my time," she said.

"You were so big I was afraid you might hurt the baby."

"I couldn't hardly carry the weight," said Christie, writhing with another contraction.

"Let me give you some powders to ease you," Dr. Foote said. "You just lay back. We may have a long night ahead yet."

"You better get her up and bend her over," said Alma. "She can't get nothing out a-laying down."

"No, I can work better with her in this position," Dr. Foote said. "Keep that knee up, Mrs. Wheeler."

Christie kept her face hidden from the doctor, but by now she wouldn't care even if it were the preacher looking at her privacies. When the pain got worse, Amanda reached behind the quilt and held her hand. And Hattie was still there, her soft voice smothering Alma's rough bark. Mrs. Willy paced around the kitchen nervously, ready to hand the doctor towels and water. When Christie began to move violently and scream, Amanda snatched the baby and held him safe. Christie could hear Amanda singing softly to the baby, as if he were afraid of the dark.

5

THE DRUG THE DOCTOR GAVE HER MADE HER FEEL SWADDLED IN gauze. Sensations mixed together: James's smell of sweat from his hard night ride, the sight of him holding the new baby like a little loaf of bread under his chin, the slow rattle of the four o'clock freight train passing by. Her mind confused the noise of the train with the turmoil in her belly. She saw the dim shapes of the people moving around her, saw the doctor shoo James aside, saw Alma take the baby to the kitchen table. From the sound of Alma's steps, Christie thought she had gone to the washstand behind the partition formed by the cupboard and pie safe. The other women seemed to disappear while the doctor probed her under her tent. He kept her on her side with her knees drawn up. He placed a pillow between her knees. Christie thought she would gladly die rather than hold such an uncomfortable position for long, but it was too embarrassing a position to die in. A powerful lurch shoved her insides down again. Christie strained and blew and got the pain out. It felt warm. Her opening yawned.

"There it comes," said Alma sometime later.

"What have we here?" said Dr. Foote, pulling something slippery from her.

A frog, Christie thought. Maybe a pig.

"Quick, here's a rag. Let me hold it," said Mrs. Willy.

"Don't let it strangle."

"This one ain't no bigger'n a puppy dog," said Alma.

"What is it?" Christie said. "Does it have a tail?"

"Shhh. You've got another baby—a baby girl," said Mrs. Willy.

Christie glimpsed the squirming piece of red flesh, like something hacked out of her, an organ that had worked loose. In what seemed just a moment—for she drifted away somewhere—it was a baby beside her, rolled in a blanket and moist with oil and enthusiastically clutching her nipple.

"Is this a baby?" she asked. She felt stupid, numb. "I thought it was a devil," she murmured. "He was so loud in my womb."

Then she saw James by the fireplace with the first baby.

"Put him down here," she said. Usually, women would make a man leave.

Her husband's face was in shadow and she couldn't read him. He laid the baby down by the other breast. The second baby lost her hold and Christie guided the nipple to her, and she took it. The first baby began to cry.

"She fed you," James said to the boy. "Now let your little sister eat."

Little bird feet, little bird claws. She was stunned by the delicateness of the babies' features, and by the differences between the two. The girl was smaller and paler in color, with lighter hair and eyes set farther apart. Her hair curved against her head, and she nursed more quickly than the boy.

"James Lake," she said to James, nodding at the boy. And she almost cried then, nodding to the girl, in an inspiration that seized her. "Emily Sue. For my sisters."

"Susan," said James in a low tone.

She couldn't tell whether he approved. His face was still shadowed. She didn't see the doctor now. Had he finished and left? She wanted to sleep. Her head had been erratic so much of the time for several months now. She longed for some clarity, like the clear, serene weather that comes deservingly after the stormy season. She heard Alma talking, fretting about something. She remembered Alma several months before, fussing when she learned that Christie had been pregnant when she went to the camp meeting. "Why, that baby'll be stirred up by all that talk," Alma cried. "It'll hit the ground in ever direction. It'll be born a-kicking."

"It'll be *lively*, Alma," Christie had said. "And if the earthquake comes, he'll be ready to run."

Alma said, "I ain't getting worked up over no earthquake. I've got too many arns in the fire."

Exactly when did Alma say that? Did Christie laugh to her face? Was that when Dulcie, Alma's serious-minded daughter, said, "But what if we did have an earthquake here? What would we do?"

"Gather in the wash, I expect," said Alma. "And run for the storm hole."

"We better pray," said Dulcie. "We better start right now."

"I don't think we could stop it," said Alma. "If it's going to come, it's going to come."

Dulcie wasn't satisfied with that. She was old enough to be saved, but she was afraid of having to face the congregation. She had refused to go to the camp meeting when Amanda asked her. Dulcie said she had beans to work up. Beans to work up! She said that in a matronly tone, the way a small girl playing with her doll tried to sound like a weary mother. Dulcie was only fifteen.

"What does it feel like now, Mrs. Wheeler?" Dr. Foote was saying.

"Fat," she said. "It feels full."

"Like you're not done?"

She nodded. Her head whirled. The babies lay quietly. The little girl sucked.

"It's getting first light," said Alma. "I hope Mandy can manage breakfast for everybody. Mammy has to have her oats and eggs and sausage by sunup or she starts growling. And the boys will be raring to get out. And Wad'll be bellering like a scrub bull in a canebrake during cucklebur season if he don't get his cornbread made just so. But he married her, he can eat whatever she throws together."

"Fried pies," said Christie. She could almost taste one of Amanda's dried-peach pies. Amanda knew how to make them crisp, not too greasy.

Alma snorted. "Fried pies is about the only thing Mandy can cook fitten to eat."

"I didn't mean that," said Christie, feeling protective toward Amanda. "Where's Hattie gone to?"

"She got mad and left," said Alma. "She was a-fixing to walk home in the dark, but Wad carried her. Let me have that one." She took the little girl from Christie's breast. Alma raised her voice. "James, why don't you just go on up to the house and get you some sleep? You're in the way, and Christie's doing good."

Christie heard James's voice from the kitchen, true and clear, saying, "I can't go off and leave her like this."

"I may not die after all," Christie said. The quilt was hanging between them, but she could see his shape move like a shadow against the log-cabin pattern.

The doctor said, "James, you could go on and catch some rest. You'll need your strength."

"He has to milk before too awful long," said Alma.

James tiptoed around the bed to the side next to the stairway. Christie could feel him staring down. She opened her eyes and saw his wild grin, like the day she met him. "Lord God," he said quietly. "Two for the price of one. You done me proud, Chrissie."

"James Lake. Emily Susan," said Christie, aware of the little flannel-shrouded shapes beside her. Little rabbits in a nest. Twins meant the monster inside her was smaller. Two rescued from his clutches. Maybe she *would* die. Maybe those fibroids were eating into her. Or the afterbirth was stuck. But the sight of these two tiny, perfectly formed little creatures kept her from being so scared now. She felt herself float a little, her weight lessening. The babies' faces moved simultaneously, as though they were asking a silent question of her. James went out the front door, and she could hear him talk to the dogs. She heard Dark-Fire's light whinny, like the screech owl. She was relieved that James had gone. Then the weight inside—the entire weight this time—moved down with a flood of pain. She pushed and pushed. Mrs. Willy took the babies out of the way as Christie grew violent. She was wet all over, her legs warm and sticky. Alma shoved newspapers under her. The doctor leaned his head under the tent, hiding from the women's eyes. Her husband had left her with a man looking up her naked crack. Alma and Mrs. Willy had been making nervous jokes about the doctor being there, but Dr. Foote did not acknowledge their humor. Where was Hattie, her warm voice like heated molasses?

"That must be the afterbirth," said Alma.

"No. I don't believe so," said Christie, as something slipped from her. "You might be surprised."

"This is a first for me," said Dr. Foote, handing a bloody newspaper to Alma.

Morning came. The moon faded, washed out by the rising light. The room took on a different air, with the light of dawn coming in from the kitchen. Mrs. Willy pushed the kitchen curtains back. The doctor went out to feed and water his horse, then checked in once more before he went home to breakfast. He wouldn't eat anything Alma offered to make him, saying he needed to go home to see about his wife, who had been poorly since the January snow.

Christianna Wheeler had given birth to five babies by then, and she was falling asleep, exhausted.

6

ON THE BOLSTER BESIDE CHRISTIE THE FIVE BABIES LAY IN A ROW, each wrapped up snugly, like a store package without the string. They used all the outing flannel that Christie had ready for one baby. They were asleep. Alma had buried the afterbirth to keep the dogs from getting it. As she dreamed herself awake, Christie kept telling herself she should have realized what she was carrying. She had felt all those arms and legs thrashing around in her, but she had feared they were connected—a single organism flailing to get free, swelling her womb unbearably. She knew if it had been one freak creature, it would have killed her trying to get out. She hadn't imagined there could have been five sweet, perfectly formed babies in there. Getting them out had been so uncomplicated, after all, simpler than her previous labors. The sun was shining broadly through the kitchen window, and she felt her smile burst her face open before she even opened her eyes. She felt like giggling with glee, as if she had played a huge joke on everybody in the family.

"Great day in the morning!" cried Wad, barging into the kitchen. "James is out yonder strutting around like a banty rooster."

"Shut the door," said Alma. "You don't want these babies taking cold." She was folding the quilt she had just taken down from the bedposts.

"Good God a'mighty," said Wad, standing over the babies. "So that's what you was a-carrying, Christie." He tugged at his hat. Christie rarely saw James's uncle in a moment of awkwardness, and she enjoyed the sight. Wad was thin and fine-boned, with straight, pale brown hair that was lightening into gray. His face was deep-creased, like weathered planks.

Mrs. Willy was asleep on Nannie's pallet, curled up in her bonnet and dark dress. She stirred under the thunder of Wad's voice.

"I don't reckon I'll be setting much tobaccer for you this time, Wad," said Christie, trying to adjust her pillows without disturbing the babies. "I've got my hands full."

"Dad-burn it, girl, I need a good pair of hands. I don't need five more mouths to feed."

"They're little. They won't eat much."

Christie had already nursed each one of them during the early hours, and now she was starved. "Bring me some sweet-milk, Alma. There's some down in the cistern."

"James just brought in some," Alma said.

"You're going to have to get you a fresh cow to feed them young-uns," said Wad doubtfully.

"We ain't feeding them babies cow's milk," Alma said to Wad.

Christie struggled to sit up when Alma handed her a glass of milk. The babies stirred, two of them working their mouths—James Lake and the girl with the blond hair that seemed to curve into a topknot.

Alma said, "I'm cooking you some oats."

"I could eat eggs and bacon," Christie said. She drank most of the milk.

"You ain't ready for that," said Alma. Christie gave her the glass back.

Amanda was at the door. "I just had to see these precious things," she squealed as she came in. She removed her fascinator and adjusted a hairpin.

"Shut the door," said Alma.

Amanda's voice bubbled merrily, like sweet grape juice boiling. She made over the babies with squeals and gibberish until another one woke up. "James said there was two boys and three girls," she said, touching the one whose eyes were open. "Let me look and see which is which."

"Them two's the boys," said Christie, touching the outer two. "And them three's the girls. This is James Lake, and this is Emily Sue, and the others we ain't named yet."

"How are you going to tell 'em apart?"

"They're all different," said Christie. "This one, James Lake, was born first, and he's got the black hair—"

"Mandy, don't make her talk. She needs her strength," said Alma. "And Wad, you've gawked enough. Get on out of here and get to work."

Wad shook his head in wonder. "She done dropped a litter, like a sow and a gang of little pigs."

"Joseph sent word to your mama, Christie," said Amanda, glaring at her husband.

Wad wandered into the kitchen, and Christie began to nurse the baby who was awake, the girl with the blond topknot. Wad's words had jabbed her like a fork.

She managed a smile. "Mama never imagined I could do anything like this," she said to Amanda.

Another of the babies began fussing, and Amanda picked her up. It was one of the girls, the tiny one who had thin lips and a shallow forehead like Christie's Aunt Sophie. "There now," Amanda said, touching the little nose. "It need some titty. Christie, how're you going to make enough to feed all these?"

Christie didn't waste her strength answering. It was one of those questions thrown out into the air and left to settle like dust. The little girl at her breast was feeding vigorously. Five babies could drink her dry, Christie thought.

"You done good, Christie," Amanda said, as she rocked the baby in her arms. "You didn't suffer anywhere near as bad as I did with Lena."

"When I had Thurman, I labored over thirty-six hours," said Alma. "He didn't want to come out."

"I think this one's hungry," said Amanda, placing the tiny last-born at Christie's left breast. Christie tried to sit up, but it was awkward, with two babies nursing at once. Alma brought the glass of milk to Christie's lips.

"Here, finish this," Alma said.

"I'm hungry," said Christie, after draining the glass.

"I don't know if your system's stout enough for no bacon and eggs."

"I believe I could even eat butter beans," said Christie.

Alma hooted. "Well, hold your taters, I'll commence to cooking."

"Everybody's going wild up at the house," said Amanda. "I told 'em they couldn't come yet till I saw how you were. Little Bunch claims she's going to move down here, so I guess I'll have to lock her up, and your little boys are acting like wild horses."

"How's Nannie?"

"Well, Nannie cried and wouldn't eat her oats. She misses you."

From the kitchen, Wad said, "Are you done feeding them babies yet?" He was at the washstand, behind the pie safe.

"Come on back in here, Wad. I never saw you at a loss for words," said Christie. Amanda pulled at the sheet to hide Christie's breasts from Wad's eyes.

"I ain't never seen nothing like this," said Wad. "I ain't never knowed anybody to have five before."

"I knowed a woman to have three oncet," said Mrs. Willy, suddenly awake and walking the floor in a curious nervous gait, her hump seeming to bounce behind her.

"I ain't never heard of five," said Alma.

"Nobody has five," said Amanda, as if the thought had just occurred to her.

Wad said, "You've gone and done it, girl, you've done the beatin'est thing to hit this country since President Jackson bought it from the Indians."

"Since that earthquake way back yonder," said Alma.

Christie felt a little stronger with the glass of milk, and she could smell the intoxicating odor of bacon frying. Mrs. Willy looked drunk. Lack of sleep had affected the old woman. She must be at least fifty, Christie thought. Just as she relaxed against the pillows, two more of the babies woke up and cried.

"They wants their titty!" squealed Amanda happily.

"I'm leaving," said Wad. "This could keep up all day."

"You packed manure in on your shoes," Alma said.

The babies squirmed like kittens looking for a nipple. Christie almost expected them to purr. Already she had studied them closely enough to know each one. James Lake, the oldest and biggest; Emily Sue, his stout, curly-haired sister; the boy with James's nose; the little girl with the blond topknot; the girl with the faint birthmark on her ear and Aunt Sophie's shallow forehead. All of them had round, unwrinkled ears and sharp little noses. James Lake had a large, full mouth, and he sucked eagerly; Emily Sue—maybe Christie imagined it—had Susan's questioning look and her quick responsiveness; the blond one with the most hair had been slow to nurse at first but responded to encouragement. The babies bore no resemblance to the violent, stormy creature she had imagined was inside her. She touched their hands and toes in renewed surprise. She knew James had gone to the barn to fix them a temporary bed. She couldn't remember what James had said. She didn't think he had said anything. Surely he did not believe what he saw.

After Christie ate her breakfast, Alma kept the other family members out while Christie tried to doze. Her belly hurt again, and she took some more of the powders Dr. Foote had left. During the nap, one of the babies nursed while Mrs. Willy held him in place. Christie was only half asleep, not daring to roll over.

Mrs. Willy had a touch of sickness—her bowels were running badly—and went to the outhouse. Amanda left, and in a moment of quiet, Christie said, "Alma, you needn't stay down here and do for me. I hate to depend on you."

"Just hush and don't think a thing about it," said Alma. "We've all got a hard time coming. So you just grab your rest."

"I didn't know you would be this good to me, after the way I've acted."

Alma stomped across the kitchen, her rag swishing, her big shoes falling like anvils.

II

Desire

1890–1899

1

CHRISTIE'S RELIEF MADE HER MIND WHIRL DIZZILY. THE TERROR IN her womb made sense now. And it even seemed fitting that there were so many babies. She and James had gotten carried away with their secret pleasures, and finally it had caught up with them. Sometimes Christie would brim over with laughter just thinking about the delicious privacy of it. No one had known how industriously she and James went at it. She could feel herself blushing, even now in her semiconsciousness, as she struggled to comprehend the truth of what she had achieved. Five babies lay on the bed beside her. She thought she must be dreaming. She had often wondered what people would think if they knew what she and James had done—how often and where, how they had enjoyed it shamelessly. Now they would suspect.

There wasn't even a word for it. She had never heard it spoken about, except in the vaguest terms. Vulgar schoolgirls snickered about "making babies." It was "what they did in the dark," "the matrimonial union," "the marriage bed," "planting seed," "joining like animals." Mama referred to it as "the wifely duty." Christie and James found a whimsical word of their own for it—"plowing." Sometimes, when they ventured into unexplored territory of surprising sensations, James talked about plowing new-ground. She knew it was shameful to enjoy it so much. It was sinful if you weren't married. There were words for that in the Bible: fornication, whoring. A woman who sinned got herself talked about for the rest of her life. Besides, Christie had heard that a person could overindulge, causing the body to be drained of energy and health. A man who didn't marry was likely to engage in the worst vice, self-abuse. Christie's Uncle Zollicoffer took Lion Tonic to build up his strength, and her mother had hinted at the reason, warning

Christie of the temptations the devil would strow in the path of the righteous.

Years before, back in Dundee, when Christie and James started sparking, Mama said, "We don't know his people." Mama was rattled by his rough, dashing ways—precisely what attracted Christie. He would ride up to her father's blacksmith shop, straight from working in his mother's tobacco patch. He would halt the horse so quickly it would rare up with him. From the garden, Christie would see him coming and run into the house to hide herself, for there she was in some faded old dress and that ugly green sunbonnet that had too much stiffening in it. Through the window, she would watch him shooting the breeze with her father, who was out shoeing a horse or straightening a buggy axle. James acted as though he had just been passing by. He was tall and limber, with thick, glistening chestnut hair and a sly grin. He didn't go to their church. He seemed to be set slightly apart from the community, because he had been born and raised a hundred and fifty miles west—over in Hopewell, beyond the two big rivers. If I marry him, he'll take me away from here, she thought.

All that season, she concealed her excitement. She found herself churning butter to a rhythm of "James loves Christie, Christie loves James." She unmolded the butter and furtively traced his initials at the edge of the fern design pressed into the yellow surface. She saw meaningful patterns in the fan of sunrays beneath billowy clouds; in clusters of baby chicks; in the glow of a hen egg; in the way a pair of birds sat on a branch, careful not to get too close to each other. "We don't know his people," her pa would say out of the blue, several hours after her mother said it.

Papa judged James to be well-intentioned but doubted he would be able to provide for Christie. James lived with his mother and sister on some poor land that ran on a rocky slant, and they had only one cow.

"He don't have no place to carry ye to," said her pa. "He'll be carrying ye to live with his mammy, and then ye'll be waiting on her hand and foot."

"She's feeble," Mama put in. "I see her name on the sick list in the paper ever so often. She had a congestive chill back in the winter."

"Maybe she'll die," said Christie impatiently.

"Christianna!" said Mama, looking hurt.

Papa shook his head. "Wash Simmons down at the sawmill told me I needed to marry ye off to get ye out of that schoolhouse. Wash says he never seed a girl to keep on after the twelfth grade, when it's done over with."

Mr. Maynard had let her continue coming to school, insisting she would make a good schoolteacher if she didn't marry. He furnished her with additional history books and drilled her in the subject each morning. The maps of China and Europe intrigued her most, places so far away they almost could not be believed. But then she asked him for a history of Kentucky, and she memorized facts about Andrew Jackson's purchase of land from the Chickasaws in 1818. The western tip of Kentucky, the upper portion of the Purchase, was hemmed by rivers. It touched the Mississippi River like the toe of a boot, the book said, but Christie's father said the shape on the map looked more like a pile of hen drop. The ball at the toe of the boot—the New Madrid bend of the Mississippi River—was the center of the devastating earthquake that in late 1811 had rumbled all the way to the East Coast and rattled dishes at the White House. Paducah was the main city in the Purchase now, but Hopewell was a thriving town of two thousand souls who entertained themselves with oyster suppers and hops and Valentine drawings, according to one of the accounts Christie eagerly read. The surrounding land, part prairie, begged for grain and tobacco. One book said the rivers provided the humidity to keep the summertime green, so green that when the first white settlers floated down the Cumberland from Nashville and turned onto the Tennessee River, they selected the area because it reminded them of Ireland. But another history book said it reminded the settlers of England.

Her parents let James come on Sunday afternoons and sit with her in the shut-off parlor, while her younger sisters, Eunice and Emily, giggled in the hallway. Or he would take her riding in his buggy if the weather was fine. Once, though, they were caught in a surprise rain and took shelter in a schoolhouse, where they sat side by side at a desk made for two small children. He nudged her, pretending he didn't see he was scooting her out of the seat. She nudged back, pushing him playfully. Then her awareness of their bodies pressing each other in their damp clothes made her cheeks flame. Her fingers caught hold of the inkwell hole in the desk, and she yanked herself upright. She marched to the blackboard.

"I'm the teacher," she said, teasing. With chalk, she wrote her name: *Christianna Wilburn.* "Recite this, please," she said.

"Yes, ma'am! Chrissie-tanna Will-be-yourn," he said solemnly. "Where's your middle name at?"

"I ain't got one. Mama thought my name was two words. Christie Anna. But it's one word. What's your middle name?"

He shifted position, draping his long arms languidly over the small desk, his legs jutting out into the aisle. He was as loose-limbed as a jumping jack. He stood up and came forward. She thought he was going to kiss her. Instead he wrote his full name on the board, *James Reid Wheeler.* He stacked the three words vertically, so that *Wheeler* came to rest just after her name.

CHRISTIANNA WILBURN WHEELER

Her eyes raced past his smooth good looks to the rain outside. It was letting up, and already the hot summer air was steaming.

It was true that the Wilburns didn't know his people over in Hopewell, but they knew his local relations. His mother's kin, the Reids, were early settlers of Dundee. As for James's adventuresome father, John Wheeler had come to Dundee as an itinerant carpenter and wound up marrying Pernecia Reid. He took her to Hopewell, to the Wheeler family farm. When James was sixteen, his father was kicked in the head by a mule with a loose shoe, and he lived only a week. After that, Mrs. Wheeler returned to Dundee with her children. Now James helped his mother run the small farm her parents left when they died. James didn't finish school.

He told Christie he burned to go back to Hopewell, a climate where dark-leaf tobacco thrived. He claimed the dark tobacco, which was cured by fires burning beneath it when it was hanging in the barns, was more satisfying to work than the golden leaf raised in Dundee.

"One of these days, I im to go back and live on my daddy's place, where I was raised," he told Christie's parents. "I aim to have fields of dark tobaccer and a fruit orchard and a herd of cattle and a stable full of horses, as well as pigs and hens and geese. I aim to have just about everything that'll grow or walk—just as soon as Uncle Wad turns loose of that section of land I'm supposed to have. I get fifty acres, and then I want to buy some more from him."

"Gooseberry bushes," Christie said, as if she were asking for the moon.

James promised her gooseberry bushes and a flock of banty hens if she wanted them. A peacock too.

"He talks mighty big talk," Papa allowed that evening, after the younger children had gone to bed.

"He's young," said Mama.

"He could charm the pants off of a snake," Papa said.

"Hopewell is too far away," Mama said, knotting a thread.

Mama seemed to have forgotten that Lake Wilburn had courted her down in Tennessee and brought her all the way up from Smith County, her home, to live in Dundee. Her full name was Mary Tennessee Rhodes, and he always called her Tennie, as though she were a souvenir of that state.

"Go on and marry him, Christie," Granny Wilburn said. "A young girl needs to marry and raise a family." Granny was always dispensing advice, which Christie ordinarily ignored.

But gloomy Aunt Sophie Rhodes, Mama's sister, who had lived with them for as long as Christie could remember, said, "So many girls marry too young and it kills them."

"Hush, Sophie," said Mama. "You'll give the girl bad dreams."

"But you know it's true. They can't wait to start out. And their constitutions can't stand it."

Aunt Sophie coughed and spit into her brass spittoon, a little cup shaped like a rooster, with a hinged lid. All her life, Christie had seen that rooster tail pop down, the rooster rare back to crow, and Sophie spitting into the little cavity beneath. She'd spit and say "Cock-a-doo-dle-do" almost in the same breath and motion.

Christie's parents gave the preacher a ham and two silver dollars. One Saturday in July, Mama killed a fattened hen and made lady cake, and the neighbors and family brought more meat and cakes. The next day, James brought his mother and his sister in a wagon, along with a ham and some new-potatoes. The kinfolks from Tennessee brought watermelons, which were already ripe down there. The flies were buzzing, the horses gave off hot oat-breath, and the chickens fluffed their feathers lazily in their dust bowls. A child collected a jar full of potato bugs. In the middle of the afternoon, Granny Wilburn had to lie down with her racing heart in the front room, where the breeze rippled the dotted-Swiss curtains. Christie's mama laughed, recalling how Granny had behaved the same way the day Mama married Lake. Both Emily and Eunice, Christie's sisters, spilled lemonade on their fresh white dresses, and during the ceremony their brothers, Luther and Jack, got in a little fight over a bluetick hound that had turned up. Christie felt a swelling desire churn through her, an anticipation of lying in James's arms at last. They were standing under the largest oak tree in the yard, and a spider was dangling down over the preacher's head, spinning and wrapping her silk around a grasshopper that had just blundered into her web. The spider rolled the grasshopper with silk, over and over, like a store clerk wrapping a package and tying it with string. Christie felt her desire winding around and around. She almost broke out laughing when she heard the preacher say, "Christianna Wilburn, do you take this man . . . ?" She forgot what to say. Brother Woodall had to repeat, "Christianna Wilburn, do you take this man?" James elbowed her; Papa cleared his throat. She heard her little brothers fussing, her mama threatening under her breath to get the switch. The stray bluetick got beneath the long table, where the food waited under white tablecloths. Christie was taken outside of herself, as though she had been knocked out of her senses and thrown sprawling for a tumbling somerset across the sky before floating back down to earth. Everything was unbelievable. And so funny she thought she would not be able to restrain the runaway inner mirth that boiled like a mineral spring.

There was an electric charge in the air, like the atmosphere before a summer storm. But the sun was shining and there were no clouds.

"I do," she said.

"I got you now," said James after they kissed. His grin spread out like a slice of mushmelon.

A while later, after almost everyone had finished eating, Christie caught James on the back porch.

"I hope the preacher leaves early so we can dance," she said when they stole an embrace.

"You naughty girl."

"I want to dance."

"We've got plenty of time for dancing," he said. "We'll be dancing through the cornfields and up the creek and down the tobaccer patch."

And then he grabbed her hands and whirled her around. He danced her out into the yard, as if there were music. The preacher's mouth flew open and he dropped the chicken leg he was eating. The bluetick hound grabbed it. Christie's cousins—two dozen of them—gasped, but the younger ones giggled and joined the dance, spinning around giddily. Aunt Sophie hacked, and her cock-a-doodle-do sounded louder than she probably intended. Mama cried, "Christie *Anna!* Don't drag that hem in the dirt. All them hours a-hemming on that."

"This ain't dancing, Brother Woodall," James said as they romped through the yard past the preacher. "It just looks like dancing."

"The devil will get you on your wedding night!" said Aunt Sophie with a frown. She disapproved of everything pleasurable, including sunrises and boiled custard.

"Get that grin off of your face, Aunt Sophie," Christie said, prancing away with James through the hot, thick grass.

Wash Simmons laughed. "Look at them young people go. Durn, I wisht the preacher would let me play my fiddle."

Christie heard Aunt Sophie mutter, "It's nine months from the marriage bed to the deathbed."

Brother Woodall had found another piece of chicken and was holding it up high, away from the dog.

The women packed the wagon with pies and cakes and salads of chicken and ham; watermelon-rind preserves; extra watermelons; bread; fresh eggs. They set the presents in: vegetable and flower seeds, hair ribbons, brushes, butcher knives, coal-oil lamps, and a twenty-piece set of china dishes that several of the Tennessee relations went in on together. Mama piled Christie's feather bed in the back of the wagon, along with the sheets and quilts and coverlets she had helped Christie make over several winters. Aunt Sophie gave Christie a chair doily she had been tatting for years. It was familiar, and Christie was surprised to learn it was for her. "I was tatting it for you all along, Christie," said Aunt Sophie. Christie thought she would cry.

In James's wagon, with two patient old horses, the newlyweds traveled a mile and a quarter to the plain white house where James lived with his mother and his sister. In a small, dark room upstairs, after Christie dressed the spool bed with her feather bed and sheets and quilts, they began the part nobody ever talked about.

2

IN THOSE FIRST FEW YEARS OF MARRIAGE, CHRISTIE FELT SIMULTANE-ously giddy and ecstatic, mentally agitated and surging with fire and ambition. During her first pregnancy, she was haunted by Aunt Sophie's warning, but after she gave birth to Clint without any trouble, she laughed to Aunt Sophie's face. She was glad to be out of that claustrophobic household, filled with Aunt Sophie's seminary quotations and Granny Wilburn's bad breath, and the conspicuous absence of Susan, which seemed to make the whole house creak with grief. Having her own children and leading her own life was like having her own playthings in a secret place. Even though she was married, she still felt young and gay. Because she and James lived with his mother and sister, their intimate life remained furtive and secret and exciting, and they stole kisses behind doorways, in the stable, in the barn. James often teased Christie, saying "Give me a buss" when he knew his mother was just steps away, startling Christie into embarrassed giggles.

Mrs. Wheeler was gentle and frail, and Christie took advantage of her scared-sheep nature much of the time. But Christie liked her and could see some of James's sweetness reflected in her features. Mrs. Wheeler had a flaw in her speech. When she said her name, Pernecia, it came out "Mermetha." Christie wasn't patient with the older woman's groping efforts to be understood, and she often wished James's mother could write the words down. Secretly, she was tickled by the oddness of the words shaped by her mother-in-law's struggling tongue. Cruel, young Christie kept trying to maneuver her into saying "preserves," or "shortening bread," or "shush."

Christie called her Mermetha. "Mermetha," she would say. "Tell me what it was like when you lived over there in Hopewell. Was it pretty? Did you have Valentine drawings? Or hops? Were there funny people, interesting to talk to?"

She had been homesick the whole time, Mrs. Wheeler told her. She said she never felt right among strangers. She didn't seem to remember the landscape, the flowers and trees, the roads, the stores in town, all of which Christie was avid to know about. Christie was eager for the company of strangers. She saw the same people every week, and the church suppers were dull. She wanted to get away from busybodies like the Calvin sisters, who gossiped in a mean spirit about all the churchgoers who couldn't carry a tune.

Out driving with James in his buggy early in their acquaintance, Christie had let him kiss her, but she always pulled back primly, worrying about wrinkling her clothes and whether her breath was sweet. But the ache between her legs increased with prolonged expectation. When he led her upstairs at his mother's house, on their wedding night, she was alive with mingled shame and joy. She made him wait in the hallway. Trembling, she wrestled clumsily with the feather bed she had brought. She flopped it onto the straw mattress on the spool bed and plumped it up with her fists. Then she spread the sheets of bleached muslin. She laid her double-wedding-ring quilt on the sheets, then unfolded the coverlet and spread it on top. The pillow slips had hand-tied lace borders, and the sheets were edged with fine stitching learned from her mother. The quilt had been pieced over three winters, and Mama and Aunt Sophie and Granny Wilburn had helped with the quilting. The coverlet was white, with leaves and flowers she had embroidered in white. All that white, like bird tracks in the snow.

"It's too hot a night for all that cover," James said after she let him into the room.

He pulled out her hairpins one by one, and her hair fell down, the tresses swinging almost to her waist. Her clothes loosened, and as the garments slipped away she could feel her hair hot against her back. The room was dark. She could hear an owl hooting mournfully. Mama had told her to do what James asked, implying it would be unpleasant. She had spoken of it in the same tone she would use for emptying slop buckets or dressing hens. The mystery of how the man connected with the woman and planted his seed was something that had never been explained. What Christie had witnessed among the horses, cows, and chickens seemed to confirm Mama's hints—especially if it involved the long, threatening thing Christie had seen hanging from a stallion's belly. But Christie surged with desire, her head whirling with questions. The marital union made as little sense as one of those perplexing Bible stories—casting pearls before swine. It was like that, she found out—just beautiful nonsense. Surrendering, she dropped all her questions then. She kept seeing mental pictures of her father's forge: the squeeze of his bellows, the fire of his furnace. She was warming herself near James's fire, close enough to scorch. The soft wisps on his chest, his beard, her own hair—all brushed against her like comforting nesting material. His arms were strong, his chest was smooth; he was hard and tight and smooth all over. She supposed it would always hurt—an inexplicably delicious sort of pain—but when the next time it didn't, she began to crave it more. Sometimes a garden had to be replanted, she thought recklessly whenever she and James escaped to the small upstairs room. The preacher had warned that the devil tempted Eve with this irresistible bliss. Adam and Eve weren't married, he said, and Eve's sin hurtled down through time to threaten all of the human race. Mama had spoken of the act as a troublesome duty. But it wasn't like that at all. It was like the pleasure of reaching under a hen to clasp a new egg, or petting kittens, or icing a cake. It was very much like the growing glimmer of a sunrise. Christie knew now why women wouldn't speak of it to each other—admitting the pleasure would be too embarrassing. Even with James, at times it was like something they did in secret from each other, in the dark, as if they were both having dreams—doing something in their sleep that they could admit no knowledge of later.

The surprise of it, the mechanics of it, and the tenderness of it were so different from what she had observed in the horses, or the cows with their hovering bull. She could not get enough of holding and caressing. The rooster clamped onto the hen's reddened comb and held her in place while she squawked piteously. The horses had such clumsy bodies, they could not lie together, entwined in an embrace. Their hard hooves seemed like weapons. The dogs got stuck and ran together in panic. But Christie thrilled to the pleasures of touching and barely touching and glimpsing and inching closer and feeling in the dark a bit of flesh that she couldn't name immediately—would this be his shoulder or his forearm or a patch of neck? She'd hold her finger still and try to identify the spot by its texture until he moved and she would know. Those first few years, they were both insatiable, desiring at all hours the carefree dabbling, the fun of hiding, the sweet expectation as they labored through the day thinking of the night's luxurious promise. Even while pregnant with the boys, and to a lesser extent with Nannie (who was a larger, fussier baby in the womb), she savored James's touch, his way of teasing at her flesh, strumming her chord like one of those noisemakers called a dumb bull, in which a vibrating string made a noise like a bull bellowing.

She recalled all the giggling and murmuring and moaning and caresses, the little jolts of surprise, the unexpected touches—the irrepressible sounds that Pernecia and Elizabeth must have heard.

In no time, it seemed, they had two boys and a girl.

Christie had married a fine man, her parents admitted. Papa judged a man by the way he took care of his tools. "A man that cares for his tools will care for his wife and younguns," he said. "I never see James throw his tools in the dirt or let them get wet. And he keeps his horses shoed good." Actually, Christie observed, James had had his horses shod more often than necessary as an excuse to tarry around her father's blacksmith shop during the year before they married. But James did take good care of all his animals, and he thought of his dogs as companions, talking to them as though they had lively minds. He had a fice named Floyd and a tree dog called Mose. They were always with him in the fields. As the children came along, James treated them like little farmers. Even before the boys could walk, he made them popguns and tom-walkers—funny little wooden stilts. James always took his time with a job, whether it was currying the horses or sickling weeds or making playthings for the children. He did everything as though he had all day.

When Mrs. Wheeler died unexpectedly, soon after Nannie was born, Christie regretted the way she had treated her. A nasty attack of remittent fever took her swiftly, before Christie learned to appreciate and forgive the older woman's more difficult ways. In his grief, James rented the farm to Elizabeth, who brought her new husband and baby to live there.

"Now we'll go to Hopewell," James told Christie. "I'll build you a new house and plant you some gooseberry bushes."

"We can't afford to build a house," she said.

"Uncle Wad will let me borrow."

"Papa told me never to borrow," she objected.

"But I'm aiming to grow dark-fire tobaccer. It brings good money. And we can live with Uncle Wad and them till we get the house built."

He was insistent, and as enthusiastic as a boy going fishing. He knew she had always wanted to go to Hopewell, or anywhere. But now she was cautious.

"What would I do out there if something happened to you and I owed a debt like that?" Christie asked him. She couldn't imagine living without seeing his slate-blue eyes, or his thick hair—brown like a thrasher bird.

"The Wheelers would take care of you," James said earnestly.

"Uncle Wad and Mandy, and Aunt Alma—you won't find better people in the whole world. They'd do anything for you."

At last, Christie and James, with enough savings for seed and a cow, set off for Hopewell in a new red wagon with their baby girl and two small boys. Reluctantly, James gave his dogs to Elizabeth. They were too old to go, he said. A frisky team—a black gelding, a bay mare, and two roans—pulled the wagon. Christie stored the furniture in the Wilburns' stable, expecting to send for it as soon as James got the house built. Christie brought her churn and her bedding, and Mama gave her a new quilt, a red log-cabin figure on a gray ground. Papa had made them a set of fireplace tools and a hoe.

The red wagon reached Hopewell late on a Saturday. Christie and the children sat on the wagon boards, behind James. She held herself upright and self-conscious, fidgeting with anticipation. She had never been so far away from home. James, bouncing on the spring seat, drove the team past the courthouse square. Although it was late and most of the day's trading had been done, there were still many mules and horses tied to the racks around the square and some men gathered here and there. The large courthouse, in the center of the square, was made of red brick with white trim, with a Seth Thomas clock in its tall tower. The town square had several dry-goods stores, cobblers' shops, a buggy-and-wheel shop, a confectionery, a ladies' millinery shop, and two drugstores. The buildings were all elegant brick, with stores on the bottom floor and offices above; painted signs for doctors, lawyers, and land agents gleamed on the upper-story windows. Long's Hardware had an engraving just beneath its third-story cornices: WAGONS PLOWS STOVES.

They turned south and followed the highway running parallel to the railroad. The sun was low in the sky. After they crossed a bridge above the railroad track and passed a tobacco warehouse and a sweet-feed mill, the land flattened out; along meandering creeks, intricately patterned lines of hickories and oaks and tupelos separated handsome cleared fields.

The place waiting for Christie and James was only a mile from town, close to the railroad track and not far from the stockyards and feed mill. The Wheeler farm was a rough square of about three hundred acres, and James owned fifty acres of it, land that had come to him from his father. He owed Wad for another twenty acres. Crossing the fields diagonally was a tributary of Wolf Creek. When James turned the horses down the road that bisected the property, they saw the clear, open fields, the winter-bare fruit orchard, and the deep creek, and, in the distance, a large white tree-shaded house with several outbuildings. The farm had the look of a secure settlement.

"That's Uncle Wad's house," James said, halting the horses. "Our house will be over yonder behind those trees."

"Here, hold Nannie a minute."

Christie set the baby in her husband's arms and ran out across the open field. She tried to see everything: the railroad bed on the bank by the road, the intersection of the road and the railroad tracks, the cows in the pasture, a flock of blackbirds taking off from an isolated dead tree. Toward the north, the grain elevator of the feed mill in Hopewell was visible. This was her new home, the fields where her children would play and work, where she'd raise her chickens and work her garden. The fields were well situated, with the creek crossing them. The curly-bark birches standing along the creek line resembled scraggledly-bearded men. She saw the carpet of leaves under the trees and the frozen ridges left by the plow in the fields. A dusting of snow had sifted across the fields, causing the winter wheat to take on a bluish tinge. Dull gray clouds boiled above. She imagined the sunrises and sunsets from this spot. The exhilarating freedom that ran through her now was like the stir she used to feel when she watched James on his horse, in her front yard, talking to her father while she hid inside. She ran through the stubby, dead cornstalks in the field, with her arms spread open to the sky.

Now, she thought.

3

EVEN IN THE CROWDED WHEELER HOUSE, WHERE THEY STAYED THAT
first year, James and Christie could not stop their reckless plowing.
Didn't the whole household hear it? she always wondered afterward.
Christie and James and the children bunched into one of five small
upstairs bedrooms. Clint and Jewell slept on a pallet, and Nannie slept in
the crate she had traveled in. During that first night, Christie heard the
train coming; it was so close she thought doomsday had arrived. The
train took a long time to pass. The boys stirred; James squeezed her
hand. The train roared past like a romping child with a mind of its own.

The house was packed—Wad and Amanda and their two girls,
Lena and Little Bunch; and Wad's sister Alma and her husband,
Thomas Hunt, with their five children; as well as Boone, Wad and
Alma's sickly brother, and Mammy Dove, their mother. Everyone
except Mammy Dove slept upstairs. Boone had a bed on the landing
outside James and Christie's door. At night, she heard trains and animals outside, and snores and wheezes and clocks inside. She never
heard any sounds from the other rooms that she could identify as what
she and James were doing, and she had to wonder what that meant.
The spool bed they occupied had a latticed-rope bottom that tugged
on its wooden frame with a loud creaking sound. James whispered
once, "This sounds like a wheat thresher. I reckon we better thresh
some wheat, now that we've plowed a right smart." Christie couldn't
help snickering. Some mornings after a particularly noisy session in the
uncooperative bed, she would go downstairs and everyone at the table
would stop eating and stare at her as if she were the loosest woman in
all of Sodom and Gomorrah combined.

The daytime sounds of the Wheelers grew as familiar to her as rain on the roof. She was as intimate with their voices now as she was with the contours of the fields and the arrangement of the trees on the farm: Alma yelling after the children, her voice ricocheting off the walls; Wad grumbling and cussing, a raspy catch in his voice, as if he had used a file on it; Amanda's lilting, murmuring laugh; Boone's cough and bellowslike wheeze; Mammy Dove's infrequent little whine. The mantel clock ticked loudly; Amanda's cuckoo clock cuckooed. There always seemed to be the sounds of bacon frying and dogs barking and dishes clattering. And on top of it all, there were the sounds of the children laughing and screaming and fighting.

Amanda told Christie, "We've got to stick together or these Wheelers will be the death of us." At first Christie thought Amanda was joking, but as they became friends, she heard the seriousness in Amanda's words. Amanda was a pale, delicate woman with fine, light-brown hair. She often wore a brooch at her breast, as if she were dressed up to go somewhere. She was like a rose blooming in a tobacco patch, Christie thought. She was a sweet person, eager to please, and out of place, it seemed, among the Wheelers. Christie loved the girlish way Amanda laughed at herself. Amanda even laughed over her own fears. If a black cat was hanging around, she wouldn't go outside. She said if you broke a dish on Monday, you would get sick on Thursday. When she found a measuring worm on her dress, she said if a measuring worm measured your whole length, you would die. She exploded with surprise over the simplest things, as if she expected any day that a hen would lay something other than an egg. She involved the children in everything she did—hoeing, sewing, shelling beans—making a teaching game of each task. She still had a slim figure even after bearing two children. "After Wad's first wife, Mary, died, he needed somebody for his young boys," Alma told Christie. "But I believe he married Mandy purely for decoration. He found her with a bunch of barefooted brothers and sisters on a wagon in town one mule day. He just brung her on home." Amanda was sixteen years old then, not much older than Wad's boys. She had been raised over in Lyon County, in a puncheon-floored plank shack with ten brothers and sisters.

Christie couldn't imagine how Amanda could sleep with a man twenty years older. Wad had a foul breath, rounded shoulders, and white whiskers that Christie thought must be as prickly as a cactus. One day she saw Wad spit tobacco juice onto a hollyhock Amanda had trained up the drainpipe near the back door. The juice stained the bottom blossom. Amanda appeared in the doorway then, looking like a flower herself. She said, "Wad, the clock's winding down. It needs you to wind it." Christie could tell that the way she said that—it needs you—pleased him, and he looked at his wife as though he had just fallen in love.

4

BUT IT WASN'T JUST AN EXCESS OF LOVING, CHRISTIE THOUGHT. THE fuss over the earthquake prediction had affected her pregnancy, too. So many people she knew believed babies could be influenced in the womb by outside happenings. Last summer, when she got pregnant, everybody in Hopewell was talking about the coming earthquake, and all the anticipation had stirred her as much as dreams or the wrong foods. For virtually the entire nine months, her womb had rumbled and roared like the earth about to split open.

A noted prognosticator had foretold a cataclysmic upheaval in the earth. He said it would occur at the end of the year—the dawn of the new century. Every week the newspaper reported new details of his predictions: the land throughout the Mississippi River Valley would turn inside out, leaving nothing but a shimmering sheet of liquid clay; all the houses would sink; the earth might not stop shaking for months. The disaster was on everyone's lips. Preachers turned to the Book of Revelation to read deep meanings into the prophecy, for the new century was likely to bring the Day of Judgment. Some people, figuring it was now or never, spent all their money. Others gave all their possessions to the poor.

Christie didn't want to believe the talk, but her condition made her apprehensive. Amanda had worked her girls, Little Bunch and Lena, into a state of terror. The other children turned hide-and-go-seek into an earthquake game. Jimmie Lou, Alma's older daughter, scared the little ones with tales about the earth cracking open and catching afire.

"Do you believe that earthquake will happen?" Christie asked James one Saturday morning at breakfast.

He shrugged. "If it happens, it happens. Nothing I can do about it." He sliced his fried eggs rapidly, crisscrossing them with his knife aimed through the tines of his fork. He had shaved his beard off for the summer, and Christie still had trouble adjusting to the altered lines of his face.

"Mandy's in bad shape over it," Christie said.

James paused, his fork halfway to his mouth, and said thoughtfully, "You know what Wad said to me when I first laid eyes on her?"

"What?"

"He called her a orphan—his orphan wife. I felt sorry for her. I thought I felt sorry for her because she was a orphan, but later I knew it was because he *called* her that."

"She told me she felt like he picked her out that day on the square the way he'd pick out a mule," Christie said.

"He carries her around on a piller, though."

"She's got legs. She can walk," Christie said, a little too sharply. "You sound like Alma. Alma never gives her credit for anything."

James regarded her silently, the way he always did when she had one of her little rebellious outbursts. Sometimes, for no reason, she wanted to spite him, to do something perverse. Then she was so shocked at herself that she tried to pretend nothing had happened. She had a way of turning him off when talk got difficult, her stare piercing him like hot irons, her tongue like a hot poker. But the mood passed in a moment, as if the poker had been dropped into a tub of water, and she felt her protest drowning, hissing into silence.

Christie contemplated her husband's strong body, his thick hair. His face was rugged and weathered. Her love for him had gone through twists and turns as casual as the meandering of a creek. Since coming to Hopewell, they had been so busy working that they sometimes lost sight of each other. They used to catch little glimpses of one another at the same instant and share a jolt of happiness, like a puff of smoke from a chimney. But now their work wore them down, and apart.

She hated the dark-leaf tobacco James loved so much. She hated working with the gummy plants. She choked on the acrid smell of the hanging tobacco curing over hickory fires in the barn. James had counted on the dark-fired tobacco to flourish, but prices were going down instead. They owed Blankenship's Planing Mill for lumber, and they owed Wad over a thousand dollars for land. James had said they shouldn't have any more children for a while.

She hadn't told him she was pregnant again. The night she conceived, she figured out later, was a Saturday in early June. She remembered that night. James had been plowing corn until nearly dark. She saw him out in the far field, gripping the plow handle as he trudged behind a red mule. He had traded their fine bay mare for a pair of sorrel mules. She had desired his touch and had thought about it with a building need throughout the day as she hoed and ironed, but at bedtime they sank fast into sleep the instant the lamp was shut out. Later something awoke them both—one of the children calling out in sleep, or a jackass braying in a far field—and they turned to face each other in the dark. A sudden passion gripped them, and they plowed and plowed with renewed fervor, and the train whistle sounded, merging with the long, slow release of desire. She was swinging on a grapevine, her hair flying.

"The ground will open into a big ditch and swaller us up," Clint was saying now. "And down deep inside the ground it will be on fire." He waved his fork through the air in illustration.

James said, "Clean your plate, Clint. We can't waste that syrup."

Clint and Jewell were soaking their biscuits in sorghum molasses. James had brought home a new bucket of sorghum from a neighbor's syrup mill last week, and the children had begged for some at every meal. Christie wiped Nannie's face. Nannie had been sucking a rag Christie had strained tomatoes with the day before. Nannie was three. Her hair was fine and light, and her eyes were still blue.

Nannie squirmed away from Christie and sat down on the floor with the wooden crank toy James had made for her. It was the figure of a woman at a pretty red-cedar churn. When Nannie turned the handle on the box platform, the woman lifted her churn dasher up and down. Christie had made the figure a calico dress with a bonnet to match. Nannie called her plaything Churn Girl.

James said, "Quit cranking that thing so fast. You'll break it."

"Churn Girl's got to make butter 'fore dinner," said Nannie.

"You can't hurry butter," Christie said, removing James's plate. The yellow stain of the egg on the plate struck her like spilled sunshine.

James drank the rest of his milk and scooted his chair away from the table. Rising, he said, "Wad's aiming to start cutting tobaccer Monday if the weather holds out. He figures if we all get out there, we'll get it cut without having to hire any hands."

"I need to wash a-Monday," Christie said. She dreaded tobacco cutting.

"I can cut," Clint said, licking his fingers.

"Not till you're bigger." James laid his hand on Clint's head. "Boys, get on out to the corncrib and tote those cobs down to the hogs soon as you're done. We'll carry the corn to the mill after I get done milking."

"Jewell can't tote a whole bucket," said Clint.

"Be fair," said James, wiping his mouth on his sleeve.

"I hate tobaccer," Christie said, but he didn't hear.

She ate her breakfast and finished her morning work quickly, so they could get to town. She gathered vegetables from the garden, eggs from the henhouse. She cleaned the kitchen, swept. She made up the beds. Her muslin sheets were gray with wear and the harshness of lye soap. She needed to buy bluing. She wished she could have some fragrant soap, something other than homemade.

With Nannie at her heels, she carried a basket of eggs out to the wagon in the shed by the stable. As Christie set the eggs in the wagon, Amanda came through the back gate with the mail—a circular and a letter from Christie's mother. The mail carrier was riding away on his horse.

Amanda handed over the letter excitedly. "Mr. Letcher says he talked to a woman out on his Star Route that's got her husband to building a boat!" Amanda loosened her bonnet and let it fall to her neck. "When the Mississippi River spills out, she'll be ready to row!" Amanda laughed merrily. "Alma said last night she had too much to do to set around waiting on no earthquake!"

"I feel all stirred up," Christie said. But she wasn't ready to tell Amanda about the baby yet. She said, "It's like I want something—I don't know what—but I'll know it when I see it."

"You miss your people back in Dundee," Amanda said.

Christie nodded. She stared at her mother's handwriting on the envelope. It was wiggly, like worm trails under tree bark. "Mama's birthday's next week. I'm going to send her some trimming for a dress. Maybe some lace."

"I wish I could buy some new material," said Amanda with a sigh. "I need something new to wear to the earthquake! I told Wad if the earthquake catches me in my drawers, the Lord won't know me!" She laughed, pretending embarrassment.

"Are you really scared of that earthquake?"

Amanda shivered. "Maybe the world will end. I hear tell it might could."

"But Mandy, why would the Lord want to destroy His creation? The world is grand."

"Maybe it's just to make everything new again, like spring." Amanda touched Christie's cheek gently. "Don't fret, Christie. We need to have faith."

Christie turned to the house to get a knife to open her letter. Just then James and the boys appeared, leading the mules, Slow and Boresome. Christie pulled Nannie out of the way of the mules. The boys were quarreling over a dirt-dauber nest Clint had knocked down from the porch post. Clint wanted to keep it for his treasure box, but Jewell—behind Clint's back—had started picking the spiders out of the tunnels of the nest.

"Mandy, reckon that earthquake's a-coming tonight?" said James with a grin. He had been teasing her about it for days.

"I'm going to laugh at the expression on your face when the ground cracks open, James," Amanda said. "I want to see it. And Wad's face, too!" She leaned over to inspect the dirt-dauber nest in Jewell's hands. "Don't pick out the spiders, hon," she said gently. "Them's for the baby dirt daubers to eat on when they hatch out."

Nannie, pulling at Christie's apron, said, "Churn Girl put a spider in her churn and she churned it up into butter."

"She did not," Jewell said, his finger in one of the dirt-dauber tunnels.

"Don't be silly, Nannie," said James, giving her a pat.

"It was play-like," Nannie said quietly, almost in a whisper.

"I don't want to hear another word about that dirt-dauber nest, boys," James said with finality as he began to hitch the mules to the wagon.

Christie washed Nannie's face and hands and got her dressed for town. Then she put on her own good blue-figured dress and her freshest bonnet. She changed shoes and began carrying baskets of green beans and turnips out to the wagon. She was tired and angry. It had been a hard week. They were running out of clean clothes. She still had peaches and green beans to can, and the stock peas were starting to come in. She was behind on the tomatoes.

Her mother wrote that Emily had received a ribbon at the fair for her cross-stitching. Christie felt proud, but the news made her sad, too. She missed seeing her brothers and sisters grow up. Christie put the letter in the pocket of her dress, as if by keeping it with her she could be closer to her folks. She rode to town in silence, holding Nannie and a necklace of buttons for her to play with.

Just as they crossed the railroad track and turned onto the highway, they could hear the express train's whistle coming from the north. It was the Memphis Princess, going south from St. Louis. The train passed them, gliding on the shiny rails like a skater on a frozen creek bed. The train's shadow flattened the weedy embankment.

5

"WE'LL DARE THE EARTHQUAKE TO COME AND GET US. WE WON'T BE afraid," Amanda said, patting Christie's hand. "We'll test our faith."

"The Lord wouldn't bring us all the way down to Reelfoot and then spring an earthquake on us," Christie said with a laugh. "That wouldn't be fair."

They were on an excursion train. It was late summer, and the crops had been laid by, so there was a lull in the field work until harvest. They were going to a camp meeting—a "brush-arbor"—at Reelfoot Lake. Christie had been to camp meetings all her life, but this one was going to be different. Reelfoot Lake had been formed by the dreadful earthquakes of 1811 and 1812, and multitudes of the faithful were drawn to the site now—sure that another earthquake was coming, soon after Christmas. Christie didn't imagine the world would end just because it was the end of a century, as some said, but Amanda believed it might. Actually, both of them just wanted to go somewhere. James said it would do them some good. Amanda brought along Lena and Little Bunch, but Christie was glad none of the other Wheelers could come. Wad said he had enough religion to last him through the winter.

Christie and Amanda wore beribboned straw hats and carried ginger cakes and bottles of lemonade. On the train, their hands were idle, for they could no more do embroidery or mending on such a trip than they could in church. It was a Wednesday, but they had on their Sunday go-to-meeting clothes. Amanda wore a slim, brown skirt with tucks on the flounce and a waist with a lace-trimmed yoke and rows of tiny white buttons. Until she married, she had never owned a dress that wasn't handed down. She learned to make her own clothes on the machine that had belonged to Wad's first wife, whose dresses were too small for Amanda.

"Church picnic," said Christie. "Say it the way Mermetha would."

Amanda doubled over with giggles. She hadn't known James's mother very well, but Christie had described her often enough.

Amanda said, "Thurth mick-mick," and squealed.

Christie relaxed, glad she had told Amanda about the baby. She thought she could feel it jumping around already. It seemed much too soon.

Amanda called to Little Bunch, who was prowling in the aisle. "Go get you a drink, Bunch. You don't want to get too hot."

"She ain't had a fit since Easter," Lena said to Christie.

"Alma said she was growing out of them," Amanda said.

"I knew a man to have fits," Christie said.

"Was he married?" Amanda whispered to Christie.

"I don't believe so."

Amanda whispered, "Men that have fits? When they get married they don't have fits anymore because being married works off the poison."

"I never heard that. What an idea!"

Christie had told James she had been feeling wild in the head lately and needed to pray. He said she was mentally alienated. If he had known her secret, he would not have let her go to a camp meeting. When the train lurched, she felt off balance, as if her stomach lagged behind the train's motion. The blood rushed through her veins in an anxious tide. She had been having morning sick-spells. Many foods didn't suit her anymore. She had developed a distaste for cabbage and she didn't like black pepper on her mushmelon now. The nausea and dizziness were familiar, but they seemed worse this time. She thought that meant it would be a large baby, probably a boy. She remembered her mother having bad spells when she was carrying Luther. "It ain't like me to get down like this," Mama kept saying. Christie and Emily were frightened when Mama had a round of bloody flux that summer, weakening her for the delivery. Aunt Sophie gathered in the kinfolks and made sure Uncle Zollicoffer Rhodes made the trip from Bundle, Tennessee, right in the middle of threshing time.

Amanda fanned herself with a folding fan she had brought. It had a picture of Jesus on it, standing in front of a tobacco warehouse. "Lena, go see if you can get me some water," she said, handing her daughter her tin cup. "And hold on. This train jerks so. And wet this handkerchief for me." She whispered to Christie, "If it's this hot here, can you imagine how hot it must be down in Hell, on the Devil's hearth?"

Amanda often fixed Little Bunch up like a doll, and today she had curled her hair into perfect, fat tubes and fastened a blue bow atop her head. Little Bunch, a sad-faced, purposeful child, slept much of the way. When she was awake, her sharp fingernails dug into her scalp, worrying some sores she had made. Her curls were already falling out.

"I'm going to tie them hands behind your back," Amanda threatened, as she tore Little Bunch's hands away from her head. Then she drew the child lovingly to her breast and held her close as if the threat had come from someone else.

The camp followers sang rejoicing songs during the trip. A red-haired man led the singing. "Bringing in the Sheaves" was so popular it was repeated twice as they approached the station. Christie imagined bringing in sheaves during an earthquake, a festive notion. She always loved the spectacle of a camp meeting—all the singing and good cheer and food, the chance to see new people.

"Mm-ringing in the thieveth," Amanda said with a mischievous glance at Christie.

From the train, several coaches and wagons hauled the passengers to the campsite, in a clearing near the lake. Christie could see the lake through the margin of trees. Many of the cypress trees grew out in the water. Their roots—smooth, tanned "knees"—surfaced here and there. The lake was enormous and blue, with inlets and coves making a jagged shoreline. She saw a pale, long-legged bird wading in shallow water, its head occasionally ducking under the surface. It was a steamy day with a hazy sun that spread distinct, gauzy beams through the trees onto the lane leading to the camp. Christie's mother called sunbeams like that heaven-beams. The camp was crowded with buggies, slat-sided farm wagons, horses, rigged-up tents. Most families traveled to camp meetings in their wagons, bringing provisions for a week's stay. A camp meeting could go on that long, but Christie and Amanda were staying only one night.

"This is the biggest camp meeting I've ever been to!" Amanda said, gasping at the extent of the gathering. "I bet there's already a thousand here."

"Let's explore," said Christie, swinging her skirts away from some bushes. "Come on, girls."

Several canvas-shrouded pavilions had been erected, as well as a brush-arbor, a raised platform with a roof made of cut leafy branches to shelter the speakers. People were stringing up tents, cooking, singing in small, spontaneous groups, laughing, pitching horseshoes. Children ran around loose. The main event scheduled for late afternoon was a talk by a man who had survived the great earthquakes long ago. He was said to be nearly a hundred years old. In the meantime, a number of preachers were already at work, some holding forth behind tall stumps. They were talking away, gathering in all who would stop to listen. It seemed to Christie as she walked around the grounds that most of them were crying out gloomy news about the coming century.

One preacher had built himself a platform up in a shagbark hickory. His voice stormed down the Ten Commandments through thick hickory boughs. Another preacher, standing below in a damp, dirty shirt, his sleeves rolled up above his elbows, brandished the Bible, open to Revelation. A piece of paper fell to the ground. "My New Year's resolutions, folks," he said, stooping to snatch the paper. "Number one—give up the evil weed." He urged all Christians to turn over a new leaf with the new century. "The 'baccer leaf wrinkles and dries and shrivels and is subjected to the hand of man in the stages of manufacture—the cutting, the firing, the bulking, the stripping, the prizing," he said. "And in the end it all goes up in smoke. The leaf of man's days is like that, cultivated and worried and treated and cared for, but in the end it shrivels to dust, to ashes."

"He's right," Amanda said. "Besides, tobaccer is nasty."

"It's right toilsome," Christie agreed.

They wandered through the grounds, listening to the preachers call out their messages about the earthquake, Judgment Day, a new age, heaven on earth, and crop forecasts. They told prophecies: the coming winter would be the hardest in memory, a winter to test every Christian's faith; the new century would bring evils and wonders in equal proportion; if Christ didn't return in person on New Year's Eve, he would at least send an angel who would walk among us, like one of us, carrying a ledger, counting up our sins. The Book of Life for 1899 was shorter than it had ever been, as sinners' names fell off the rolls in huge numbers. Christie stopped to hear a thin, wasted-looking man who seemed earnest and sober, with a philosophical, reasoned way of presenting himself. He held a Bible but didn't thump it. In a low, subdued voice, he explained his plan for carrying God's word to the inhabitants of the moon. The plan involved a great deal of ammunition and some very long expanding tubes. Christie didn't know whether to laugh. The man had a dab of custard on his coat that she had the urge to remove.

"When do you aim to go to the moon?" Amanda asked the man. "Can I come along?"

"Don't be silly, Mama," said Lena.

"I'm just having fun," said Amanda. "Christie would go with me, wouldn't you, dear?" Amanda's eyes twinkled like dewdrops.

"You wonder if some of these preachers even have a church,"

Christie said doubtfully as they walked on. She thought they were probably enjoying themselves too.

Courting couples strolled around, ignoring all the preachers. Christie felt her spirits charged by the lively atmosphere. It did do her good to get away. She kept trying to imagine her great-grandfather, Thomas Wilburn, who had become a Methodist minister late in life. Inspired by the Cane Ridge Revival, he was ordained by Bishop Francis Asbury himself, then spent his last years as a circuit rider, traveling by horseback through the rough frontier of Middle Tennessee, bringing fresh news of the Lord to lost souls in the wilderness. The story told in the family was that he had heard God call to him, "Thomas Wilburn, get out there into the world and commence to preaching." He obeyed the call, not knowing until fifteen years later, on his deathbed, that one of his sons had been hiding in a tree and had issued the call himself as a prank.

An elderly couple with a barrel of water in their wagon ladled water with a tin dipper to anyone bringing his own cup. The man had erysipelas of the foot, he said, but he hadn't wanted to miss the camp meeting, so he had whittled some crutches out of hickory sticks, and his wife drove the mules.

"I just had to come and hear old Mr. Ledbetty tell about that earthquake way back yander," the man said.

"He's over a hundred year old," said his wife. "But the one I want to hear is that good Brother Cornett. They say he knows everything there is to know about the Bible."

"Why, he used to play cards," the husband said with a derisive snort. He was still whittling on a crutch.

"Oh, shut up, Phillip. If he used to play cards and then made a preacher, then that's good."

"He used to play cards and he dranked and run wild with women."

"I don't care. If he played cards and then made a preacher, he's done good. They say he knows everything there is about the Bible."

"I doubt that," said the husband. "I purely doubt it."

"Why, Phillip, he's *been* overseas!"

"She's got a hankering for this Brother Cornett," the man said to Christie and Amanda as he filled their cups with water.

"He sure sounds like the beatin'est," Amanda said with a wide smile.

Amanda was friendly to everyone she met, but Lena was shy, standing with her head hunched down because she was growing so tall. Little Bunch was slow and distracted and had to be led like a calf. Amanda said of one enthusiastic preacher, "I like this one. He's got fire." And of another, "That man's so ugly, how do you reckon he can even preach out of that face?" Christie enjoyed letting Amanda take the lead, her high spirits propelling them. She and Lena followed her, dragging Little Bunch along, working to keep the child's hands out of her hair.

A little later, someone pointed toward Brother Cornett, and they pushed through the crowd to catch a glimpse of him. He was leaning against a cypress tree talking with some other dark-dressed preachers. He was young and slender, with a wavy mop of black hair and exuberant, mobile eyebrows. He kept kicking at a cypress knee, a root that protruded from the ground like a rising on skin.

"Look at that hair!" said Amanda. She whispered to Christie, "If I wasn't married, I'd climb all over him!"

"Mandy!" Christie was shocked.

"Do I sound sinful, Christie?" Impulsively, Amanda kissed her on the cheek. "I'm just talking, dear. No harm in talk."

But Christie let her gaze linger on the black-haired preacher. She felt her blood tingling, as it rushed nourishment to her baby.

Following a short late-morning prayer service, dinner was spread on planks set on trestles. Christie and Amanda had brought some ham and chess pie and dressed eggs and cold slaw. The previous year had not been a bountiful one, so the meats were meager, but there was plenty of green beans, corn, cornbread, sliced tomatoes, cream peas, crowder peas, and Great Northerns. Christie was glad to see pear halves centered with dollops of mayonnaise and grated cheese, like Granny Wilburn's pear salad. She noticed some people hogging bread into baskets they carried.

In the sultry afternoon, one preacher after another ascended the main platform, where he was protected from the sun by the brush-arbor. Now and then there was a good breeze. Amanda kept raising her hat for air, and locks of hair tumbled out. She crammed her hair back under her hat and waved her paper fan.

"I'm hot as a tater," she said, sweeping her fan to include Christie.

After a while, Christie and Lena went to the ladies' tent, leaving Little Bunch and Amanda under a tree talking with a woman who was tatting an edging for a dresser scarf. Amanda could talk about the end of the world and tatting in the same minute with equal enthusiasm.

"My mama could tat as easy as shelling beans," Amanda was saying as Christie walked away. "Why, she could tat the birds right out of the trees."

On the way down a path through the woods, Lena confided to Christie that she was starting her first period. She was near tears. They stopped by a tree, away from the path.

"I'm afraid to tell Mama," Lena whined. "She'll get mad at me."

"Why, no, she won't."

"I got blood on my drawers. I saw it when I went to the tent while-ago. Mama will get mad if I flower my skirt."

"Hasn't she told you what to do?"

Lena dropped her head and wouldn't say. "Does it cause fits?" she asked. "Dicey Jane Burnett, a girl at school, said her aunt has fits every month, when she starts."

"You ain't going to have no fit, Lena," Christie said impatiently. "Get that thought out of your head. It's got nothing to do with this."

"Little Bunch saw a woman here with the jerks. She said it was just like one of her fits."

Christie took Lena by the shoulders and spoke straight into her little pasty face. "Look, Lena. This means you're grown now. It means you can have a baby."

"I can't have a baby if I'm not married."

"Don't be so sure. You needn't go fooling around with boys, hear me? You've got to be real careful. And if you don't know what I mean, you'll have to talk to your mama."

It bothered Christie to discuss this subject here, with Lena. Lena was just a child. Did she feel that dangerous desire already? What would Amanda tell her about what lay ahead? Christie felt something jump in her stomach. It felt loose. All the blood in her body seemed to be rushing to the warm spot in the center of her womb. She didn't know what to say. Quietly, she took Lena's hand and led her to the ladies' tent. Inside the tent, Lena bit her fingernails.

Christie hadn't brought any rags with her. She hadn't expected to need any. With her scissors, she began to fashion something for Lena from a towel.

"You'll have to tell your mama," said Christie, trying to rip the heavy selvedge of the towel. "This is a serious thing."

"Maybe you could tell her."

"If you can tell me, you can tell your mama."

Christie cut the towel into manageable pieces. "When you get through with these, save them, and when we get home we'll wash them out."

"Will this be enough?"

"No. We'll have to find you some more."

Christie waited until Lena was behind the curtain, then proceeded to ask a large woman who was waiting if she had any extra cloths. The woman obligingly gave her a rag, but it was so dirty Christie hid it under a rock outside the tent as soon as the woman had gone. Finally, she obtained some clean bird's-eye linen from a preacher's wife. The woman had a cultivated manner and a hat with a broad brim that shaded her face. In a South drawl, she said cheerfully, "You know what I do, and I don't know a soul that does this? I roll up a rag in a tight little tube the size of my finger and stuff it up inside. A rag plug like you patch a wash pan with. It stops the leak! I try to get my friends to do it, but they're afraid to try it."

The woman powdered her face. Most Methodists didn't use face paint or wear ornaments, but this woman had an expensive watch on a gold chain. She said with a self-satisfied sigh, "Wasn't that a fine melting time at this morning's service? It's a sweet day to many souls. Melting time is the sweetest part of any brush-arbor."

"We didn't get here that early," Christie said. Melting time, when all the true believers came together to rededicate their souls, always made her feel as though she would smother. What she liked was the stomping and shouting and singing later in the day. There hadn't been enough singing yet today.

She and Lena returned to the tree where Little Bunch was sitting with her mother, getting her head massaged and combed. The preaching was continuing nearby. A courting couple under a tree fed each other bites of cake.

"I could stay here a week listening to all these good people," Amanda said with a loud sigh. "Little Bunch, your head is just full of scabs." She suddenly shouted, "Hallelujah!" and laughed. "I just felt like calling out," she said. "Precious Jesus," she cried, "I'm coming soon!"

Christie felt queasy. Members of the congregation were shouting randomly. The preacher on the main platform called loudly for a prayer then, and people bowed their heads. Christie bowed hers, but she peeped. The hot, pinched faces around her seemed fierce, drained of joy.

"We're on the brink, Lord," the preacher called up to heaven. "Lead us over the edge."

Christie prayed for understanding. She feared for her baby. What would James say when he learned they were bringing another baby into the world at this uncertain time? Why couldn't they have controlled themselves? She prayed that the new century would not bring a cracking open of the earth but a multitude of blessings from it. She thought with a pang of sorrow about the girl she was, back in Dundee, when she felt the first sunrise-glimmer of passion.

"Amen!" shouted Amanda when the preacher finished. "Lena, your face looks like a mule eating briers. Straighten up and smile!"

6

THE CROWD HAD SWELLED, LIKE A WASHTUB SPILLING OVER WITH SUDS. People in front sat on log benches. Men and boys perched on tree branches for a view. By now several preachers had described—with little variation—what the new century would bring. The crowd was eager to hear old Rollie Ledbetter tell the true details of the great earthquake. Christie kept telling herself that all the earthquake talk was no more than a scary bedtime story told to children. It wasn't serious. Still, it *was* scary, and it gave her shivers.

Rickety, ancient Mr. Ledbetter stumbled up the steps to the platform, helped by two of the preachers, one of whom was Brother Cornett. Some wild whoops sailed forth from the woods, where the rowdies tended to gather. Brother Cornett called for quiet. He propped Rollie Ledbetter against a tree at the edge of the platform and jauntily approached the high stump that served as a lectern. As he began to introduce Mr. Ledbetter, two straw-hatted young women in lacy dresses stood up, gasped, and began running toward the lake. They disappeared in the trees. Brother Cornett's long mane of black hair fell into his eyes, and he flipped it back with a toss of his head. His hair was as dark as a blackbird.

"Ain't he handsome?" Amanda whispered.

"Mandy, watch yourself!" Christie said. But he *was* good to look at, she thought. His face was smooth-shaven, and his white shirt, brown coat, and twill trousers were all well fitted.

"His face looks as soft as a baby's butt," Amanda whispered, making Christie laugh.

Rollie Ledbetter started to waver, and Brother Cornett rushed over to catch him.

"There now, Brother Ledbetter," Brother Cornett said. "We don't want you falling through a crack."

The old man wobbled over to the stump, then, and began to talk. Brother Cornett hadn't finished his introduction, but he let it go.

The old man clutched the stump for support. His head glowed pink through his sparse white hair. "It was deep in the night," he said, his voice stronger than his thin and shaky frame suggested. "And I thought the Lord was a-knocking on the door. It got louder and louder, like thunder, and then the bed commenced to shaking. I heard the horses a-whinnying; the barn had fell in on 'em. Outside, the trees was swaying back and forth, and the birds was a-crying and the chickens thought the fox was after 'em—chickens don't think too large and couldn't feature the end of the world.

"I lived in the settlement of Birdie in the Territory of Missouri, and there was still Indians. Some said this combobulation was something the Indians was behind—some secret of the yearth and the mighty Mississippi that they knew. They said the Indians could command the deeps of the yearth and the flow of the river. Later on, the Indians claimed it was just a love storm between two young Indians, that crippled one they called Reelfoot and his bride.

"At the height of the event, the mighty Mississip commenced to go back'ards, the episode was so stormacious, and it flowed t'other way for a few minutes. The whole *bedrock* had upheaved. I felt the tremendious violence of the quake and the roll of the river. The atmosphere was sulfur and smelled; the air was yaller and dirty and stung the eyeballs.

"My mother and father takened us younguns into the wagon bed and hitched up the horses and we started off, but there was nowheres to flee to, nowheres a-tall."

"Amen," said Brother Cornett, with a shake of his black waves.

Christie's eyes kept wandering back to Brother Cornett, and she saw that Amanda was fixed on him too. There was something exhilarating just about the sight of him. Married women weren't supposed to notice men this way—especially a preacher. She felt ashamed.

The old man, whose creaky frame leaned against the high stump like a windfall, seemed lost in his memories, as if he longed for the recurrence of what must have been the great adventure of his life. He went on, speaking dreamily, almost lovingly. He told how the earth's rumbling furor terrorized man and beast all through the night. The skies thundered violently and the river roared. He said the shocks continued—of a night and of a day—for days on end. Then a month later the land seized even more violently; for two weeks the earth rolled and rocked, and the sky grew dark and made noises like the Devil belching and gave off the smell of brimstone, and the river gathered up its water into the middle like a mountain and then threw the water back at both shores violently, breaking off patches of cottonwood trees along the banks. The river's edge was covered with boat wrecks and stranded fish and animals torn to pieces and birds reduced to piles of feathers, and the earth vomited up its sand and water and other substances—black infernal matter from the bowels of the earth—through deep cracks in the riverbed and the bottomland by the river.

For months afterward, the hard thunder and the shaking continued off and on. And then all was still and peaceful, and doves flew in bearing olive branches. "People may say them was hazelnuts, but they was olives," the old man said. "I seen olives a-growing on a bush back in the swamp. And I et some and they was olives. And all the land was different. And no sign of houses. And this big lake was here, and these here cypress trees come in now and directly.

"Now its time has come round again, and I wait for it, to carry me on up yander on the tides of faith. It's going to come and dreen this here lake."

The old man turned to Brother Cornett, who had been at his elbow all the while, and said, "Did you mean for me to go on?"

"No, that's fine, Brother Ledbetter," said Brother Cornett. "We're happy you shared your recollections.

"Hear that, ladies and gentlemen," Brother Cornett called out. "Brother Ledbetter, more than any soul present at this meeting, has seen the jaws of Hell, smelled its sulfurous fumes, caught its foul, tree-bending breath. He has seen the goodness of God in resurrecting the land, in creating this beautiful lake you see here today, in taming the mighty Mississippi River, showing us what His power can do."

He steered the old man off the platform.

"Go on and set down, Brother Ledbetter. We'll draw the meaning for you."

"That old man's buttons are gone on his britches," whispered Christie to Amanda, but Amanda didn't hear. She breathed heavily, clutching fiercely at Christie's and Little Bunch's hands. Little Bunch struggled to get away, and with her free hand she pulled at her hair.

Brother Cornett picked up Rollie Ledbetter's tale of the earthquake as if it had been a dropped ball. He rolled on with it, barely pausing to pat the old man's arm before plunging headlong into the coming earthquake.

Rollie Ledbetter sank down onto a log. The crowd, already moved by the old man's tale, was growing agitated, shouting "Amen!" and

"Glory!" And as Brother Cornett's honey voice seemed to melt into the sunbeams darting down through the openings in the brush-arbor above him, everybody began to stir in time to his cadences. Christie stole a glance at Lena, wondering if Lena was overcome by Brother Cornett's sermon or whether she was too absorbed in her new state. Lena, pale and listless, stared straight ahead. Amanda was drinking in Brother Cornett's words. He strutted about the platform, thrashing his arms in an extravagant manner. He was a well-formed man, muscular and lean, with a straight carriage and flexible limbs.

In a hushed tone, Brother Cornett said, "For the Lord says, 'Old things were done away, and all things become new.'"

He repeated Brother Ledbetter's story, drawing out the essence of its dire implications, his voice growing surer and louder. He removed his coat and flung it to the side of the platform, all the while striding to and fro. He began dripping with sweat from his exertions. He plucked his handkerchief from his breast pocket, swabbed his face, and pushed back the forelock that had tumbled into his eyes.

The crowd, on its feet, seemed to sway like willows in the wind. Amanda was twisting her hands together and moving her mouth in nonsense syllables. A few people were jumping up and screaming, "Christ is come!" and "The end is at hand!" and "Repent! Repent!" Some yelped wordlessly in fear. Christie loosened her hat to get air. The thin waist she was wearing was damp under the arms. The earthquake the old man had described seemed so real, and it had happened right here under her feet. The people around her seemed to imagine the ground slipping away now, for they rocked and bobbed. Christie, between Lena and Amanda, held their hands. They were like a chain of paper-dolls.

On the far side of the platform, Brother Cornett lowered himself to his knees. He threw his arms and head forward over his knees until his hair spread out against the flooring. Abruptly he rose and dashed to the near side of the platform, where he sank to his knees again and repeated the movement. Rising, he dipped a tin cup in a water bucket on the edge of the platform and poured the water on his head.

"I baptize myself!" he cried.

"Hallelujah!" some voices cried.

"I believe it!" squealed Amanda.

"Are you ready for the day of reckoning?" yelled Brother Cornett, looking straight at Christie. "Are you ready to feel the earth tremble, and the thunder roll its voice of doom crosst the sky, setting forks of flames down to the ground, like tongues of the Devil sent by God to punish the wicked? Are you looking for eternal darkness or do you want eternal light?" He pranced away. "Do you repent of your sins today and tomorrow and for all time? If your very mama and daddy was backsliding into the pit of the Devil, would you plunge in and yank 'em out? Could you leave behind your comfortable beds and your homes and your land and your horses and them good, strong mules and them big, round punkins and meaty hogs and succulent 'maters and all them good old taters down in the ground?" His voice softened and was barely audible. "In the ground, folks; them taters live in the ground and they flourish in dirt until they are cleansed of that dirt and made ready to nourish the human body. That bears thinking about, ladies and gentlemen." His voice rose up again. "For that lowly tater is like the human soul, washed clean in the blood of the Lamb, fit then to nourish the body of the Lord, for the Lord needs us human souls to reflect His light, so we can see Him, so He shows up good, and then we, too, bake in His glory."

He paused to survey the crowd, which was suddenly hushed. "I'm talking about a time of weeping among sinners and the doom of the wicked," he said calmly. He slapped at a bug on his cheek. "I'm talking of the place where the lion roareth and the wang-doodle mourneth for his first-born."

A large, fleshy woman in a grease-stained dress jumped to her feet, shouting, "I'm happy, praise God!"

But others around Christie leaped and stomped like frightened horses in a storm. Amanda's cheeks glowed and her eyes flashed. Christie felt something rise in her, a growing desire. She had been keeping so many feelings to herself that she was like a setting hen, but now she couldn't hold them. They were about to jump out in one streak. She was on her feet, waving her arms and shouting the responsive note: "Hallelujah!"

"We have to be ready, Christians," Brother Cornett exhorted. "We have to learn about keeping ready to die, so that we shall have life everlasting. We will cast all the evils and the devils into the lake. Water is cleansing. Us Methodists know what to do with water. We sprinkle the heart and the soul. The blood of the Lamb is the true soap for the soul, for it washes away the sins and leaves the soul pure and ready for its heavenly reward. Great God, we are ready for our reward!"

There might have been an explosion of joy and weeping then, but Brother Cornett wouldn't let the congregation fly apart yet. He had his voice trained on them, as if directing their movements. His eyes flashed and his voice rose to a falsetto. "We're ready to go, Lord!" he cried. "We're ready for the storm."

Christie was exhilarated. The energy of the man's performance surged through her, lifting her up like a bundle of hay being forked into the loft of the barn. He had pierced her with his direct stare. She felt chosen. She and Amanda were both swinging their arms—stomping a little, too. Suddenly she thought she heard Aunt Sophie's spittoon, her cock-a-doodle-do. It was a woman in the crowd, crowing. And nearby, a man began howling like a hound dog at a train whistle.

"It's up to you, ever individual soul, to take that step," cried Brother Cornett, clutching his shoulder. "I feel the pains of Hell in my body and soul."

"Mercy, Lord, release me, Savior," a man cried. Christie felt something turn a somerset in her stomach.

"I know a sickness that spreads like a eating cancer," yelled Brother Cornett, raising his fist to the sky. His eyebrows lifted like the silhouettes of distant birds in flight. "That sickness is all over the land, in ever tree and bush and moving creature, in ever tobaccer patch and horse barn and pitchfork, even in the wood you burn to keep you warm. The world is being eat up with sin, and Judgment Day will be here soon, maybe sooner than we want it to, but when it comes we'll thank the Lord for coming to take us home.

"The dawn of Judgment Day will be like any other. It'll catch us by surprise. The sun might be shining, and we'll be going about our business, and the Devil and his imps will be going about their work, sneaking around and laying in wait for us, but then the sky will start to change. You won't know it at first. You'll just think she looks like rain. And then you'll hear the birds stop singing, and you'll see the horses and the pigs getting riled and running into the fence like they was scared. But you don't see it yet. Then the ground starts to tremble— just a little bit at first—and then it starts to rolling good, with a noise only Mr. Ledbetter here has heard before, and then it grows, and it won't stop, and *you* start to roll. The ground commences to move up and down like big waves, waves you've never witnessed before, and with all that moving, the ground starts to crack, and out of the ground comes *brimstone breath!* The foul-smelling breath of the Devil exploding right out of the middle of the earth, for that's where he dwells, under the ground waiting to trap us in the dark—when we're asleep, when we're not thinking, when we're out in the woods in the night, without any light to lead our way.

"And just when we think we're going to be swallowed up into the bowels of the earth, to be worked over by that old Devil, a spreading light starts through the sky—from the east, like a new sun rising up, and it sends out such light that we can scarce look. It's a calming and peaceful light, but so strong it seems to devour everything earthly. The smoke dissolves, and the fires a-shooting up from the bowels of the earth start to go out, and the upheaval of the land starts to draw back, and when it's all quiet the birds commence to singing again, and you look around and everything is changed. Nothing you knew is there anymore. And many people you knew ain't there no more. They're swallered up, gone. You look around, and everything is light and golden. You reach down and touch the ground under you, and it's solid gold. You look out at a big light coming, big beams of light, and a crown of gold is lit by the light of day so bright you can barely see His face. It is Jesus' face. And He is a-smiling on you, with His grace. *You* are in heaven on earth, for a thousand years of peace and harmony."

Amanda was waving at Brother Cornett, who glanced her way. Amanda gasped and stared, as if he might be Jesus, looking right at her with love in His eyes. Her eyes were glassy, and tears ran down her cheeks. Christie wanted to cry too, for Brother Cornett's energetic performance had touched something in her that had been all knotted up, and now it seemed to be coming unraveled. She had felt this once before, when a fever broke.

The threat of the coming earthquake seemed real to her now. Yet she couldn't visualize the heaven Brother Cornett pictured. If the world ended, her child would never get to know it.

Brother Cornett cried, "Let us sing." He began shouting out the lines of the hymn, and the congregation joined in.

> *Why not now?*
> *Why not now?*
> *Why not come to Jesus now?*
> *Why not now . . . why not now?*
> *Why not come to Jesus now?*

After the first verse, Brother Cornett threw back his head and bellowed like a bull. Then he cried, "A feller come up to me and told me I'd live forever, here on earth, as a man. He claimed to be an angel. And I said to him, 'Why, I believe you smell like brimstone. If you come from anywhere, you come from Hell, where they burn brimstone to keep warm.' That feller's heart wasn't true, and the Devil had snared him. Why, Hell is already so full of sinners you can see their feet sticking out the winders. We don't want to be with that bunch."

Brother Cornett swung his fist into his Bible and yelled, "The gates of Hell shall not prevail!"

The whole crowd, shouting and singing, moved in time to Brother

Cornett's exaggerated gestures. He marched and twirled and high-stepped. When he brandished his fist skyward, the crowd raised theirs. When he pointed to one section of the congregation, it rose and shouted, and when he whirled to point at another section—scattered back in the trees to his left—that section rose with a responding whoop too. Christie turned to Amanda, trying to read her. Amanda was muttering and gasping, her hands fighting the hot air, and Little Bunch seemed to be working up to a tantrum. Her face was red and her cheeks puffed with air. In the row ahead of them, a woman in a thin, faded calico dress fell over, sagging to the bench and then slipping down to the ground, where she lay in a heap.

For several weeks Christie's mind had been going at cross-purposes. But now it was clearing, and all her feelings were concentrating into one large wave inside her. If she hoped to bring her baby into a good world, she couldn't be afraid. Why would God take away a mother in birth? Was that why Aunt Sophie never married? Was she afraid? Did Aunt Sophie love herself more than the children she might have had? Christie placed her hand on her stomach. It was rumbling, she knew, but she couldn't hear it. Amanda was starting to shout out the hymn, shout out the name of Jesus, as though she were calling a missing child.

The singing and shouting grew more turbulent. The worshipers had glazed eyes, as if they wouldn't recognize their own families in front of them. Off to the edge of the gathering, near the cleared dining area, someone bowed to a tree and raised his head up high and howled an eerie, long wolf cry. Christie recognized him as the fellow with the plan to travel to the moon. Two other men joined him, pawing at the tree and barking like dogs.

"Go on," Brother Cornett urged. "Get that old devil-dog on out of there. Don't carry him around in you, on a free ride. Oh, I see him going now. That old Devil's up in that tree. They done treed the Devil, where he can't get away. Lord have mercy and bless us all."

Amanda was on her feet now, embracing a crying woman. "That's all right, honey, come to the Lord."

The woman fell over and crumpled up on the ground, twitching, and then Amanda—her head tottering like a sunflower—fell down too. Several others nearby keeled over and lay rigid as planks, while the rest of the congregation kept shouting and writhing. Brother Cornett didn't stop. Christie held Amanda's head in her lap and slapped at her face. She was motionless and pale. Then she began quivering, and she came to life as quickly as she had fallen, with a big smile on her face.

"Come to Jesus just now," she said weakly.

Her hat was on the ground, and her hair had escaped. Her head looked like a hen with its feathers ruffled.

"I saw Jesus," she said.

Little Bunch, red-faced, was alternately screaming through clenched teeth and picking her nose. Lena, looking mortified, tugged at Christie's wrist. Christie's mind raced. She felt a particular thrill at the anonymity here. Amanda had fallen to the ground so easily, with such abandon. Christie remembered the way James had whirled her around on their wedding day. Dancing that wasn't really dancing, their exuberant joy erupting right in front of the surprised preacher, the shocked aunts, the tittering cousins, grim Aunt Sophie. She closed her eyes, picturing the scene, wishing she and James could do something like that again. She remembered that hound grabbing the preacher's chicken leg. She wondered whatever happened to that dog. Her mind drifted and shook the way the ground had shaken during the creation of Reelfoot Lake. She felt her brain fluids astir, her head in a wave, as if it were trying to locate the source of her desire and discontent.

"Just let yourself go, Christie," Amanda was saying. "Just feel the spirit."

"I do!" Christie cried. "But I don't want to bark at devils or fall over like a tree."

"You should let yourself have faith, Christie," said Amanda, with her unceasing, gentle smile.

Little Bunch was screaming, her eyes wild. She kicked at a stump.

7

LATER, AFTER THE SERMON WAS OVER AND THE FERVOR HAD DIED down somewhat, Christie and Amanda and the girls made their way along a deer path to the lake. With a long stick, Christie beat the weeds on the path, to scare away snakes. The sun shone through the stately cypress trees, creating a sheet of light across the glassy surface of the surprisingly peaceful lake. It was still hot. There was no breeze. The mosquitoes were already out. A pair of snake doctors buzzed through the air. The wading birds were stalking through the shallow water, dipping their heads.

"Was I out for long?" Amanda asked.

Christie shook her head no.

"Did I have the jerks?"

"No, you were stiff," said Christie.

"You had a fit, Mama," said Little Bunch. She hiccupped loudly.

"It wasn't a fit," said her mother. "It was a visit from Jesus."

"Christie had one too," said Lena.

"No, I didn't, Lena."

"When Mama fell down, your eyes were closed, and you fell over," Lena insisted. "Didn't she, Bunch?"

"I've got the hee-cups," said Little Bunch.

"I was resting my eyes," said Christie. She did feel drained, as if she had been visited not only by Jesus but by the Holy Spirit and about a thousand angels. "Let's go eat," she said.

"I could eat Adam's off-ox," said Amanda.

When they returned from the lake to the clearing, they saw some women removing the sheets that had protected the food tables from flies. Several other women were crying hysterically, and one of the men who had been barking under the tree was devouring a piece of fried chicken. Christie glimpsed Brother Cornett splashing water from a cup on his face. A woman handed him a plate of meat. Christie felt her cheeks burning. Brother Cornett, standing by a tupelo tree, began eating—apparently with great enjoyment—nodding as the woman talked earnestly to him. Christie could not hear what they were saying, but the woman kept touching her hair self-consciously.

Some people couldn't eat; they kept shouting and singing. A mother unable to stop her shouting of praise for the Lord nursed her baby in front of everybody. One woman stood on a wagon bed and sang hymns at the top of her voice until dark closed in. A bonfire was burning on the shore, to draw mosquitoes.

That night Christie and Amanda and the girls slept on the straw-carpeted pavilion under a large dormitory tent with open sides. They had brought pallets, and they hung a sheet between two trees for a wall. They wouldn't undress or wash, with so many people around. They didn't know what desperadoes lurked in the woods. Lena made numerous trips to the ladies' tent. Amanda had forgotten to bring her curlers, and Christie needed some liniment for her feet, but some of the other women let them borrow their things. More than a dozen women occupied the pavilion, most with young children. One woman had lost her husband recently in a fire; another woman's husband had mangled his leg in a wagon accident and couldn't work. Amanda was quiet. Christie felt wrung out, as if she had taken a round of calomel.

Flickering pine-knot torches and tallow candles cast long shadows and pools of glowing light, illuminating leaves and bushes and the brushy roof of the arbor. Christie could hear rustlings in the drying, wilting leaves of the cut branches. She could see the ghostly shapes of the cypress trees standing out in the water, like guards. She thought about the people here, taking off in lay-by time to restore their souls before they had to bring in the crops. Bringing in the sheaves.

Noises—babies crying, rowdy laughter from the fringes of the camp—kept her awake. She heard more wolf howls and roosters; people couldn't stop whooping and praying. She heard someone singing "Sweet By and By." Firecrackers went off.

"Somebody couldn't wait for Christmas," whispered Amanda when a string of firecrackers popped.

"Do they think God's deaf?" Christie said. She rolled over toward Amanda, and the straw under the pallet crunched. "Are you afraid of the earthquake now?" Christie asked her.

"I don't know. I guess if the Lord wills it, then I have to be ready."

"Would you be ready to die, Mandy?"

"Brother Cornett talked about keeping ready to die. I reckon we have to keep ready."

"I'm not ready," said Christie.

Amanda giggled. "That man was larruping. I declare I could eat him up."

Amanda's childlike acceptance of the end of the world was calming. "He has a way about him," Christie said.

Amanda said, "You might of told me about Lena. I was hurt that she told you first."

"She wanted me to tell you, but I left it up to her."

"I'm so proud," said Amanda. "I wish my mama had lived to know my fine girls."

"It's hard," said Christie, hearing Amanda sniffle. "It's awful hard not having your mama around. I had my mama with me for ever one of my babies." She slapped at a mosquito noise. She said, "I can't think about the end of the world and having a baby in the same frame of mind. They just don't go together."

"Don't be scared, Christie," said Amanda soothingly. "The Lord knows what's best."

"Oh, I don't believe the world will end. I just don't see how it could."

"Well, then, you've got nothing to be afraid of."

"But I'm afraid something's wrong. This baby's moving too soon. It feels different. It's so loud—already!"

"That's probably just the baby telling you he wants attention. All the Wheelers want attention." Amanda patted Christie's head. "They all just want to be babied and carried around on a piller. The men, I mean. The women—well, sometimes I think Alma would just as soon kick a man in the head as look at him."

"She could make doodlebugs behave!" Christie said.

They snickered. Christie imagined Alma in her big shoes going out to milk the cow herself out of impatience with the men; Alma with a sassafras stick stirring lye soap in the kettle like a medicine man whipping up a potion; Alma teasing Amanda about her mail-order cuckoo clock.

Christie said to Amanda, "If something happens to me, would you take care of my chillern? Don't let Alma have them."

"Don't worry your head, Christie," said Amanda. "Nothing's going to happen to you."

"Except the end of the world."

They laughed, and Amanda said, "I don't know what I'd do without you, Christie. If it wasn't for you, I think I'd die." She rearranged her pallet and the straw crunched. "But you're so lucky to have a mama."

In the darkness, Christie prayed for guidance. She hadn't been fair to James. He worked so hard, fighting the weather and the land. When they topped the tobacco, he had worked late, despite a strained shoulder and blisters on his hands. She resolved to treat him better. If she died, what would he do? She asked the Lord how she could fight the demons of dread in her mind. The poisonous notion her Aunt Sophie had put there was resurfacing now.

The light from the climbing moon entered the tent. Nightmarish shapes passed in a procession through the light as she drifted toward sleep. She imagined breech births, childbed fevers, pinhead babies. When she finally slept, she dreamed of the earthquake. She dreamed she was ravaged by a fever, her body trembling all over. A powerful rumbling rolled through her. Then she saw herself sitting at her churn, the dasher plunging and slamming in time to a fast song. An urgent voice was singing. She could hear Brother Cornett speaking softly and soothingly, and her frantic churning turned into a slow, drawn-out release as his voice, plush as velvet, caressed her—first her hair, then her breasts, then her legs. She could feel him in her, his long, hot tool churning in her, to the rhythm of "Bringing In the Sheaves."

"We shall come rejoicing!" he cried.

The sensation of deep pleasure was so vivid, its force flung her into consciousness. She woke up with a gasp, her heart beating like a horse with the thumps.

"Christie!" Amanda raised up on her elbow and reached toward her.

"I had a nightmare!" Christie told Amanda the dream, whispering, still feeling the pleasure of the dream beneath the horror. She trembled with disbelief, her mind still under the dream's sway. It had felt so good; she had never felt anything so sweet. But now the sensation was fast fading away, leaving her trembling with shame.

Amanda whispered, "Christie, I was laying here thinking about him, too, and trying to stop myself. What did he do?"

"I'm not sure. Everything. All over. It was so real."

Amanda let out a long, slow breath. "Well, he makes me want to pull my clothes off and go climb a tree. If I could do anything in the world I wanted to? I'd run off with somebody like that." She sat up and hugged her knees. "Christie, did you ever lay down with anybody but James?"

"Of course not—why?"

Christie could see Amanda's profile in the light. Some torches were still glowing, although everyone had been cautioned against fire. Amanda turned and drew close. She spoke in a soft whisper.

"Before I married Wad, I knew this boy who took me to the corncrib and showed me how—you know. He was a pretty boy—black hair and blue eyes and red cheeks and tall, with the kindest heart—and he touched me all over. I knew it was bad, but it thrilled me more than anything I ever did before or since. It felt like being set afire, but without the pain. And then he had to go away, and I didn't see him anymore. When I met Wad, I thought getting married meant you'd have that all the time and it wouldn't be a sin. But it wasn't true."

"Did it get boresome?"

"I hate it. The way he grunts and wallers in the bed—I'd rather sleep with the mules." Amanda sighed. "I guess that's my punishment. I keep remembering that boy in the corncrib. His name was Robert. And just thinking about him gives me chill bumps." She pulled the quilt over her shoulders. A mosquito hummed. "I wonder what Brother Cornett's given name is," she said with a giggle. Christie laughed with warm relief. Amanda said, "Christie, don't feel bad about that dream. It sounds to me like it was a right good dream!"

"I'm so ashamed. A dream like that could affect the baby."

"Nothing happened, Christie. Don't dwell on it. You'll cause that baby to be fretful and not mind you, if you get too worked up."

"Y'all hush," a cranky woman cried out from a nearby pallet. "You're laughing in the face of the Lord."

In the morning, the sunrise service was interrupted by firecrackers. Babies squalled. Christie ate a piece of fatback and a biscuit with molasses, and in the middle of the morning love feast—the communion where they took bread and grape juice at the altar—she vomited up her breakfast.

The mess slopped onto Amanda's hem. Christie was startled and appalled, but Amanda put her arm around her and said, "That's all right, Christie. Go on and get it all out."

"That's the same thing Brother Cornett was saying to all of us sinners," Christie said.

She saw Amanda smile, then grin. Christie began to laugh. Overcome with laughter, they hurried away from the altar, into the trees, where they sat on a log and laughed together, rocking with a giggly mirth that wouldn't stop, like the mud and sand bubbling out of the bowels of the earth when Reelfoot Lake came into being.

III

The Babies

Spring 1900

1

With the delivery of the five babies, Christie felt peaceful and drained—the pain gone, the horror evaporated, no devils left inside. The babies nursing made her feel her womb shrinking, as if they were sucking the air out of it. She felt such relief. She was no longer insane. The commotion in her womb had been these five sweet babies, probably just innocently battling each other for attention—like all brothers and sisters, she thought. She was so ashamed that she had not recognized them as her own. Her dream about Brother Cornett faded from her consciousness now, his ludicrous leer disappearing like a bird in the sky.

She tried to open her eyes. The drug Dr. Foote had given her made her groggy, but she was aware enough to feel the babies' tiny butterfly hands and their wet mouths like dewdrops. Their cries were shrill, like cricket chirps.

"They won't all last," she thought she heard the doctor say. "The best thing to do is keep two and find somebody with milk to take the rest."

Christie had been dozing intermittently. Her breathing was heavy at times with exhaustion, and the squirm of babies against her made her body seem to be crawling in all directions. She wanted to sink into sleep again so the doctor's words would be only a dream. She heard James argue with the doctor.

"How would you pick which ones to keep?" James said angrily.

"I'd keep the two strongest ones. Why, if she tried to feed all of them, they might not any of them make it." The doctor's voice was a conspiratorial murmur, a slight sound like a handkerchief fluttering on the wash line. "This littlest one might not make it. I'll be surprised if any of them do. You better just let her feed these two here, the biggest ones."

She opened her eyes. James wasn't there. Alma pushed back the curtains in the front room and the paper shade flew up, snapping onto its roller. Sunlight splashed onto the brick hearth. Christie glimpsed an unfamiliar speckled hound in the field, visible through the stark winter trees. She vaguely remembered eating bacon and eggs. She thought Alma and Mrs. Willy had been there all night—cleaning up, wrapping and unwrapping the babies, rubbing them with olive butter. Water was boiling. Christie was drifting, her mind mingling with the steam of the boiling water.

Growing more alert, with her astonishment widening like the light of day, she watched cautiously as the doctor examined each baby, probing it and listening to its heartbeat through the long tubes strung from his ears. He turned each baby this way and that until he got it to cry. He seemed to be talking to Christie, as he recommended plentiful olive butter for the skin and warned against direct air—nothing she didn't already know. She saw mysterious metal pieces in his black bag.

"Have you ever seen any teensier babies, Dr. Foote?" Alma asked. Her voice was like a clatter of plates.

"Not this many in one brood," he said. "You put all these babies together and the weight would make two good-size babies, I'd allow. All divided up this way, though, it'll take a right smart while for those little lungs and tummies to start working good."

His big fingers pulled the babies' faces, tugged at their ears, poked inside their mouths. The black tubes dangled from his ears like some foul, snaky matter drawn from inside his head. Christie tried to sit up, to see what she could learn about the man who made it his business to care for people's bodies. How could a person do that? To touch a stranger's body, to take authority over it—it would require either courage or cruelty. The preachers cared for the soul, and the doctors got ahold of the body. She remembered him touching her during the dark hours of the night. But it didn't seem to matter anymore. She knew he would examine her again when he finished with the babies; she would cover her face and open her legs.

The doctor handed an infant to Mrs. Willy, saying, "This one's a little damp."

It was the one who made Christie see the dark winter branches of a rain-soaked tree, with the deep blue sky coming through from behind. She heard him cry—a strong, healthy cry.

All the babies were crying now from the doctor's prodding. Their cries grew piercing and loud. The baby with the hint of a curl in her brown hair made Christie see the brown-orange shoots of fescue in a fallow field late in the fall. She could imagine that vivid burnt-orange, and the fading green of the field behind.

When she woke up again, all their names were clear in her mind. She had dreamed the names of the last three babies, but the story of the dream had faded. The babies were all lying beside her, sleeping, nearly motionless, their tiny breaths barely discernible.

James Lake was the oldest, the one with the large full mouth that made her see the red-pink of a rooster's comb. James for her husband, Lake for her papa.

Emily Sue, from the feel of her, was stout, with wisps of brown hair that would be curly, she thought. Emily for one sister, Susan for another.

John Wilburn, the one who made her think of blue sky behind winter trees, had James's nose.

Mollie Lee, with the blond top, made her think of hot biscuits breaking in half. Mollie, the yellow of sunlight and corn.

And Minnie Sophia, so still, a gray cloud thinning out into air.

The colors were shimmering, frothy curtains. John Wilburn's deep blue was the most vibrant color among them. She was still half dreaming. The reality of five babies kept startling her, as if it were fresh news each time she remembered. But giving birth to five babies was no more remarkable than that she gave each one a color, or that just the right name had appeared in a dream. She and James had given no thought to names, although once he had said, "I always liked the name Sary." Christie didn't see a Sarah here.

Christie opened her eyes and saw Amanda smiling down at her.

"I'm so proud of you, Christie," said Amanda. "They're the sweetest little things you ever did see!"

"Dr. Foote said they wouldn't all last." Christie tried to sit up. John Wilburn's eyes were open.

"Shush, Christie. They're all just fine," Amanda said, touching the baby's cheek. "That Foote don't know everything," she said indignantly. "He made like Hattie couldn't handle it. But she could have."

John Wilburn's face squeezed into a frown. Then his mouth formed a hard circle. Amanda lifted him and jiggled him gently. "Hush, little babe," she sang softly. The baby's face relaxed, puzzled. "It don't know where it is," Amanda said with a squeal.

"He's hungry," Christie said, smiling at Amanda's delight.

Amanda whispered, "Christie, the doctor didn't even know there was five. Hattie knew that, but she was afraid to say. She didn't want to scare you. She told me she could feel more than one—maybe four, she thought. I couldn't believe it at first."

"I knew it," said Christie, reaching to take the baby from Amanda. "I knew there was something all along." She shuddered.

She held John Wilburn to her breast. Her breast seemed heavier than the baby. He yawned, and in closing his mouth found her nipple and began sucking.

"Mandy," Christie whispered, raising a hand to pull at Amanda's arm. "Did I hear the doctor say they wouldn't live?"

"I didn't hear him say that," Amanda said, touching the nursing infant fondly. "But he was afraid you wouldn't have enough milk. Just look at that baby at his titty!"

"Did I dream it?"

Mrs. Willy had built up the fire, then curled up on her pallet to nap. Alma went home to cook dinner, while her daughter Dulcie came down with Nannie, Clint, and Jewell. The children stood around bashfully, now and then poking a timid finger at one of the bundles. The blankets were so large that the babies appeared full-sized except for their tiny heads. Nannie's old baby bonnets swallowed them. When it was time for Christie to nurse one of the babies, Dulcie whisked Clint and Jewell away, leaving Nannie, who worked with some paperdolls in a corner.

When Alma returned with a bucket of dinner, Mrs. Willy shot up from her nap.

"I was as sleepy as a dead pig in the sun," she said.

Mrs. Willy helped Amanda change Christie's stained cloths and sheets. Alma ordered Nannie to stand in the corner and not look. Then Little Bunch appeared, alone. She slammed the door and headed straight for the babies. Alma slapped her hands as she grabbed at the babies' faces.

"Quit that, or I'll jerk a knot in your tail," Alma said. "Let 'em sleep when they will, or they'll be a-crying their eyes out."

Little Bunch grunted. She didn't take her eyes from the babies.

"I'm carrying you right back home, Bunch," Amanda said. She pulled on her coat and wool cap and hauled her daughter out through the back door.

Always in the past, Christie had been able to nap between feedings. But now the nursing seemed nearly continuous, the babies nibbling at her like mice.

The babies' names swirled through her mind, awaiting James's approval. Minnie Sophia, the weakest baby, had a faint birthmark on her ear. All of the babies had little round, unwrinkled ears and sharp little noses. They were all sleeping now, wrapped in the outing blankets Christie had made, individually wrapped little packages. She had made only six blankets. Amanda had brought down some extra bonnets she had found.

"That littlest one ain't stirred none," said Mrs. Willy. "But the other ones have got more lively to 'em."

Christie's mind fuzzed over like mold on bread. She was afraid to ask what the doctor had said. She must have dreamed it.

Alma brought Christie a washing rag. "Your hair's a sight," she said.

"Bring me my comb and brush," said Christie. "They're on the dresser in the bedroom."

"I'll get 'em, Mama!" cried Nannie, off in a run.

"Where's James?" Christie asked Alma.

"He was in, but you were asleep. Now he's gone to see if the Smiths down the road can spare that oldest girl. She's had a fresh baby and might could lend a hand—or a tit." Alma laughed. It was unusual to see Alma laugh, or care about hair.

"Well, I need about three extra tits."

Alma shook her head doubtfully as she looked at the line of babies on the bed. "We never will be able to tell them babies apart," she said.

One of the babies was making a sucking motion with its mouth. It was Emily Sue. Christie thought of pinning something on their bonnets to help the family tell the babies apart. Blue and orange and yellow and gray and pink.

"Nannie," she said. "Be a good girl and bring my workbox."

"You ain't a-sewing!" cried Mrs. Willy.

"No. I need some ribbon."

Nannie fetched the little cedar box with her threads and needles. Christie's pins were scattered, loose, on the bottom. She had heard of a woman fifty years old who was just now on her second paper of pins and was still using the same five needles she started with. Christie gave Nannie some scraps of calico and a needle to play with. She threaded and knotted the needle for her, but the task took her strength. She smelled chicken. She was starving. In her workbox she found snippets of ribbon wound around a card. She found bits of blue and a light red. She'd have to embroider the names as soon as she was able. She had a small bit of yellow, some gray, something brownish-gold that would do for orange. She had bought the ribbons from an Irish peddler last summer. She cut the little pieces of ribbon and attached them with tiny safety pins to the bonnets.

Alma brought a plate of fried chicken and vegetables and a glass of milk to Christie. "What's them ribbons supposed to tell?" she asked.

Someone was on the front porch. Alma set the plate on the table beside the bed and went to the door. It was the mail carrier, Edward Letcher. Christie could hear his squeaky voice, a hawk's cry, on the other side of the stairway. "I told Mrs. Pritchard I didn't believe it, but she said James was there and told her you had five babies here. Is it so?"

"That's how many we've counted," said Alma.

Mr. Letcher, a short, dark-haired man of middle years, walked in with the mail, followed by Alma. Christie was glad she had combed her hair.

"Howdy, Mr. Letcher," said Christie proudly. "Look what I got." She could hardly believe her own voice. It was as though she were listening to someone else talk.

"By Jubers, Mrs. Pritchard was speaking the truth. And she didn't even know for sure. She was just going by what James said. She thought James might be telling a story. It's like James to tell sech a story." Mr. Letcher set the mail down on the lamp table by the window. His feet shuffled nervously.

"What have you got there? All boys?"

"Three girls and two boys."

"I'll be dogged. The girls *would* outnumber the boys," he said. "They all look just alike."

"Nobody will ever be able to tell 'em apart," declared Alma.

"Have you done named 'em yet?" asked the mail carrier.

"I have to talk to James about that," said Christie, reaching for a biscuit. She had finished a chicken leg.

"They're sleeping mighty good!" said Mr. Letcher. "My lands. I expect they're a sign of good luck—or something bountiful, I'd say."

"Mr. Letcher," said Alma. "Do us the favor of going ahead on your route. Christie needs her strength."

"Why, I'll be going," he said, backing away from the babies. He said to Christie, "You got yourself a handful, Mrs. Wheeler."

Through the front window, Christie watched Mr. Letcher ride away, switching his horse smartly. She always liked it when he stopped in with the mail. He usually left the mail in the box at the end of the lane, unless she got a letter from Dundee. Then he brought it to the house and sometimes visited for a while. Alma picked up the mail he had set down.

"This ain't even yours," she said, squinting at the envelope. "This is for Mack Pritchard—from his boy in Jackson. And here's the Pritchards' new wishbook."

Before Christie could finish eating, she had to nurse two of the babies. Holding them—even though they were light as feathers—was awkward and strained her arms. She felt the milk flowing, but it seemed thin. The first milk was supposed to be yellow and thick—the butter that gets churned to the top by the labor of childbirth, her mother had told her years ago.

Because they were so light, she thought she could eat while nursing the two—they were Emily Sue and Mollie. She didn't want to ask anyone to feed her while she was nursing the babies. But in her stranded position, she couldn't reach the little table. James had made the table when she became mostly bedridden, and it had been handy when Alma brought the meals. Thinking back to the hard winter since Christmas—when every step across the floor was like pushing a barrel of flour, and turning over in bed at night always woke her up and presented new challenges for arranging her thickened limbs—she knew she had to readjust all her memories of her pregnancy in terms of what she knew now.

James had eaten dinner up at Wad's. He stopped in later, with a lightness in his step and a grin he couldn't wipe off his face. But Christie recognized worry underneath the grin, so she didn't bring up the names yet. It might be too much for him to think about now. He touched each baby's blanket awkwardly. Then he squatted down by the bed close to her and grinned foolishly.

"Did we overdo it, James?" she whispered. "Plowing?"

"You can't overdo that," he said, touching her breast. He leaned forward and kissed her lightly.

They were whispering, aware that Alma was washing dishes nearby.

"We'll be talked about," Christie said, with a little snicker. "They'll say we didn't know when to stop."

"Let 'em talk," said James, still grinning. "These babies ain't what you thought," he said.

"What?"

"All that mess about Reelfoot."

"Oh, don't bring that up."

She didn't remember telling him her fear that a monster had lodged in her while she was at Reelfoot. Somehow he knew, and she was surprised. But he didn't know about Brother Cornett, she was sure.

"That's all over with, Chrissie," he said gently, touching her forehead. Then he grinned with the modesty of a man brought onstage for a prize. "Now look what we got." He turned his head from side to side in amazement.

"What did the doctor tell you?" she asked hesitantly.

James said, "He couldn't find nothing wrong with them. But he said we needed to get help. He didn't think you could make enough milk."

"I believe I can," Christie said, her voice wavering.

"I've engaged that neighbor girl—the Smith girl—to help out," he said, rising to his feet. "I spoke to her pa. She'll be here after-while."

Christie hadn't realized she would feel so hurt. Her breasts had grown so large, she thought she ought to be able to nurse her babies. Her mother always said if a woman couldn't nurse her babies, they would never grow up to mind her. Christie didn't reveal her hurt to James. Things had been so hard between them these winter months. She felt easier with him now. She had completely misinterpreted what had happened at Reelfoot, she realized. Her imagination had carried her away. Aunt Sophie always said Christie had too much imagination.

Hattie Hurt came by for a while to see the babies. She washed her hands and examined the babies tenderly, as though she were sorting peaches and was afraid of bruising them. She kept murmuring, "I declare."

"Could you tell I had all these in me?" Christie asked.

Hattie nodded. "I thought you had four, but I didn't want to say. That least one was hiding from me, I'd allow!"

"They played hide-and-go-seek in there. And on sunny days, they played here-we-go-round-the-mulberry-bush."

Hattie laughed. "Well, Christie, I can't say as I ever saw five come at one time." With great care, Hattie unwrapped John Wilburn. "I was glad the doctor was sent for, Christie," she said, as she began massaging the baby, wiping him with oil from one of her bottles. "I didn't want to say in front of you, but I was afraid I couldn't get them all out."

Hattie wrapped up the baby and set him down by Christie. He squinted at the light.

"They're looking stronger," Hattie said. "If they can get enough milk, I don't know why they won't do good." She paused over Minnie Sophia and stroked her cheek. "They're all fully formed, and they weren't early."

"Then they'll be all right, won't they?"

"Just don't give up, Christie."

"I won't. I couldn't."

Later, gathering her things, Hattie told Christie she was looking good and getting her color back. She said she'd stop in again when she got time. "And if you need me, send for me."

"We can't pay you and the doctor both," said Christie.

"You just send for me," Hattie said.

Christie stared at the double-wedding-ring pattern in the quilt on the bed. With her fingers, she traced one of the large circles. Here we go round the mulberry bush. She had to remember to tell James to give Hattie a ham.

She fell asleep again. When she awoke, the Smith girl was standing over her, removing her coat. Alma had said the girl was unmarried and that the father of her baby was a Beecher who had gone up to Illinois to live. The girl looked about sixteen, with buck teeth and fine hair.

"I left my little baby with Mama and them, and I run up to see if I could help you out," the girl said. She didn't seem surprised by the number of babies. "Give me one," she said.

Casually, she lifted the one most awake, Emily Sue. Settling herself in the rocking chair by the bed, she nursed her awhile. Then she said, "This little thing's so light, I could take another one and still have some milk left over. The more you nurse, the more you'll make, Mama says."

"Not with five," Alma corrected her. "There must be a limit."

"Take this least one," said Christie. She almost said "Minnie Sophia" aloud. Already the babies had grown into the names. Naming them seemed so private, she wanted to talk to James alone—when they got a chance.

The young girl, Elvie, wore a long white apron over a brown house dress. The veins in her breast were blue. Her hair was uncombed, and she had twisted it up in a knot on top of her head. Her air of carelessness explained how she got her baby in the first place, Christie thought.

"My little girl's already eating from the table," Elvie said, rocking as she nursed. "She eat some mashed-up green beans and taters. She just loves taters, and today I mashed up some beans and give her. I didn't know having a baby was so easy. They just eat and dirty their didies, over and over, and just grow. That's all there is to it. Mama says I'll be old before my time having a baby so young, but I don't care. I don't care if I have ten or fifteen younguns."

Minnie Sophia sucked a little, but seemed fussy and didn't want much.

"Here, this one's had enough," said Elvie, handing the baby to Alma, who placed her back in the row beside Christie. Minnie Sophia would live, Christie believed. The doctor's words suddenly made her angry—he wasn't giving the babies a chance. They just needed attention and care. She stroked Minnie's cheek and the baby gurgled. Christie made a point of touching each baby, holding each one close to her and caressing it. Their bonnets engulfed their little heads.

"This one with the blue ribbon's hungry," Alma said. "Do it next."

Elvie pulled at her hair and looked out the window. "I wish it would snow," she said. "It didn't snow enough for me this winter."

"What are you talking about, child?" said Alma, in the act of handing John Wilburn to Elvie. "You'd change your mind if it was up to your knees and you had to get water out to the calves."

"Claude wrote that there was snow up in Illinois. He was in a foot of it and his horse just wallered in it." Elvie laughed, then smirked. "He thinks Illinois is the beatin'est place on earth."

"Are you going up there?" Christie asked. She liked the idea of a foot of snow, clear and glistening and beautiful. She loved snow cream.

"I don't know." The girl sniffed. "Mama's against it." She fell silent as she nursed the little boy.

"I don't believe you'll ever go to Illinois," Mrs. Willy piped up. "You're a mama's girl, and I don't think you'll ever stray that far from your mama."

"You better get your pappy up there after that boy," Alma said sternly. "Drag him back down here to take care of you and give your youngun a name."

"You don't know Claude," Elvie said. "Claude does just whatsomever he pleases."

Alma, seeing their neighbor Mack Pritchard coming up the front path, went out on the porch to greet him. When she returned, Alma reported that he seemed just as surprised as Mr. Letcher by the news of five babies. He had brought a jug of cow's milk for the babies.

"I told Mack to set that milk out there in the springhouse, but I don't know what we oughter do with it," she said. "I believe sweetmilk is too rich and they might take the milksick."

"Let's ask Dr. Foote when he comes back," said Christie. She felt her milk flowing again—she was able to nurse. Minnie Sophia was still awake, and Christie tried to get her to eat. She sucked a little, but her face grimaced as if the yellow fluid tasted bad.

"I forgot to give Mack his mail," Alma said.

"James can take it next time he goes by," said Christie.

Through the day, between naps, she kept tending to the babies, bringing them one by one, or on occasion two at once, to her breasts. It was too soon for them to take much. Still, she was fearful of going dry. She didn't know where James was. The Smith girl had left after finishing with John Wilburn and Emily Sue. Mrs. Willy was wandering around the house, picking up bits of mud from the floor and throwing them into the fire. Nannie played paper-dolls in her corner and didn't say a word, as if the new babies had scared the sound out of her. Alma flew through the work at hand like a swift-running horse—determined and not turning to look at the scenery. Without sleep, she cooked, carried in water, washed, fed the fire, shut out the older children, and somehow kept up with the needs of the babies. Amanda popped in three times to see the babies, and each time Alma sent her back home to look after Boone and Mammy Dove and the children. Amanda was so distracted she misplaced her fascinator and had to borrow one of Alma's oversized dark bonnets, the kind of drab thing Amanda had sworn never to have on her head even if she lived to be a hundred. Christie laughed at Amanda in the big bonnet. It was a typical sun-bonnet, with gathers in the back to hold it snug around the head, while the tail protected the neck. The broad brim jutted out over the forehead to shade the eyes. The arched shape of a mature woman's bonnet always reminded Christie of a covered wagon.

"Jimmie Lou could take better care of things than Mandy can, and that ain't saying a whole lot," Alma muttered after Amanda had left. She heaved a log into the cookstove and slammed the lid in place. Mrs. Willy, like a bird swooping to a scattering of crumbs, flew after her to pick up little pieces of bark from the floor.

Alma said, "They'll wag their tongues over this at church. Yessir, there'll be plenty of talk." She shook her head. "I can just see Wad now, carrying on like he done this hisself. And Thomas will tell ever'body from here to Mississippi."

Christie hated to be talked about. One of the worst things in the world was for a woman to be talked about the way the Smith girl was. Christie wished Wad would keep quiet. Alma always fussed with her brother, but beneath Alma's bossy ways was a fierce defensiveness of her kin. Christie didn't think Alma had much feeling for her, no more than she had for Amanda or the other wives who had come into the family. Christie hadn't seen James's Wheeler nature at first, but now that they had lived in Hopewell for a few years amongst his kin, she thought she saw it in him too. It was a kind of self-satisfaction and a fear of others.

"How's the weather looking out there?" Alma asked Dr. Foote when he arrived at about three o'clock.

"It's coming on dark a mite early," he said. "Might be something about to happen."

"I think I'm going to get on home if she's fixing to rain," said Mrs.

Willy, rising from a cane-bottomed chair. She had been hemming diapers hastily fashioned from a sheet. "If y'all want me back, I'll come in the morning."

"You don't have to come, Mrs. Willy," said Christie. "We'll manage."

"I don't mind helping out one bit," said the woman, looking nervously out the window at the shadowy sky. "I'll finish these diapers at home."

Dr. Foote was doubtful about the cow's milk Mack Pritchard had brought.

"It's too early to try it," he said. "They need as much mother's milk as they can have the first day or two."

"Won't they get the milksick from a cow anyway?" Alma asked.

"We don't get that around here much these days." Dr. Foote was fingering the babies, turning their heads from side to side as they lay sleeping.

"We had the Smith girl here this afternoon, but I don't think we can count on her," Alma said.

"I've got hold of a colored woman that's going to come about six o'clock," said Dr. Foote. "If you ain't got no objection. She's got a baby and milk to spare."

"We need all the help we can get," said Christie.

"Will your husband care?"

"If it's all we can get—"

"Well, if he aims to try to save 'em all, he better not care what color the milk comes from," said Dr. Foote. "Now I believe these two biggest ones have got the best chance."

"The least one eat," Christie protested. "She eat two times. And Hattie said they looked good."

"Well, they look better now," he said. "They might do better if you could find somebody to take two or three of them."

"No, we won't split 'em up," Christie said. "I ain't giving away none of my babies."

"You heard her, Dr. Foote," Alma said.

"We can take care of 'em," Christie said weakly, although she was not sure.

"Who's this colored woman you've got coming?" asked Alma.

"She's called Mittens Dowdy, and she can't get here till six o'clock because she cooks for Dr. Cooley. But she's a good soul and she'll come out early and late, she said."

"What will we have to pay her?" asked Christie.

"I don't know, but I'd allow you wouldn't have to pay her anything but a few scraps if you let her take one home with her. It'd be a lot easier on her."

Christie was too tired to argue. It occurred to her that Dr. Foote might charge five times his regular fee—he was liable to charge by the baby.

The doctor punched his tubes into his ears and unwound the blanket from James Lake. He listened to their hearts, pried into their diapers, turned them over, made them squall. Alma started changing their diapers.

"You didn't make enough of these things, Christie," she said. "But I believe we could divide 'em in two, these babies are so little."

"They'll grow," said Christie.

She couldn't nurse. Her milk hadn't built up again. If she could sleep until the Negro woman came, maybe she would feel better. The doctor asked some questions about her bleeding and seemed satisfied that she was doing normally—no fever or infection—so he didn't examine her again. She felt relieved. Her cramps had stopped, and the throbbing between her legs had subsided. She was sore, but her opening did not seem as stretched as it usually did when she gave birth, and she did not believe it was torn at all. The babies were so small, they had popped out like loose teeth.

2

When she awoke, the doctor was gone. James was gazing down at the babies as if he had just seen them for the first time. He had changed into his milking clothes, which smelled of cow manure.

"My lands," said James softly. "What in the world have we done."

"I know what all their names are now," said Christie. "They come to me when I was waking up this morning. I've been thinking those names all day, so already I think that's who they are."

The babies were sleeping, and James knelt by the bed as she whispered to him about the ribbons, pointing out each in turn. "James Lake is the oldest one. Look at his big mouth. And Emily Sue has the curly hair, and John Wilburn—he looks like you. This one's Mollie Lee. Look at all that blond hair she's got. It could almost make a top-knot. And the littlest one is Minnie Sophia. Dr. Foote said she was weak, but she's been eating good and she's got real strong fingers."

"I never thought you'd name one after your Aunt Sophie," James murmured. He seemed mesmerized by the row of infants.

"I had a soft spot in my heart for her all of a sudden. Poor old thing. She didn't ever get to have a baby."

"This one's got a red face," said James, pointing to the baby with the blue ribbon. "Which one did you say this was?"

"John Wilburn. He's got your nose."

"All the noses look alike to me."

"Well, they're all little and pointy, but John Wilburn has a little-bitty bump on the end. See."

"It takes sharp eyes to get to know this bunch."

"Well, we'd better look hard while we've got them," said Christie, her voice wavering. "But Hattie said they had a good chance. They just have to get enough milk."

James nodded and gazed out the window. A robin redbreast flew past, its russet front glowing faintly in the fading light. "I couldn't find nobody but that Smith girl, and she's so young I don't know if she'll do much good."

"She fed three of them, and I've fed 'em all since you were here— they don't take much yet, they're so little. And Dr. Foote's sending a colored woman."

"A colored woman?"

"Is that all right?"

He held his head in his hands. "Sometimes you do things you never thought you'd have to do."

"Rich people do it. I guess it's all right." She gazed down at the sleeping bundles. Their breathing was so shallow, so slight. They could flutter out of life like moths.

"Well, I ain't rich, and I don't want to act like rich folks neither," said James, pushing his forehead against the edge of the bed.

He looked up. The babies were stirring, making little whimpers.

"They all wake up at once," said Christie. "Help me hold some of them while I get to work on them."

Alma came into the kitchen from the back porch. "Here we go again," she said, reaching for a baby and a diaper. "I've got the first diapers washed. They're going to run through 'em right quick."

Christie nursed John Wilburn and Mollie Lee while James held them in position for her. The others squirmed impatiently beside her. John Wilburn had a strong tug, stronger than the last time he nursed. The Wilburn name gave him strength, she thought. At moments, she could scarcely comprehend where she was. She felt overwhelmed. With all the people coming and going, it was like being in a dark barn, with the bulky shapes of cows moving around her.

After the babies had been changed and fed again, James went out to milk, and Alma left for home to fix dinner. Amanda and Lena stayed with Christie then. She rested while Amanda and Lena fussed over the babies.

Amanda rocked one of the babies in her arms. "Christie, I told Nannie and the little boys they could come down after supper if they were good. If you don't want them here, I'll just tell them they were bad. They've been running up and down the hall and the stairs, and Boone even got up from his lofty-bed and got after them."

"Don't let them run wild," said Christie, distressed.

"Oh, they're all right. I shouldn't have said anything. Me and my big mouth. Dulcie's watching them. They won't get into anything they oughtn't to."

"Dulcie's hogging the new book," said Lena, who had been regarding the babies with awe.

"We got a new wishbook," Amanda said. "And Little Bunch wants to cut out dolls, but I won't let her since we haven't had a chance to look at the book yet—not that we'd ever get to order anything out of it." Amanda sat on the edge of the bed, the baby cradled in her arms.

"Did you get it in the mail?"

"Mr. Letcher brought it today. Didn't you get yours?"

"No, he brought us the Pritchards' mail instead. It's over there on the table. I forgot to ask James to take it to him, and then Mack Pritchard was out here, but we forgot to say anything. I wouldn't want to open the Pritchards' wishbook."

"I hope yours don't get lost! It's got some of the new fashions. You can't imagine who would wear them. The dresses look too hard to sew, and you could never buy them—some of them cost seven or eight dollars."

"I don't need any new clothes," said Christie. "I'm still too big."

Amanda exclaimed over the babies. "They're all as pretty as little pups," she said. "Such good color! I think they're looking better than they did, Christie. I think that old Foote's wrong."

"This littlest one's still weak," said Christie, touching Minnie's bonnet. Minnie still appeared terribly fragile, like a newly hatched, fuzzy and raw bird, but Christie definitely thought she was stronger. "I don't know what we're going to do with all of these," said Christie, suddenly laughing at the enormity and strangeness of her situation.

"I'm sure they'll be all right," said Amanda.

"Mandy, you sure are good to me," Christie said. "I've been awful to live with all winter. I've been so awful to James."

"But I believe everybody forgives you, now that they know what was going on. Didn't I tell you not to worry about that dream you had at Reelfoot?" Amanda glanced out the window. "There comes somebody." She set the baby down on the bed, in the vacant place between Minnie Sophia and James Lake.

"It must be that colored woman Dr. Foote's sending. She's a little early, though."

"He's sending you a colored woman? Does James know?"

"He said it was all right."

"Don't tell Wad. He'll have a duck fit."

"I don't care," said Christie, leaning back against the pillows. Her breasts felt drained, and her eyes were tired. She was hungry again. Her blood was dancing as hard as spring runoff.

"It's not her," Amanda said, standing at the window. "It's a man, in a good suit of clothes."

In a moment the man was at the front door. Christie heard Amanda let him in. She could hear them talking. Then Amanda rushed around the staircase and called excitedly, "It's Mr. Jenkins from the *Hopewell Chronicle!* He wants to see the babies!"

"What in the world?" cried Christie. "Don't let him in! Everything's all strowed around, and I'm in a mess. My hair, my face. I'm in the bed!"

"Ma'am, I don't mean to bother you," said Mr. Jenkins, stepping around the stairway into the room. Christie could see the side of his face. He had politely averted his head.

"We've got her in the front room for the warmth of the fireplace," Amanda explained. "But she's not fixed for company."

Mr. Jenkins said, "I just want to verify for myself that there was five babies born, so that I can inform our readers of this wondrous event."

"I don't know why you want to make a fuss," Christie called out. "But I'd be much obliged if you'd come back some other time."

"When do you have to have this for the paper?" Amanda asked the man.

"Tomorrow," he said. "I'd be much obliged if I could come back tomorrow morning—say about nine o'clock? Would that be all right?"

"Is that all right, Christie?" asked Amanda.

"I reckon."

The man said, "And could I peep, just to see if there are really five babies?"

"There's five all right," said Amanda. "Christie, he's just going to peep. You can hide under the cover."

The man stepped forward and Christie pulled the cover over her head.

"Glory be and praise the Lord," he said. "Why, it's really true."

"Pretty, ain't they?" chirped Amanda.

Christie heard him step back, imagined him tipping his hat. "I'll be back tomorrow morning, then," he said.

"The Lord willing and if the creek don't rise," said Amanda, shutting the door. She scurried back to Christie's side. "Well! What do you think of that! Christie, the newspaper! You're going to be in the paper! You and your babies, in the paper."

"That ain't nothing," said Christie, pushing the cover down. "I was in the paper when I moved here, and when we had that hog to stray, and you were in there when you went to Bowling Green. And our trip to Reelfoot was in. Why, everything that happens is in the paper."

"But that's just little stuff in that letter Mrs. Ray sends in. They didn't send a man out here when your hog strayed. Or when we went to Reelfoot. This is different."

"What will they say in the paper?"

"Well, I don't know. Probably 'Mr. and Mrs. James Wheeler are the proud parents of five babies,' and they'll say where you live and give their names—you'd better settle on 'em by tomorrow—and maybe how y'all moved here a few years back. What else could they say?"

"I don't know. But I guess that'll be all right."

"But don't tell him about that colored woman helping out."

"They wouldn't put that in. Would they?"

"I don't know."

Christie straightened up and readjusted her pillow. "Well, I reckon I ought to be right proud," she said.

She patted Emily Sue, whose head seemed to be circling, trying to escape from her blanket and her position between James and Mollie. The doctor had set them down in order of their size, as if to make a point. But Christie had moved Minnie to the center, so she would get the warmth from the stronger ones. The babies' eyelashes were like faint fringes of down, and their skin was red and wrinkled. Their fingers were as tiny and new as green beans setting onto the vine, when the bloom starts to shrivel away.

3

"I HOPE THAT COLORED WOMAN DR. FOOTE'S SENDING GETS HERE soon," Christie said. "I'll feel better knowing we can get enough milk."

Amanda said, "Did I ever tell you about the time some colored women come here to help out? Alma and me, you know, had babies the same year. I had Little Bunch, and she had Hub. And when Alma's down, everything stops dead. So Wad got one colored woman to wash and clean up and another one to cook."

Amanda laughed, her bird trill. But she was careful to talk softly in the babies' presence. She kept a sharp eye on Little Bunch, who had appeared again and was sitting cross-legged on the small braided rug near the hearth. She was rocking back and forth. Amanda was sewing, making little bonnets.

"How did it work out?" asked Christie, trying to shift her legs without disturbing the babies.

"Mary and Sarah were always trying to outdo each other. They'd fuss all the time about some little something. Each one would try to do the best job so they'd get the most praise. We thought it was funny because *we* got the advantage. Mary had a hard time doing a washing that would get as much praise as one of Sarah's cakes, so she went to great extremes to turn out a fine-looking wash. She was an artist with an iron! I can still see her now. Poor woman. She died about five years ago."

"What about Wad?" Christie noticed Little Bunch perk up like an alert mother bird when two of the babies stirred.

"Wad didn't like for them to be in the room when he was eating, so Sarah would fix all the food and bring it in and not come back in till he was done. I never did understand that. He didn't mind eating what they cooked, or sleeping on sheets they'd ironed, but he didn't want to be in the same room with them—if he was eating or working with the younguns or something like that."

"Maybe he was embarrassed."

"Why would he be embarrassed? He was the head of the house. They worked for him. And he's been around Negroes all his life."

"I'm sure I can't figure your husband out," said Christie, thinking it odd that Amanda, too, should find him hard to know.

"But I loved those women," said Amanda. "I loved having them around. They brought life to the place. Life here was a misery till you came, Christie."

In the chair beside Christie, Amanda rocked slowly and worked her needle through a baby bonnet. The ribbon in her hair was loose, and the hair fluffed down around her eyes, making them shadowed and blurred-looking. At Reelfoot last summer, Christie had realized Amanda had a strain in her personality that she kept secret. There was something a little dangerous about it, as if she might consider doing something unthinkable—as though she had, in fact. Christie remembered seeing Amanda come out of the smokehouse one day last fall, looking flustered. And a while later Christie saw Thomas Hunt, Alma's husband, emerge. She couldn't be sure the two had been in there together, but since then Amanda and Thomas had been paired in her mind like the swirl of colors in a candy stick. At Reelfoot, it was a hot day and Amanda's shirtwaist was spotted with sweat stains. Christie remembered the way Amanda looked searchingly around the congregation, as if she were looking for someone she knew.

During the nightmarish months of carrying the babies, Christie had wondered whether she was being punished for enjoying the act that created them. It was as though she had partaken of too much of a good thing, and it made her full and distended—as if her sins were lust combined with gluttony. Even now, seeing the five new babies, so perfectly formed, she was astonished by the overabundance of blessings. She couldn't really believe that the intensity of her "plowing" with James had itself resulted in making so many babies simultaneously. But it seemed so. It occurred to her now that maybe physical intimacy had to be a secret, for if everyone realized how much pleasure it could be, there would be more babies than women could ever handle.

Mittens Dowdy arrived soon after the clock struck six, in a wagon driven by her husband, who waited outside. Mittens was a small, skinny woman wearing a blue head-rag and a man's frayed overcoat. She warmed her hands by the fire as she gaped at the babies.

"I told Sam, my husband, this white lady needs milk for five babies, and I had to repeat it three times for him, and he still can't believe it. Wait till I tell him I seen five all-at-once-babies with my own eyes!"

Mittens, who had four children of her own, had left her two-month-old baby with her mother. She was about thirty-five, Christie guessed.

"These is the littlest babies I ever seen!" Mittens gazed in disbelief, then laughed. "One great big baby divided five ways."

"Bring your husband in," said Amanda. "He'll freeze out there."

"Oh, no, he wouldn't come in for the world. He be all right, ma'am."

"I never thought I'd have to get anybody to help out feeding a baby," Christie said apologetically. "But I didn't expect to have five."

"They'll suck you dry," Mittens said, reaching down to pick up a baby. "Well, I'll get started on two of 'em. Maybe I can handle 'em all and you save your milk for tonight."

Mittens sat in the rocker Amanda had vacated. She whipped open her dress and expertly set two babies—Mollie and Emily—at her breasts. Her strong arms held their weights like shelves. Christie relaxed.

"I'm much obliged," she said.

"I expects you tired, ma'am."

"I'm *so* tired."

"Where's yo' husband?"

"Milking."

"Bet he don't know what to make of all this," said Mittens. "Bet he stays away as much as he can. Mens don't know what to make of babies."

"No, he's sure surprised."

"They always surprised. Can't believe what they made just by sticking a poker in the fire." She laughed, showing brown, hollowed teeth. "I seed Sam one time stirring the poker in the fireplace, looking just as thoughtful. I'd just told him we was having a new baby. I knowed he was thinking, Now how did I get that to happen? It's just an unbelievability."

Christie lay quietly, listening to the clock tick as the woman fed Mollie and Emily. Mittens' voice was soothing. She murmured sweet-talk to the two babies. When the others began stirring, Amanda picked up the loudest and rocked him in her arms. It was John Wilburn, who was already developing as the fussiest. Eighteen hours had now passed since Christie began labor. Her memories were confused, but she thought she'd always remember the whirl of sensations—pain and dream and sound. The clock chimed six-fifteen. Out the window, she saw the speckled hound again. The dog had something bright red in his mouth. She wondered if Alma had thrown out some of the bloody rags.

She woke up just as Mittens was leaving by the back door. Christie heard Mittens call to her husband, "Sam, you froze? You oughter see them little babies—five of 'em, all in a row."

A mule slobbered and snorted, and a blast of air filled the room for a moment. Amanda and Little Bunch got their coats on when Alma appeared with a basket and a bucket. Christie could smell cornbread and ham and stewed dried apples. Nannie and the boys followed Alma, rushing in boisterously and bouncing over to the bed.

"Shhh!" said Christie.

Nannie and Clint and Jewell stopped short. Quietly, they stared at the row of babies.

Eight children. Christie had eight children.

4

THE MIDNIGHT PASSENGER TRAIN, THE ROBERT E. LEE, ROARED AND clacked past as if nothing had happened. Christie woke up, her heart jolting into a rapid beat. She lay motionless, unable to hear the babies above the sound of the train. Then, after the rattling subsided, she could hear the faint whisper of their breathing.

Beside her, James slept soundly, with an occasional snore. He had volunteered to sleep in the north bedroom, so he wouldn't disturb her, but she wanted him in the bed. The babies had a bed of their own now. James hadn't expected to need more than a cradle for some time, so Nannie's old baby bed had been left in the loft of the stable. But after supper, James had retrieved the baby bed and cleaned it up—brushing out the dust and cobwebs, and washing and oiling and rubbing it. Amanda folded a feather bolster in two, creating a little feather bed that just fit inside. She covered it with an oilcloth and an old quilt. The babies fit in the bed sideways, in a line, each one wrapped in outing flannel, with an outing blanket laid over all of them. Amanda created a hood for the bed by draping a light quilt over the posts and letting it hang down on three sides.

In the glow from the fireplace, Christie could see the babies each time she awoke. They didn't cry much. John Wilburn and Emily Sue cried the loudest and wanted to nurse the most. Minnie Sophia was quiet and still—so delicate, not like forceful Aunt Sophie at all. Christie had nursed them at eight o'clock, and at about ten she fed John Wilburn and Emily Sue again, but it didn't seem fair to the others. Yet Dr. Foote said if she tried to feed all of them, they all might suffer. She didn't know what to do. Her milk wasn't flowing white yet, just the preliminary yellow dribble. With all the weight she had gained, why wouldn't she make enough milk for them? Would God make a mistake like that? It would be like a simple error in arithmetic. The Almighty ought to know how to count better than that. He did make mistakes, she thought. Things so often went wrong. But that was supposed to be God's plan. His vision was so large and intricate that ordinary folks couldn't see the whole. When the predicted earthquake failed to occur, most people decided that God never meant it to happen after all. He had just put forth the idea, to stir everyone up.

So for all practical purposes, God was leaving the babies' fate up to her and James. She knew she couldn't neglect little Minnie. Or any of them. That would be like leaving a baby out in the cold winter wind. Maybe it would be better to lose one of the babies before they started to mean too much to her, but she thought it was probably already too late for that. An image of her little sister Susan jumped through her mind. Susan was eating apple pie with the sharp paring knife, laying the blade flat against her tongue, as Papa had taught her to do.

Lying awake now in the dark room, in the flickering shadows thrown by the fire, Christie remembered Wad's cruel remark—that her babies were like a litter. She had seen sows with their litters, cats with theirs. If a sow had too many pigs, the vigorous little ones pushed the weakest ones out of the way. With cats, there were usually plenty of tits for the kittens, but even so a kitten always claimed the same tit, grabbing it as his own and spreading his elbows out possessively. Her little creatures didn't have such strength to fight each other for her milk. Was it up to her, then, to choose which ones should live? She had noticed that when they woke up, they stirred helplessly, waving their limbs like the legs of a bug that had turned over onto its back and couldn't get itself righted. Their mouths opened and faint little cries came out, growing louder with their hunger. Earlier that night, Emily Sue had had a tiny wrinkle of oilcloth digging into her back, and she screamed until Christie discovered what was wrong. Tending to the babies was like playing dolls, the creatures were so tiny, so light. She had become accustomed to feeling huge, but now, even though her body was significantly lighter, she still felt ungainly and awkward, with the bulk and strength to crush her babies by accident.

She wanted a glass of milk, but she didn't want to wake James up. He needed his sleep. She wasn't supposed to get out of bed, but she thought maybe she could make it to the kitchen without aggravating her bleeding or disturbing him. She eased her way out of bed and stood up slowly, waiting for the dizziness to subside. She bent closer to the babies, staring at them until she was sure all of them were breathing. She didn't know where her shoes were.

James mumbled, "Where are you off to?"

"I need some milk."

"Get back in the bed. I'll get it."

Groggily, he got up and pulled on his shirt. She heard him go through the kitchen and open the door to the back porch. She heard the wind sing. Raindrops hit the window. He brought the jug into the kitchen and poured out a glass and brought it to her.

"Did you want some more?"

"No. This is plenty."

He returned the jug to the porch. On his way back, he paused by the baby bed for a moment and stared in disbelief, just as Mittens had described. Then he stoked the fire and placed two small logs on the embers.

"The rain's stopped, but it's cold out there," he said, shivering as he got into bed again. "Do you think they're cold?"

"No. They're all wrapped up," she said, drawing her knees up so that they rested against his thighs. James heard her soft snicker.

"What's so funny?" he whispered.

"That colored woman had some funny words. She talked about where babies come from—she said a man has a hot poker and he stirs the fire."

He touched her leg. "My poker's freezing off," he said.

"Well, my fire's out anyway," she said. She relaxed, snuggling against James.

He whispered, "I can see you blush, right through the dark." He got tickled. Then he whispered, "Mack Pritchard said, 'Why, James, you must have plugged her five times at oncet!' I won't tell you what else I heard."

"Do men always talk so dirty?"

"I told 'em they just wish they could do something that big." He shifted his body, making a little trough of heat between them. "Are you all right down there?" he asked.

"It's the easiest time I've had."

"Because they were so little?"

"Unh-huh. I guess it wasn't them fibroids after all."

"Who would have thought?"

"I don't know. I can't think." Her mind spun like a rolling pin.

"I can't think either."

"Maybe we'll wake up in the morning and it will all be a dream."

"I hope so."

"James!"

"But what are we going to do?" he said worriedly. "You can't feed 'em enough now. And how are we going to feed five more growing younguns? We're too deep in debt as it is."

"If what Dr. Foote said is true, we might not have all of them for long anyway."

"What the doctor said about letting two or three of them go—is that what we oughter do?"

He had turned away from her, and he was talking so quietly he seemed far off, the sound coming around his head from the other side of the bolster. He sighed wearily into the bolster.

"Hattie told me not to give up," she said. "She believes they've got a chance, if we just take care of them good." As she spoke, she thought she felt her milk charge, ready to flow. And then she remembered that her mother would be coming sometime soon. Her mother would know what to do.

In the daylight, their dark thoughts passed and James was proud all over again, going out to milk humming. The day dawned clear after the night's uneventful rain, and even though the fire had died down, the house seemed warmer. Christie had nursed all the babies during the night, and they were hungry again when Mittens came.

Mittens rode out early with Dr. Foote, who seemed pleased with the babies' progress. He said their color looked good; even Minnie had rallied. Christie had eaten a good breakfast, and she was gaining strength.

Dr. Foote said, "I've got Dr. Cooley coming by after-while. He wants to take a look at the babies." Dr. Foote seemed rested and cheerful today, with a bounce in his step. The black tubes hung from his ears as if they had grown there.

"We can't afford no extra doctors," said Christie. "And if we're all right, then you needn't stop by so much."

"Dr. Cooley won't charge. He just wants a look, out of scientific interest. Why, girl, we haven't seen the likes of this before. We want to know what to expect next time."

Mittens, with a baby at each breast, said, "Dr. Cooley rides on one of them railroad tricycles. He tried to get me to ride in it, but I don't want to go meeting no freight train in that little buggy!"

"Have you seen that?" Dr. Foote asked, throwing his arm in the general direction of the railroad track. "He pumps away and goes lickety-splitting down the track."

"I've seen him pass," said Christie.

"He can take it wherever the railroad goes, so I imagine he'll use it to come out here. That feller takes to every new notion that comes along."

"He ain't scared of nothing," said Mittens. "He ain't even scared of the night."

The household seemed to whir, as everybody got down to the business of caring for the babies. Christie helped change them because she wanted to examine every spot on their bodies. She could find no abnormalities in any of them. The babies had the tiniest fingernails. Their wrinkled skin was plumping up with the milk they were taking in. She felt hopeful now. Their little belly sores, beneath the greased cloths wound around their middles, were darkening and hardening well, and none of the babies had taken cold.

Amanda reported the doings up at her house: the boys popped corn last night; Lena's hair got washed; Boone lost a button; Thurman dropped a log on his toe but wouldn't admit it hurt. Amanda had finished the five little bonnets.

"Nannie and the boys are having a big time with Boone," Amanda said. "He's making them some trains out of cardboard. And even Mammy Dove's carrying on about the babies. She's got it in her head that you had five babies at once, which is true, but the way she's carrying on, it's like one of her notions, something she knows she's got all cattywampus. She keeps going over and over it, trying to get it straight, when she's already *got* it straight. And yet, it's purely unbelievable, which I guess is why she's having such a time with it."

Amanda fussed over the babies, changing their diaper cloths and washing them with a warm rag. She changed their bonnets. Suddenly she let out a wail.

"I can't remember which one's James and which one's John. I got the ribbons mixed up when I took off the bonnets."

"This one's John Wilburn," said Christie. "He's the one with James's nose."

"Why didn't you name the one with James's nose James?" Amanda asked.

"Oh, I don't know. I just didn't."

"You could change it."

"But I don't want to. He's already got his name. That's who he is."

Amanda said, "I'm going to get Lena to make some name labels for them to wear around their wrists. She's so good at embroidering. But their arms are too skinny. Maybe we'll put the names around their waists instead."

"I can't even remember all their names, much less tell which one is which," joked James, who had come in through the back porch with an armload of firewood. Usually Clint and Jewell brought the kindling, but they had forgotten their job now that they were staying at the other house.

"You'll get used to 'em, James," said Amanda.

Mrs. Willy entered the front door then, in her black galoshes. She had news, which she spilled out breathlessly. "I've found a woman who lost her little baby, a Mrs. Bowden? And she's still got milk, and she's a-suffering from it. But she said she would only take them at her house. She can't leave because she has to stay with her mammy, who's feeble. Her husband ran off and left her when she got with child."

"Why, Mrs. Willy, you've been a-wallering in the mud," said James, as Mrs. Willy tracked mud onto the carpet.

"Yessir, the road will suck you right up this morning." She loosened her galoshes. "I'll clean this here up."

"Does this woman live hereabouts?" Christie asked.

"Down near Ulster. I got word to her last night, and then she sent word this morning. I was waiting to hear, is how come I'm late."

"That's too far away," Christie said. "And I believe my milk will be coming in, now and directly."

"But we might need her," said James. "And we better get her before she goes dry."

"I know. But not yet," said Christie. "Somebody else might turn up. We're managing, so far. Don't they look better this morning?"

James gave her a troubled glance when he went out to work. It would have eased his mind to send one or two babies out temporarily, but Christie feared she wouldn't see them again. Whatever was done had to be done here, she thought. Later, she wondered if she was selfishly denying the other woman the satisfaction of a baby at her breast. But if Mrs. Bowden had lost her baby, no one else's baby could replace it, she reasoned.

Everyone from the main house, except for Mammy Dove and Boone, came in soon after breakfast to see the babies, and Christie showed them off proudly. She felt stronger today, and the babies were picking up by the hour, she thought. Wad had been out at daybreak spreading manure on a cornfield, and after he had spread his first load he came down, tracking in filth on the floor. Alma put him out after only a few minutes. Then the young ones came—all five of Alma's, as well as Amanda's girls and Christie's three. Alma's daughter Jimmie Lou rolled a pie crust while Dulcie and Little Bunch and Lena made over the babies. The boys clumped together awkwardly in the corner as far from the baby bed as they could get. Christie laughed at them and teased them for being afraid of little babies.

"What good are babies?" said Hub contemptuously. Arch seemed too shy to look at them. Hub and Arch were Alma's youngest boys.

"You were babies once," Amanda told them.

"Not that little," said Arch.

"You don't remember," said Amanda. "Babies and old people are blessed by not having to remember anything."

"Mama, did you really find them in the woods?" Jewell asked.

"Not me," Christie said. "The hoot owl found them in the woods and brought them here."

"The hoot owl said, 'Who, who, who wants a baby?'" Amanda said.

"I don't see how a hoot owl can carry one of them things," said Clint doubtfully.

"They won't all live," said Hub. "That's what Uncle Wad said."

"Shut up, Hub, or I'll smack you," said Alma. "Wad don't know a baby from apple pandowdy. So don't believe a word he says about babies."

"Is that what Jimmie Lou's making?" Arch said, his eyes lighting up.

Thurman hardly acknowledged the babies. He had grown tall this winter and was too big to go to school. His skin looked raw from the winter wind. He kept slapping his misshapen gloves against his leg nervously. To Christie he said, "I've been helping Uncle Wad spread manure. We're loading up the second load."

"Good. That's what we need, more people packing in manure," Christie said.

Jimmie Lou, in the kitchen doorway with the rolling pin, said, "You won't get a girlfriend in them clothes, Thurman."

"I ain't looking for no girlfriend. Especially not anybody as ugly as you."

"Jimmie Lou can't be your girlfriend, eejit," said Lena. "She's your sister."

"I know that," said Thurman. "You think I don't know she's my sister?"

Alma said, "You good-for-nothing boys get on out now. We don't have room for ever'body."

Dulcie picked up Emily Sue and fondled her. Rocking the baby in her arms, she cooed, "Little-o, little-o, little-o. Look, Aunt Mandy, she likes this."

"How can you tell it's a girl?" asked Jimmie Lou.

"'Cause she's so pretty," said Dulcie into the baby's face. "Why, she looks just like a little girl, a sweet little girl."

Christie had forgotten that the newspaper man, Mr. Jenkins, was coming. When he showed up at the stroke of nine, everyone in the house got flustered. Amanda shooed the boys out then, but the girls were allowed to stay in the kitchen. Wad's older sons, Joseph and Henry, were liable to show up with their wives and children any minute, Christie realized.

Mr. Jenkins said, "I didn't mean to disturb you, ma'am, but our readers are going to want to know about this blessed event—or should I say five blessed events?" He had a tablet with him and a large black fountain pen.

"I forgot you were coming, but I do have my hair combed this time," said Christie with a laugh. She bunched up her bolster and leaned back against it. She was feeling so much better. The man's Adam's apple was large, as if he really had an apple stuck in his goozle. It was hard for her to keep a straight face as it bobbed up and down.

"That's quite all right, Mrs. Wheeler," said Mr. Jenkins. "I'm sorry I dropped in on you like that."

"Be seated, Mr. Jenkins," said Amanda, pulling forth one of the good cane-bottomed chairs.

From the kitchen doorway, Alma glared over the room like a hawk watching for a mouse to misstep. She grunted and said, "Be sure you get it right, now."

Mr. Jenkins, still standing, had his eyes on the babies. "Could I just look for a minute?" he said. "I've never seen anything like this!"

"Well, we hadn't neither," said Christie. "It was a surprise."

"I guess you didn't know you were fixing to have so many."

"No, sir." Christie felt uneasy, wondering what people would think.

Mr. Jenkins set his hat on the floor beside him. He had been carrying it in his hands like a collection plate. He reached to take one of the babies whose eyes were open—Mollie Lee. She was looking lively today. Her blurry eyes washed over him like water. When she began to cry, he set her down and petted another one, John Wilburn, until he peeped like a chick.

"Babies need lots of petting—to tame them and make them loving," Amanda said, taking up Mollie and rocking her in her arms.

"They look right healthy," observed Mr. Jenkins. "I imagine you're going to have yourself a handful when they get to crawling around."

Christie laughed. "A handful? I don't imagine I'll be able to hold five babies at once. I'd be afraid of spilling them." The whole situation seemed funny. She imagined herself in the rocking chair, rocking five wriggling babies.

Mr. Jenkins asked all kinds of questions. What did they weigh?

What hour were they born? What time did Dr. Foote get there?

"I weighed a hundred and eighty pounds, I'm right certain," Christie said. "I gained and gained and gained." She was uncomfortable talking so directly to a man, but Amanda encouraged her by jumping into the conversation.

"Christie used to be skinny," Amanda told the man. "Didn't you, Christie? And she's tall."

"Where's your husband, Mrs. Wheeler?" Mr. Jenkins asked Christie.

"Up at Wad's barn. I think they're getting ready to burn plant beds today."

"I've heard of Wad Wheeler. He's a fine feller."

"My man is James, Wad's nephew."

Mr. Jenkins chatted pleasantly about tobacco for a while, predicting a warm spring and a good growing spell. He made notes, ogled the babies some more, and apologized again for his intrusion.

"Did you want to talk to my husband?" asked Christie, afraid she had said all the wrong things. "I forgot to tell him you were coming. We've had so much commotion here." She felt her breast drip, and John Wilburn was awake, needing to drink. She couldn't waste any milk, but it would be rude to ask the man to leave.

"I'm mighty sorry I've bothered you, ma'am," said Mr. Jenkins, rising to go. "Maybe I'll run into your man out at the barn. But I think I have enough for the paper." He ran down the list of names again and took another good look at the babies.

Amanda clasped her hands and squealed. "Oh, Christie, you're going to be in the paper with your babies. Why, nothing like this ever happened to us before!"

"Well, I don't imagine anybody in Hopewell has had such monumental news lately, ma'am," said Mr. Jenkins politely as he took his leave.

After he had gone, Christie said, "I oughter have let James be the one to talk to him."

"Your baby needs you," said Amanda, picking up John Wilburn and feeling his dress tail. "Uh-oh, this littlun has rivered all over hisself! All through his didy."

Christie was gazing out the front window. She could see Mr. Jenkins riding away on a beautiful horse, a shocking-white stallion. A nursery rhyme shot through her mind. "Ride a cock horse to Banbury Cross, to see a fine lady upon a white horse." If Amanda saw the horse, she would have to make a wish. But she was busy changing the baby, humming something to him. She lowered his dress tail, then placed him at Christie's breast.

5

HAVING MITTENS DOWDY IN THE HOUSE WAS A NEW EXPERIENCE FOR Christie. She had seen Negroes out and about—in the square, or going along the road, or in the fields—but she hadn't been around them much close up. Back in Dundee, an old black man used to do odd jobs around the farm for Christie's family, and they would often give him provisions and dry-goods (blankets and old clothes) to take home. He was called Uncle Obie, and he loved snakes. This made some people avoid him, since a person without fear of snakes was said to have the Devil in him. Christie remembered little about him but knew he had been found dead along a rutted road one chilly morning. People said a whip snake had come along and thrashed him to death.

Mittens was afraid of snakes, the shadows of birds in flight, bad dreams, and objects that fell to the floor and weren't picked up immediately. She sat in the rocking chair with her back to the window while she nursed the babies. The girls came down from Wad's house just to gawk at her. Her dark breasts were like coconuts, Jimmie Lou said. The boys hung around outside with Mittens' husband, Sam, who waited for her with his mule and wagon. The boys got Sam to show them knife tricks and odd contortions he could do with his hands. When Christie mentioned Sam's tricks, Mittens laughed heartily and said he should join the circus. Christie couldn't tell whether Mittens was laughing at Sam or was actually proud of his abilities and his way with the children. Mittens wouldn't look out the window at her husband. It would be bad luck to look at him through glass.

Christie paid Mittens a dime from her egg money each time she came, and they gave her extra milk from the springhouse.

"Set down and drink this cup of milk to get you started, Mittens," said Amanda when Mittens arrived early the next morning. "We've got milk running out of our ears, and you need your strength." Amanda was enthralled with Mittens and didn't want to miss any of her visits. She was intrigued that they had many of the same notions about bad luck and signs.

"And carry a piece of ham home with you," said Christie.

"Let me eat that piece of ham right here and now," Mittens said. "If I take it home, Sam'll get ahold of it. He gets to the good things first and won't let me have any. He won't even let the chirren have it."

When she finished eating, she said, "Sam goes to the store of a Saturday and he gets a sack of meal and a bucket of 'lasses and a piece of fatback and that lasts us to the next Saturday, and then he goes back and loads up again, if he's got the money. Long as I got dried beans and my chickens and a mess of turnip greens in the back yard and a smidgin of fat, I can get along. And Dr. Cooley—he awful good to help us out."

"How many chickens have you got?" asked Christie.

"I got near a dozen, and they give me plenty of eggs, but I ain't had no milk since Dr. Cooley sold his cow. He'd give me milk, but now he don't even have no milk for hisself."

Mittens and Sam lived in a little house behind Dr. Cooley's. It was not much more than a fireplace and hearth, she said, but it had a front porch and a shed in the back.

Mittens chuckled. "Sam says it's a pure wonder your man put that many babies in you at oncet, Mrs. Wheeler. He never heard tell of that many."

"You can take a bucket of milk home with you for your young-uns," Christie said.

Mittens laughed. "Oh, them chirrens don't like milk as much as they like dirt. They be eating chimley dirt. I tell 'em it holding up the chimley—but it taste so good! I know it does, but we needs the fire-place!"

"Your chillern need milk," Amanda said.

"I don't want to take milk away from you. You needs it to make mama-milk for these babies."

"No, we've got so much, it's going to ruin," Christie insisted. "The neighbors keep bringing us milk, when we've already got plenty. Why, James milks two cows."

"I'd be scared to put them babies on cow milk." Mittens shook her head solemnly. "It too rich. I hopes yo' little babies don't have to drank it. But my little baby is a-fussing. He big enough to eat mashed taters and beans, so I done started him in on that. Lord, my appetite's picked up since I'm coming over here. Sam say he never saw me put away as much supper as I did last night. I fixed hoe-cakes and beans and a scrap of ham. I shorely went after them hoe-cakes. I reckon I can help out as long as I keep up my strength and till they all get too big for me to handle. I had one oncet to keep on a-sucking till she was nearly three year old, so I reckon I won't go plumb dry."

Mittens wore a figured apron and brown cotton stockings, snagged and runnered in an intricate pattern of fluffs and balled-up fibers. She carried a wool scarf around her shoulders and wore a heavy blue head-rag. When she took the head-rag off and retied it, Christie could see that Mittens' hair was tight and dense, like Dove Wheeler's yarn ball—a furious tangle of leftover bits of string that she kept in a feed-sack under her bed.

Mittens rocked the babies and sang what sounded to Christie like nonsense songs. She made up new words to old tunes. "Five little babies, two on each tit, one left over, out in the sorghum, don't you cry."

In a low, whispery voice, she told the babies stories. Christie couldn't make out the plots, but from the drift of Mittens' voice and the movements of her body, she thought the stories seemed scary and full of surprise. Mittens told the stories as if she were passing on secrets to the babies.

"You're breathing hoodoo on those chillern," Alma fumed when she heard Mittens. "They can't hear any sense to sech tales. What do you want to tell stories for?"

But Mittens kept on talking under her breath. Then she hummed—a lyrical, low tune deep in her throat. Long after Mittens left, Christie could hear the humming going through her mind, reverberating there, a lovely melody she couldn't get out of her head and didn't want to. It kept repeating while she fell asleep and was still there when she woke up. She didn't understand how a melody could catch hold of a person like that. The song entertained her but bothered her too. It was as though something had possessed her, and she didn't know what it was.

6

On the third morning, Dr. Foote told Christie to go ahead with the cow's milk, to get the babies used to it. They appeared to be thriving, but they would be needing more and more milk as they grew. He said to weaken the cow's milk with water and a little sweetening and boil it, so Alma heated a stewer full—far too much for the babies—and set it out on the roof of the porch to cool. The sun was shining, and the mercury had shot up. Christie saw that Alma had gone outside without her coat.

"Cow milk for cows," said Mittens.

"I'm fixing to keep nursing Minnie and give the cow's milk to the others," Christie said. "I want to make sure there's enough for Minnie."

"That Foote doctor's changing his tune," said Mittens. "First, he wanted to give 'em away, didn't he?"

"He saw we wouldn't do that," said Christie. "Anyway, he said it was hard to find a woman that's clean and ain't sick."

James was doubtful about cow's milk too, but Christie didn't argue with the doctor now. She had to do something, even if she had to give the babies solid food. The babies were thirsty all the time, it seemed, drinking both Christie and Mittens dry. Christie's milk was coming freely now, but two women probably couldn't continue to produce enough milk for six babies, counting Mittens' little one. Elvie Smith had not returned. (Amanda guessed that Elvie was mad at Alma for shaming her about not having a husband.) Mr. Letcher, the mail carrier, had allowed that cow's milk was worth a try. Wad and Alma were both unsure. Joseph's wife, Mary Ann, had used it for a week with her oldest when she had a breast infection, and the baby hadn't gotten sick.

But Mrs. Willy knew of four cases where babies died after they were put on it.

"I think it's cool enough," said Alma a while after Mittens and the doctor had left. She had brought the stewer of milk indoors.

"It needs to be the temperature of skin," said Amanda, taking the spoon and putting a drop of milk on her hand. "That feels all right. But how are we going to get it down this little babe?" Amanda set down the spoon and lifted Mollie Lee into the crook of her elbow. "Dr. Foote didn't say how to do this."

"I don't imagine he would even know," said Alma. She took the spoon and dipped it in the milk. "Hold still, Mandy. A drop at a time and maybe she'll lick it."

"She can't lick," said Amanda. "She needs to suck it. Maybe she'll suck it off of a finger. Won't you, littlun?"

"Mollie Lee," said Christie.

"We'll have to make a sugar tit," said Alma.

"Mittens said make a sucky rag," Amanda said.

"Same thing," Alma said. "We need a dropper."

"Let me have her," said Christie, exasperated. "Here's what we'll do." Amanda brought the baby to Christie in the bed, and Christie placed her close to her breast. "Now, give me the spoon." She took a spoon of milk and dribbled it on her breast. "Now, hon," she said to Mollie.

"Suck it, little precious," cooed Amanda.

Alma wasn't impressed. And Christie's plan didn't work. The milk smeared on Mollie's face and dripped down to Christie's stomach and on the baby's dress. Christie tried to poke a few drops of milk down Mollie's mouth with the spoon, but Mollie made such fitful gurgling sounds that Christie had to quit and pat her on the back. Patting the fragile little thing was like burping a bird. Then Christie tried again. This time the baby got a taste of the milk.

"I think she likes it now," said Christie. But it was difficult to keep from choking her. Again Mollie spluttered, but her lips and mouth moved in a sucking motion. With a sigh, Christie guided the baby to her nipple and she grabbed it. "That's all right, hon," Christie said.

"I'll make a sucky rag right now," Amanda said.

Neighbors had brought so much milk that Alma had set crocks of cream onto the hearth to clabber, so that it could be churned into butter. Now Jimmie Lou was churning in the kitchen, and Dulcie was minding the younger girls, who had all crowded in and were whispering in the kitchen. Nobody had gone to school. Little Bunch, with a bright red ribbon on top of her head, seemed unusually well behaved that morning. Christie let her hold Mollie Lee for a moment after she had been burped. Little Bunch cuddled her, rocking her and talking baby talk, mostly "titty, titty."

Amanda, hovering near, said, "Don't squeeze her too hard, Bunch. Set her down now. She's had enough."

"Set her down, or I'll smack you one," said Alma, looming over Little Bunch.

Without a word, Amanda quickly retrieved the baby from her child. She rocked Mollie Lee for a moment as the baby began to fall asleep. Then she set Mollie Lee down and whispered to Little Bunch, "You said you'd be good now, Bunch-Berry."

Christie was growing sleepy herself. All the fuss and care made her feel more relaxed than she had been in a long while. Mittens' song had been going through her head all morning.

"Can we take the babies up to see Mammy?" Dulcie asked her mother. "I'll wrap them up and pull them in the little wagon."

"No," said Alma. "What are you thinking, youngun?"

"It's warm out today."

"I don't care if it's a hundred and five. These babies ain't old enough to go traipsing around, out visiting. My word." Alma swished a broom around the room and almost swept Mrs. Willy across the hearth.

"Imogene, I nearly got you by the tail," said Alma.

Mrs. Willy said, "I feel so out of place, but I want to help." She pulled up one of her stockings that was falling down.

"Don't move a bone on my account, Imogene," said Alma sarcastically. "I'll just sweep around you."

"It would do Mammy so much good to see these babies," Dulcie whined, as she dragged Little Bunch away from the babies. "Mammy just lays there and looks out the window, and she don't even seem to see anything. She ain't even looking, she's so sad."

"I know what she sees," said Alma, whisking at the hearth. "She sees how lucky she is that she don't have to lift a finger to keep this place running now. She can look out and see Wad spreading manure and think, Ha-ha, not me."

"But she misses going outside," said Dulcie. "And she wants to ride to town."

"This child has got a foolish, tender heart," said Alma.

"Well, I wish I could get out in the field," said Christie. "I feel like I've been laying here a year. I 'magine Dove might be tired of being laid up."

The sounds going on around her seemed so loud—the fireplace

tools knocking, the stove lids clanging, the broom scratching, the slop-slop sounds of diapers punched down and swirled in a tub of water. The lace curtains threw patterns of light on the floor. Outside, the oak tree made black webs on the sky.

"Why, here comes Boone!" said Amanda, looking out the front window.

"He must be a-wanting something," said Alma. "He wouldn't go out-of-doors if he didn't."

Boone came in, hunched and shaggy, in several layers of worn-out clothes, and rattling his cane. He said, "I bundled up against the cold, but it's spring out there! I got plumb hot. Your March flowers is blooming, Christie. And I see by the looks of you, you're blooming too!"

"No, I'm drooping," said Christie, shifting her position against the bolster. She was still weary, but she was being propelled along by all the excitement.

"Why, you look good. And let's see them babies I done heared so much about. Why, they're all just alike, like shelly beans in a hull!"

"Don't say that to her, Boone," Alma said. "She'll get all over you. She can tell 'em apart in the dark. She can hear one of 'em cry and know which one it is."

"That beats all," said Boone.

Boone studied the babies as though he were a judge in a contest, trying to pick the best. Christie smiled.

Boone pulled off his overcoat and drew out yesterday's Hopewell paper. It was a weekly, published on Tuesday afternoons. The Wheelers got it a day late. "Here you are," he said. "I had to read about you in the paper before I even laid eyes on these babies."

"You needn't to be out, Boone," said Alma as she and Amanda crowded around him to see the newspaper.

"Let Christie see it," said Boone, cracking open the paper for her. The announcement was on the fourth page, at the top.

MRS. WHEELER
IS BLESSED WITH
5 QUINTUPLETS

"Quintuplets," said Christie. "So that's what they call them."

"I heard Dr. Cooley use that saying when he come out on that railroad tricycle this morning," said Amanda.

"It's like triplets," said Boone. "Only triplets is three. Quintuplets is five."

"Why, Boone, you know everything," Amanda said.

"Quint means five in Latin," said Christie. "I remember that from school." She quickly scanned the paper. "It says the babies are doing fine and the proud parents operate a tobaccer farm south of town. It gives the babies' names and says only the mother can tell them apart!" She groaned. "And he tells how I gained so much weight and have a big job on my hands nursing five babies."

"Don't you get chill bumps, Christie?" asked Amanda, hugging herself in a little shiver.

"A little bit. But what will James think?"

"He'll be proud."

"Everybody in town will see this!"

Christie felt her face go red. She shouldn't have talked so freely to Mr. Jenkins about gaining weight and nursing her babies. Now everybody in town would be having unwholesome thoughts. She wondered what Boone thought. He looked ridiculous standing there with that monkey grin on his face, wrapped up in his rags, afraid he'd catch a sniffle. She didn't know if Boone had ever had a woman friend or why he never married, although it was clear why most women wouldn't put up with him. She usually felt sorry for Boone, but at this moment he seemed silly, playing with the babies so awkwardly. He seemed prouder of the newspaper story than of the babies.

"What do you make of these babies, Boone?" she asked softly.

He looked under their blankets, checking for their feet, naked little things no bigger than the tip of his thumb. "They're like doll-babies," he said, glancing toward the window. "I sure wisht I'd a-been here when Dr. Cooley drove up on that railroad tricycle. I've seen it go by and always wanted to get a good look at it."

"Dr. Cooley didn't say two words the whole time he was here," said Amanda. "He come in and poked at the babies and left."

"There's somebody in the yard," said Alma, going to the door. In a moment she returned with two large parcels. "A boy brought this from the drugstore. It has a letter for you, Christie."

Amanda read the note aloud while Alma cut the strings of the packages. The note said, *Congratulations on your new family! We hope we may be of service in supplying all your baby needs. Harmon B. Howell, Howell's Drugs and Sundries.* Amanda passed the note to Christie.

"There's diaper cloths in here," said Alma. "Store-bought diapers!"

"And look, there's some bottles with nipples!" cried Amanda. "Now we can try that cow's milk again." She lifted one of the bottles and revolved it through her fingers.

"If the drugstore's selling these, then the sweet-milk must be all right," said Christie, as she examined one of the bottles.

"Don't you imagine Dr. Foote had something to do with sending these?" said Amanda. She held a bottle up to the light.

The bottles were flat, oval glass containers with graceful necks that curved upward like handles. The glass was embossed with a woman's head, surrounded by stars, and the words FORTUNE NURSING BOTTLE. The nipples were black rubber, and they fit onto the bottle necks with rubber tubes.

"Ain't they queer?" said Amanda. "They look like what you'd keep your whiskey in." She laughed.

Mrs. Willy, who had been sitting in a corner sewing, sashayed across the floor to get a good look at the contents of the package. "Now, ain't that nice," she said. "Everybody says folks uptown ain't nice. But I call that nice."

"That *is* nice," Christie agreed. It occurred to her to wonder why Mrs. Willy and Boone didn't make a pair. She could imagine that more easily than they probably could.

"I think there must be five or six dozen here," said Alma, whipping through the stack of diaper cloths. "Law, the washing. We could use a pair of hands on the didies," she hinted loudly to Mrs. Willy. "We've got a load ready to scrub out at the wash-house when the water gets hot."

"They used to jest hang 'em out and air 'em," said Mrs. Willy.

"They don't do that now, Mrs. Willy," said Amanda. "Times is a-changing all the time."

"The diapers is made out of bird's-eye," Alma said approvingly.

"Bird's-eye is good," Christie said, feeling the material. It was faintly patterned with diamonds, each with a dot in the center.

Boone left when one of the babies, James Lake, began to cry. Amanda handed the baby to Christie to nurse. Christie scooted into a sitting position against her bolster. Her legs were heavy, but the place between her legs was feeling better and there wasn't much blood. Her nipples were red and sore. She thought ahead to having five babies crawling around the house, all into trouble. Washing and sewing and cooking for five babies and three older children. Eight children! It was almost funny. That morning she had heard James laughing to himself in the kitchen when he was washing. She missed her other children. Amanda had said Nannie woke up with a little cold that morning, and she didn't want her to be around the babies. Christie worried about Nannie, but she couldn't help feeling cheerful. Maybe it was the spring air creeping indoors. Just then Alma walked out the back door with a basket of dirty clothes to take up to her wash-house. Alma was keeping up James's work clothes, as well as the children's clothes. Those sturdy brogans of hers planted her feet firmly and left her free and strong as an oak tree in the spring wind.

Amanda washed the bottles in soda water and scalded them. Then she tried feeding James Lake. The bottle seemed nearly as large as the baby and could hold enough milk to drown him. But he sucked the nipple eagerly.

"I'll fix some more bottles," Amanda said happily.

7

ALL DAY THE FAMILY DRIFTED IN AND OUT, DISTRACTED FROM THEIR work and not wanting to miss anything. They came to see what the drugstore had sent. Wad's daughters-in-law, Mary Ann and Maggie, came down together, with their children. Maggie was carrying another baby herself, and she was getting big now. She brought some boiled custard, saying Christie needed extra nourishment. Mrs. Willy went home, claiming she was in the way. Some of the neighbor women who had seen the newspaper came by—Mrs. Pritchard and her daughter; Mrs. Culpepper; and Mrs. Jenny Smith, who said her daughter, Elvie, hadn't come back to help Christie with the nursing for fear of bringing some disease to her own baby. Christie thought the woman was just apologizing for her daughter's lack of consideration and was managing to insult Christie in the bargain. Mrs. Smith must be so ashamed of her daughter, Christie thought. Wad and Alma's sister, Delphinia, sent word from town that she'd be out as soon as she got over her influenza. The men were sowing tobacco in the burned-off plant beds, but James ducked in a few times to see how the babies were doing. He reported that Wad said if people saw Mittens nursing the babies they would think of marshmallows floating on hot chocolate. "I told him the babies loved hot chocolate," James said with a grin.

Brother Jones came and offered a short prayer for the babies and then told Christie they were "little lambs personally sent by Jesus as a sign." When Christie asked a sign of what, Boone, who had returned, got the preacher involved in a discussion of planting by the moon and whether the phases of the moon had biblical validity. Brother Jones said he didn't have personal knowledge of moon signs although his grandmother swore by them, and she always had a bountiful garden.

"I wouldn't be surprised if these babies were a sign of Jesus coming back," Brother Jones declared. He rubbed his shiny chin in thought. "When you think about it, it makes a whole lot of sense." Brother Jones spoke in authoritative, booming tones that seemed surprising, coming from his small, rotund frame. "Mrs. Wheeler, as soon as you're able to get these precious lambs into the church, we'll sprinkle 'em."

Christie laughed. She thought of Alma sprinkling down sheets to iron. Alma always sprinkled with such purpose and verve, like a strong summer shower. Alma could probably sprinkle a new baby forcefully enough to impress the Lord.

The preacher said, "Some people can never get it straight whether effusion is better or the full-plunge immersion, but I for one believe that full immersion is not necessary for a soul to enter the Kingdom of Heaven."

Christie remembered Amanda at Reelfoot saying, "Wad would get a kick out of all the argufying over baptism."

"You won't dip these babies in the creek, Brother Jones," said Christie teasingly. "They couldn't stand it."

"No, ma'am, I sure ain't for dipping babies," Brother Jones said earnestly. He was pacing between the foot of the bed and the hearth just as if he were striding before his congregation.

Boone reminded him that babies did not have to be baptized to get to Heaven. He began giving the preacher a history of the practice of effusion. Christie's own knowledge of the mechanics of heaven was scanty, as though she hadn't been paying full attention all these years. She had no idea what to think about effusion. Brother Jones seemed to have purposelessly introduced an unnecessary controversy, something else for her to worry about. She had never had so many bewildering choices: first it was the matter of choosing whether to nurse only the strongest babies; then it was the cow's milk; now it was baptism. And what were the babies supposed to be a sign of? A good crop year? She had grown especially wary of predictions since the earthquake flopped. Amanda hardly mentioned the earthquake anymore.

Mittens hooted when she saw the black nipples on the baby bottles late that day.

"Black as tar," she said.

"Wonder why black?" said Christie. "Must be some reason."

"It's so the light won't get through," said Mittens. "Light hurts milk."

"But the bottles are clear."

Mittens grunted. "How'd they take to that cow milk?"

"They just sucked them nipples like they was flesh and blood. But Mollie spit up a lot of it."

"People babies wasn't meant to have cow milk," said Mittens. "But some says white babies wasn't meant to have colored milk, so maybe it's all owing to what you believe."

"I don't know," said Christie, as Mittens pulled aside her shift and prepared to nurse. "Mittens, do you believe in prophecies?"

"Long as they don't cause no trouble. My sister's littlest girl done flew off the coal-house last week after the preacher prophesied how before the end of time people be flying through the air like birds."

"Did she get hurt?"

"No. Just banged up a knee." Mittens fitted James Lake and Emily Sue to her bosom. Mittens was small, but strong and agile. She clapped the babies against her like poultices. "When's you mama gonna get here?" she asked.

"I don't know. I wish I hadn't sent for her. She's got bronchitis, and she won't like to travel out in uncertain weather. But I didn't think she would want to miss this, so James sent word."

"You need you mama," said Mittens, nodding and rocking.

"Did your mama give you that name—Mittens?" Christie asked.

"Oh, it just a nickname. White folks called me that when I was little."

"How come? Or don't you want to tell?"

Mittens laughed. "Oh, t'ain't nothing. When I was seven year old, I used to wash dishes for Mrs. Thompson up on Third Street, and she used to see me a-scrubbing and scrubbing those old heavy pans, and she tease me, saying I was trying to scrub my hands plumb white. One day I come to work in the wintertime in some white mittens my mama made me out of some old sacking, and Mrs. Thompson got to calling me Mittens, saying she thought my hands was white when she saw me." Mittens laughed so loud the babies both jumped with the heaving of her chest. "She got a kick out of calling me Mittens, but it made me mad 'cause my real name is a pretty name—Clary."

"Do you want me to call you Clary?"

"Naw. I done use to Mittens now."

James came in later, tired from working on the plant beds. He said Boone had been out to show him the newspaper, and several men from the neighborhood had stopped by to ask how Christie was doing. They were shy about peeking in to see the babies, surrounded by all the womenfolk.

Gleefully, Christie showed him the rubber nipples and pointed out the new stack of diaper cloths. "Store-bought didies!" she cried. "With a paper of safety pins! From Mr. Howell at the drugstore. He wants to serve all our baby needs, he says in the letter. What could he mean by that?"

"He means if we want to buy any baby medicine or ointments or teething powder, he'll be glad to take our money," said James, stepping closer to the baby bed to examine the babies. Mittens had left, after nursing all five, although she claimed she didn't give them enough. "Mr. Howell's thinking of business. But I expect people *are* trying to help. Mack Pritchard brought some more sweet-milk, and I put it in the springhouse. It's getting so warm out I don't know if that milk will last long. Ever'body must think we're helpless, having five all at once to take care of."

"Well, you were worried about how we were going to manage."

"But I don't like to take handouts."

"It's just being neighborly. I carried Mrs. Perkins some custard and a dozen dressed eggs when she had her last baby."

"I reckon."

As James was washing up, Alma arrived with supper. She walked in, rattling as if she had been talking all the way down to the house. "Wad got on to Boone about some kindling, and Jimmie Lou's all sulled up about that box supper at the church she made that pie for. And Hub and Arch got in a fight and Arch skinned Hub's chin, and I have to wait for Thomas to get home to give Arch a whipping. He's getting too big for me to whip, and I don't want him and Wad to get into it. I tell you, it's a madhouse up there. Amanda's got her hands full. Wad's in a ugly temper. We don't have no clean clothes. If it's a good drying day tomorrow I've got to put out a wash. I can dry diapers by the fire, but I can't handle all the jeans britches."

"How's Nannie's cold?" Christie asked.

"She's better. I put a taller-rag on her chest. She's crying for you."

"Is she fevered?"

"No, I don't believe so," said Alma, slamming plates on the table.

While Alma's back was turned, James leaned over and kissed Christie. "The babies look good, and you look pretty as a peach."

"Somebody else said pretty as a peach," said Christie.

"Who? Somebody said you was pretty as a peach?"

"I can't think who. So many people have been by. Oh, it was Dulcie. She called the babies peaches."

"Well, they are," said James with a grin, as he bent over the babies. "They're little peachy pusses."

It flustered Christie for James to buss her while Alma was in the house, but he made her feel good all the same. With the babies filling out, she was beginning to beam with happiness, a feeling as deep and exhilarating as desire. She needed to change into a clean dress. Her shift was stained in the front from milk she couldn't afford to leak.

Alma piled food on James's plate and set it on the kitchen table. Christie had a good view of the table and stove from her bed, only a few feet away. James sat down to eat. Instead of sitting at his usual spot, with his back to the front room, he sat in the opposite place, so he could see her and the babies.

Alma poured James some milk, then brought Christie a plate of food. She set the vinegar on the table in front of James. She said, "James, you act like somebody that's had his name in the paper."

James smeared butter on his cornbread. He broke out in a wide grin. "Well, Alma, I must admit it is kindly special. Different."

"I thought you'd think it was awful," said Christie, biting into her cornbread.

"Why would I think that?"

She shrugged. "I was afraid you'd be ashamed."

"Why, James is a man who likes some attention," said Alma. "I reckon with a wife as big as you've been and ain't able to move except to grunt, he appreciates a little attention. All I've heard all day is how much strutting James is doing."

"Alma!" Alma's presence unnerved Christie.

As soon as Christie and James finished eating, Alma left with her bucket and dishes. She was in such a hurry she forgot to put away the milk.

"Come here," Christie said to James when he got up from the table. "Sit here close and look at these babies. Look at James Lake. Doesn't he have Papa's cheekbones? And little Emily Sue. When she's awake, she's got a fire in her eyes. And John Wilburn. I know he's going to take after you, with that nose and the way he whimpers."

"I don't whimper."

"You do sometimes."

He caressed John Wilburn clumsily, poking his own immense finger into the set of matchstick fingers. The little hand waved and tried to close around his finger. The eyes opened—fluttery, deep, murky, blue marbles.

During the night, John Wilburn got sick. His crying merged with the train whistle, and Christie did not realize at first that she was hearing one of the babies. She sat up and held him and patted him and tried to nurse him, but he wouldn't nurse. His arms flailed. James turned on the kerosene lamp by the bed. Christie changed the baby's diaper, but he kept on crying. It was the first time any of them had cried so loud or so continuously.

"He's just crying, ain't he?" asked James anxiously. "The way babies do?"

"No, he don't feel good," said Christie, holding him close, trying to pacify him. "He hurts." She loosened his bonnet and aired his hot neck.

Then Mollie started crying, a high-pitched wail.

"It's that cow's milk," Christie said, setting down John Wilburn. "I was afraid of this."

James took Mollie in his arms. It was almost frightening to see a man holding such a tiny creature. Awkwardly, he curved his arms around her, enclosing her so that in the dim lamp light her shriek seemed to come from his heart.

"Let me change her," said Christie. "Set her down here and take the other one."

"We oughter had somebody stay with us," said James, setting down Mollie on the bed. He was reluctant to take up John Wilburn.

"I'll ask Mrs. Willy tomorrow night," said Christie. "She can sleep in the children's bed. Mrs. Willy said take catnip tea for colic, but where am I going to get catnip this time of night—or year?"

"I could go after the doctor."

"No. I believe they're all right. He'll come in the morning anyway."

"I could go after Jimmie Lou or Mandy."

"No. But you can help. Just pick up John Wilburn and pet him." She demonstrated, rocking Mollie in her arms.

They were awake for an hour, holding the two babies, who refused to nurse. The others were willing to eat, though, and Christie fed them while James tried to calm the first two with a sugar tit.

"It was a stomachache," Christie said, as the babies quieted down. "But I think it's better now. I won't try to feed them yet."

James brought Christie some milk. She was drinking milk every two or three hours during the day. She drained the glass, still cradling Mollie, rocking her soothingly against her breast. She hummed that melody Mittens had put in her head, thinking it would be familiar to the babies by now. Mollie made a sucking motion with her lips and grew quiet.

"She's asleep," Christie said finally, handing the baby to James. He placed her back in the bed. Christie said, "Did I tell you Brother Jones wants to sprinkle them when we can get them to church?"

"What a sight that would be." James touched Mollie's bonnet.

Christie could imagine them standing before the preacher, the babies in their arms. He would be holding a full-blown rose soaked in water. He would sprinkle the water on the babies' heads, one by one.

She didn't sleep well. She kept dreaming about standing at the altar with the babies, and the preacher squirting water on them with a big black rubber nipple. How could she and James hold all five babies? she kept wondering. Five babies in four arms. She saw one of them perched on top of her head. At first light, she inched out of bed, and after checking to see that the babies were breathing normally, she crept into the kitchen, so she could watch the sun come up. James found her there, barefooted, upright but wobbly. She gazed out at the wraiths of pale pastel light glowing through the silhouetted trees, and then the pink blush extended its arms wide. It was the first dawn she had seen directly in several days, and she felt reassured to know the sun still rose.

8

LATER THAT MORNING, A STRANGER IN GOOD CLOTHES RODE UP IN A hired rig from the depot. He had thinning brown hair, with a wispy mustache curling around the corners of his mouth like little arms, and he carried a brown satchel. He was so completely outfitted in brown that Alma told Christie later she thought he might have been wallowing with the hogs. But Alma let him in when he said he was Mr. John W. Roberts, from a newspaper in St. Louis.

"I'm down here to confirm with my own eyes that what I've heard is true and to take back further news to my paper," he said, stepping into the front room. "We printed the news as soon as we learned of it from the *Hopewell Chronicle.*"

Christie was sitting up in the bed, wearing a striped flannelette wrapper over her shift. With so many visitors arriving, she had taken care to fix herself. She wasn't used to men coming into the house when James wasn't there. The mail carrier was the only man who would stop and visit with her, and even he did not come indoors unless James was nearby. It wouldn't be polite. But Christie had heard that Northern men had less respect for their womenfolks.

"You took the train all the way from St. Louis?" said Christie, astonished.

"That I did, Mrs. Wheeler. The overnight train." Mr. Roberts stepped forward to see the babies. "Could I hold one?" he asked.

Christie had just been getting ready to nurse Minnie and James Lake, but she had hurriedly gotten her clothes back together before the man appeared around the staircase. She was too startled to know what to do now. Mittens and Dr. Foote had left two hours before. The only family members present were Alma and Amanda. She didn't know where James was. John Wilburn and Mollie Lee had recovered from their colic, and the babies had all nursed well that morning. Dr. Foote wasn't worried.

Mr. Roberts laid a newspaper on the bed, and Amanda snatched it up. On the first page was a large news article entitled THE HOPEWELL QUINTUPLETS.

"Look what it says here," she said, rustling the newspaper excitedly. "It says this is so rare as to be unknown in this part of the world."

"Read it out, Mandy," said Christie. She was holding Minnie, who seemed heavier.

Amanda held the paper near the window light and read aloud. The first part of the article repeated what the Hopewell paper said. Then Amanda read, in an astonished voice, "'In most known instances of quintuplets, the babies have been born prematurely, and most of them do not survive. There are no previously recorded cases in the United States of quintuplets being born fully developed. In the Hopewell case, the babies are said to have been born at the proper time, each weighing almost four pounds. The report from Hopewell is that mother and all five children are thriving, probably due to the mother's uncommonly large weight gain, which aided in providing their nourishment.'"

"This never happened in the whole country?" asked Christie, stupefied.

"That's what they tell me," Mr. Roberts said. He had picked up Emily Sue and was cuddling her in his arms. All the babies were awake now. He said, "I telephoned doctors and hospitals in several large cities, and no one had ever heard of any cases on record. I would have telephoned you too, but there's no service down here."

"Hopewell's getting telephones this summer," said Amanda defensively.

"Not that anybody will have anything worth saying," said Alma, who—despite having let the stranger in—was still eyeing him up and down. He had sallow skin and sunken eyes. He set Emily Sue down when she started to fret.

Christie said Mr. Roberts looked in need of refreshment, so Alma gave him a glass of tea and some biscuits and ham left from breakfast.

"Much obliged to you, ma'am," he said, lighting into the food. He sat at the kitchen table, too near for Christie to feed the babies.

"Didn't you eat at the train station?" Amanda asked.

"No, ma'am. It was late. I had some apples and candy on the train."

"I'd love to take the train to St. Louis," Christie said. "But I'll be tied down all my life now with these babies." She smiled. In Christie's arms, Minnie seemed to smile too.

After Mr. Roberts finished eating, he got up and stared at the babies. "Are they all the same size?" he asked. "Which one was born first? Which ones are boys and which ones are girls?"

His direct manner made Christie uncomfortable. He kept asking questions—birth weight, precise time of birth, their feeding schedule. He wanted to know how long they were and what they weighed now. He asked about the attending doctor.

"I can tell the runt," said Alma. "But I get mixed up on the others."

Mr. Roberts wrote down the answers to his questions in a book. He asked further questions. He wanted to know how Christie was going to manage that many babies. He wanted to know their names. Christie handed Minnie to Amanda, who set her with the others. Then Christie went down the row of babies, naming them and describing them for the man. It came to her that Mollie Lee's fine blond hair favored Granny Wilburn's, but she didn't say this. When the babies started crying—all at once, it seemed—Alma told him he'd have to wait on the porch while the babies had their dinner.

"That's all right," he said, screwing the cap back on his fountain pen. "I'll be on my way."

Amanda showed Mr. Roberts one of the nursing bottles, and he held it admiringly. Alma grabbed it from him.

"You don't need to see that, mister," she said.

He opened his pen and scribbled something in his writing book again. The babies continued to cry, and Christie and Amanda tried to quiet them. Amanda picked up the loudest one, James Lake.

"My, my, those babies have healthy lungs," Mr. Roberts said. "I can't but wonder how you get them all fed."

"It ain't easy," said Christie, holding Mollie Lee close and jiggling her.

"We've got a colored woman helping out," said Amanda.

"They look normal," the man said, running his fingers across the dress tails of the babies in the bed.

"The least one was poorly for a while," said Christie. "And they don't much like sweet-milk. But they're all doing tolerable well."

"That sweet-milk made them sick last night," Amanda said.

She set down James Lake and took Mollie. Minnie was whimpering lightly.

Christie was relieved when Mr. Roberts left.

"My best wishes to you, Mrs. Wheeler," he said as he backed toward the door. "This is certainly a wonder of the world."

"Read me that paper again, Mandy," said Christie, after they had quieted down the babies and two of them were peacefully drawing milk from her breasts. "It don't hardly seem real."

Amanda read the whole story aloud a second time, shaking her head in disbelief as she read.

"Law, that feller sure made a lot out of this," said Alma, wringing out a rag. "Come all the way from St. Louis."

Christie laughed. "He didn't tarry too long—after he come all this way! I reckon the notion of raising five younguns kindly scared him."

"He had that hired man waiting for him with that buggy, and he was probably charging by the hour," said Amanda, who was diddling with Emily Sue, plucking at her hair to see if it sprang back into curls.

"You oughtn't to have said we had a colored woman helping out," said Alma, who was wiping the kitchen table. "Now he'll put it in the paper."

"I didn't say Mittens was giving 'em titty, did I?" Amanda protested. "Maybe he'll think she's doing the cooking and sweeping."

"He'll think we're mighty grand, having hired help," Christie said.

"I never had hired help in my life, except that time with Mary and Sary," said Alma. "But when I was real little, Mammy and Pappy had slaves—two or three of 'em. Then Pappy went off to the War."

"Jimmie Lou said she wished she had a slave," said Amanda.

"Jimmie Lou thinks she can have anything she wants," said Alma. "But I didn't spoil her. It was Thomas, going out all over the country and coming back with pretty doodads—all kinds of samples."

"The samples is always nicer than what you find in the store," said Amanda. "But just feature the stores up there in St. Louis!"

"When's Thomas coming home?" Christie asked Alma. "He don't know a thing about these babies. Won't he be surprised!"

Alma dunked the rag she had been using into a tub of water. "He'll get here when he gets here, I reckon," she said. "He was supposed to be here yesterday."

"Maybe he's read about it in the St. Louis paper."

"He won't see no paper from St. Louis," said Alma. "He went down towards Natchez. He'll take the train back up when he gets through his rounds for that spring line of women's drawers. I wish he'd go back to peddling seeds instead of women's underclothes. It ain't nice."

"I want to see his samples," Amanda said eagerly. "Would you ask him for a sample for me?" Then she blushed. "Don't tell him it's for me."

Alma grunted and slapped her rag open. "Ask him yourself," she said.

When James came in for dinner, Christie told him about the newspaperman from St. Louis and showed him the paper. She read it to him because James was a slow reader, having stopped school after the tenth grade. He ate as she read, nodding now and then thoughtfully.

"What do you make out of that, James?" Amanda asked. "All the way from St. Louis."

"Don't know," he said, breaking open his cornbread. "Don't know what to make out of it."

Amanda said, "The feller acted like he'd been in such a hurry to get here, but then he didn't stay too awful long."

"He stayed long enough to eat," said Christie.

"He eat like he was starved," said Amanda. "He looked half sick."

Christie finished nursing John Wilburn and handed him to Amanda to change him.

"The real milk is coming now," she said. "It's kindly blue. It was sorter green-looking yesterday and now it's just blue."

"That's good. Those babies will pick up now," said Amanda. She lifted John Wilburn's dress tail. As she changed him, she made playful baby noises in his face.

James was studying the newspaper, calling the words to himself.

"I sure don't know what they think about us in St. Louis," he said.

"Oh, they don't know us," said Christie cheerfully. "They can think what they want to." She was sitting on the edge of the bed. Her breasts were sore and heavy, but she felt like stirring. The floor was cold, so she slipped on some knitted socks.

"I don't know," James said. He shook his head as he swabbed his plate with a piece of bread. He had a stunned look in his eyes.

"Do you want some milk with your pie?" asked Amanda.

"If it ain't ruint."

"No, it smells all right. We've already churned about five pounds of butter, and there's more cream here a-clabbering." Amanda refilled his glass and dug out a hunk of deep-dish apple pie.

"What are you doing after dinner?" Christie asked.

"We've got the ground ready to sow clover," he said. "And we're ready to break ground for taters. It's dried out enough." He shook his head. "It's the latest spring I've seen in years."

"I hope we get enough taters this year," said Amanda. "We ain't hardly got any taters left, and they're all swiveled up like little old men." She laughed.

"I'm thinking we have to clear out some more ground this year to get more corn in," said James. He finished his pie, then stood over the babies and gazed at them.

Little Bunch slipped in the back door just as Amanda was carrying the milk jug to the back porch.

"I thought I told you to help Boone pick out seeds," said Amanda.

Little Bunch rushed over to the babies. Her eyes were wild, her face contorted.

"What is it, Little Bunch?" said Amanda. "Say something."

Little Bunch clenched her teeth and pointed at the babies, trying to grab at them.

"Come on, Bunch," said Amanda, pulling at her child. "Let's go see what Alma's fixed for dinner."

She tried to pull Little Bunch, but the child wouldn't move. Christie started to say something, and it came out a gurgle. Her saliva went down the wrong way and she had a spell of coughing. Little Bunch seemed not to hear the commotion as Amanda tried to drag her away.

"They're too little for you to hold," Amanda said. "You're liable to squeeze the wind out of them."

Little Bunch's teeth were clenched so hard Christie was afraid the child was having one of her fits. She was breathing with difficulty, and her eyes became glazed. Finally Amanda broke the child's hold on the floor—she seemed to be suctioned onto it and had to be pried off—and limply Little Bunch allowed herself to be guided out the front door.

9

SINCE THE ST. LOUIS NEWSPAPERMAN HAD COME TO SEE THE BABIES that morning, a breathless excitement surged through Christie whenever she saw the five babies, lying in a row in the little hooded bed. The man said it hadn't happened before, at least not that anybody remembered. She didn't know what that could mean. Now she remembered what Brother Jones had said, that the babies' birth might be a miracle, like the birth of Jesus. He had called the babies a sign from God, although he might as easily have been talking about an odd-shaped cloud in the sky. Other preachers had said the same thing about the predicted earthquake. It was odd to recall how agitated everybody had been over the earthquake. She remembered old Rollie Ledbetter telling about the year the earth rolled like waves of water. His earthquake story had seemed so vivid it was smothering. She remembered Amanda's hot impatience and sly grin as she gazed across the crowd, and she remembered people falling over, caught in fear and wonder, each one seizing up like a dog having a fit in the heat of August. They all believed something was coming: Jesus.

Christie had never imagined that she would do anything truly out of the ordinary, or that she would be chosen as a vessel for something so much larger than herself, of significance to people far away, people she didn't know. Now everybody was telling her she had done something amazing. But there was nothing odd about these little babies. They were just innocent babies, not angels or devils. It occurred to her that even Jesus in the manger must have wet his diaper, if they had diapers back then. She tried to imagine the sacred baby in those ancient times. Mary would have used some rough cloth made of flax fibers. Probably Brother Jones believed that Jesus didn't dirty his diaper, if he had even thought of such a thing. Babies wore swaddling clothes back then, and people wore big sheets wrapped around their bodies. She'd once seen a picture of the grown Jesus dressed in a blue sheet wrapped around a white one, and the white one was drawn up to reveal leather-thong sandals. He was flanked by a choir of angels, with enormous white-swan wings and wedding-ring halos.

She knew it was a sinful thought, placing her babies in a category with Jesus. They were just babies—hers, her flesh and blood. Mollie Lee's fine hair kept reminding her of old Granny Wilburn's hair, and sometimes she thought she saw her mother's mouth outlined in the babies' mouths when they cried. She wondered if those narrow lips were a main trait of the Rhodes line. Christie barely remembered her mother's mother, Granny Rhodes, who had died of paralysis when Christie was still a child, but she remembered her oval, thin-lipped mouth. Now and then she saw Wheeler traits, too, in the babies, but they were less familiar, more like underlying disturbances that erupted only occasionally.

Alma's husband, Thomas Hunt, had his own notion about what the babies signified. He had arrived home full of reports about the famous Hopewell quintuplets. The news of the miracle births had reached Tupelo, Mississippi, where he had passed a recent night with a cotton-farming family. And this morning he had heard from a farm-machine drummer at a crossroads store that people were saying the babies had been born in response to the assassination of Kentucky's new governor some weeks before.

Thomas came in with Alma when she brought Christie the clean wash her daughters had ironed.

"It means that these babies are destined for leadership," Thomas said, staring at the five helpless infants. "I see governors and presidents a-laying here."

"Three of 'em's girls," Alma pointed out.

"They'll be first ladies, at least," said Thomas.

"Don't listen to him, Christie," said Alma. "He's got the tom-foolin'est notions from going out drumming. I think that hot sun down South hits his head and addles his brains. The whole country's just bumfuzzled. People are liable to believe anything."

"Well, I believe the assassination was what God had in mind," Thomas said. "Not that-there earthquake Mandy was so worked up over."

Christie suppressed a laugh. This man, bony and lank, stood before her in his store-bought clothes—too extravagant for church and truly silly for wearing out here in the country. He wore galluses and stripes and polished his boots. Growing tobacco hadn't suited him. He had tried his hand, unsuccessfully, at running a country store. Then the life of the traveling salesman lured him off. Christie secretly thought Alma was glad to get him out of her sight for weeks at a time. She had noticed that Amanda always seemed so much more pleased to see him than Alma did. Alma didn't care what was out there in other places. But Amanda did. Amanda was starved for the news Thomas brought from distant towns. That was all it was, Christie told herself.

Mr. Letcher brought the mail late. Christie snatched her mother's letter and read it while he ate some cold biscuits with damson preserves. Alma was in the kitchen washing the babies.

"Listen to this," said Christie, deep into the letter. "Mama's coming as soon as she gets over her bronchitis! She wrote this three days ago, and she said the sun was baking out her passages, so she might even be on her way by now."

Mr. Letcher said, "Folks here didn't realize what a big thing it was till they heard about it a-being in the St. Louis paper. They didn't know it ain't never happened before."

"It never happened to anybody I know, but I thought it probably happened *somewhere*," said Christie.

Her mother had written, *The Lord is testing you, Christie.* She added, *You poor girl! Five babies to feed. How will you ever do it?*

Mr. Letcher said, "You think nothing around here amounts to much, but come to find out we got something here that they never heard of in St. Louis."

In the afternoon, waking from a nap, Christie was startled to see Mrs. George Blankenship standing by the bed. Mrs. Blankenship reeked of lilies of the valley. Amanda and Mrs. Willy were still there, fussing with the babies.

"I just want to say how proud I am," gushed Mrs. Blankenship.

Christie sat up and smoothed her hair. She knew she needed to comb it out. It had been pinned up in a knot since Tuesday. She was speechless. Mrs. Blankenship was one of the last people she ever expected to see in her house. George Blankenship owned the planing mill where James had had their lumber planed. James still owed him nearly a hundred dollars.

Mrs. Blankenship said, "Oh, would you look—five of them! And all just as perfect as baby-dolls." She turned to Christie. "Why, Mrs. Wheeler, that day when you fainted on the street and I rushed up to help you, I had a little suspicion that you were in the family way, but I could have had no idea you would have five! Congratulations, darling.

Oh, I've just got to hold one." Mrs. Blankenship snatched up Minnie. Minnie's mouth formed an O, then twisted out of shape. Her eyes squinted; she gurgled.

"That one's been peaked," said Amanda, rushing forward.

"She's the runt," said Mrs. Willy. "But she's just as sweet as any of 'em!" Mrs. Willy's humped back made her dress hike up behind, Christie noticed.

"I'll hold her real gentle," said Mrs. Blankenship, squeezing Minnie to her bosom. "I've had two babies myself, so I know how to hold them." She set down Minnie, who continued to fret, and picked up James Lake. "Now here's a healthy little boy, am I right? Ooh, you sweet thing, I could just eat you up."

"Their dresses are a mile too long," said Christie apologetically.

She thought of that day in town when she fainted. Christie had been in Madison's Dry Goods, among all the bolts of silk plushes, velveteens, and sateens. Mrs. Blankenship was buying some Japanese lawn for a tea gown. Christie's own need for a new work dress made her feel shabby, as she listened to Mrs. Blankenship's silky voice, which seemed to match the bolt of material she was caressing. Mrs. Blankenship was wearing a hat adorned with pieces of calico cleverly arranged to resemble a field of small flowers.

Today Mrs. Blankenship had on a broad-brimmed felt hat with large gray and black plumes clumped around the brim and a bright red bow at the back. She removed one of her white gloves and caressed each of the babies' cheeks with a long, slender finger. She had brought a powder box and puff for the babies. It was a dainty box decorated with a baby's cherubic body entwined with gold filigree and violets.

"I heard you got Dr. Cooley's nigger to help out," said Mrs. Blankenship, scrutinizing the furnishings in the room.

"She's got a growing baby, but she helps out in the morning and evening," said Amanda. "Mittens is a big help."

"I've heard she's good with babies," said Mrs. Blankenship. "Dr. Cooley said she's raised his two little ones, and he never has the slightest problem with her. He said she's real clean."

"Mittens was personally sent by the Lord," said Amanda. She set Minnie down among the other babies.

Mrs. Blankenship laughed—a polite tee-hee. Christie was bothered, remembering that day in the store, where the air was thick with the strong smells of new material. In a ray of sun from the window, she could see the dust from the material swimming in the light. As she grabbed Nannie and hurried out of the store, she saw Mrs. Blankenship staring at her, her hat settled squarely on her head. A wagon

loaded with fresh corn drifted by, the horses stomping heavily, sound-
ing like a train snorting. Christie felt her face burning, and she paused
by a lamppost. "Nannie," she said, as her sight dimmed. A mule was
passing by, and the smell of manure in the muddy street was strong.
She saw black. Suddenly Mrs. Blankenship was towering over her, that
flowery hat about to jump off. Christie was in a heap on the sidewalk,
her skirts twisted to the side. Mrs. Blankenship's skirts billowed above
her like a pot boiling over.

"Come on, darling, breathe this." Mrs. Blankenship held a blue
vial under Christie's nose. The vapors stung her eyes, but her head
cleared, the way the spectacles she sometimes used for reading or
sewing cleared her eyes.

"You fainted, poor dear."

Christie grabbed at the air. "Nannie!"

"She's here," said Mrs. Blankenship.

Nannie was puckered up, about to cry. Christie held the lamppost
and hoisted herself up, feeling mortified. She always wanted to be neat
and clean in town. Her dress was ironed, her bonnet was starched. But
in her fall, her skirt had flown up and her underskirt had gotten soiled
with manure. Her bonnet had fallen back to her neck. Several people
had gathered around. Mrs. Blankenship wore gloves made of a gos-
samer material with dainty pearl buttons. Christie looked down at her
own hands. She saw the hangnail, the cut from butchering the
chicken, the knuckles rubbed raw with lye soap, the purple brier-
pricks from picking blackberries.

Now John Wilburn was crying and wanting to be fed. Christie
took him from Mrs. Willy and patted his back, talking quietly to him,
so Mrs. Blankenship wouldn't hear—the way Mittens talked to the
babies under her breath. Remembering the scene in town was painful
to Christie, and seeing Mrs. Blankenship again—a woman so different
from herself, a woman who never had to slop hogs or sucker
tobacco—made her face burn.

She was relieved when Mrs. Blankenship left, gliding across the
floor like a person on wheels, traveling backward in her flowing skirts,
waving her way out. Christie hoped she hadn't been rude.

"Why did she come here?" Amanda asked.

"I don't know," said Christie. "At least she didn't bring up that bill
we owe."

"That powder box is too pretty to use up on babies," Mrs. Willy
said.

"I'll save it," said Christie. "Put it on the mantel, Mrs. Willy."

Amanda grabbed the box from Mrs. Willy and tested the powder on her hand with the puff. "If I had her money, I wouldn't get stuck up," she said. She prissed across the floor, waving the powder puff. "Well, I declare," she said mockingly. "Them babies is the dearest little lambs."

Christie laughed. "Do you think I should wear my morning tea gown of Japanese lawn to receive the visitors tomorrow?" she said. "Or should I haul out the French henrietta?"

"Oh, the French henrietta by all means," said Amanda. "I'm aiming to wear mine out to the garden when I plant taters."

"She just looks down at us," said Christie.

Amanda set the powder box on the mantel and then went to the window, as if she were waiting for someone to arrive. "I hope Mittens gets here early," she said, glancing at the clock. "I need to get up to the house and start in on my ironing. Wad will need clean jeans britches tomorrow, and I'm going to iron some for James too."

Through the window, Christie had a view of the field where she had run the day she arrived here. She remembered her first view of the place. It was late winter, like this. The milkweed pods had shattered on the muddy furrows where she walked. She remembered seeing the smoke unfurling from Wad's chimney, a cluster of blackbirds whirling over the field, a brown-and-white dog trotting purposefully toward a creek, a row of hog shelters inside a pen on the slope above the creek, and a large, dried-up garden. The trees were black, like gloomy scarecrows. And now Christie and James had their own house at the edge of that field. She saw James out there now, breaking ground for this year's corn. She could see him steadying the plow handles as the mule lurched forward. She saw the muscles through his shirt, for he had shed his coat. She could already envision the abundant field, the corn silking, then the ears filling out. It was warm outside, they said, but Alma wouldn't open the windows yet. Soon, Christie hoped to take short trips to the henhouse, the smokehouse, the springhouse. She longed to be out, to run in the field the way she had that first day.

10

MORE AND MORE VISITORS WERE COMING OUT TO LOOK AT THE babies. Everybody was talking about the newspaperman who came down from St. Louis. The proprietor at Crittenden's Inn on the square said the St. Louis fellow had been in there for dinner before catching the afternoon train. The man sat by himself in a corner of the room, writing in his book and drinking large quantities of water, flavoring it from a silver flask in his overcoat. He dined on fresh oysters and chicken salad and beef roast with potatoes and gravy and Mrs. Crittenden's chess pie. Christie heard Mr. Crittenden's report from Mr. Letcher, who had heard it from Mrs. Humphreys, a War widow who was half blind and yet walked three miles to town every day.

Near the end of the babies' first week, Mittens Dowdy said, "They be big enough to use a pee-bucket before you know it!" Even little Minnie was stronger. Christie hadn't tried the cow's milk on her yet, but the others were taking some in the bottles. Weakening the milk further and adding a bit more sugar seemed to prevent the colic. There was an art to holding the bottles, which were made to fit the hand, with a narrow, crooked neck to prevent all the milk from rushing forth if the tubing popped off. Amanda said the black rubber nipples seemed too hard for babies, but they sucked them willingly. When the holes in the nipples got plugged up, she jabbed her needle into the dark rubber.

Except for James Lake, who always seemed hungry, the babies preferred breast milk, and Mollie preferred Christie's left breast to her right. She wouldn't eat from the right one—a sign that she would be left-handed, Amanda allowed. James Lake was going to be a good eater, Christie said, the type of child who would take a bucket of molasses biscuits to school and devour every one. He had more personality than the others; he was the most forceful and demanding. But Emily Sue was her most unusual child—that sassy look and that hint of curl. Christie was relieved to have a girl with curl to her hair. Christie's own hair was so straight and characterless. She was too old to let her hair down now, but she longed to release it, to let it fly in the wind.

The men were working long hours, getting ready for the spring planting. They complained that Alma's green beans weren't cooked down enough and the cornbread wasn't made to her usual perfection. The women bustled around the babies—washing their dresses and undershirts and diapers, giving them baths and bottles, and keeping the house warm. The door kept fanning. Dust settled everywhere. Someone was always churning, it seemed. Mrs. Willy got such a blissful look on her face when she churned.

"These babies are going to eat you out of house and home," Dr. Foote said to Christie as he examined the babies on Saturday morning. "I meant to tell you, I won't be charging my usual fee. I already mentioned this to James when I ran into him down the lane. I told him all Wheeler babies are free."

"Why, I was afraid you'd charge by the baby," she said, stupefied by his generosity. "I didn't know how we could ever pay you."

"Well, this whole blessed event is my pleasure, Mrs. Wheeler," he said as he wiggled John Wilburn's toes. "I won't take a cent."

"We're much obliged, Dr. Foote."

"If you had called on Dr. Cooley instead of me, I wouldn't have got to be in on this and have my name in the St. Louis paper."

"That is an amazement," Christie agreed, still baffled by how far the news had traveled.

When Alma arrived with Christie's dinner, Christie said, "Alma, after I get through eating, I may be strong enough to get out and hoe. I feel like hoeing."

"You ain't setting foot out in that garden!" Alma cried.

Christie laughed. "I'm just fooling with you, Alma. I'm glad you brought me some onions. I do love a green onion in the spring."

She ate while the babies slept. The fried chicken was crisp outside and juicy inside; the potatoes were seasoned with black pepper and bacon grease; the cornbread was laced with cracklings cooked tender. Christie ate everything Alma brought.

"Who's that on the porch *now?*" Alma said from the kitchen where she was washing the dishes. She strode through the front room, her brogans slamming the carpet, and brought in a set of strangers.

It was a group of five smartly dressed men from town, all apologizing for their muddy shoes. They lined up at the foot of Christie's bed.

Christie recognized Mr. Jenkins, from the Hopewell paper. And the editor, Mr. Redmon, was there. The squat one with a watch chain on his weskit said he was the mayor, Marcus Webb. Christie was astonished to see the mayor right there in her house.

"This is a significant thing you've done, ma'am," said the mayor, pulling down the hem of his coat nervously. "You've brought honor to our town."

Alma stood in the kitchen doorway with a dishrag, looking as intimidated as Christie had ever seen her. Christie herself was speechless. The mayor untied a red ribbon from a scroll and handed the ribbon to one of the men, who rolled it around his fingers, then dropped it on the bed.

Unfurling the scroll, the mayor read aloud. "'Whereas, I have in me the power to issue proclamations in favor of our fair citizens and their good works; and whereas, Hopewell is the distinguished home of the Wheeler Quintuplets; and whereas, Mrs. Wheeler is the esteemed mother of same, I hereby proclaim Mrs. Wheeler to be Hopewell's Mother of the Year. And whereas, Mr. and Mrs. Wheeler have brought forth this eighth wonder of the world in the form of five healthy babies at one time, thereby raising the population of our fair city by a significant and goodly number, I hereby declare the Wheeler family to be the First Family of our city, for now and the indefinite future.'

"Congratulations, Mrs. Wheeler," the mayor said, handing Christie the scroll, which rolled up again on its own. "We wanted to have an official ceremony in town, but realizing you wouldn't be able to attend, we wanted our good wishes made known immediately. Mr. Jenkins here is writing this up in the *Hopewell Chronicle* for next week."

Mr. Jenkins shuffled his feet and lifted his fountain pen. Christie remembered his huge Adam's apple. He said, "Don't forget, Your Honor, that the City of Hopewell is taking up a collection for the babies."

"Oh, I was getting to that! Even as we speak, the merchants are getting together to provide supplies for you in this unusual time, Mrs. Wheeler. You're going to need extra goods, and your neighbors, the citizens of Hopewell, are rallying to the cause."

"I don't know what to say," Christie said shyly. She wondered what James would think. "The drugstore sent some things we needed," she said.

Mr. Redmon said, "They're getting together a whole wagonload of goods—hams and meal and sugar and coal oil, and even furniture from MacNeill's. Five little beds, I heard."

"But my husband can build a bed!" Christie protested. She was sure the babies wouldn't want to be separated. Children usually slept together in a bunch and kept warmer that way.

"We'll have this news in the paper again," said Mr. Jenkins. "This time we'll do you proud."

A tall man with a dangling forelock and broad, flat face said, "By gravy, we didn't like the way St. Louis made us out to be so indifferent to such an extraordinary happening."

"And so the town of Hopewell may be a little slow getting to its feet, but I reckon you are too, ma'am—no offense," said Mr. Redmon. "Five babies are bound to get you down awhile."

"I'm weak from laying, but I'm raring to go." Christie's enthusiasm made them laugh. "Thank ye kindly. I'm much obliged."

Mayor Webb handed Christie the newspaper he had been carrying. "Here's what the St. Louis paper had to say after their man got back up yonder. You can hold on to this."

Christie glanced at the article. It was on the top page, as if it were the account of an important event, like an election or a battle in a war.

After the men left, Alma exploded with laughter. "Did you ever hear such high talking?" she said.

"You was mighty bashful, though," said Christie. "I never saw you bashful before, Alma." She had thoroughly enjoyed the sight of Alma standing back, dumbstruck.

Emily Sue began to cry. Alma picked her up and handed her to Christie. Christie held the baby close and she grew quiet.

Alma swung the dishrag at an early fly that had gotten in. "What-all you reckon they'll send?" she said. "I swan, Christie. Wait till Wad and them hear about this. Mandy'll be a-squalling when she finds out she missed seeing the mayor."

Christie couldn't believe it. It was like a dream—the stores coming to her, with a wagonload of things she could never have afforded. Fancy goods, novelties like those in the wishbook. Maybe even play-toys and games and slates and books for school.

"The mayor said I did a significant thing," said Christie, rocking Emily Sue in her arms. "But did you notice how they didn't hardly even look at the babies? Or pick them up?"

"They didn't want to get do-do and vomick on their fine suits of clothes," said Alma with a snort.

Christie was bothered by some things in the St. Louis article. She showed it to Amanda when she arrived. Mr. Roberts had written that the quintuplets were "born to a simple country woman and her yeoman farmer husband."

Amanda scoffed at that. "He don't know you, Christie. You ain't simple. Why, nobody's as smart as you. You're smarter than a schoolteacher."

"And he called our house 'a humble three-room abode.' Why, we've got six rooms, not counting the loft."

At suppertime, when James came in from milking—after several more visitors had come and gone—Christie told him about the fellows from town, her words tumbling over themselves in excitement.

"James, they all said I done good!" she said softly. "They're so proud."

She played with the ribbon while he studied the lettering on the scroll.

"They're going to help us feed them," she said. "We won't have to worry."

James moved slowly toward the baby bed, as the news sank in. He patted Christie on the head and stared hard at the babies. A grin he seemed to have been saving up spread over his face.

"I looked out across the field this evening about three o'clock and I counted ten horses in the yard," he said. "And four buggies. It was looking like a camp meeting over here."

He sat on the edge of the bed beside Christie to unlace his shoes. "I didn't know how we were going to manage," he said. He paused and straightened up, then said, "You know, when I'm out there plowing, staring at a mule's behind for hours on end, I go over and over it, and it hits me by surprise all over again ever time I put my mind on it. I don't think I'll ever get used to what's happened."

"Oh, I knew something big would happen when I married you," she said playfully. "I knew marrying you would turn into *something* grand."

"We're behind on the spring plowing," he said, laughing into her hair and holding her close for the first time since the babies were born.

"Not yet," she gasped. She heard steps on the back porch. "And I'm afraid we'd have to crawl under the corncrib to do it."

11

MITTENS HAD GONE HOME. IT WAS DARK NOW. CHRISTIE HAD SETTLED the babies down, and they were all sleeping. James was taking a hot bath in the kitchen. In case somebody came in, he hid the washtub behind a curtain Amanda had strung up. A bath at the end of the week always put him in a good mood. After his bath, he started teasing Christie, saying he had a surprise. He urged her to comb her hair and get cleaned up for company. Then Dulcie and Jimmie Lou came in the back door. Jimmie Lou had crimped her hair with the curling iron, making fat curls as big as eggs.

"Your head looks like a Easter basket, Jimmie Lou," said James.

Jimmie Lou ignored James's teasing and charged through the kitchen toward Christie. "All right, Cousin Christie, get on out of that bed," she said, tweaking Christie's toes under the quilt.

"What's going on?"

"A surprise, Chrissie," said James, pulling her hand. "Come on. We're going to carry you outside."

"What in the world?" she said, her eyes on the babies.

"You're coming up to the house," said Dulcie, who had on a good skirt with a shirtwaist and weskit. "Let's go!"

"The young folks are getting up a blow-out," said James. "They're having a play-party! Everybody wants to see the babies."

"A party! But we can't carry the babies up yonder."

"They'll fit in the clothes basket, and they won't never know the difference," James said. "I'll cover the whole thing with a quilt."

"Well, what brought this on!" cried Christie. Her feet landed in her house-shoes. Jerking up a little too quickly made her sight dim.

"Wad liked the sound of that wagonload of presents coming,"

James explained. "And Thomas brought home some peanuts and pep-permint candy for the chillern. Some neighbors are coming—the Stokeses and Pritchards. Wad's threatening to get his fiddle out."

Christie laughed. "But I'm too big to carry."

"We'll get all the pallbearers in the family to haul you out," James joked.

"Oh, we'll get to sing," she said happily. "I wish I could dance."

"I'm ready to swing around, I tell you right now," said Jimmie Lou, skipping across the hearth.

"I'll dance in my mind," said Christie, brightening. Her hair was falling down, she saw in the glass Jimmie Lou handed her.

"Aunt Mandy said she wasn't going to swing around, even if Uncle Wad got out his fiddle," Dulcie said. "She's mad at him."

"She said she'd come down here and take care of the babies if you didn't want to carry them up there," said Jimmie Lou, who was root-ing under John Wilburn's dress tail to tickle his toes. He was awake now, and he seemed to be peacefully studying his surroundings.

"They'll be all right in the basket," said James. "I want to show them off."

"Are you able to do this, Christie?" asked Dulcie worriedly.

"If it's not too cold. I've been dying to get out of this bed all week. But you'll have to go in the north room and bring me something out of the clean-clothes closet."

"Will the babies cry if there's singing?"

"No, they like songs. Mandy and Mittens sing to them all the time."

Christie thought if she could hear some singing, she could get that humming out of her mind. It had gotten stuck there. By now she had supplied words to Mittens's tune, nonsense phrases—lick the skillet, tear down the tree, chase down the lamb, and don't catch me.

Excitedly, she got herself washed and ready, while Dulcie prepared clean bottles to carry with them. People would want to see the babies drink from the bottles, Christie thought. As she transferred the babies to the clothes basket, she held each one close, wondering if it was a mistake to take them out so soon. She realized how much she loved them—their tiny features, their wriggling limbs, their unceasing hunger. They were growing, and gurgling like creek water, and she imagined that the flicker of a smile threatened to break out on their little faces.

"A significant thing." The mayor's words played like a harp across the humming in her head.

At Wad's house, James set the babies in a warm corner of the kitchen, near the stove, and Amanda settled Christie in a large, soft chair next to them. Amanda surrounded Christie with pillows and wrapped her in a log-cabin quilt that Christie remembered sleeping under when they lived here. After wrestling with her bolster in bed all week, she was glad to rest her back against comfortable cushions, but the kitchen was so warm she soon pushed away the quilt. The girls flocked to the babies, and Nannie and Clint and Jewell crowded around Christie, excited at first and pulling at her for attention. But when they seemed assured that she was really there, they resumed their squealing and romping through the house. It pleased Christie to see them enjoying themselves. She loved to see a playsome child, set free from daily chores. The children had already filled up on the peppermint candy and peanuts Thomas had brought, and Boone had promised to make Nannie some doll furniture out of the peanut hulls. Her pinafore pockets were full of hulls. She was sucking on a piece of Boone's cough candy. He kept a supply of horehound sticks for his throat, and he had given Nannie a piece.

Christie pulled Nannie toward her and kissed her hair. "How's them sniffles, sweetie?"

Nannie shook her head. "All gone," she said. "That old taller-rag hurt. It made me red."

Christie spied down the neck of Nannie's dress. "It's better now," she said. She kissed the place to make it well.

The house was crowded—all the Wheelers, including Wad's sons, Joseph and Henry, with their wives and small children, and three neighboring families, all of whom had older boys and girls eager for a frolic. Everyone tried to squeeze into the kitchen to see the babies in their basket next to the stove. The babies slept through most of the excitement, and when they woke up the women helped feed them with the bottles. Christie remembered nursing Nannie on their first night with the Wheeler family. When they lived in this house, the family had seemed at war, with everyone at cross-purposes, but now they seemed to belong, like all the daisies in a field standing out against the clover and johnson grass and timothy.

"There's the proud pappy," said Mack Pritchard, the neighbor who had brought so much sweet-milk. "Nobody believed you had it in you, James."

Alma's voice carried over to the men, who had cornered James, teasing him. She said, "You oughter seen James knocking around the corner of the barn yesterday morning on them tom-walkers he whittled down out of some planks. He liked to scared Nannie to death!"

"He was about eight foot tall," said Henry, raising his hand above his head. "He was as pleased as a skunk in a churn."

Joseph joined in. "I told him he don't need no tom-walkers now," Joseph said. "He seems tall enough, with what he's done."

"They're talking about you all over town, Christie," hollered one of the Stokes women from the far side of the room.

"You need you about five titties, Christie," said Ethel Pritchard, Mack's wife. She was in the kitchen picking out hickory nuts Wad had cracked.

Christie blushed, and everyone around her laughed. Suddenly the cuckoo bird sprang out of the clock on the wall and cuckooed eight times. The loud-ticking mantel clock said five of eight. She saw the men gathered around the fireplace, teasing James. By their hand movements and loud whoops, she knew what they were saying. James caught her eye. She heard one of the young men say, "Reckon you ever got five birds in one shot, James?" She could see James's abashed grin. She couldn't hear all the talk, but she could see his lips saying, "You shut up now, Howard. Don't let the womenfolks hear that."

The kitchen was separated from the front sitting room only by the long oak dining table, so that from the kitchen Christie could observe all the goings-on. The children played checkers and soldiers and dolls, while the older folks played rummy. The front room was shadowy, with brown walls and small rag rugs braided of wool strips from old winter clothing. Several upholstered sitting chairs and rockers hugged the walls, and a small table with a coal-oil lantern on it stood between the two windows. Another lantern burned in the center of the dining table, casting a glow on the lace curtains and green paper shades of the tall windows. The double doors to the parlor had been opened up, and Christie could see that the carpet had been rolled and pushed to one side. The men had moved some of the parlor furniture out on the porch. Alma had oiled the wood floor and dampened it to keep the dust down. At a play-party, the young people played singing games so they could dance when musical instruments and dance leaders couldn't be found in a hurry. Wad Wheeler played the fiddle, but he couldn't always be persuaded to bring it out.

Boone, his white hair sticking out in all directions, sat on the top step of the stairway, holding on to a post.

"Come on down, Boone," Christie called to him. "You need to bounce around with the young folks."

From the kitchen, Christie watched the circle of alternating players, boys and girls and older folks all together. They sang verse after verse of "'Liza Jane," swinging around in circles and stomping forward and back, lacing hands and parading down the length of the room. They sang their way through "Toddy-O," "Skip to My Lou," and

"Killie Kranky." The songs exhilarated Christie. She remembered her wedding day, when she and James danced across the grass right past the preacher. Christie noticed that Jimmie Lou had her eye on Bob Stokes, a blond-haired boy with a cowlick that seemed to run a course parallel to his crooked grin.

"You're going to get enough jars here for a canning, Alma," said Bob Stokes's mother, when her husband went out to check his buggy jug, the squat wide-mouthed whiskey jug that fit under the seat of his buggy.

James went out too, with Wad's sons and some of the neighbors. James rarely took a drink of whiskey, but Christie didn't mind right now if he did. He was happy and full of laughter. She was the focus of everyone's admiration. Everybody was talking about the babies and the newspaperman from St. Louis and the men from town. To go from the heaviness and fear of her pregnancy to the shining light of attention was like getting saved at church. Or it was like the rush of anticipation at a box supper when a young man who caught a girl's eye bid on her cake. James had done that, many years ago when they were sparking. She carried a sunset cake to a box supper, and she was frantic for James to bid on it. More than anything, she wanted to pass the night with him, eating that cake together. Her sisters laughed at her because the cake was her own invention—layers of white, yellow, orange, and pink in descending order, like sunset flames. The cake was held together with pineapple filling and boiled white icing. James did bid the highest, paying a dollar. He told her he had mistaken her cake for angelfood, because he thought an angel must have made it. His serious tone made her laugh so hard that cake crumbs flew out of her mouth into his glass of cider. That feeling she had at that box supper was being in love. She felt the same now.

Thomas Hunt approached Christie with a coconut and a shriveled orange and some headache powders he had left over from samples he had distributed through Mississippi.

"Thank ye kindly, Thomas," said Christie. "I'm surely glad to get this coconut."

"Let me open it up for you, so you can have a delicious drink of milk."

"No, not now. I want to save it till I'm able to make a cake."

"It's hard to get oranges now, but a feller traded them to me for some shoelaces. These was from Christmas."

James came in to get a handful of corn Thomas and Alma's son Thurman had popped in the fireplace. Thurman's sisters had bragged on his popping skills, but he couldn't pop the corn fast enough to suit the crowd. James brought a handful of popped corn for Christie. He said, "Thomas, I thought you were going to bring us some samples of them ladies' drawers you're trading in now."

"Oh, I reserve my samples for only the most promising ladies," said Thomas, casting a mischievous eye at his wife.

"The very idea," said Alma with a frown. "Scattering out women's drawers all over the country."

"Do you let 'em try 'em on, Thomas?" asked Wad, who had just come in from the porch.

Christie thought she heard a threatening note in Wad's tone. There was a lull in the singing, as the young people crowded around Thurman and his corn popper. Alma picked up a popped kernel that shot out on the floor.

When Thomas went upstairs to find his jar of whiskey, Wad said, "There goes a feller that acts above his raising—the way he goes out a-bragging his way around the whole country, like he's something on a stick." Wad laughed. "Thurman told me he saw some of them samples out in his pap's buggy. He said Thomas was using one of 'em for a feed-bag for his horses." Wad slapped his knee as he laughed.

"I ain't saying a word to that," Alma said, glaring at her brother. "I've made up my bed, and I'll lay in it."

"I'm jest humoring you, Alma," Wad teased. He turned to face the basket of babies. "How're you gonna tell them younguns apart, Christie?" He laughed, his high-pitched wheeze. "They'll have you fooled the rest of your born days. You'll tell one to go hoe some taters, and when you catch him out playing ball and ask him why ain't he hoeing them taters, he'll lay it onto another one. He'll say, 'I didn't hear nothing about hoeing no taters! You got me mixed up with somebody else!'"

Wad had a childish habit of jumping up and down—or drumming his feet if he was seated—when he joked and teased. Christie laughed.

"Play me your fiddle, Wad," she urged him.

"Well, being's the whole family's here, from baby up, I'll do it—for you, Christie. As long as we ain't got any Baptists here."

"The young folks is getting tired of singing their way through a bounce-around," Ethel Pritchard said with a perky smile. "They need a little music to go with it."

When Wad started fiddling, it was as though he were saying with his bow on the strings what he could not begin to say in words. He played the fiddle like sawing wood, with irregular, screechy sounds. But he had fire. The whole crowd joined in the singing, which smoothed over his defects.

Old Dan Tucker was a fine old man,
Washed his face in a frying pan;
Combed his hair with a wagon wheel,
Died with the toothache in his heel.
Run away, all run away, Tucker,
You're too late to get your supper.

The girls in the circle all ran to the center, and the boys tightened the circle around them. They giggled and gasped as they changed positions and Wad began playing another verse. Watching him, Christie realized what a well-respected man he was, and also how much he could get away with. Amanda hated for him to drink whiskey, and tonight she wouldn't join the singing games at all, preferring to help out with the children and babies. She was heating milk for the baby bottles.

"Come on and play, Mama," Lena said as she dashed out of the circle into the kitchen for a moment.

Amanda shook her head no. Lena grabbed some popcorn and rejoined the circle.

"This ain't like you, Mandy," Christie said. "You always like to swing."

"Wad's been at that whiskey all evening," Amanda said disgustedly. "He's mad 'cause Thomas give me one of those sample corsets he brought back."

"What did Alma say?"

"She don't know about it." Amanda tested the milk on the back of her hand and removed the stewer from the stove eye. She said, "It's a Talk-of-the-Town corset. And it's a featherbone style."

Mrs. Stokes got up from the card table and came over to the babies. "You're looking poorly, Christie," she said, pinching Christie's jaw. "Having five of them babies pulling at you is taking your strength."

"But I feel good," Christie said. "I'm just weak from laying. And I'm fat! I need one of them featherbone corsets to hold me together." She started laughing, but Mrs. Stokes wasn't amused.

"I was glad to hear you wasn't letting your babies suck from that Smith girl," Mrs. Stokes said. "I don't believe a girl such as that ought to be a-fooling with your babies, Christie."

Alma had always defended Mrs. Stokes's habit of finding fault, saying she was just being honest, but Christie suspected Alma might be having second thoughts about Mrs. Stokes, now that her son Bob was sweet on Jimmie Lou. Christie remembered what James had told her so often, how she had to get along with everybody. Now that she was the center of attention, she felt it was easier to forgive Mrs. Stokes. But at the same time she almost felt she could get away with making a disrespectful remark to her now. Her mind was whirling around like a child's hoop.

Christie's attention shifted to Thomas, who was joking and laughing with Alma. Amanda had her back to them. Amanda spilled some of the milk she was pouring into a bottle. When the next play began, Thomas dragged Alma out onto the parlor floor. She clomped along in her Sunday boots. She had pulled off her apron and bonnet, and with a ribbon in her hair she looked ten years younger.

> *Possum up the 'simmon tree,*
> *Raccoon on the ground;*
> *Raccoon says to the possum,*
> *Shake 'em 'simmons down.*

Christie was surprised. Alma and Thomas had never seemed like husband and wife, and here they were playing one of the swinging games. The babies seemed to have transformed everything. The singing accentuated Christie's feeling of limitless possibility. Wad's fiddle screeched along, making up with good intention what it lacked in skill. But the real music, Christie thought, was the children shrieking as they ran through the halls and up the stairs. Clint and Jewell and Nannie romped up the stairs and across Boone's loft, leaning down daringly over the railing to wave at her. Then they ran back down the stairs and arrived at her knees, red-faced and breathless.

The dancing circle was singing.

> *I wouldn't marry an old maid,*
> *I'll tell you the reason why.*
> *Her neck's too long and stringy,*
> *I'm afraid she'll never die.*

When James came near, Christie reached her hand up to touch him. He bent down, and she whispered in his ear, "Remember what I said in the wagon on the way out of Dundee?"

"No, what?"

"That it was the happiest day of my life. But that's not true anymore. Today's the day."

"I remember that," said James, squeezing her hand.

She watched her husband walk through the room, his bearing so confident, his stride more manly than it had ever been. They were no longer young folks, Christie thought.

"That husband of yours don't know what hit him," said Ethel Pritchard, unaware she had stepped in the milk Amanda had spilled.

"How will you ever feed all these younguns?" Mrs. Stokes said. "And where will you put 'em all?"

Christie didn't reply. She noticed Amanda, sitting in a chair feeding John Wilburn from a bottle, singing to him softly and holding him almost desperately close.

"Mandy," Christie said.

Amanda looked up, her eyes scared. She looked down at the baby.

"He hungry," she cooed. Her hair was falling in loose ringlets around her face. She wore a brooch on a ribbon at her throat, with the silhouette of a woman, like a hidden person about to leap out of her.

Boone, in a cheerful mood, descended from his loft then to sit in a corner near Christie. He always wore the same old threadbare britches. Some of the visiting children gathered around to see his picture-card album. Christie had seen it so many times she knew it by heart.

"This is my Museum of Humankind," he told the children as he opened the small album. He had picture-card portraits of Napoleon, Abraham Lincoln, and Jenny Lind, as well as pictures of Pygmies and Bushmen and witch doctors. He had one picture of several women with lips like platters and ears with jam pots hanging from them.

"I'm making an album too," Dulcie said. "Pa brought me some trading cards." She pulled them out of her pocket and showed them around. Thomas had brought his daughter several colorful advertising cards for Scott's Carbolated Salve, Dr. Humphreys' Witch Hazel Oil, Vegetine Blood Purifier, Dr. Ayer's Cathartic Pills, Turkish Pile Ointment, and Dr. Koenig's Hamburg Breast Tea. The cards featured pictures of cherubic children and delicate women.

The babies were fretting from all the warmth, and Dulcie helped Christie remove their bonnets. Little Bunch kept hovering around them, pulling at their bonnet strings. Finally, Dulcie complained to her uncle, and Wad took Little Bunch upstairs and locked her in a bedroom. During a lull in the music, they could hear her kicking and screaming. Amanda, who had been quietly helping with the babies, ran upstairs and stayed with her.

"Little Bunch always causes trouble," said Dulcie, exasperated. "When I carry her to school, I can't do a thing with her. We have to tie her to a desk."

"She just wants to love on the babies," said Lena, defending her sister. Lena herself seemed afraid of the babies, and she tiptoed around them.

Christie could see that Dulcie was shy and didn't know how to act at a play-party, while her older sister's eyes were shining. Jimmie Lou blushed and giggled every time she got near the Stokes boy.

"Why don't you go join the circle?" Christie said to Dulcie gently. "You'll have fun."

"Go with me to see Mammy Dove," Dulcie begged. "Let's show her the babies."

Mammy Dove had been feeble this winter and had taken to her bed.

"All right, if you'll get James to help us carry them." Christie reached for Dulcie's hand. "And if you'll dance a little when we come back. For me."

Dulcie nodded. The child had on an oversized apron, and her hair was hanging down in plaits.

Dove was sitting up in bed in her tiny room behind the parlor. Dulcie carried a small lantern and set it on a washstand near her grandmother's bed. Christie stood at the foot, clutching the spool post.

"Look who's here, Mammy," said Dulcie.

The old woman squinted in the lantern light, and Christie sat down in the rocking chair beside her. Dove's wedding photograph was hanging on the wall beside the bed. In it, Dove looked young and pretty, with fine features and thick hair. Her husband, Lige Wheeler, James's grandfather, was just a boy in the picture. He was still fairly young, a father of five, when he died in the war—of measles. Whenever she saw the picture, Christie was amused to imagine wrinkled, old Dove meeting her young soldier-boy husband up in Heaven. Brother Jones once said that after Judgment Day, God made adjustments for a situation like that.

"How come you're out, child? Where's them babies I hear tell of?" Dove spoke with a rasping in her throat, like a bug buzzing.

"They're here," said Christie, smiling. "James is bringing them."

"You don't need to be out of bed, child," scolded the old woman.

James brought the babies in, setting the basket up on the bed, out of the draft. Dulcie set the lantern so Dove could see them. Dove's face lit up. She had heard all about the babies, and she even knew their names.

Dulcie said, "They're telling about the babies everywhere, Mammy. Nothing like this ever happened before, and a wagon full of presents is coming from town."

"Well, I declare," said Dove, grasping at the edge of her quilt.

The lantern light played on the ridges and brown spots on the old woman's hands as she ran them across the blankets in the basket. Her hands were so old and spotted, her skin was rough and scaly, and her fingernails splintered and cracked. But the texture of the babies' tiny faces was as delicate as the tip of James's privacies.

12

THE YARD WAS FULL OF HORSES AND WAGONS AND BUGGIES. PEOPLE tromped on the March flowers and the clump of red tulips Christie had divided from her mother's bulb bed. Since the St. Louis newspaper's second report on the quintuplets, the news had been drifting out over the nation like smoke from a chimney. Mrs. Blankenship returned, bringing her two small children, an aunt, and a niece. She said the babies looked as healthy as pups, and when she tried to hold James Lake he spit on her lace cuff, which made Christie laugh. She felt better about Mrs. Blankenship's second visit. Now Mrs. Blankenship was just one of many. Seeing so many strange faces, some from faraway cities, made Christie swell with a rumbling exhilaration, as though she were pregnant again. More newspapermen came—from Paducah and Louisville and Memphis. An outfit of doctors from a hospital in Memphis came to observe the babies. When they drew up in their hired rig from the depot, Dr. Foote was just leaving, but the emergency he had been on his way to suddenly vanished. He escorted the doctors in, prancing around them, taking credit for the babies' survival. Christie couldn't resist telling the doctors that Dr. Foote had diagnosed fibroid tumors, but that she knew fibroids couldn't wiggle. The doctors wrote in their books with fountain pens.

She was up now, moving around and tending to the babies. She felt better and Amanda said she looked better, but James came in from the fields so tired he didn't notice how she looked. He couldn't keep the babies straight, either. He seemed to be in awe of them. Christie had plaited some colored embroidery threads together and made identifying bracelets. The bracelets—not much bigger than a wedding ring—were red, yellow, white, orange, blue. James couldn't remember what color went with which name, but he was able to distinguish the babies by size.

"It won't make no difference which one's which till they're old enough to get in trouble," he joked.

Wad persuaded Lena, who was good at lettering, to print DONA-TIONS GRATEFULLY ACCEPTED on a piece of tablet paper. He came in one morning and placed the sign and one of Alma's blue fruit jars on the pine hope chest at the foot of Christie's bed.

"That was the preacher's idie," Wad explained. "A man familiar with the rewards of the collection plate."

"This ain't church," Christie said. She was in the rocker, nursing the two boys. She had learned how to shield her breasts with a folded diaper.

Wad laughed all the way out the back door.

"You packed in manure again," she yelled after him.

Christie showed Lena's sign and the fruit jar to James when he came in from milking that day. "Wad just busts in here and takes over," she said. "I've never known a Wheeler to knock on a door."

"I reckon he figures he owns the place," James said with a sigh.

"And they never say 'howdy-do,'" Christie went on. "They just jump right in with some notion. Are you going to let him take up a collection?"

James picked up the sign and traced the letters with a dirty finger. He said, "You know I never begged for anything in my life. But I can't go against Uncle Wad in this."

"But it's our house, and our babies."

"I know, but Wad give us our start here, and we owe him some-thing."

He meant more than just the thousand dollars they owed him, but Christie knew the thousand dollars came first. She wished James were in a position to stand up to his uncle more, but she knew he had little choice. He was behind on his work, they were low on flour and sugar, and they needed cash for seed. The price of tobacco had been falling, and the prospect of ever paying off their debt to Wad seemed remote unless they did try to collect donations. James was right, she thought, gazing at the row of babies. The babies were more active, their arms and legs twisting, their little faces wrinkling and looking upward as if straining to figure out what went on above them as they were lifted and petted and cuddled and changed and wrapped by a succession of huge hands. Everyone assured Christie that the babies would thrive on all the special attention. Amanda believed that kittens handled at an early age made better pets.

On Tuesday, the *Hopewell Chronicle* had a new article about the quintuplets—with emphasis on the St. Louis newspaper and the mayor's visit to the babies. Dr. Foote was mentioned prominently. With that, even more people from town began arriving. By the next day, the Wheelers had collected twenty-three dollars and eighty-six cents in the blue jar. Mr. Letcher brought twenty-six pieces of mail that morning and stayed for an hour out of curiosity while it was opened.

In the middle of the afternoon, when James and Wad started plowing a field beyond the creek, something happened that Christie later decided was the turning point of her life. It was the tenth day of the babies' lives. The 3:03 train from Memphis, the Friendship, was whistling in the distance, as usual. Earlier, Alma had gathered in her wash because it was sprinkling rain, but then the sky cleared up and now she had gone home to hang the damp clothes out again. Amanda had just reported that one of the March flowers was opening and she had set a row of bricks around the flower bed to protect it. She had come into the kitchen to help Lena make dried-apple stack-cake. Christie, sitting on the bed against her bolster, was breast-feeding Minnie and Mollie in the presence of several women from town, who were all eager to feed the other babies from the funny milk bottles. The women's husbands were standing around under the trees in the yard, probably talking horses and crops. Christie was thinking how odd it was that people had taken time in the middle of the afternoon, in planting season, to dress up and go visiting as if it were Sunday. Through the window, she could see a man she vaguely recognized as a clerk who worked behind a counter at the drugstore. She wondered if he had brought the goods the drugstore and other merchants had promised. The wagonload of presents had grown in her mind, and Wad had mentioned it often. She was musing about the presents and the strange casualness of people visiting on a workday, Minnie and Mollie were tugging at her nipples, the women were prattling about bird's-eye twill and rocking the three other babies, when Christie glanced through the window again and cried out. Hurrying across the field was an enormous throng of people. Women, holding on to their hats and skirts and stepping high through the muddy pasture. Children, running. Men, striding behind and alongside, like dogs herding a flock.

"Lord, the train's stopped!" cried Mrs. Wilson, a fat woman with pretty teeth.

Mrs. Wilson set Emily Sue down in the baby bed, and Mrs. Creech set James Lake next to Emily Sue, and Miss Mattie Bailey set down John Wilburn. The three women rushed out front to see.

Christie tried to reach for something to cover the babies in their bed. They had been set down so abruptly—and out of order—that they were squalling. She could see the crowd advancing. Minnie and Mollie still smacked at her breasts. They wouldn't let go, and she hesitated to tear them loose because they had been nursing somewhat poorly that morning.

"Mrs. Willy!" she cried.

But Mrs. Willy had stepped out to the back porch. Even Amanda had rushed outside to look. Christie was on the bed, clumsily shaking open a folded diaper to hide herself, as the crowd burst in, like picnickers who had found shelter in a rain. The three crying babies were soon snatched up and kissed and patted. Amanda darted back inside to watch the babies, who stopped crying as three young women in sailor-style suits rocked them in their arms, exclaiming over their tiny features and spouting a stream of baby talk. Other visitors marveled over Minnie and Mollie, who were still sucking vigorously, their faces hidden.

"Be careful with them babies," Amanda warned the women in the sailing suits. "Lena, you watch the back door. They can't all bust in here. There ain't room."

They were coming around through the north rooms, circling around to the kitchen, entering the front room from both directions. Men crowded their way forward to Christie's bedside, their mouths hanging open at the sight. She cringed. Amanda unfolded the diaper Christie was struggling with and placed it across Christie's chest, adjusting it so that the babies could get air.

"There, Christie," she whispered.

Christie felt paralyzed. The crowd filled her house. There must be fifty people in her front room. They were dressed in such a variety of fine clothes that Christie felt ashamed of her small, plain house. Could it be seen as a "humble three-room abode"? The wallpaper, though new, looked suddenly shabby, the handmade furniture too modest, the place too small. It was suffused with smells of cooking and babies and close human habitation. She shrank from the newcomers. She felt naked, like a picked chicken. And she was speechless. But the people supplied the talk. The rush of excitement propelled their words. They couldn't contain their glee at finding the eighth wonder they had heard about. Christie smelled the stack-cake burning.

"I can say I held one of them," said a young woman in a sateen cloak. "My mother will be so envious."

"She won't believe you," said her companion, a tall, mannish woman.

"You'll vouch for me, Lucy," said the girl. "Promise."

"They're so little," a pop-eyed man said. "My lands!"

"Little possum babies!" a woman cooed.

Christie knew they took her for an ignorant country woman, and her cheeks flamed at the thought of her powerlessness against them. More of them were coming across the field, like an army advancing. Amanda threw up her hands and cried, "Christie, what in the world are we going to do?"

"Mandy, watch the babies—don't let them get away from us!"

Then Mrs. Willy charged in from the back porch as if she had come to the rescue, but she stopped short. She couldn't drive out a trainload of people.

"I expect we'll have more rain by night," she said cheerfully. "Have y'all had any rain down your way?" She seemed to assume they all lived in Memphis because the train came from there. But Christie figured most of them were on their way home in the North after their excursion to the Memphis exposition.

She was afraid to close her eyes. Her hands cupped the little bottoms of the two babies she held, her middle fingers splinting their backs for support. She felt Minnie let go. Minnie gurgled. One-handed, Christie held her—a bundle of feathers—against her shoulder and patted her back with the same hand that supported her. Then Mrs. Willy took Minnie and rocked her in her arms. The other three babies were crying again, as people were handing them around and reaching to touch them. Amanda was watching them as carefully as a stalking cat. Someone handed Emily to Christie. Emily was crying loudly. Christie had difficulty getting the baby hidden at her breast in front of the men and children, who were all eyes. Amanda draped the diaper across Christie's shoulders.

"Have to change you, punkins," said Mrs. Willy to Minnie, as she cradled her in her arms. "She's the least one," Mrs. Willy said to the room at large.

"There's always a runt," said a young man in a straw hat.

Mrs. Willy said, "I'm sorry we can't ask you men to set a spell, but these babies have to have their dinner."

Everybody laughed, and Mrs. Willy pointed to Mollie, feeding from Christie's left breast. Mrs. Willy said, "Mollie here won't eat from the other side, she always has to have the left."

"That's a sign she'll be left-handed," a woman said.

Emily started tugging at Christie. Mollie was still going strong. The people were talking to each other in such a clamor that Christie hardly distinguished their words. She could feel Emily's familiar pull, sharper than the boys', stronger than Minnie's or Mollie's. She was aware of the yellow cherries or plums on a woman's hat and the way they moved as she spoke, a young woman's handkerchief clutched and balled in her hand as if she had shortly before been weeping, her young male companion who reached for the hand with the handkerchief as if the couple had some private business the train stop had interrupted. Christie saw a smile of flirtation between them and detected a note of embarrassment, perhaps at the realization that they could be producing babies together if they were married. Some of the other people in the room spoke with a Northern brogue. Through the window Christie saw James crossing the field, just as Jimmie Lou burst in through the back with an apronful of wrinkled lime-spotted potatoes she had been peeling.

"I didn't take time to set these down," she said, letting them roll onto the kitchen table. With her paring knife in her hand, she turned to face the visitors, some of whom were by now drifting out, only to be replaced by others. The crowd from the train was enormous, two or three cars full.

"Jimmie Lou, go help Lena at the front door," Amanda yelled. "Don't let any more in. And take your knife."

"Oh, we'll go now," a woman said apologetically.

"We'll make room for the others."

"The conductor said he'd stop till we all got to go through."

"Is it true the President named the babies?" a man in a silk-plush hat asked Christie. He squeezed between her and the baby bed.

"No, I named 'em myself," murmured Christie, craning to keep her eyes on all the babies. The three who weren't nursing were growing fretful. Amanda and Mrs. Willy were trying to keep people from snatching them up.

The man in the silk-plush hat lit his pipe and puffed thoughtfully. "If this ain't the dad-blamedest," he said. "Wait till I tell Mama and Daddy. They won't believe I saw this."

More and more people swarmed in. By now Alma had returned from her wash-house and was standing guard over the babies. Lena and Jimmie Lou watched the doors. "Take turns now," Alma demanded in a loud voice of authority. "The babies had their dinner and they need to have their nap, so don't try to hold them now. They're fussing."

Christie took care to keep her breasts covered as Mrs. Willy lifted Mollie from her. Mrs. Willy carried Mollie aside to change her, but nobody in the room would leave until they saw all five babies together at one time. The chatter was much the same from person to person. Christie wanted to be friendly, but she thought she was caught up in a bad dream. Her head felt light, and she wondered if she really had had five babies. She clawed at her hair, combing it with her fingers and smoothing it. She had to keep alert. She felt she would sink into this bed and be trampled over like her March flowers.

James charged through the crowd as though he were driving his mules forward. "Christie!" he gasped.

"The babies are all right, James," said Amanda quickly. "You've got company!"

"What in God's name," James said, his voice drowning in the babble.

"Everybody watch out," Alma thundered. "This here's the daddy."

James looked frightened enough to shoot off a gun.

"Here, James," Christie said to him. "We're all here."

A loud sigh followed by a hush washed over the crowd, as attention shifted from the babies to James. James reached the foot of the bed, and he seemed to swim forward to get to the babies. Christie noticed how the women from the train devoured James with starved eyes.

13

THAT NIGHT AFTER SUPPER, WAD CAME DOWN TO TALK BUSINESS. IT
had rained since the train stopped. He left his boots on the back porch
and entered in his sock feet. He had to duck under a wet sheet hanging on a line across the kitchen. He was still wearing his work clothes,
caked with mud that flaked off onto the floor. Mrs. Willy had swept
the floor after the train crowd left, and Alma washed it.

"How much did you take in from all that?" asked Wad, picking up
the jar and eyeing it.

"I already counted it," said James. "It was two dollars and ten cents
all day."

"They come in so fast, they didn't even notice the jar," said
Christie. "They went straight to the babies."

Wad said, "Well, we oughter be getting something more out of
this." He sat down next to the baby bed, in the squeaky rocker
Christie had heard so much during the last week. It was beginning to
be like the clock, making a sound that was always there. She meant to
ask James to oil it.

"Tell what you've got in mind, Uncle Wad," said James.

From the way Wad grinned at James, Christie suspected they must
have planned whatever it was they were springing on her now.

Wad said, "We've got so many folks tromping in here through
that-there bean field, what we need to do is charge, not just ask for
donations."

"There's liable to be even more people," James told Christie.

"Boone talked to the conductor, and he said he was going to stop
the train again tomorrow," said Wad, taking out his plug of tobacco.

He laughed. "Boone sure gets on his feet in a hurry when he's a mind to."

Wad pried open his pocketknife with his thumbnail and carved off a corner of the plug. Christie said nothing.

"I was studying on ten cents," Wad said. "If we charged a nickel, then they'd all come for sure. But this way we'll make just as much, even if some stay out."

"We ain't getting much in that jar," said James. "That's for sure."

"I saw somebody give a quarter," said Christie.

"We can leave the jar in here, in case the spirit moves anybody to give extra," Wad said. "I'll get one of the girls to stand out on the porch and help me collect the dimes."

James said, "Uncle Wad's right, Chrissie, we might as well make 'em pay."

She sighed uneasily. "I know we need the money," she said. "But they scared me, busting in here like that. I believe those train people would have busted the door down."

Wad bent over and pulled at his socks. He said, as kindly as he knew how, "If we collect the money at the door, it'll slow 'em down and they won't all bust in at oncet. That's what I was thinking."

"That sounds better," Christie acknowledged.

James laughed. "We can set Alma out front with a pitchfork."

"But that many people swooping in here around the babies—it ain't good for 'em." Christie stopped, not wanting to voice her worst fear, that her babies could be stolen right in front of her eyes.

Wad slapped his leg. "Christie-Belle, you've got to show people what we got here. We've got a wonder of the world! It said so in the paper! And Brother Jones says this is like the borning of Jesus, it's a thing of wonder. It's like the Wise Men coming with presents. You have to let 'em come! How does Brother Jones put it? You have to share this gift with all humanity." Wad stumbled over words unfamiliar to his lips as he tried to imitate the preacher. "I say it's a good opportunity. And whatever it is, we have to get what we can out of it."

"Besides, we ain't seen them presents from town yet," James said.

Christie straightened up against the bolster, shifting the baby she had been holding—Minnie. She had been holding her close, even after she had finished sucking. Facing Wad, Christie said, "Neither one of you's giving me any say-so about this."

"What?" said Wad. "What can we do about it? These people's going to come anyhow. You can't keep 'em out. And you can't tell people they can't come in your house. That ain't neighborly."

"I know. But they could have hurt the babies."

"We'll work that out," Wad said. "We'll slow 'em down."

James said, "Well, it's going to be hard feeding five more. We have to do something."

He stood over the babies and picked at them as if to check that they were still alive and hadn't turned into something else. Rats or pups. Christie was weary and confused. She had been so caught up in the excitement of the last few days. She loved seeing Amanda's eyes shine. She was proud of her babies. She had enjoyed thinking that reports of them were spreading to faraway places. But now she was afraid.

Wad rocked fast in the chair, making it squeak like a train braking. He said, "It's like anything. Take a crop. Corn or hogs, say. You save the nubbins and you save the stalks and the leaves and the seed. You feed the corn to the hogs. You put the manure back in the soil. You use ever smidgin of the hog—the tail, the ears, the lard, the snout, ever'thing but the squeal. And if you got five babies instead of one, you make them work for you. That's the principle of thrift and it's in the Bible and you can't set them aside on a silver platter and make out like they was better than the other chillern and don't have to work or con-tribute to the family. And if people will pay to see 'em, then I say it's like putting 'em to work. Why, even a mule can work."

Christie felt peculiar, as she always did when she overheard men talking business. This time she was the business. "I don't know, Wad," she said. "These babies ain't mules."

"Christie, don't fret now," Wad said, softening. "Ever'body wants to see these littluns. You oughter be right proud to show 'em off."

"I am," said Christie.

"Why, ever'body's proud," said Wad.

"Nothing ever happened and now everything at once." She thought about what Brother Jones had said. Were her babies really a miracle? Not knowing what to say, Christie let the subject drop.

Later that night James said to Christie, "I don't see nothing wrong with what Wad said, Chrissie."

"I know what he means," she said. "But we have to be careful with the babies."

"We will. Wad and me will be here," he said, drawing his arm around her. "And I'll get Henry and Joseph too."

"I don't want people to see me feed them. If we could move into the other room, it would be better."

"No, you need to be in here close to the fire, and they want to see you with the babies. When the train comes, you can feed them with the bottles. Mandy and Mrs. Willy can have the bottles ready."

During the night, James Lake and John Wilburn were colicky and wouldn't suck. Minnie slept peacefully. Emily cried for a while until Christie lulled her to sleep. Christie fell in and out of sleep, reaching for the babies, confusing their cries with rain crows calling out for rain. Later on in the night, it did rain again, a downpour with a fast, hard wind that muffled the babies' cries for a while. As the storm dwindled into a slow drizzle, Christie dreamed about Reelfoot. In the dream, she was at Reelfoot Lake just as the gigantic tremor opened up the earth and the angry, muddy water flooded in to form the lake. Then she was on the lake, in a flimsy canoe, waiting for the destruction of the world to appear before her like a theatrical production all across the heavens.

14

EARLY THE NEXT MORNING, AMANDA WAS FOLDING CLEAN DIAPER cloths at the foot of Christie's bed, where she could keep out of Mittens' way. She said, "I swan, Christie, I can't get over all them people parading in here from the train. I've seen so many new people I can't even remember them. Imagine! But I've never seen Wad act like this. His mind is way out yonder, and he just takes off like a skyrocket. He don't stop to think about who he might run over. I talk to him and he don't hear a word I say. I'm still mad at him anyway."

Amanda jabbered on, her smooth white hands undulating like fish.

"Lena's making a present for the babies—I won't tell you what it is, but you'll see that child has a talent with a needle—and Little Bunch don't talk about anything but the babies; you can't get her onto any other subject. I've a good mind to send her to school again and see if the teacher can knock some sense in her. Last year they wouldn't take her on account of her fits, but I know she's smarter than all the rest of them, with a mind of her own. That teacher at Sunnyside said they couldn't make her look at the books or learn the numbers or the words. Wad says she's just stubborn; he don't really care if she goes to school or not. Alma's younguns are just running wild through all this. Nobody's going to school today. I told Clint and Jewell they didn't have to if the big ones didn't. I believe Jimmie Lou wanted to go so she could be the center of attention, but she didn't want to miss the goings-on here either. You know how Jimmie Lou wants to be in the middle of things, but Dulcie's real quiet and won't take more credit than she deserves. That girl's dependable. I was more like Jimmie Lou, and I can just imagine how she feels. She wants attention and she'll do what she has to to get it. It comes from Alma not giving her enough loving. Stop me before my mouth runs away with me. I'm just beating my gums. I got carried away by that train stopping." Amanda paused as she folded the last diaper cloth. "Well, the babies are doing good! Nobody's crying and nobody's wet or hungry."

"You spoke too soon," said Christie, as Emily Sue started crying. "James Lake and John Wilburn were a little colicky last night, after all the commotion." She picked up Emily Sue and patted her, but she continued to cry. Christie sat on the edge of the bed with her.

"Hand her to me," said Mittens. "And take this one here."

The babies always seemed glad to drink from Mittens' breasts. She bounced them so softly Christie thought it must feel to the babies like floating.

Amanda took John Wilburn from Mittens and burbled her baby talk at him. "You're just a little froggy-boo, just a little froggy-boo!"

"They've been crying too much," said Christie, peering into Emily Sue's face. The little eyes seemed to whirl with confusion.

"They looking for they teeth," said Mittens. "That's why babies cry, 'cause they ain't got teeth."

"That's plumb crazy, Mittens," Christie said affectionately.

"I never heard that," said Amanda, setting down John Wilburn carefully and turning to touch Emily Sue. "Here, take this one. Her hungry!" She took Emily Sue from Christie and gave her to Mittens.

As Mittens rocked Emily Sue, she hummed that familiar melody of hers. The baby quieted then and began to suck.

Christie walked around a crock of cream Alma had set on the hearth to clabber. On a cane-bottomed chair, a bowl of dough was rising. She reached for the key on top of the clock and began to wind the clock. James had forgotten to wind it last night.

"What's that song, Mittens?" Christie asked. She replaced the key.

"Oh, it's jest something in my head."

"Did you learn it from your mama?"

"My mama didn't have time for no songs. She busy being a slave."

"Didn't she tell you any stories?" asked Amanda. "I always told little stories to my younguns."

"Colored people ain't got no time for stories neither."

"But I hear you telling these babies stories," said Christie.

"Oh, that jest foolishness I make up."

"Alma says it's hoodoo," Amanda said, laughing. "I wish somebody would hoodoo my man."

"That train what's hoodoo," Mittens muttered. "It breathe like it's got the TB, and it wheeze and fire come out like a 'baccer barn a-blowing up, and all them people it belch out right into your house and you don't know who they is. They liable to steal ever child on the place, and they come in here all in the way so I expect you can't hear yo'self think."

"You should have *seen* all the people out here, Mittens," Amanda said. She set the pile of fresh diapers inside a drawer of the chifforobe. "The field out there was purely dark with people rushing in from the train. It's true!"

"It was like being in the middle of the stockyard," Christie said. "With all the cows and calves and pigs and horses. And the men."

"The men." Amanda nodded. "And that newspaperman from St. Louis. And those men with the mayor. The mayor of Hopewell was right here in this house, and I didn't get to see him."

"He talked big," said Christie. "When the train stopped—I was so scared at first! But then the people were so excited by the babies."

"You can't get away from that train," Mittens said. "That train *after* you."

Later that morning, when Mittens had gone and the babies were all sleeping, Amanda worked on Christie's tangled hair. Christie intended to wash it when she was able. Standing for very long made her feel faint. The babies had taken more of her strength than she would have expected.

"Go look at yourself in the glass," Amanda said, when she finished pinning up Christie's hair. She had twisted it in the back and fluffed up the top.

Christie stood, and as she turned she was startled to see a woman standing by the baby bed, a woman in coiled hair, with spectacles shining like gold. Christie saw her own reflection in the woman's specs— two small witches beaming out of the woman's eyes. Christie's head swam and she caught the edge of the table. The woman said, "I brung you this telegram."

The word "telegram" was like the word "snake." Christie snatched the paper. It could only be bad news. It had to be about one of the folks back in Dundee. In the instant of grabbing the paper, Christie imagined tragedy—Mama dead, Papa distraught, her sisters wailing, Christie traveling by train back to the funeral. She saw her father's clothes, wrinkled and spattered with blood. The Wilburns had received a telegram once—when Uncle John Rhodes died down in Smith County, Tennessee. Christie was about fifteen, and a man on a horse had brought the telegram in the night, so late even the dogs didn't hear the man come up the road.

But this telegram was from Louisville, and it made little sense. REQUEST PERMISSION TO NAME PRECIOUS BABES, it said. LETTERS

POURING IN WITH NAMES FOR BABIES. SUGGEST RUNOFF FOR WINNING
NAMES. FREE SUBSCRIPTION FOLLOWS.

"I catched a ride with the doctor," the woman in the specs said.
"He's tying up his horse out yonder. I tell you, that man drives like
something wild. I've a good mind to walk back."

"This says they want to name the babies," Christie said, fluttering
the telegram in Amanda's direction. "What do they mean by that?"

The woman said, "Where's your man at?"

"Out there by the stable," Christie said, waving the telegram at the
kitchen window. She could see James hitching up one of the mules,
the sorrel they called Slow, to the plow.

The woman peered out at James. "That's who done that-there?"
she said, turning her head in the direction of the babies. "That's who
made them babies?"

"He's my husband."

"Law me," the woman said, staring again at James. "He must be a
mighty powerful man."

Christie could see James glance at the house, then turn to adjusting
the mule's collar. She could see that he was whistling a tune, for the
mules liked to be entertained.

The woman said, "Could I trouble you for a drink?"

"On the back porch," said Amanda, opening the kitchen door.
"The dipper's on the east wall. Let me see that telegram, Christie."

"You didn't tell her to strain the wiggletails out of the water,"
Christie said after the woman went out the door.

"They won't hurt her." Amanda giggled.

Dr. Foote came in then, in high spirits over the clear, dry weather.
"Everybody in Hopewell's feeling a little frisky, I believe," he said as he
dropped his overcoat on a chair. He rubbed his hands together before
the fire.

"I believe the babies like all the company we've been having,"
Amanda said to Dr. Foote. "They quieten right down when somebody
holds them. I know they're getting spoiled."

"They're still not used to sweet-milk," Christie said. "Two of them
had a touch of colic last night."

Amanda started warming a cup of coffee for the doctor, the only
person they knew who would drink coffee so long after breakfast.

The woman who had brought the telegram drifted in from the
back. She had a narrow forehead and large, gray eyes made larger by
her gold-rimmed specs. She wore a fringed shawl over a gingham dress
with a high collar.

"Who are you?" said Christie.

"Nobody you know. It don't matter." The woman bent over to jerk up a loose stocking. "I'll wait in the buggy," she said to the doctor.

She left and Amanda looked out the window at her, puzzled. "Dr. Foote, why didn't she give the telegram to you to carry out here?"

"She wanted to see the babies, so I let her ride."

"But she didn't really look at them," Christie said.

"She don't know us from Adam's off-ox," Amanda said.

"Nor me," said Dr. Foote. "Well, Mrs. Wheeler," he said as he turned his attention to the babies. "I hear the train stopped here yesterday evening."

"Yes, sir. We just about had the World Fair out here."

"Mittens told me this morning, and I thought she was going to fly right up to the sky, she was so full of the news. And oh, my, I've been getting letters from all over and even telegrams—one from Detroit, Michigan, and one from Pittsburgh, Pennsylvania." He chuckled and wagged his head. "They all want to know how we achieved this miracle. I tell 'em Hopewell is a good, clean-living town, and we know how to take care of our people. Why, we're not a bit surprised that one of our fair citizens produced quintuplets. What's your telegram say?"

"It's from the *Courier-Journal* in Louisville."

"That's a big newspaper," said Dr. Foote, impressed.

"They want to name the babies." Christie set the telegram in a basket with the other letters she had received. "They've already got names," she said, sitting on the edge of the bed. "I'll have to let this paper know."

Dr. Foote busied himself with the babies, looking into their eyes and mouths, pulling at their skin. All of them woke up and cried. One by one, he removed their dresses, untied their undershirts, then turned them over and thumped them in various places. He listened to their hearts.

"How's the runt been doing today?" the doctor asked as he began examining Minnie. He had saved her for last. She whimpered at his cold instrument on her chest.

"I can just hear Clint and Jewell calling her Runt," said Amanda.

"I'll get after them for that before they even commence," said Christie. She wanted to object to the doctor for using the word, but she held herself back for fear James would find out. Dr. Foote wasn't charging, so she shouldn't fuss at him.

After probing Minnie, he handed her to Amanda to be dressed. The babies had cried throughout the examination. Dr. Foote removed his stethoscope and placed it in his bag. Then he said to Christie, "If they get to crying too much, I want you to get some of that soothing-syrup the drugstore sells. It's got an opium base, and that will ease them. They'll use up their strength with too much crying."

"They weren't crying when you came in," Christie said, exasperated.

"Sometimes they're wet," said Amanda. "But these little things don't hardly put out a drop. Mrs. Willy's been airing out some of the diapers instead of washing them."

"I'd increase that cow's milk now," Dr. Foote said.

Amanda dressed Minnie and wrapped her in her outing blanket. Christie rearranged the babies, with Minnie in the middle. She had been trying to keep them in an order that put the largest ones, the two boys, on the outside and the smallest one in the center. The two boys enclosed the three little girls like parentheses.

"They stop crying when somebody holds them," Amanda said. She lifted James Lake, who was puckered up again.

"A little sugar water would help their appetite," said Dr. Foote. "Make a sugar tit."

"We did that," Christie said.

Standing by the fire, Dr. Foote drank his coffee, with no mention of the woman waiting out in the cold. Christie read the telegram again. She would have to reply, but then she realized she couldn't send a telegram—it cost by the word. And she had so many letters to answer.

As soon as Dr. Foote departed, three of the babies started crying again. Amanda warmed up some sweet-milk in the bottles, and after about an hour the babies quieted down. Christie intended to send to the drugstore for some of that soothing-syrup.

"I wish people wouldn't call Minnie the runt," Christie said to Amanda.

Amanda touched Christie's shoulder. "We won't let Dr. Foote get away with that next time," she said.

The ground was still muddy in places, and James laid some planks across a low spot in the lane that held water. He hid some of the pictures and valuables in the unfinished rooms upstairs and stored some of his tools and horse rigging in the loft of the stable. He got Joseph to keep an eye out on the grounds and Henry to guard the back door. With Amanda, Alma, Mrs. Willy, and Jimmie Lou right there with her, Christie felt more prepared for the train today. Dulcie was watching Nannie and Little Bunch.

At three o'clock, Wad appeared on the porch with a cigar box. Lena had lettered a sign for him: THE AMAZING 5 BABIES. ADMISSION 10 CENTS. She had drawn some fancy wreaths and flowers around the letters. Christie had finished nursing all the babies about an hour before, and Amanda had fixed three bottles of milk and set them in a pan of warm water. She made two sugar tits in case the babies cried. Boone came down, bringing some of his newspaper cuttings and one of his albums of picture-cards. The boys all clustered outside, planning to show off the knife-throwing skills they had learned from Mittens' husband.

Wad stuck his head in the door and called, "Mandy, you get on back up to the house and tend to Mammy. She's by herself up there."

Amanda rushed across the room and fussed at him.

"That ain't fair!" she cried. "You can't make me miss the train people after all the time I've spent with the babies."

"I'll go," said Dulcie, exasperated. "Nobody cares about Mammy except me anyway." She stomped off, dragging Little Bunch, with Nannie tripping along behind.

"Ever'body settle down," Alma said.

At three minutes past three, the Friendship whistled and slowly crunched to a halt. The smokestack continued to pour out smoke and huff loudly as the passengers descended into the field. Apprehensively, Christie watched the throng approach, the women lifting their skirts out of the muddy furrows and clutching the arms of obliging men. She saw the excited faces as the crowd climbed the steps and the quizzical looks when they encountered Wad on the porch. She saw him laughing, his hand raised in a jubilant greeting.

The spring air rushed through the door. The people streamed past her, a bit more quickly than yesterday. Alma pushed them along. Christie sat up against the bolster, fully dressed, on top of the bed comfort, with the babies lined up close to her for their protection. She watched the people pass through her house in a bewildering tide of laughing, crying, snorts, and high-pitched spurts, whistles, squeals, barks, mews, and shouts—a babble of baby talk. She saw the pleasure Amanda and Mrs. Willy took in showing off the babies, who did not cry. Alma stood beside the bed holding a sassafras stick in a commanding pose like a general in the War. Christie giggled at the sight. At this moment, she loved Alma. She felt safe with her there.

One man with a florid face told Christie his wife had died in childbirth, and a woman in a large straw hat unaccountably wept when she saw the babies. Christie—sensing the woman's sorrow, whatever it was—was touched that her babies had caused people from so far away to reach into their hearts and bring forth their troubles. Several visitors had impenetrable brogues and thick, dark hair. She had rarely seen foreigners. A storm of contradictory feelings rolled through her. As she watched the parade before her, it seemed almost as though she had been granted an opportunity to travel widely, to see strange faces from distant lands. She wasn't the show—she was watching the show.

15

Wad burst in with his cigar box of cash. He was dancing a jig and going "hee-haw, hee-hee-hee-haw." He sounded just like the old jack that used to bray by the barnyard fence. Christie laughed.

"Wad, you beat all," she said. "Here you are just when I was about to give this baby a suck." He suddenly seemed silly. Maybe that was how Amanda saw him much of the time.

"Now you didn't mind a baby sucking titty in front of a trainload of people, did you, girl?" he teased.

"Christie didn't do that, and you know it," snapped Amanda. "We fed them off of a bottle."

Ignoring his wife, Wad dumped his cigar box of coins onto the bed. "Look how much we taken in," he said triumphantly. He began to count the money.

Christie fit the baby to her breast, hiding her breast behind a square of outing.

"Which one's that?" Wad asked.

"John Wilburn, the one that favors James."

"Oh, is that so? Why, that baby don't favor nobody." He studied the back of the baby's head and his ears. "You must mean the way he's going at his titty. James always was a good eater."

Christie held the baby close to her, feeling how his little form had filled out, his middle heavy with all the milk he was getting. But he was still a tiny baby. His dress was long enough to knot at the tail.

Wad sat on the edge of the bed and beat his sock feet on the floor, in glee. He counted the coins rapidly, dashing them into the box as he counted. He was like a squirrel with his nut pile. Throughout, John Wilburn sucked steadily.

"Twenty-six dollars and ten cents," Wad announced. "We're gonna be rich!"

"Did they all pay?" asked Amanda. "Didn't anybody stay back?"

"One or two had to dig deep, and some of 'em borried off of one another, but there was only a couple of boys that didn't come in. I could have charged a quarter, I believe."

Wad swooped up Mollie, who was starting to fret, and held her awkwardly.

"Little-o, little-o," he said. "No bigger'n a hoppy-toad. And about as ugly."

"You can't say that where the mama can hear," said Christie, amused.

"All babies is ugly. But their mamas can't see that. They're ugly so nobody else will steal them, and their mama don't see how ugly they are so she's fooled into keeping them."

"Wad Wheeler!" Amanda said, pointing the poker at him. "Get out of here."

He set the baby down, as carefully as setting an egg on a table.

"You ain't got no heart," Christie said. She spoke teasingly, but it was what she really thought. The babies had elevated her onto a stage of importance, and all the unaccustomed attention from Alma and Wad made Christie feel resentful and reckless. Her indebtedness to them seemed to increase daily.

The rest of the day was busy. All the family was in and out, comparing impressions of the train passengers. Mollie and James Lake cried for over an hour, until Henry brought the soothing-syrup from town. Christie gave each of the babies a few drops, and it made them sleep. Christie's other children were in a state of high excitement; Dulcie declared they were unmanageable. Nannie's hair looked stringy, and she had soot on her face. Clint had been stung by a bee. Before joining James in the field, Wad instructed Arch to sit on the porch and collect admission from any other visitors who might come by that afternoon. Neighbors weren't to be charged, he said, only people they didn't know. Arch tried to make Mrs. Willy pay a dime every time she went in the front door, but she threatened to fasten him in the pigpen if he didn't quit pestering her. She had a toothache and had packed up her jaw in a clean diaper.

When Mittens arrived, Arch poked his head inside to ask, "Do niggers get in free if they use the back door?"

"Scat, youngun," said Mrs. Willy, shooing him out with the broom.

Mittens aroused the babies and got them to suck. The soothing-syrup had increased their appetites, and they nursed contentedly while Mittens sang to them—rather loudly this time, a song about going to glory. The babies sank back into sleep.

At bedtime, James turned out the coal-oil lamp and groaned with a pleasurable tiredness. He sat on the edge of the bed, facing the babies, and removed his britches. The room was still bright from the flames in the fireplace.

"That soothing-syrup stopped 'em from hollering, didn't it?" he said.

"I reckon they're all right now," Christie said, covering the babies. She had told Alma not to send Jimmie Lou to stay tonight, since the babies weren't fretting.

James stood up and walked around to his side of the bed.

"I never saw Uncle Wad so excited," he said as he lay down. "I reckon we're going to get a crop out now," he said with satisfaction.

Christie joined him in the bed. She was quivery from the day's events. She shut her eyes tight, trying to imagine how many people would have to shove their way past her bed for Wad to collect enough dimes to settle their debt. Thousands.

"If we didn't owe him and Blankenship's Mill, we'd be rich," she said sleepily.

"It's easier for a camel to pass through the eye of a needle than it is for a rich man to get to heaven," James said.

She heard him yawn. She tried to imagine a camel squeezing through the eye of a needle. The hump kept getting stuck.

During the night, Christie and James were awakened by the dogs barking, the throaty roar they used on unknown people in the dark, not the frenzied yap they saved for other animals. James pulled on his britches and lit the lantern. Carrying the lantern, he went toward the front door. Christie heard him grab his shotgun from the cabinet under the stairs. Then she heard him talking with a man on the porch. A few moments later, he brought the man in—a skinny scarecrow who twirled his hat nervously in his hand.

"I just had to see," he said. "I got on my horse at Carbondale, Illinois, and rode all the way down here. I didn't mean to wake y'all up. I was going to wait till daylight, but it was so cold and dark."

"We're up now," James said, setting down the lantern and the shotgun.

The man shifted his hat from one hand to the other and nodded apologetically to Christie. "I hope you'll forgive me for this, ma'am. I just had to come and see. I can't explain it. I thought I couldn't miss this. I lost my own little girl when she was four. And my wife and I want to have another child, but so far we haven't been blessed. It's been ten years."

Christie hovered over the babies, who were in various stages of wakefulness. Her loose dress was hanging on her. The man gazed at the babies, then reached out to touch John Wilburn, who was starting to squirm. James lifted the baby and the visitor's eyes gazed on him, greedy with hope.

"It's a true miracle," the man said. "Forgive me, I just had to come. And I didn't mean to wake y'all up, but then I heard your dogs and then your light come on." The man laughed nervously. "I figured anybody with a new baby is up in the night anyway."

"That's for sure," said James, handing John Wilburn to him.

The man held the baby up in his face, stared at him for a moment, then handed him back to James. James set John Wilburn down with the others. The visitor touched each of the babies, one by one, and each responded with a slight sound—notes on a piano.

"I have a good estate up in Illinois and raise plenty of corn and cows and good horses. All that—and nobody to leave it to."

"You're still a young man," said James.

"A man thinks of his heirs."

"Don't you have other family—brothers and sisters and their chillern?" Christie asked.

"Oh, Lordy. Enough kinfolks to fill up a church. But it just ain't the same as having your true own chillern. I just kept asking myself how in the world you done such a thing."

"Don't know," James said.

James stoked the fire and added a chunk of wood. Christie fussed with the babies, talking softly to them and petting them. She wanted to start nursing, but the stranger stood by the fire, his eyes on the babies. The babies had slept through the time for their middle-of-the-night feeding. They didn't seem to be hungry. Minnie's eyes fluttered open, then relaxed into sleep. Christie shuddered beneath the shadow from this stranger. He probably didn't mean harm, but she was afraid his presence was unlucky. Amanda would see it as a dark omen.

The stranger soon left—refusing any warm nourishment and promising to send them a ham.

"Why didn't he bring a ham with him?" James asked. "Would have saved him the trouble of sending it."

"He wasn't thinking about ham," said Christie, adjusting the cover.

"I don't imagine he'll think about it when he gets home, neither." James pushed the rolled rag rug up against the bottom of the door and placed his shotgun under the bed. He said, "Wad would have had that dime."

"Not after he rode all that way," said Christie. "I wouldn't take it."

She couldn't get back to sleep till almost first light. When she woke up again, she lay there waiting for the babies to stir. But she didn't hear a peep from them. The soothing-syrup made them sleep soundly, and Christie thought they were probably tired from all the company too.

After the others woke in the morning, Minnie slept on. Christie nursed Mollie Lee and John Wilburn, but they took very little. She began feeding Emily Sue and James Lake with somewhat more success. She was getting used to balancing two at a time against her stomach. When Christie set them back in the bed, Minnie opened her eyes and blinked. Christie held her against her nipple, but Minnie took only two or three tugs, then moved her head aside, struggling feebly.

"James, this ain't right," said Christie. "They must have had too much of that soothing-syrup."

"It's that sweet-milk," he said angrily as he stomped his boot to get his foot and heavy sock to fit inside it. He tied the boot fast and hard, as though he were roping a calf. Christie knew he'd have to loosen the lace and retie it. He had slept badly after the stranger's visit in the night.

James unloaded the shotgun and returned it to the cabinet, stobbing the butt down as if he were setting a fence post. He shut the cabinet door. "Is that littlun cold?" he asked as he paused by the baby bed.

"No, she's warm. But she don't have a fever. She just seems weak. I think they've had too much excitement. Maybe Mittens can get her to suck."

James let out a sigh of disgust. "What if it's nigger milk causing this?"

"That don't make sense."

"I had misgivings about both of those," said James. "It ain't natural. Neither one—cow's milk or nigger milk."

"We drink sweet-milk ourselves. The chillern drink it."

"We have stronger constitutions. But ever kind of baby creature has its own food from its mammy. Birds chew the worms up first so the littluns can eat. A baby don't start out on fried chicken and turnip greens. Even a calf don't go to grazing right off." James was spitting his words at her, making her feel to blame.

"We ain't talking about turnip greens," Christie said as calmly as she could. "Dr. Foote said try the bottles. And those doctors from Memphis."

"I don't know." James finished relacing his boots and went into the kitchen where Alma was already frying bacon. She had come herself today instead of sending one of the girls, as if she had anticipated trouble.

The sun peeped over the hickory grove and blazed through the kitchen window. It was going to be a cloudless, blue day. Christie didn't know what she was supposed to do. She remembered what Dr. Foote had said about sacrificing the littlest ones. The memory crossed her mind like the shadow of a hawk over a mouse. She shuddered. She couldn't imagine only four. Or three. Or two. There had to be five babies. She couldn't imagine losing a single one of them.

Mittens came in the back door just as James was going out. He had eaten his bacon and eggs quickly, as if he had to escape.

"Let me at them babies," Mittens said, heading across the kitchen. She saw that they were awake.

"They don't act hungry," said Christie. "That syrup made them sleepy. They're not ready to eat."

"I'll get 'em to eat," Mittens said confidently.

Alma set eggs and bacon on the kitchen table for Christie and poured her some coffee. She handed Mittens a glass of milk.

"We've got plenty of sweet-milk," Alma said. "Enough to feed half a dozen calves."

"You got so much milk, you got milk's mammy," said Mittens, laughing. She drained the glass in one draught and handed it back to Alma.

"I brought you a hambone to carry home with you, Mittens," said Alma. "There's still some meat on it. And you can have some bacon and eggs when you get done, if you ain't eat yet."

"Oh, you so kind," said Mittens, turning to the baby bed.

She picked up the two outer babies, the boys, and plunked herself down in the rocker. She hummed her haunting tune awhile, then started to sing.

> Going to roll in my Jesus' arms
> On the other side of Jordan.

The babies bounced against her as she hummed and rocked. When they tried to turn loose, she held them tight and pushed their heads against her breasts.

"Is this one James or John?" she asked Christie, ducking her head toward the one on the left.

"John Wilburn."

His face curled up in a little soundless cry.

"I'm getting so I know 'em," Mittens said, pushing his face against her again. "Another week and I'll know 'em good. Lordy, Lordy," she sang. "I's coming soon."

"Hush that, Mittens," said Alma, as she poured bacon fat into the meat-grease can on the stove. "Them babies don't want to hear sech songs."

"I's singing about the promised land, is all," said Mittens, singing louder.

"Them babies don't need to be hearing news from the promised land," said Alma, wiping up a dribble of grease. "You get that notion out of your woolly old head." She handed Christie a stick of cornbread.

"The promised land is the place for me," Mittens said. "That's where I's a-going."

"I reckon you thought you was headed there when that earthquake was a-coming," said Alma.

"That earthquake still coming," said Mittens. "God changed His mind and decided to wait on that earthquake awhile, is all. He gonna wait till the world get really mean and no-count, then He gonna punish us."

"Oh, great balls of fire!" scoffed Alma. "That's foolishness."

"If I's foolish, it's just the Wheeler in me, ma'am," said Mittens.

Alma straightened her shoulders and swished her long apron at a fly. "What in the name of Moses are you talking about?"

Mittens looked straight at Alma, then quickly swung her gaze away. "My granddaddy on my mama's side come here with the first Wheelers in this here country. Just him and yo' granddaddy."

"Oh, well, yes, I've heard he brought a slave with him," Alma said, reflecting.

"He weren't no slave." Mittens studied Alma again. "That were yo' granddaddy's bastard son. That's how come I be so light-complected." Mittens grinned. "So I's a Wheeler."

Alma scowled and took a step backwards. "That don't mean you're blood kin to me," she said. She swished her apron again, at the fly but also at the subject. "Foolishness," she said. She spluttered as she dropped some eggshells into the slop bucket. "Dad-blamed foolery." She jabbed a finger at Mittens. "Don't you go telling sech a story, if you know what's good for you." She stomped out to the back porch with a water pitcher.

"Hallelujah," Mittens sang. "He's coming again!"

Christie had picked at her breakfast. She slipped into the closed-off north room to use the pot. She was amused to imagine a branch of black Wheelers. It was probably true, she thought. No white Wheeler would acknowledge it, so the connection would have been lost to memory. But the black cousins probably knew the history very well. She listened to Mittens still singing away, singing such sad notes with a contradictory joyous vigor.

"These babies is feeding just fine," said Mittens when Christie returned. "Look at 'em go. They didn't want no white milk, or cow milk. They want colored milk! Now hand me that least one. I'll show her what taste good!"

Not long after Mittens left, Christie's mother arrived at last. James had known she was coming, but he kept the news from Christie for a surprise. Mama exclaimed over the babies so loudly that she woke them all up and set off a frenzy of bawling. She bent over them and let fly her special brand of baby talk, like a high-pitched bird squawk. They stopped bawling. They gazed at her as if mesmerized.

Christie's mother was short and plump, with graying hair plaited and twisted into a knot. It had been over two years since Christie had seen her, and she looked so much older that Christie kept staring at her, taking in the extra gray, the pockets under her eyes, the new wrinkles around her mouth. After a while, she realized that her mother was studying her in the same way.

"You've got so fat," her mother said. "Just look at them-there arms."

"I had to have all that weight to carry these littluns," said Christie proudly. "Just look what I done, Mama."

"Swear to goodness!" Mama cried, snatching up one of the babies—Emily Sue.

"They've been peaked, but they ain't sick. They went off their feed for a while last night, but this morning they were hungry again."

Mama said to Christie, "Child, I wish I could get these tits swelled up again. I wish I could help you more than anything! I've nursed enough in my time. It seems like I oughter just be able to pick one up and my big sacks would start running again." She held Emily Sue closely, rocking her and chirping to her. "Why, Christie, their dresses is so long their little legs can't move!"

Christie was stupefied that her mother was here, in the midst of the swirl her life had become. For a while Mama seemed like one of the strangers from the train, her curiosity and amazement the same as theirs. Christie thought about the cold, late-winter day four years ago when she moved away from Dundee, in the wagon with James and the children. Mama and Papa dressed up as though they were going to town and accompanied Christie and James, riding alongside the wagon in their buggy. At midday they all paused for a fried-chicken dinner Mama had fixed that morning. And then Christie's parents turned back home.

"I'm afraid you won't never be back," Mama had said, crying.

Even then, her mother suffered with bronchitis, and Papa was hacking spit up from his lungs like an old man. Christie realized they had dressed up so she would remember them at their best.

Now, Christie's memory of her mother gradually adjusted itself to the woman present before her.

"These babies are precious and I've never seen the like in all my born days," Mama said. She had changed into a housedress and tied on one of her large feed-sack aprons. "They're like little puppies. That reminds me. Our dog Girl just had pups again. She had these ugly little spotted pups, and she's so pretty herself, but she got with a no-count mutt down the road."

Mama exclaimed over the odd bottles with the black nipples. She ran her fingers over the raised lettering and the woman's head with the stars around it.

"Mrs. Johnson at church bottle-fed her baby when her milk dried up, and that baby never did do right. He was sickly all his life. Poor thing. She didn't think he was able to go out and play with the other little boys, so she dressed him up and petted him and spoiled him rotten. Your papa says the boy was just petted too much and couldn't get healthy. That boy wore a dress till he was seven year old."

Christie's mother was never herself when she was away from her own home. She fretted, had bowel disturbances, put on airs, talked nonsense, worried about the family left behind, had delusions about catastrophes that might be taking place while she was gone, and couldn't sleep well. In her desire to see her mother again, Christie had forgotten all of these traits. But as the morning wore on, Mama began getting on her nerves.

"I'm glad you're here, Mama," said Christie. "But I don't think you'll want to stay."

"Why not, child?"

"You'll have to sleep on a pallet in the corner, and the babies will keep you awake—unless you want to sleep in the north bedroom. But the drafts will aggravate your bronchitis in there. And the house is full of people. You ain't got no idea. It's like court day at the square. You won't believe how many people are coming out here."

"Well, I don't want to miss a thing," said Mama eagerly.

"Here come some people now," said Alma, at the front window.

"They just come in. They don't even knock," Christie said. "Alma and the girls have to watch the door."

"Well, it wouldn't do to turn people away," Mama said. "When I married and moved up to Kentucky, there was a saying, 'You know you're in Kentucky, because ever door is open to a stranger.'"

Neighbors and townspeople came through all morning. Dr. Foote said the soothing-syrup had lulled the babies too much and to let up on it. Mr. Letcher brought letters, including one from a Mrs. Crockett who had moved away from Dundee years ago and remembered Christie as a child. Another letter was from Abigail Doran, a girl who used to board with the Wilburns in Dundee until Aunt Sophie asked her to leave for going with a wild Willis boy. Abigail said in the letter that she had heard about the babies and just wanted to be in touch.

"I never thought we'd hear tell of her again," Mama said.

The babies took the milk from the bottles and were less fretful now. Since it was a sunny, springlike day, Alma let the fire go out. Several buggies arrived, and one got stuck in a muddy hole, but Wad's sons pulled it out.

Mama managed to be in the middle of all the day's traffic, telling everyone about her train trip and her bronchitis. By the time the Friendship was expected, she had put out a wash of diapers; she had changed and washed each of the babies, careful to lay them in the order Christie wanted; and she had cooked cornbread, cabbage, ham, and a pot of tobacco-patch beans for dinner, as well as her special cold slaw and a double sheet of gingerbread. (She had brought some ginger with her.) Nannie, Clint, and Jewell came down for dinner, and afterward Mama gave them a nickel's worth of candy she had brought. Nannie, not remembering her grandmother, took the candy bashfully.

"What do you think of them babies?" Mama asked the children.

"They're too little," Jewell said.

"You reckon you was ever that little?" Mama asked.

The children, busy with the candy, all shook their heads.

"When will the train get here?" Mama asked for the tenth time.

"There's Wad now," said Christie. "He's taking over from Arch."

"Wad Wheeler's got good business sense," said Mama. "What we didn't eat of that gingerbread, I'm cutting into squares to sell. I think people from the train would like a little refreshment. We had a baking sale for the church last week and I made two apple pies and two spice cakes. I just know I forgot the cloves in those cakes. They won't taste right."

"I'm sure they'll be better than anybody else's, even if you did leave out the cloves," said Christie. She could almost taste Mama's spice cake.

She realized suddenly that at the moment she was nearly alone in the house—alone with just Mama and the children. Silently, she counted them.

"I'm so proud," said Mama, reading Christie's face. She gave Christie a hug. The babies were all quiet, and Christie lowered her head onto her mother's shoulder. She held her tears in so the children wouldn't think she was sad.

16

"WHEN'S THAT WAGON COMING FROM TOWN WITH ALL THAT MESS OF free things?" Alma wanted to know when she brought down some chess pies, two loaves of light bread, and a batch of soda crackers. James loved Alma's soda crackers with clabber and sorghum.

"Maybe they decided against it when I made like we didn't need it," said Christie. She was in the rocker, feeding James Lake and Emily Sue. "Then again, they said it would take awhile to get everybody together on it."

"That tickles me so much I don't know what to do," Mama said in awe. "Reckon what they'll bring?"

"I imagine they're waiting to see if these babies are going to live before they're out all of that," said Alma.

Christie said sharply, "Don't talk like that, Alma. These babies are going to be all right."

Alma grabbed a broom and whipped at the hearth. The stale ashes circulated in a cloud. It was heating up outside, and Christie could see wasps butting against the windows. Those thick, black, short-legged spiders were out too, and she watched one carry a fly across three panes of glass. Christie wondered how long a journey it would seem to the spider, and what sense the spider would make of the glass, which probably reflected the bright blue sunshiny day. The spider might feel it was walking on water, or on the sky itself.

"The way these doors is a-fanning, them waspers will get in here after the babies," said Mama, who had been pacing in order to get a kink out of her leg.

"You just have to have something to worry about, Mama," said Christie.

"If a wasper stings you on the side of the head, you'll die," Mama said.

"I'll get Lena or Jimmie Lou to stand at the door with the broom when the train gets here," said Alma.

"My dress hem's raveled out," said Mama, scooping up her hem. "Look at that. I'm liable to catch my feet on it and fall."

"Well, set down," Christie said, in exasperation.

She was trying to get the babies fed before the Friendship stopped. She was afraid all the commotion was making the babies restless, and she hoped Mittens could do something with them when she came later. Mittens had been so good with them that morning. Maybe it was her singing that revived them. Babies needed touching, and they also needed sweet-talking, Christie believed.

Emily Sue had had enough, but James Lake kept tugging. Mama took the little girl and held her up to squeeze out her air, jabbering to her all the while in baby talk.

"My goodness, that baby had too much dinner, yes!"

"I can't afford to waste it," said Christie when a streak of white fluid flew out of the baby's mouth.

"She so hungry, eat too fast, didn't she?" Mama cooed to Emily Sue.

"Hand me Mollie," said Christie.

"Which one's that?"

"The light-haired one, the one with the yellow bracelet."

Christie stared at the front window. A man outside was lifting the window sash. Startled, she drew a little outing blanket in front of her. The man, in a black coat and felt hat, swung his leg up and stepped over the sill into the room—just as calmly as if he were climbing a stile over a fence. For a moment, Christie was so stunned, she almost thought she was seeing something quite ordinary.

"You're letting them waspers in, mister," said Alma.

"Shut the winder," Mama said.

"Sorry, ma'am. There was a milk can in front of the door, and I saw everybody in here and thought this would be the best way in. Is this the babies I heard tell about?"

"Get out of here," Alma said. "And shut that winder!" Impatiently, she marched over and shut it herself.

The man wore town britches and a gold watch chain, but he had on farmer boots. His hat was frayed. He had little eyes and a gray-striped mustache. Quickly he advanced toward the baby bed. Christie moved the blanket to shield the baby at her breast, as well as herself, from the stranger.

Alma loomed between him and Christie. "You'll have to see my brother if you aim to come in here. He's out yonder in the field a-planting seed taters."

"There's a wasper!" cried Mama, setting down Emily Sue and quickly drawing outing over the faces of all the babies. "You let that wasper in," she said to the man, who seemed frozen beside the baby bed.

"Take your hat off," Alma said to him. "Get that wasper."

The man looked bewildered as Alma snatched his hat from his head and started chasing the wasp with it. "The broom ain't handy," she explained to Mama as she whizzed past her.

"I heard tell about the babies, and my Uncle Plez at Maple Grove told me where to come," the man said. "He said everybody in town was out here and you couldn't believe your eyes."

"Sometimes I can't believe my own eyes," said Alma, stalking the wasp now, the man's broad hat brim folded for a good grip. The wasp sailed past her.

She steered the stranger by the arm away from the baby bed. "Let that wasper go this-a-way, if it will," she said. "Then I can shoo it out the back door to the porch."

The wasp was flitting around near the ceiling, buzzing and flying fast.

"They have a lot of get-up-and-go when they wake up in the first hot sun in the spring," said Alma.

"I feel like that myself sometimes on a good spring day," the man said, craning his neck.

"The wasp landed on the chifforobe," said Christie, pointing.

James Lake let go of her nipple and wiggled. He was crying to be taken up, and Christie tried to give him air by lifting the edge of the blanket.

"Mama, will you take this baby?" she said. "And reach me John Wilburn."

"I don't know which one's which," Mama said.

"The one that's crying!" said Christie.

The man volunteered to be of help, but Mama told him to turn his back. Christie said nothing, and Mama exchanged the babies at Christie's breast while the man averted his eyes. (Christie was sure he peeped, though.) Mama held James Lake to her shoulder against a diaper and burped the air out of him, cooing softly to him. Mama had put on her bonnet to shield her head from the wasp, and the bonnet strings dangled across the baby's face.

"Tennie, when you get done with that baby, go and get me the broom," Alma said to Mama. "I put it out on the back porch by the shovel."

"I'll get it for you ladies," the man volunteered.

"You stay right there, mister," Alma said. "I got one eye on you and one on the wasper."

"Couldn't I just hold one?" the man begged.

"Hold your horses," Alma grumbled.

"Daddy said everybody in town was out here," the man said.

Mama set the baby down and fetched the broom for Alma. Alma brought it back in a broad swing straight at the wasp on the chifforobe.

"Got it," she said, easing back the broom and bringing the wasp to the floor. After stomping the wounded wasp, she swept it outside.

Mama said, "If a wasper stings you to the side of the head, you'll die."

Christie felt John Wilburn and Mollie Lee tugging—both weak tugs, weaker than yesterday. John Wilburn let go, and then Mollie Lee let go and started to squirm and whimper. Christie held the babies tightly against her and rocked them gently, the way Mittens had done. The rocker creaked loudly. The man's hand stole out to pet Minnie, then James Lake in the baby bed. Both babies seemed to look at him with a long, penetrating gaze.

"You got you a handful, ain't you?" the man said, grinning at Christie.

Christie felt too tired to reply. The babies were exhausted too, sinking back into their sleep. She heard the train whistle in the distance. And then she could see Wad running up to the front porch with his cigar box.

Alma said to the man who had come through the window, "We forgot to mention, but the admission is ten cents? You can give it to my brother out yonder on the porch as you leave."

17

THE TRAIN WAS AN OLD ACQUAINTANCE, CHRISTIE THOUGHT. ITS whistle was so familiar, but with new meaning now.

"I feel like I'm back on the train," said Mama, swaying to the remembered rhythm. "All night—clack, clack, clack." She coughed into her fist.

Wad opened the door. "All aboard!" he said with a conspiratorial laugh. The man who had climbed through the window had gone, but not before Wad collected a dime from him.

"Stop fanning that door," Alma yelled at Wad. "There they come, a-running across the field! A plague of locusts."

"There's not as much mud as there's been a-being," said Mrs. Willy. She dropped a diaper into a bucket of lye water.

"I'm surprised folks will pay a dime," said Mama, who was pacing around, self-consciously holding up her dress hem.

"Mama, you set down on that chair between the stairs and the bed," Christie said impatiently. "You can watch the babies and hide your dress hem, both." She was sitting with the babies lined up beside her on the bed, as before. Amanda and Lena were at her side. Dulcie was at the other house, tending to the children.

"I don't imagine anybody would just pick one up and carry it off to the train," said Mama nervously, as she took her position. "Would they?"

"Not if we can help it," Christie said.

"I'm just letting in two dozen at a time," said Alma. She was at the front window, eyeing the advancing crowd.

Alma had sent Arch out to knock down the wasp nests and drive away the wasps with some kerosene, and she stationed Jimmie Lou inside by the window, armed with a broom.

"Wad's showing out," Alma said, watching through the window as her brother exuberantly greeted the first train passengers. "Dad-blame him."

She disappeared around the stairway and opened the front door.

"Where's James?" Christie asked, but nobody knew. She could see the other men outside—Joseph and Henry at opposite ends of the house and Wad on the porch.

She felt light-headed as the people rushed in. She was proud and nervous, as well as curious about the world coming to her. But these people behaved just the same as the ones yesterday. They said the same things she'd heard yesterday. They couldn't believe five babies came from one mother. Weren't they darling—all just alike, couldn't tell them apart, such tiny features. And the mother looked well. The poor daddy, all those mouths to feed, such a shame they had such a little house and had to put the bed in the front room. Many of the visitors talked as though Christie weren't there. She saw a pair of men sniggering in a vulgar way, and one made a finger gesture that embarrassed her. Then a man who said he used to be a preacher down in Tupelo, Mississippi, offered a short prayer for the babies, asking everyone in the room to bow their heads, but during the prayer Christie noticed a young man eating a sandwich and a woman studying the tatting on a dresser scarf. Another woman gave Christie a piece of pink ribbon she had planned to take to a newborn niece but said she could spare. The young man with the sandwich dropped the wadded-paper wrapping on the floor. The babies slept, barely stirring, and many women remarked on how sweetly they behaved and what pretty little hands and faces they had. One woman in a fruit-topped straw hat said they looked too tiny to be real. Another woman in a similar hat but different fruits said she had seen a pair of twins that were each smaller.

Jimmie Lou got the broom after a big fly that had blundered indoors. She chased it into the kitchen, where it settled in the window. Mama couldn't stay put in the chair by the babies. Leaving Mrs. Willy and Jimmie Lou to guard them, she ran to the kitchen, holding up her hem, and hauled her gingerbread from the stove box, where it was keeping warm. A man in spectacles immediately bought a piece, saying he had taken the train from Memphis especially to see the babies and he was going to get out at Paducah and take the train back home again.

"I'll have a three-hour wait in Paducah, but I reckon I'll take a gander at the steamboats," he said, gobbling the gingerbread.

"Must be something to be able to just pick up and go like that," said Mama. "I had to wait till I got over my bronchitis before I could come out here from Dundee to see my own daughter."

"What'll you take for a piece of that gingerbread, ma'am?" another man asked. He was wavy-haired and had a large wart on his face.

Alma steered the people in and shooed them out quickly. Christie, her right arm curved around the babies, tried to concentrate on the crowd, all the people flowing past her, shoving to get a look. For a moment she felt as though she were in her own coffin. It was her funeral and the people were filing past. But instead of weeping over her body, they were marveling over what her body had produced. It was almost the same, she thought. Weddings and holidays were like funerals too—the same people, the same places, the same food. Everything just depended on what mood people were in. That could be important to remember, she thought. It was as though thinking or imagining could make something so, just as it was with intimacy. Sometimes with James, she was repulsed by his body, while at other times she was so hungry for him to get closer. But for a long period now, all desire had evaporated from her, drawn like smoke up the flue.

James rushed in then, pushing people aside. He was out of breath, and he reached the babies just as a woman picked up Mollie Lee, making her cry.

"Ooh, you sweet little thing," the woman prattled. "Is baby hungry?"

James took the baby from her and set her down in the bed with the others. "She's trying to sleep," he said.

"Well, who do you think you are?" the woman said.

"I misjudged the time, and that mule wouldn't hurry," James said to Christie.

The woman, realizing that James was the father, beamed at him. Christie could see his eyes count the babies. He turned to face the crowd: an elegantly dressed woman and her pie-faced little daughter; a bulbous-nosed man with a straw hat; two men in boiled shirts and wool suits and watch chains; some girls in white; several prim women who constituted a church group. James stood on the rag rug beside Christie, as if he had just stepped onstage and forgotten what he was supposed to say. Christie knew he hated to be among strangers, that he felt awkward. He preferred to stay with his own kind. Now, in his own home, as he had been so many times during the past week or two, he was cowed. Christie felt his shame, and she tried to ease it by the signs on her face when he glanced back at her. She was glowing inside, as if her soul had escaped her body and traveled to some busy scene in a stranger's house, maybe in another country. Rays of afternoon sun blasting through the window made the crowd appear fuzzy and insubstantial.

"This is my husband," she said. Her voice seemed to have an echo. "And these are our babies."

The babies were awake now, fretting. Amanda took Minnie in her arms. Minnie began to cry.

"Only the ladies get to hold 'em," James said, when a fat-fingered man with a greasy face reached for Mollie Lee.

Some of the women picked up the babies and marveled at their fragile weight, their tiny fingers, their tiny cries. They were birds, puppies, kittens, feathers, butterballs, angels. Most of the people stood back in awe, but others seemed starved to hold the babies. James watched carefully, ready to snatch the babies back to safety.

The man who had tried to pick up Mollie Lee said to James, "You really put it to her, ain't you, my friend? You must have been mighty busy one night putting it to her."

"I could tell you where to put it," James said, louder than he probably intended. "I won't have you talk dirty in front of my wife."

The man shuffled away, mumbling. Christie pretended she hadn't heard. She noticed mud on a woman's boots. The woman was examining the chifforobe and paying no attention to the babies. "The furniture is right tacky," she said to her companion. A woman in a gray traveling suit picked up Mollie and held her upright by the shoulders.

Mama cried, "Don't hold her that way!" She took the baby from the startled woman and held her closely, one hand supporting Mollie's head. Mama said, "It's dangerous to hold a little baby like you was, without holding its head. Her little head could break right off."

Several people laughed at the woman, but her companion said soothingly, "Flossie, you'll learn when you have babies of your own." Christie couldn't help noticing Flossie's blush under her rough skin. The woman looked too old to have a baby.

After the train left, Mama had a coughing spell, which she blamed on the air coming in the door. Mrs. Willy gave her a piece of horehound. The babies were all crying now, and Christie was trying to find the soothing-syrup. Remembering Dr. Foote's advice, she intended to give them only a drop this time. The syrup wasn't on the shelf by the sink, where she thought she had left it. Jimmie Lou, who had chased out a wasp, returned, saying the yard was full of lunch sacks and cigar papers and newspapers. She said she would take the newspapers to Boone, who had been feeling too poorly to come down today. New spring air tended to set him back.

"I don't believe there's a one of your March flowers left, Christie," Jimmie Lou said. "I saw people picking them."

"I didn't even get to see them," said Christie, disappointed.

"Are they from them bulbs I give you?" Mama asked.

Christie nodded. Amanda was warming bottles of milk. The babies' squalls soared above the other sounds—the sound of hands shaping dough, the fireplace tools clinking, a rolling pin flattening dough, the clock striking four, the talking. The background sounds all ran together. Christie searched through the chifforobe for the soothing-syrup.

"I'll get Clint and Jewell out to clean up all that trash," said James. "Maybe they'll find something worth keeping."

He cornered Christie by the bed. She was standing, rocking John Wilburn in her arms and trying to get him to take a sucky rag.

"Are you all right?" he asked her as he reached to touch the baby.

She nodded. "I didn't know where you went to. The train got here and you were nowhere."

He shook his head apologetically. "That little red mule just didn't have no giddy-up in her. I had to scare her on back to the stable. Are the babies all right?"

"I believe so. Look, he's sucking on this sugar tit." The baby smacked his lips.

"He likes that sweetening," James said with a grin.

"James, how long is this going to keep up?"

He didn't answer. He squeezed her hand—awkwardly, for she had the baby in her arms.

Wad wouldn't return to the field until he and James had counted the coins Wad had collected. Alma made them count the money on the porch, as if it were too nasty to have in a clean house. She was busy with the broom. She produced the soothing-syrup from the hiding place inside the clock. Christie was trying to get some of the syrup down the babies when Wad stomped in, followed by James.

"Forty-one dollars and thirty cents!" Wad announced. "We had four hundred and thirteen people to come through, in less than one hour. Sure would like that kind of money by the hour all day. What would that be?" Vainly, he tried to figure it in his head.

"It would be a heap of dimes and nickels," said Alma.

"A crowd like that could just pack off the babies and couldn't nobody stop them," said Christie quietly.

James squeezed her hand. "We ain't going to let that happen," he said.

"You ready, James?" Wad asked.

"Yeah, let's go."

"Where?" Christie asked.

"We're aiming to start breaking that ground out there where they're coming off the train," James said. "This warm spell is drying it out fast, and it'll get beat down by all them people."

"If you plow it, they'll track mud in," said Alma.

"Make you some signs so they'll go down the lane," suggested Mama.

"People won't go out of their way," said Wad.

"If we don't get that field in corn, we'll be eating hay this time next year," James said.

"You can't feed them babies on hay," said Wad. He chuckled. "But I'm thinking we'll take in enough off of the train to be eating high on the hog."

The men left, talking about replanting some clover that got washed out in last week's rain. A blast of air filled the room for a moment when the back door and the front door were open at the same time.

The babies were all feeding now, from the bottles, their appetites improved by the syrup. John Wilburn sucked from the black nipples just as if they were Christie's breasts. Mama held Mollie, Alma had Emily, Mrs. Willy had Minnie, and Amanda had James Lake. The house grew quiet, the women murmuring, the babies making satisfied little hums. Christie was restless. She should be working outdoors. There was so much that needed to be done. She wanted to get out in the garden and plunge her hands in the dirt. It was so long since she had been outside—except for the ride the other night up to the main house. But it had been dark and cold then, and she had been all covered up. Now spring was in the air, and Christie longed to feel its mellow breath and to see the new shoots emerge from the earth.

"I'm so tired of laying," Christie said to her mother.

"You ain't got good color," said Mama. "Them babies is wearing you out. You need to eat some red meat."

"But it's too early in the year to butcher a calf," said Christie.

More people arrived that afternoon, including a young couple from Memphis who had been visiting the woman's parents in Hopewell. They rode out in a fine, well-outfitted buggy that the woman said belonged to her mother. Christie could see it through the window, beneath the great oak.

The woman, in a navy-blue suit with leg-of-mutton sleeves, said,

"I realized we couldn't go back to Memphis without bringing news of this wonder. We're taking the train tonight at eight o'clock."

"It was daylight all the way up here last week, but at night we won't get to see the scenery," her husband said. He had fair skin and gentle hands, as if he had never worked.

His wife had a clear complexion and soft, shiny hair. She picked up each baby in turn and held the little bundle lovingly. "They're so light," she said. "They don't look like they'd be much trouble at all."

The couple stayed, chatting pleasantly. Christie liked them and found herself telling them all about the babies. It was as though out of all the crowd of strangers and the familiar den of kinfolks, these young people—so clearly looking forward to starting their own family—were the ones who could become friends of hers. They were well-to-do, judging by their dress and the buggy, yet they seemed humble and gracious, and they apparently felt privileged to see the babies. Mama gave them some gingerbread she had saved out and wouldn't take their money.

"You have such a comfortable home," the young woman said. "This room is so personal." She pointed to the family pictures on the mantel and the red-plush album on the little marble table. "What you have here, with your family, money could never buy."

"My husband made that chifforobe," Christie said. She couldn't forget the woman who had earlier called the furniture tacky. The remark had made Christie feel sick at heart, as if her furniture were of no more value than a cluster of whitetop weeds in the pasture—those weeds she thought were so pretty but that had to be cleared out because cows wouldn't eat them.

The young woman, just a girl, walked over to the chifforobe, ran her hand across the smooth grain of the wood, touched the knobs. "That is the most beautiful thing," she said admiringly. "How nice to have a husband so clever."

The late-afternoon sun shot through Christie's front room, lighting on the baby bed and the chifforobe and the woman's skirts. The young couple seemed so bright and airy. Christie wished Amanda were here.

"I'm going to give you our address," the young woman said, taking some writing paper from her bag. "I'd love more than anything to have a likeness of these babies if one becomes available. I'll pay you for it! I want you to write me and tell me how the quints are doing. I'm so thrilled to have the pleasure of seeing these precious things."

"Will you write me back?" Christie said.

"I certainly will."

"We wish you the very best future for yourself and all your children, ma'am," the young man said politely as the couple left. His name was Benjamin Donelson and his wife's name was Sarah, Christie saw on the paper they gave her. They lived on Wayside Street in Memphis. They had invited her to go there and see them. Christie thought they were the nicest people she had ever met. To be so high in society and yet to be so nice was remarkable. They weren't like unpleasant Mrs. Blankenship, who took such a high tone. This young couple was polite and considerate. They seemed to have time to think about how to treat people.

When Mittens arrived, Christie's mother was flabbergasted at the way the babies took to the dark woman's breasts.

"They like hers better," said Christie, laughing.

"Is Mittens your real name?" Mama demanded.

"No, ma'am."

"Her name's Clary," said Christie.

The days were getting longer, which pleased Mittens. She said she didn't like to be out after dark because of tree snakes. All of the children were outside working now, and Amanda did not get down with Nannie and Clint and Jewell until nearly dark, just as Mittens was getting ready to go. Amanda had been working in the big garden with the children. Clint and Jewell set out onion slips and cabbage slips, but Amanda had to go behind them and pull more dirt up around the tender plants.

It was getting cooler, and as Amanda built up the fire Christie told her about the nice young couple from Memphis. "I wish you could have seen them, how they talked and what they wore. They had a real fine buggy and a daresome-looking horse. They gave me a card with their names printed on it, and they want me to write them and send them a likeness of the babies."

"I was working in the garden." Amanda sighed. "I always miss out." She laid the poker down and swept up the scraps from the kindling. She said, "Wad's been after me. He got mad 'cause I tried to make him quit collecting admission and move you and the babies up there where we can keep them safer." She studied her hands. Her fingernails had fresh dirt rims under them. "But I know that with more mouths to feed, you won't be able to pay Wad what you owe him, unless you let him collect the dimes."

Christie couldn't answer. Somehow, collecting the money had grown into an unavoidable necessity. One way or another, they had to pay Wad their debt.

"He says people are going to come in anyway," Amanda said.

After a while, Amanda rounded up the children to take them back to her house. "Come on, you burr-heads," she said. "I want you to sing loud on the way back, to scare away the boogers."

"You younguns be good," said Christie, hugging Nannie close and breathing in her garden smell. Clint and Jewell, too wound up from the unsettling changes in their routine to hold still for hugs, burst away from her. The babies seemed less frightening to them now, she thought.

James came in late, tired and hungry. But after he had gotten out of his milking clothes and washed up, he took a look at the babies and beamed with pride. "Christie, you sure have floored the country," he said, shaking his head.

"I didn't do it all by myself," she said, blushing for fear her mother could hear them. Mama was fixing supper.

"Oh, good, sody crackers and clabber," said James, sitting down at the kitchen table.

James ate substantially, hauling in the food as though starved. Christie was hungry. She drank buttermilk and ate Mama's cornbread warm with butter. She didn't care much for Alma's soda crackers, and she let James have all of them. She felt like a cow with its cumbersome sack. She hadn't been out to see the cows in months. She hadn't seen the new calves.

Mama said, "If I don't get this dress hem fixed I'm going to step on it and fly right into the fireplace."

James held his plate out to Mama. "More pie, if you please, Tennie. I don't think I could have lived another day without pie."

Mama cut another wedge of chess pie for James. "It don't have enough vanilla in it," she said.

One of the babies cried—it sounded like Emily—and the front door opened at the same moment.

"I'm going to have to make a button to fasten that door from the inside," said James angrily.

A man was in the front room. He was wearing a brown wool coat and pants and a watch chain. An angular woman in calico stood shyly behind him.

"You look just like Peggy Ramsey back in Dundee," said Mama to the woman. "I swan, everywhere I go I see somebody that looks like somebody back home."

"We're charging a dime," said James, who was standing between the couple and the babies.

"Well, we don't have a dime," the man said, turning to the woman.

"I reckon we better go, Lemuel," she said.

But the couple stepped forward and got their look at the babies, and Christie could hear them talking as they turned back to the door.

The woman said, "They looked just alike! Five of 'em."

"Wait'll we tell Mammy we saw 'em," the man said.

"It's plumb dark out," James said, returning to his pie. "This even brings people out of a night. There's been so many out here the dogs don't even notice."

"Wad would have had that dime," Mama said, scraping a dish to soak.

"People that work for a living don't have time to get out in the daytime," said Christie cheerfully. "Besides, it's planting time."

"Don't I know it," said James, finishing his pie and then draining his buttermilk glass. He scooted his chair back and abruptly headed for the outhouse.

Since the weather had warmed up, Mama slept that night in the north room, where she could sleep on a bed instead of a pallet.

"When Mama's away from Papa, she sorter loses her mind," Christie whispered to James in the dark. "I oughtn't to have expected her to come here. I never saw her nerves so bad. She's not herself."

"Joseph could carry her home," said James. "If she gets too home-sick and is scared to take the cars."

"Wad won't want to spare him from planting."

"Probably not. And it looks like all the menfolks are going to have to guard the doors when the train comes." He sighed heavily.

Two of the babies started to cry. It might have been her imagination, but Christie thought their cries were weaker tonight. But maybe this was good. Or maybe they were just more satisfied because of the soothing-syrup.

Her mother rushed in to help tend the babies. James went outside, and Christie and her mother worked with the baby bottles, so Christie could save her milk for later in the night. When they got the babies quieted down and fed, Christie suddenly bawled in her mother's arms.

"I'm here, honey," Mama said gently. "Don't forget, you're my baby."

"I don't know how this can keep up," Christie said, sobbing.

"Hush. I'll tell you what I'm going to do. Tomorrow I'm going to take that twenty cents from my gingerbread and I'm going to buy you a piece of red meat. I'm going to make you some fried steak with milk gravy."

Mama started humming, some familiar song Christie couldn't recall the words to. Her overloaded mind began supplying its own words.

A white fence post
And bob-wire fence
Around the old tobacco barn;
If this was love and not so dear,
If you were me, not you.

Later, in the night, it came to her that the song was, of course, "Amazing Grace."

18

THE FRIENDSHIP STOPPED DAILY, DISGORGING A FRESH LOT OF SIGHT-seers into the cornfield. The Wheeler men—behind in their planting—watched out for scalawags and rapscallions, and Wad collected the ten-cent admission. In the field between the house and the railroad tracks, the boys found buttons, a lady's handkerchief, nutshells, cello-phane, as well as plenty of newspapers, cigar bands, and lunch sacks. Jewell found a shiny penny, which Amanda told him meant good luck. A neighbor, Amp Perkins, had lost a horse and was able to learn from train passengers that it had been seen two miles south, trotting alongside the tracks; the horse was identifiable by a spot on his side shaped like a long-necked gourd. And Boone, who had stationed himself in a chair under a tree on warm days, reported news about the Memphis Exposi-tion he had heard from the passengers: there were displays of every kind of wonder pertaining to science and industry, including an electric churn that would make butter that tasted as good as hand-churned.

Three days passed, blending together in Christie's mind. She felt stronger, but jumpy. The babies were fitful, and they didn't want to nurse regularly. They seemed moody, sometimes preferring the bottle to the breast and sometimes rejecting the bottles. Minnie didn't like the bottle at all. People thronged around the babies all day. Christie glimpsed a man withdrawing a fistful of coins from the blue fruit jar on her hope chest. A man with a camera lined the squirming babies up on the bed beside Christie and spent over an hour trying to get them situ-ated to suit him. His lamps smelled like burnt sulfur.

Letters arrived from all over the nation, even from California. A woman wrote of her own triplets, who had kept her awake night and day with their constant demands to be fed. Only one lived, she said. A college president wrote, offering free education for the quintuplets. Merchants sent free literature for elixirs, syrups, and powders; one teething powder company promised to make a baby as fat as a pig, and the pamphlet showed a picture of a little pig with a human baby's face. Other merchants and drummers sent actual products: worm-syrup to cure worms; packaged and canned baby foods; baby clothing and diapers; rubber sheeting; lactated milk; special powder-milk foods that supplemented mother's milk; root beer; a silver spoon; a picture frame; some hemstitch frilling; a nursing corset that Christie couldn't fit into. The wagon from the drugstore still hadn't come, but the lost wishbook finally arrived. Mr. Letcher had accidentally left it at the Stokeses, a mile away, and they had thumbed it well, from the ragged and greasy look of it. Many childless women wrote, offering to take some of the children off of James and Christie's hands. Others simply offered the bitter story of their dead children. One couple's child had fallen into a vat of cleaning fluid at a laundry where they worked. Another couple lost two children to freak accidents (a bull and a mad-dog).

Mama insisted that Christie had to answer the letters, until Christie pointed out what it would cost in stamps. Then Mama said, "Well, you can answer the nicest ones."

"I don't know what to say to them."

"You oughter write that woman that had the triplets. And that poor woman that lost two of her chillern. That was such a sad story."

"I couldn't bear to write her."

"But she was nice enough to write you."

Christie sent piles of letters up to Boone, who cherished each story and postmark. He kept them with his scrapbooks and albums. He was making an album for the babies. He had collected cuttings from the newspapers and souvenirs from the train—a train schedule, a leaflet from the Memphis Exposition, calling cards and addresses and signatures.

It was midmorning, during an unaccustomed lull at the beginning of the third week. The weather had turned off cool, and Mama had just built up the fire. Christie left the sleeping babies under Mama's watchful eye and went to the back porch for a pitcher of water, shooing Clint ahead of her. After she poured water from the bucket into the pitcher, she cornered Clint against the hanging popcorn popper and gave him a hug.

"Are you my little man?" she said, tousling his hair.

He giggled and squirmed loose. "Look what I found in the field." He gave her a large brown button. "Make me a spin-the-button," he said.

"That's a fine button," she said, holding it up to the window light. "From a man's overcoat, I'd allow. I'll look for some thread."

She pulled Clint close and talked to him quietly for a moment about something that had been gnawing at the back of her mind all morning. "I want you to promise me something, Clint," she said. "Listen. If Uncle Boone tells you to do anything, you go ask Aunt Alma or Aunt Mandy first."

He took the button from her and turned it over in his palm. "Uncle Boone told me to go empty out his spit cup," he said. "Do I have to ask Aunt Alma about that?"

"No. Just be sure you don't get any on you. And bury it. Don't touch it. And if he wants you to do something and says it's a secret, you run right then and tell me or Papper. Or if you're afraid to tell, then don't do what he says. But there ain't no need to be afraid to tell. Hear me?"

Clint nodded and held out the button. She put the button in her pocket. She didn't know why she was suspicious of Boone. She hated to suspect the worst of somebody just for being peculiar.

"Remember what I said," she told Clint.

Amanda opened the porch door and entered with some clean wash.

"There you are, Clint," she said. "Go on outside and start picking up them rocks. I'll be on directly and we'll get started on the garden." She stepped inside and closed the door after him. She said, "Christie, Mammy Dove was asking about the babies. She was up making a angel-food cake. I didn't bring you any 'cause it wasn't fitten to eat. Poor thing, she couldn't beat those egg whites long enough. Her angel-food cakes used to be the fluffiest, lightest things. You thought you was eating clouds. I'm afraid she's took cold, up stirring around."

"The doctor said if one of the babies takes cold, they'll all take it," Christie said anxiously. She felt the button in her pocket and tried to remember where it came from. She remembered then what Clint had wanted and wondered if she was losing her mind.

Amanda removed her gloves. She had stitched them out of jeans cloth, and the fingers were caked with dirt. She said, "Alma told me the least one ain't looking so good."

"Minnie's getting weaker," said Christie. She had been struck in the middle of the night with the certainty that she was going to lose Minnie Sophia. By dawn, she had realized it would be a natural loss that she would be forced to accept. But now with the sun high, the idea that she could accept such a thing suddenly seemed a nightmare in itself. She couldn't lose a child. She wouldn't.

In the kitchen, Christie poured some tea into a glass and drank it. It had dregs in it and tasted warm. That morning Clint had brought in the last piece from the icicles the boys had gathered in January. It was still cold out, but the hard-cold winter, when she was so heavy she could barely walk, seemed long ago.

Strangers were marching through the front room now, and Jimmie Lou had her fingers across her lips, hushing them. Christie heard Mrs. Willy chirp something. Christie stood back, watching several women in black hats and a man in blue-jeans britches. The people's faces seemed like clock faces with stuck hands. Christie held on to Amanda's arm in the kitchen doorway as she watched the women holding her babies, rocking them gently.

Amanda said to Christie quietly, "I talked to Wad again about bringing you up to the house. But he says your old room needs too much work on it. The wall's got to be replastered, and there'll be a worse draft than there is here. And he says he can't have all these people traipsing up the stairs. I said there wouldn't be as many people, and he said there'd be enough. And then he told me something else. I don't know if it's true or not, but he said he heard there's another train coming—not a regular train on schedule, but an excursion train that would come just here, and they could stop all day and have picnics if they wanted to. So Wad said there wasn't no point in moving you." Amanda tucked up the hair that was escaping from her cap. "I could just die. I'm so outdone with Wad."

"I told James I wanted to go to Dundee, but he said people would find out," Christie whispered. "He said everybody in Dundee would show up, and it would be the same thing all over again."

"We've got to do something, Christie. We can't run away. There's nowhere to run to." Amanda sighed. "Oh, I wish I'd never got mixed up with this Wheeler outfit." She laughed at herself. "Of course I don't mean that. I wouldn't have Lena or Little Bunch then. And I wouldn't have found you."

"They're not bad," Christie said. "They ain't bad people."

"Oh, I know that. I know they ain't criminals."

It felt strange to be whispering in front of all the people, but Christie and Amanda hardly had a chance to talk anymore. Christie remembered Amanda at Reelfoot, whispering to her in the dark, asking if Christie had ever lain down with anyone but James. The crowd at Reelfoot was large and loud, like the people swarming through her house. Brother Cornett seemed like such a bright light in the darkness of the nightmare of impending devastation. His hair—dark as a blackbird.

After the visitors left, Amanda helped Christie work at calming the babies again. They fed them from the nursing bottles, and the babies sucked a little. Mama washed dishes with the water that had been warming the bottles on the stove. Mrs. Willy went home to feed her chickens. Lena and Arch were stationed in the front yard, to meet visitors and pick up trash. Christie could see them, their dark coats and caps silhouetted against the sky. The sky was gray as a child's slate. She could hear Clint and Jewell shouting playfully while they worked in the garden.

She rocked James Lake in her arms, humming to him. He and John Wilburn hadn't nursed well that morning, but she had been afraid to make anything out of that. Little Minnie's tug on the nipple was gradually weakening and the milk seemed too thick for her to swallow. It dribbled back out of her mouth. Maybe Dr. Foote had been right: the strongest babies should have received Christie's milk. She couldn't stand to lose one of them, yet she'd rather lose one than all—why hadn't she seen that before? At least there was plenty of sweet-milk. Jimmie Lou was churning butter right now from some of the extra milk. Christie listened to the slop–slop rhythm of the churn. She sang softly to the baby in her arms.

> Big at the bottom,
> Little at the top,
> Thing in the middle
> Goes ker-flippety-flop.

It was an old riddle her mother used to chant while she churned, when Christie was as little as Nannie.

Alma and Amanda wouldn't allow anyone from the train to pick up the babies that day. Christie sat against her bolster beside them, rigid and alert. Mrs. Willy and Mama stood at the foot of the bed, preventing the strangers from nudging forward. Mrs. Willy put a finger to her lips. "Shhh!" she said to the passengers. She said it again and again. "These babies is sleeping. Be quiet, now!"

"We've already taken in over two hundred dollars," James said that night after supper. "Wad aims to buy a team of horses and a new plow and some other equipment we need."

"I don't care what he buys," Christie said.

"I told him I'd discuss it with you."

"The money is your doing," she said sharply.

"Chrissie! If we keep raking in money at this rate, we'll have that debt paid off before you know it. That's all right, ain't it?"

Christie was washing lamp chimneys. The lamp burning on the table was so smoked up she could hardly see by its dim light. Mama had gone to bed, and James was oiling his boots.

He was quiet for a while. Then he said, "I don't know what you're thinking about."

"What can we do? How far do you think this is going to go?"

James shook his head. "I thought the new would wear off soon and people would leave us alone. But like Wad says, we have to get what we can out of it."

"Amanda's awful put out with Wad," Christie said. "I think he's hurt her feelings real bad."

James snorted. "Wad thinks he can rule her, but she's got him wrapped around her little finger."

Christie didn't believe that. She knew Amanda wished she could live her life over, make a different choice. It was so sad what could happen with a marriage, she thought.

"You need to get that planting done, James," Christie said. "You need to get your uncle back out in the fields and away from our front porch." She heard herself speaking spitefully, as if Wad had been responsible for the attention brought to the babies, even though she knew that was not true.

"Let me tell you something about my uncle," James said in a lecturing tone he rarely used with Christie. "He's honest, and he's got principles. But he has the kind of mind that sees to what needs doing and knows how to judge what needs doing the most. The way he sees it, this opportunity is at hand, and it outweighs the planting. He told me that never happened in his life, that nothing ever took first place over getting the crops out. Even with somebody's funeral, they'd get on with the work right quick. But he said everything's changed now. All of a sudden a whole lot of new work's opened up and there's different things to be done. There's all that horse mess in the yard, for one thing. Thurman's been cleaning it up ever day and carrying it down below the barn. And Joseph and Henry have a all-day job just making sure nothing gets stole or no shady characters is hiding around. It's like washing diapers—you have to do what you have to do."

Christie regretted her hard feelings. No matter how much she resisted Wad personally, he ran the farm and James looked to him for direction. She didn't want to be ungrateful. They hadn't expected to be able to pay him what they owed him until the children were grown.

"What are we going to do, James?" she asked. "About all of this?"

"I don't know. Let's hold out awhile. If it wasn't for Wad taking admission and Alma standing guard at the door, you know everybody would just run through here like a stampede of buffaloes."

"I never give Alma credit before, but now I can't contradict a word she says."

In bed, in the dark, she could feel herself harden again—against Wad, against James, even against the babies, believing at irrational moments that it would be a relief not to have them anymore. Yet she knew she didn't feel that. She couldn't bear not to have her babies. It occurred to her that the monster she had thought was inside her after the camp meeting did in fact exist—in the spectacle the babies had generated. She didn't know if the little ones had truly grabbed her heart yet, if all five together were as dear to her as Clint or Jewell or Nannie. She condemned herself for her heartlessness. She wondered what evil was in her heart to make her feel so empty sometimes now when she looked at the row of babies.

She awoke the next morning before first light. She lay still, replaying memories of her little sister Susan as the tiny forms on the feather bolster began to stir with life, ready to battle another day. Little ones had to fight for breath and nourishment, she thought. When the babies nursed, they tugged and pulled as hard as they could. They were capable of clamping their frail gums onto her nipple and causing a flicker of pain. Sometimes lately she looked at them the way she had often looked into a nest of baby birds—mouths gaping, eyes closed, bodies naked, their mindless gulps. Nothing there to love yet. But then she pulled these little beings toward her in wonder, like creatures she had found along the road, needing her help, abandoned by a thoughtless stranger who didn't know what to do with them and so tossed them aside before continuing down the road. Now she felt she was hurrying along that road too, carried along by events she couldn't make sense of, to some destination she couldn't imagine. The people from the train were in such a good mood, it seemed, delighted to see something out of the ordinary to tell the folks at home about. She remembered a newspaper item Boone had shown her about the amazing snake lady, who was as scaly as a perch fish and shed her skin in the spring like a snake. The paper did not say what the snake lady herself thought about her condition, or what she thought when she saw herself in the looking glass. Christie had always prized her apartness, but now it seemed that with these babies she had become an oddity, as though they were part of her body and she couldn't get loose of them. Maybe she was meant to have one baby, but it had been divided up into pieces, each with a head and heart and legs; maybe the intelligence and the spirit, too, were divided into five. Maybe her love for each was only a fifth. Maybe her grief at losing any one of them would be divided by five. She wondered if the babies somehow represented herself, divided five ways. She hated the sin in her heart, but she knew she was desperately trying to turn the babies into nothing, so she wouldn't die of despair if she lost any of them.

"Are you crying?" James whispered, sitting up suddenly.

"No." She lied, and he soon knew it, from her sniffling.

"The little one ain't doing so good, is she?" he asked, turning toward her.

"No."

"She can't die on us," James said, stroking her face gently. "You went through too much for these babies."

She was crying for herself, she thought. She didn't want to love these babies. She wanted to hate them, so she could bear to lose them. James held her close and she cried softly until she heard James Lake cry too, the loudest of them, and when she took him up, she saw Minnie stir, a little bird holding on to the nest by a wisp of down.

19

"LITTLE BUNCH HAD ONE OF HER FITS," AMANDA TOLD CHRISTIE LATER in the morning, when she was washing and changing the babies. Nannie was getting big enough to wriggle away from the eager, possessive child, Amanda said, and last night Nannie was eating a cold sweet-potato-in-the-jacket while Little Bunch tried to cuddle her. Nannie, clutching the sweet potato, slid out of Little Bunch's lap, and when Little Bunch was accused of dropping her, she had one of her tantrums, which this time developed into a full-blown fit.

"It wasn't near as bad as those fits Dicey Jane Burnett's aunt has, though," Amanda explained.

Alma, who was cleaning out the ash box of the stove, said, "Little Bunch had that fit on purpose. She just wants attention."

Amanda, ignoring Alma, continued. "Little Bunch kept on a-jerking, and she had her teeth clenched, and she shook like somebody being hit by lightning. I made sure she didn't swaller her tongue."

"Was Nannie scared?" Christie asked.

"No. Nannie never even paid no attention to her, just went right on sucking out that sweet tater. But Little Bunch sure squalled after she stopped her fit."

"That child gets stuff in her head and gets it all twisted around," Alma said. "That's all it is."

"Dicey Jane's aunt got a lick on her head when she fell out of a wagon once, and it left her with fits," Amanda said. "I knew another man to have fits too, but his went away after he married."

"Bunch is just a-growing," said Alma, stirring the hot ashes in the scuttle to release the fire.

"She used to have growing pains too," said Amanda. "I'd have to rub her legs, and she'd cry and cry. And I'd wrap 'em in hot, wet rags. She was the pitifulest thing."

"She's always been touchous," said Alma. "The least little thing, like getting her finger burned on the stove or her dress tail caught in the door, and she always did squall."

"Little Bunch was worried about this littlun," Amanda said, as she rocked Minnie in her arms. "Bunch is so sweet-natured. She just wants to love on somebody all the time."

Christie worried about her children living up at Wad's house. Right now she could see the boys through the window. Clint was slicing the air with a sharp tobacco stick. He seemed to be pretending it was a tobacco knife and threatening Jewell with it. Clint had been begging to help cut tobacco this year.

"Your boys aim to kill one another," Alma muttered when she noticed them playing. "If my brats don't kill 'em first."

"They've been playing 'Kill the Governor,'" said Amanda.

"If they use my jar rubbers for a slingshot one more time, I'm going to wring their necks," Alma said.

She pulled out the soot tray of the stove and aimed it toward the back door. A fog of soot lifted from the tray.

Two days passed. Minnie was declining. Her tiny nostrils were crusted, her breathing heavy. She was fevered. Dr. Foote came out twice a day. The women were always there, rushing in at the first shade of dawn. Mrs. Willy hired Thurman to look after her chickens so that she could help Christie without interruption. Jimmie Lou helped Mama with the cooking.

While trying to nurse the babies, Christie would close her eyes and listen to the sounds of the house. They were all so familiar—the squeaking of the damper closing, the grinding of a pot sliding from one eye of the stove to another; the slop-slop noise of diapers swishing in a tub; the slap-slap sound of churning, growing softer and slower as the butter began to gather; dishes rattling; baby bottles being scalded in soda water; the rumble of a rolling pin on dough; the angry spitting of flames in the fireplace.

In the midst of all the well-wishers and curiosity seekers and the busy hovering of the women, Christie scarcely noticed James. He appeared at mealtime—eating Mama's cooking silently, with his elbows anchored on the table, shoveling his food in so he could get back to his work. He was expecting a cow to deliver. Wad had hired two hands to help plant, since the Wheeler men had to take turn-about guarding and taking care of the place. James slept heavily, but often in the night

Christie woke up startled, fearful that Minnie had slipped away. In her dreams, the babies turned into distorted forms, like something she had hatched out by mistake—as if a cocoon had turned loose a grasshopper instead of a butterfly, or a goose egg had cracked open to release a groundhog. But when she was awake and saw the babies, they were themselves again—more and more specific in their identities. James Lake had taken to moving his arms more deliberately, a sign of strength and restlessness. A birthmark was taking shape on the tummy of John Wilburn, who seemed to clench his fists much of the time. Mollie kept moving her lips in a sucking motion long after she stopped nursing. Emily Sue had little red splotches on her skin. But Minnie Sophia's skin was as pale as a cuckoo egg.

By Monday, Minnie had stopped taking milk. Then Mittens got a few drops down her Monday night, but when Christie tried again later, she was unsuccessful. Alma squeezed juice from an onion baked in ashes and rubbed it on Minnie's chest. Then she wrapped her in a flannel soaked with tallow. The next morning, Mittens couldn't get her to nurse. The baby was still, and she didn't cry. Dr. Foote listened to her chest and said it didn't sound good. He tried to get some medicine down her, but she couldn't swallow it. He removed the tallow rag and rubbed her with something that smelled like lye. That afternoon, when the throng from the train flowed in like a flash-flooding creek, Mama held Minnie back, showing her from the far side of the bed, where she sat rocking her in her arms.

"But her wants to be with her brothers and sisters," a woman from the train purred, pitching her baby talk across the bed in an attempt to rouse Minnie.

"Bless its heart," Mama said, petting the baby. "Her had too much company."

Christie could smell a pot of Great Northerns simmering in the kitchen. The four babies beside her on the bed were active, and she thought they might be hungry. The train passengers demanded to pick them up and hold them, believing they could lull them to sleep, but when an insistent woman tried to pick up Mollie, all four of the babies began crying. Their loud, piercing cries astonished the room. People laughed.

As soon as the crowd had gone, Christie took Minnie, and the women began feeding the others the bottles of sweet-milk. Jimmie Lou and Thurman were on patrol outside, told to keep new arrivals out.

"Maybe Mittens can get Minnie to eat when she comes back," said Christie a while later. Her right nipple was burning from exposure to the air, as she tried to nurse Minnie, but Minnie wouldn't take hold. Emily Sue had refused the bottle, but she nursed from Christie's left breast and was sleeping now, her face contented.

Mama took Minnie again. She peeled back the oversized bonnet and touched the infant's damp hair. She replaced the bonnet and set her down.

"She's awful hot," Mama said.

"I think we better call James in," Alma said. "I don't think she's going to last till he comes in to milk."

Christie didn't want anyone to call James. If she could put off telling James, maybe it wouldn't happen. She couldn't bear to see the expression on his face. In the past two days, the veil of worry on his face never seemed to alter. He hardly looked at the babies, and she guessed that he, too, was afraid to love them.

"I sent Thurman after the doctor," Alma said, who had just come in. Christie hadn't realized Alma had been out.

"Hand Minnie here," Christie told her mother. Mama brought the baby to Christie, who was sitting on the bed, on top of the cover, with a quilt across her lap. She held Minnie close, breathing on her face. She unwrapped her and placed the baby directly on her stomach, under her shift. The little thing squirmed and fluttered.

"Mittens will be here before James and Wad get in. Let's see what she can do."

Mama warmed a sugar tit and Christie held it to the baby's mouth, forcing a drop inside. The drop lingered inside the open lips and then oozed out.

"Oughtn't we to send for Mrs. Willy?" Mama said. Mrs. Willy had gone home when her toothache flared up again.

"No. I'm sick of that old woman being around. She's liable to bring in chicken mites, or God knows what."

"Now, Christie, Imogene Willy is a good soul, and she's been a mighty big help." Mama glanced out the window. "Dr. Foote oughter be here soon," she said.

"He won't do a bit of good," said Christie. "He's as qualified to be a doctor as a steer is to preach."

"He hasn't been charging, though, Christie," argued Mama.

"If he was really thinking about Minnie, he'd be out here already, and he'd come up with some better ideas than thumping on her chest and pretending he's found something with those silly earpieces."

Everyone seemed too shocked by Christie's tone to speak. Christie eased Minnie away from her and got out of bed. She went to the kitchen and got herself a glass of milk and some cornbread.

"I have to stir," she said. She gulped the milk and cornbread, which was cold and crumbly, and got back in bed with Minnie. The baby lay quietly. Her face was pinched, her feet cold. Christie huddled the baby against her, beneath her loose shift, leaving some room for air. Alma wrapped up a hot brick and pushed it under the quilt. Some horses neighed outside, and Christie could see Joseph, in a bright red flannel shirt like a flag, waving the strangers away. Joseph's brother, Henry, was out there too. Jimmie Lou was on the porch with the broom upended. Christie wished Amanda was with her now, but Amanda was working in the garden with the children.

The sun was low, and the men would be coming in before long. Nobody had started supper, except for the pot of beans. Alma had been in and out. Thurman had gone for Dr. Foote. No one sent for Mrs. Willy. A few visitors got past Joseph and Jimmie Lou, but Alma held them back, letting them get a look at the babies but only from a distance. Their clamor ricocheted against the walls.

At six o'clock, Minnie's little body began to stretch out full length, rigid. Her breathing rattled, loud as the clock.

"She's passing," said Christie quietly. Somewhere far off she heard a cow bawling. One of the boys would be rounding up the cows.

"I'll get James," Alma said, striding out to the front porch in just her dress sleeves. Mama knelt by the bed and rambled her way through a prayer. Christie dreaded seeing James. She heard Alma calling—that loud, echoing holler she used when calling the men from the fields. James would hear the note of urgency in Alma's holler. Christie heard Mittens and Sam pull up then. She recognized their mule from the tickle in his snort. Mittens had said the mule had a burr up his nose.

Christie wasn't sure when Minnie drew her last breath, for she had been distracted by Alma's hollering, the slant of dying sun through the window lights, and Mittens' arrival—her dark form blotting out the sun as she headed for the babies. Minnie was limp then. Christie looked from the baby to her mother to Mittens, to the outline of Alma's bonnet through the window. She could see Mittens' husband, Sam, waiting outside with the wagon and mule under the budding oak tree, and she could sense the presence of the four live babies nearby in the baby bed. She could feel Minnie's weight in her lap. Suddenly the milk and cornbread Christie had eaten surged forth, washing over the baby.

"Lands sakes alive!" said Mittens, rushing forward. "You done acting like a baby, Miz Wheeler. Set still, I'll clean up that vomick. Don't you worry about a thing. I's right here." She stopped still and shrieked. "Oh, that poor baby, that poor dead baby! That baby done dead!"

That evening, James bowed his head down at the table for a long time before eating. Christie could not force a prayer into shape in her mind. She couldn't eat. Supper was late. Mama had managed to cook turnip greens and dried apples and cornbread to go with the Great Northerns. Wad sent down a quarter of a shoulder and some hocks from his own smokehouse. Mama urged Christie to eat, for the other babies' sake, she said, and Christie tried more cornbread, but it was dry in her throat. She had stopped crying. She and Mama had cried together for a long time, and Amanda had broken down in tears, but nobody cried again that night.

Mittens had washed Minnie Sophia and tied her feet together with a cotton string. She wrapped her up in clean outing, and James put her out in the springhouse. As he left with the little bundle, Christie said one word: "Coons." James reinforced the springhouse door and stopped up a hole in the back, and for safety he put the baby's body inside the large pot Christie used for canning. He set a rock on the lid.

"Are you sure she's gone?" Mama whispered when he came back in from the springhouse. "I knew a man that was laid out for a corpse three times when he was a baby, but he lived to be an old man."

"She's blue," said James.

Jimmie Lou kept visitors out the best she could, and after dark nobody came by. The family let them alone. Amanda kept the children away. James and Christie and Mama stayed alone in the little house with the four babies, and Christie felt almost peaceful. It was so quiet. She could hear the flames in the fireplace, and a persistent pair of hoot owls courting each other half the night. She dreamed about Susan returning. It was a happy trade—a sickly, puny baby for a golden-haired sister with a sunny disposition. She dreamed of dogs tearing off Susan's pinafore. When Christie woke up, she was sweating and cold chills of fear rolled through her like a train.

20

"WHEN WILL WE BURY HER?" CHRISTIE ASKED JAMES WHEN THEY heard the first wagon drive up at daybreak. It was Mittens and Sam.

"Let's put it off a day," said James, quickly pulling on his britches. "I don't like the way the other girls look."

He didn't want to say the obvious—that if another baby died, it would be less trouble to handle the burials together. They agreed, hastily, to keep Minnie's body as cool as possible in the springhouse with the milk and the few remaining bits of dirty ice James had cut from the pond in February. And James agreed to reinforce the springhouse further against animals and to lock the baby's body in a trunk. In bed the night before, James had held Christie fiercely, while both prayed wordlessly over the sorrowful consequence of their passion. But she cringed at his touch.

As the sun inched up, Amanda arrived, bringing Boone's newspaper. The *Hopewell Chronicle,* which was printed the day before, had yet another article about the babies and the crowds they were attracting.

> QUINTUPLETS ARE
> BIG ATTRACTION!
> Mrs. Wheeler's
> Babies Bask in
> National Glory

The article said the babies adorned the town of Hopewell like a star atop a Christmas tree. By now, the *Chronicle* said, the news of the quintuplets had spread across the continent, and visitors were arriving from everywhere. The Friendship was stopping every afternoon. Local merchants were gathering gifts for the quintuplets.

"They'll forget about that wagon of presents, now that there's just four," said James over his breakfast. Amanda was reading the paper aloud to him, while Mittens fed the boys. Mollie and Emily Sue were still sleeping. Christie was quiet. With the poker, she shifted the back log in the fireplace and watched the flames lick it. She felt as indifferent as the log.

Mittens held the babies longer than usual that morning, rocking them and singing to them. When she left, she whispered to Christie, "Don't you let go now, ma'am. And you send for me, no matter if it's the middle of the night. Let's don't let these babies go to bed thirsty. They spirit will wander off and drink out of mud-puddles to keep from drying up."

When Dr. Foote arrived, he reminded Christie that Minnie had always been the weakest. "The other four will do better now," he said reassuringly.

James didn't go to the fields straight after milking. He returned to the house, and Mama tried to shoo him out, telling him he needed to be out working.

"I'll stay close this morning," he said, as he left. "It would be disrespectful to go ahead with the planting." Christie had noticed the empty look in his eyes over his eggs and sausage earlier, and she didn't know what to say. Now she could see him in the front yard, beneath the oak tree, talking with two men. Alma's girls had been stationed on the porch to keep out any callers. The yard was crammed with strangers, as it had been for days. But now James refused to let them come in. She saw Thurman and Henry and Joseph. There was no sign of Wad. The men were guarding the place, like soldiers around a fort. Footsteps hammered the porch. Faces pressed against the window.

Mrs. Willy came in, weeping, her hair straggling out of her bonnet in gray-streaked loops. As she bent down into Christie's face, she seemed larger, her loneliness magnified under her bonnet brim.

"The Lord just couldn't be without that littlun," Mrs. Willy said. "He had to call her home."

Mama, already busy cooking dinner, sent Mrs. Willy out to the garden. The weather was cool again, but the ground was dried out enough to hoe. "The weeds are taking hold of the lettuce," Mama told her.

Christie's eyes telegraphed gratitude to her mother, who saw that Mrs. Willy's high-pitched wail annoyed Christie. Mama had already sent word to Papa and Aunt Sophie. Christie wondered if the family would come from Dundee. She wished she could be by herself, with just her children, but she couldn't take care of them all, alone. Mama was taking care of her. Mama had a pot of ham hocks on the stove, and Lena had promised to find her some potatoes and cabbage to go in it.

Just as the clock was striking eleven, Mrs. Blankenship showed up with a jar of boiled custard. Mama allowed her in. Christie was in the rocking chair giving a bottle to Mollie, who had been fussy and active all morning. The rocker's familiar squeak seemed synchronized with the clock's ticking. In a conspiratorial near-whisper, Mrs. Blankenship said, "Christie, I have a family friend I want you to see because I believe he can help you out in a way that none of the rest of us can. He's one of our most upstanding citizens. He's versed in the skills of sympathy and puts me to shame in extending my condolences at a time like this."

"Who?" Christie asked. The bed hadn't been made up. It smelled. Her hair needed washing. Mrs. Blankenship was perfumed, and her sweet odor mingled with the sour stink of babies. Christie could smell the ham hocks simmering. She had been able to get down an egg early that morning, but she was afraid it would come back up.

Mrs. Blankenship proceeded blithely. Her watch on a gold chain swung against her chest like a plumb bob. "Mr. Samuel Mullins," she said. "My husband is a friend of Mr. Mullins, and Mr. Mullins is equipped with the most appropriate advice at a time like this." The woman touched Christie's shoulder, and with her other hand she fingered Mollie's blanket. "He makes it his business to help people when they lose loved ones. His business isn't on the square. It's over on the east side of town. He has a fine, well-appointed house, with the best furnishings and the most up-to-date techniques for caring for our loved ones."

Mrs. Blankenship should run one of those newfangled funeral parlors herself, Christie thought. She had the morbid sensibility for such an enterprise. Christie—her head bowed, not answering—clutched Mollie against her chest. She refused to cry. Mrs. Blankenship stayed for a few minutes more, pouring out syrupy words in a slow stream. Then she said she was anxious to get back to town, to send word to Mr. Mullins.

"He can talk to James," Christie said tonelessly.

She ran her tongue along a cavity in a back tooth. She wished Mr. Mullins would take the matter off their hands so they wouldn't have to think about it. It seemed that everything else was being done for them these days.

She could see Jimmie Lou and Dulcie out on the porch, their faces animated and glowing with the cold. They let the mail carrier, Mr.

Letcher, inside. He stuck his head around the stairway and set down a tow sack full of mail.

"I'm mighty sorry, Mrs. Wheeler," he said to Christie. "Mrs. Letcher sent you some boiled custard." He looked as if he might cry.

"Thank ye kindly, Mr. Letcher."

"You got a letter from the new governor. I imagine he wants to help out." Mr. Letcher had the important-looking letter in his hand.

Amanda read it out. "He wants to come and see the babies," she said. "He says congratulations. Oh, Christie, we'll have to write and tell him not to come."

"He'll come if he wants to," said Christie. "There's no stopping anybody like that."

"What if he gets assassinated while he's here?" Amanda asked.

"We'd have everybody here then, for sure," said Alma. "The whole town, the whole state, the militia, the trains. It would just be open house from here on out."

"Let her go daisy!" said Christie, shoving a quilt from her lap and rising from the rocker. "I don't care."

Mama had gone to talk to the children about what had happened. "They're too little to understand," she said when she returned. She coughed into her coat sleeve. "Clint did say something about how the other babies would do better now. I believe that *is* a blessing to come out of this. Now you won't have to spread your milk around so far, Christie."

Christie said, "You're coughing again, Mama."

"There's a little bite in the air today," Mama said. She touched the top of Christie's head, then ran her hand lightly across the blanket covering the four babies. "The Lord never gives us more than we can bear, Christie," she said. "You remember that. When I lost Susan, I thought I'd never live, but I did somehow."

The babies were asleep. There seemed to be an empty space in the middle of their row, Christie thought. She wondered if they could sense it too. She had tried to keep them placed in the same order. Now Emily and Mollie were side by side, instead of enclosing Minnie. They knew the difference, Christie thought, when the two of them began fretting at the same time.

"That feller's here," Alma, at the front window, announced.

Mr. Mullins was a small man in a black suit with a shiny watch chain and creased trousers. Christie couldn't remember if she had made herself presentable. At the door Mr. Mullins told Alma that he insisted on talking with James and Christie together alone. Everyone else would have to stay out for a time. He acted with the authority of a preacher. But for once Christie appreciated the protectiveness of the people around her and did not care to speak with Mr. Mullins so personally. She persuaded him to let Mama stay. Alma went out and hollered for James as if he were in the far field, although he was only at the stable, just beyond the great oak tree. When he came in, the babies woke up, and Mr. Mullins had to wait while Christie nursed them. He went outside and talked to Wad, who was in the front yard now. Wad hadn't been in to see her. Christie figured the dying of a baby was one of those things that Wad thought didn't call for words. She had heard the family express as much sorrow over a dead cow or a burned-up tobacco crop as she had heard over her baby. But she knew that farmers like Wad Wheeler weren't the sorrowful type. If the seeds got drowned out by early rains, then they waited a spell and replanted. They had to.

Her mind swirled, and she couldn't speak. She knew if she did, the words would be as garbled as geese talking when dogs got near. Mama sat in the rocker feeding a bottle to James Lake, and Mr. Mullins sat on the best mule-eared chair, the one with the needlepoint seat.

As Mr. Mullins, stiff in his black suit, began talking to her and James, she wondered what such a man was like. What had he and Wad talked about? Corn? Had Mr. Mullins ever cut tobacco? Had he ever chopped up a black racer? It was almost funny, trying to imagine this man out in the fields. He seemed to have been raised in that dark, formal clothing—a man who couldn't touch dirt. And yet here he was talking to her and James about putting their baby in the ground. He wanted to do it for them.

"James can dig a hole," she said. "I can dig a hole myself, no bigger'n it'd take."

"Have you thought about where?" Mr. Mullins asked. "A family graveyard? Does Mr. Wheeler have a place on his property?"

"Dundee," said Christie suddenly.

"We can't go all the way back to Dundee," James said.

"Susan's there. All my family's there."

"The Wheeler graveyard on Amp Wheeler's old place," James said. "The Wheelers do all their burying there."

"There's a fine cemetery out at Maple Grove, east of town," said Mr. Mullins. "I can get you a place there—large enough so that your future needs will be taken care of."

Christie wanted to cry, but she refused. She was filled with despair, like a hollow cistern full of dank air.

"I reckon we can make do right here," said James firmly. "You're talking about more money than we've got."

Mr. Mullins plucked at the material in his pants, parallel plucks at mid-thigh. "Forgive me. I didn't make myself clear. In light of what you have done for this town, my services and what we can provide you at Maple Grove would not be of any expense to you. You've done this town proud, and the loss of your baby doesn't detract from this honor." He leaned forward. "I have another proposition if you'll listen carefully."

James and Christie looked at each other—possibly the first time their eyes had actually met since Minnie died. James was hollow-eyed and his face was gray.

Mr. Mullins continued, "What I propose to do is preserve your little Mindy and keep her in an appropriate case until you are able to hold the funeral service. We have remarkable new techniques that make this possible. Now, I hate to put it like this, but Mrs. Wheeler, you have your hands full with these babies, not to mention all your company, and you want to devote all your time and energy to caring for these precious babies—the little darlings who I'm sure are the treasures of your life—and having a service now, involving a great many people, might detract from caring for these babies. And I suspect, Mrs. Wheeler, that you're not in the best of health and you need your strength. Therefore, I propose to keep the little body until such time as you're ready. We can preserve her little body just as it is indefinitely. And, I apologize so much for this thought, but if it should happen that one or more of the others should not last, but are called to join their little sister, then we could have them together. We could keep them all together, if—heaven forbid—it comes to that. We could keep them in such a way that you could see the precious babies perfectly preserved, for always."

Christie shuddered, and James rose abruptly, as if he were about to threaten the man. But then James sat down again with a sigh, letting the man's words sink in. He had said "babies," as if he expected to get his hands on more than one.

"None of this would be any expense to you good people," Mr. Mullins repeated.

When Mr. Mullins left, he took with him the little form of Minnie Sophia from the springhouse. Christie went outside with James and they opened the trunk and saw her again. She was blue and cold, and the outing flannel surrounding her was damp. Mr. Mullins placed the trunk in a little wicker buggy and rolled it to the front yard, where his carriage was waiting. He traveled in a fine carriage, outfitted inside with black velvet and gold tassels. From the back he pulled out a small oak chest, lined with sky-blue plush, and he started to lift Minnie from the trunk, but James quickly pushed his hands away. James picked up the baby himself and placed her gently inside the chest. She was so small inside it, like a single jewel in a jewel box.

As she watched Mr. Mullins drive away, Christie realized she was out-of-doors in broad daylight for the first time in many weeks. She was looking out over the same fields from almost the same vantage point as when she had first seen the place four years ago. The freshly plowed fields rolled ahead of her like angry, rolling creek water high in the spring runoff. The land had the contours and colors of a spring flood. She stood there, rooted, for a moment until James nudged her elbow.

"Feel the air," she said. "It's spring."

21

"COME ON AND LET THIS BABY SUCK, CHRISTIE," MAMA SAID AFTER dinner. "Your eyes look lost. Pay attention now. You don't want to lose these other babies."

"Where's James?"

"He's out tending to the stock. He's turning the cows out to pasture."

"Did that cow have her calf?"

"Not yet."

Christie pulled Emily Sue closer to her breast and felt the baby clamp on to her nipple. She wondered if a cow had ever had five calves. Somewhere in the world, sometime in history, it might have happened. That was the kind of thing Boone was likely to know. She wondered if Joseph and Mary had been troubled by all those shepherds and wise men bearing gifts. The preacher had brought up the name of Jesus again when he came out just before dinner, uttering bland comforts that Christie barely heard. She wondered how Mary's family regarded her situation. They probably refused to believe Joseph had nothing to do with it.

Mama wound her apron around her hands, as though they were lively creatures she had to keep still. She said, "Christie, when you were little, you'd set for a hour holding a chicken, just a-waiting for it to lay a egg in your hand."

"I don't remember that."

"Well, you did."

Amanda came in the front with an iced yellow cake a neighbor had dropped by. Christie saw the neighbor out on the porch, talking to Jimmie Lou. She was a Skaggs woman Christie barely knew. The yard was full of strangers. The people were always out there. The newspapermen were there again. The doctors. The townspeople. Neighbors had left their work and cleaned up, most of them bringing a dish. Jimmie Lou sent them to the back door, but most just handed over the food they had brought and quietly left.

"We just didn't know how people cared," said Amanda repeatedly.

Christie couldn't eat, and yet she desperately needed to. At dinner they had cut into a new ham the Culpeppers had sent. Some food had arrived at the other house too, Alma reported—enough beans to drive a mule team, Wad allowed.

"Look at all that grub—all on account of one little baby, the least little thing you ever saw," Mama said sadly. She surveyed the surviving babies, as if she expected the banquet on the table to nourish them into tall, fat children right away. On the table were two apple pies ("made from old swiveled-up apples," Mack Pritchard's wife explained in apology), a white cake, a yellow cake, a coconut cake, green beans simmered with hog jaws, shelly beans, cold slaw, cornbread, green onions, and preserves.

"I hope them apple pies go down good, Christie," said Mrs. Pritchard. "Mack laughed at me for bringing them, but I had to make do with what I had."

"We're much obliged, Mrs. Pritchard," said Christie. Ethel Pritchard was such a sweet, gentle soul, a kindly woman who raised the prettiest zinnias in the country.

"Are y'all going to set up all night?" Mrs. Pritchard wanted to know.

"Well, we don't have the body to set up with," Mama explained. "Mr. Mullins, in town, took her, and he's got a notion to keep her just like she was, for all of time, though I don't reckon that's what he really means. Anyhow, they're not going to put her in the ground yet."

"Well," said Mrs. Pritchard, folding her apron hem while trying to digest that information. "Has Brother Jones been out yet?" she asked.

"He come out this morning," said Mama in a quiet voice. She had calmed down considerably, and now her sadness depressed Christie. Mama said, "Brother Jones talked to James out by the stable a right smart while. They didn't work out the service yet. Mr. Mullins has got to have his say in it, so I don't know what they'll do."

Mrs. Pritchard twisted her bonnet strings awkwardly, examined the babies, and started toward the kitchen. "Take care of them babies good now, Christie," she said. "I hope they don't get what the first one had."

Mama said, "This change of weather is hard on littluns. My bronchitis is coming back, I'm afraid, with this dampness."

"We're having a wet spring," acknowledged Mrs. Pritchard.

"I don't know when to start home," Mama said. "My husband will be running out of clean work clothes, so I don't know how long I'll manage to stay."

"I need to get on along," said Mrs. Pritchard.

"Can't you get that baby to suck?" Mama asked Christie after Mrs. Pritchard had gone.

"No. She didn't want any. Here, take her." Christie handed Emily Sue to her mother, who shouldered and patted the infant.

"Go boop-boop," Mama said.

"She didn't eat," Christie said. "I believe I'm running low on milk."

Mama set the baby down, and all four started squalling, their plaintive screeches blending in a chorus like birds at dawn.

"They're hungry," Mama said, cooing. "Blessed babies is hungry."

Christie shut her eyes. The crying echoed the turmoil that had been inside her all those months. She realized the stir inside her during her pregnancy must have been soundless, yet it had seemed loud and noisy, like the babies' hollering now. All along, these babies had clamored for something, as if they wanted something they couldn't explain, as if they would never be satisfied with anything she could give them.

Mama started warming some sweet-milk in a stewer for the babies, and then she poured some of Mrs. Blankenship's boiled custard into a cup for Christie.

"Try this. You got to make you some milk."

Christie sipped the boiled custard from a spoon. It was sweet and thin, with too much nutmeg—little red-brown flecks like dried blood. "Let me try some of that other—Mrs. Letcher's."

Mama went to the back porch and got the other boiled custard. She dipped it out into another cup and brought it to Christie.

"It's better," Christie said. "It's got more body. Mrs. Blankenship's custard's a mite too sweet."

"You're bound and determined not to like that Mrs. Blankenship, ain't you now, Christie," said Mama.

"I don't know why I can't like her. She ain't done nothing to me."

"Well, I know how it is," said Mama sympathetically. "A woman like that seems to have everything, and she can't understand what it's like for everybody else. She thinks she knows, but she don't really. People like that, they don't know how miserable they make everybody else. I'm sure they don't mean to. It's just their raising."

"You're too forgiving, Mama," said Christie. "And we owe Blankenship's Mill nearly a hundred dollars on this house."

"Yes, I know you do. Your papa always told you never to go in debt. He never owed a penny in his life." Mama drank some of Mrs. Blankenship's boiled custard. She gazed at the babies. "Lord, honey, what do you think will become of these four younguns?" She set the dish down on the bedside table in order to pet James Lake and caress Emily Sue's cheek. Then she let loose a streak of nonsense burbles that made Christie relax and close her eyes. She felt like a child again, bathing in the soothing talk of her mother. The babies quieted down a little as long as Mama talked to them. When Mittens came, they nursed—all except John Wilburn—and then slept as if exhausted from the exercise.

"I's so sorry, Mrs. Wheeler," Mittens said over and over. "I tried and they did good, but that little Minnie, she just didn't want my milk."

"It wasn't your fault, Mittens." Christie believed losing Minnie was a punishment for her own wrongs. She was afraid more evil thoughts would enter her and eat her up from the inside. She twisted the edge of an outing blanket.

Later, as Mittens prepared to leave, she said, "I couldn't rest all night. People coming in here and just about take these babies off. That train hauling in a thousand peoples right through yo' house."

"The train didn't stop today."

Dr. Foote had gotten a telegram through to the station manager in Memphis, who told the conductor what had happened. And the news had been in the Memphis newspaper. That afternoon the train let out three long, mournful sounds, distinctly different from the usual two hoots. As the train chugged past, Amanda whispered to Christie in a corner of the kitchen, "I swan, I think Wad would charge a dime to let people see Minnie if you'd let him. But if he did that, I think I'd just get on that train and go as far as it went and never come back."

"Where would you go?"

"I don't know. I'd go find that nice couple you talked about."

"How would you buy a ticket?"

"I don't know."

By nightfall, everyone in the family had come in to eat, digging into the food with more enjoyment than they would have had for the cooking they were used to. But Alma said Mrs. Pritchard had been right about her apple pies. Jimmie Lou and Dulcie kept washing plates so others could eat. Mama made the children wait till the men had finished. Everyone urged Christie to eat, but she couldn't.

"Good Lord, there's enough grub here for a wheat threshing," Wad said.

"I brought down these pickles you give me last year, Christie," said Amanda. "Christie did up these pickles," she said to the rest of the family.

"Is that right, to take her own pickles on a day like this?" asked Mary Ann, Joseph's wife.

"What difference does it make?" said Lena, who had been moody lately.

"They're good pickles, if I do say so myself," said Christie.

Clint and Jewell and Nannie were eating on saucers in a corner, bent over their food silently and intently. Little Bunch wasn't eating. She wore a blue bow in the center of her head and had a handkerchief knotted on her wrist. She kept her other hand busy working it, knotting and twisting it. She stalked around the babies like a wary cat. Amanda slapped her hands. "Somebody has to watch you ever minute," she said.

"I can't stand being around her," said Lena. "She might have a fit right in front of me."

"The paper sure made a big fuss this week," said Alma, pointedly ignoring Amanda and her daughters. "But they're behind. Next week they'll be blaring out the sad story."

"It's already in the Memphis paper," said Joseph.

"It's so sad," said Mary Ann. "It's just the worst shame."

"Where'd the little-bitty one go to?" asked Jewell, eating a piece of bread. He went over the babies like a dog sniffing.

"She's gone to Heaven, precious," said Mama, catching hold of Jewell and making him squirm.

"What do you reckon that Mr. Mullins will do, James?" Amanda asked.

James shook his head and worked his knife from the pocket of his blue-jeans britches. "I didn't ask too many questions. I figured I didn't want to know."

"They can keep her in a glass case just the way she was when she was alive," said Wad.

"How do you figure that?" Alma asked.

"Boone read it somewhere. He's always reading something." Wad laughed.

"You're starving yourself, Christie," said Alma. "Here, eat some ham, and I'll bring you some bread and butter. Mrs. Pryor made the best light cornbread, 'east raised."

"Put some preserves on it," said Christie.

Alma laid the lid of the preserve stand on top of the plate of ham. The table was so crowded there was no place else to put it. She scooped out more strawberry preserves than Christie wanted, but they did stimulate her appetite. They were bright red and had a deep sweetness, cut by a tart vinegar flavor.

"Who made these preserves?" she asked.

"I did. Don't you remember?" said Alma.

"Oh. I oughter known your strawberries."

"Why, yes, ma'am. Them's my strawberries. I could tell 'em a mile off."

"Are you trying to make me laugh?"

"No. Just trying to make you eat."

The children had finished eating and were playing a card game. Dulcie was embroidering a pillow slip, and Jimmie Lou was still washing dishes. Christie punched her bolster and sat down on the bed. She felt stranded. She felt the house closing in on her. It was hot and the air didn't stir. The men lingered at the table with their pipes, talking about tobacco plants. Then they started teasing Henry about Maggie's expected baby.

"Maybe she'll have six and outdo Christie here," joked Wad.

"Don't say that or it'll come true," said Maggie, blushing.

"Nobody wants that many babies," said Hub, Alma's youngest child, waving his fist full of cards. "There ain't enough titties."

"Christie has to give these babies their dinner now," said Alma, when two of the babies started crying. "Now don't you menfolks pay any attention." Mama helped Christie, holding the babies up against her and jiggling and singing to them. Alma pulled sheets in front of Christie till she got John Wilburn and Emily Sue situated. Nannie came and sat with Christie.

"Nannie wants her titty too!" Jewell said. The children laughed.

"Sounds to me like Jewell wants some," Henry joked. He was good-natured, the babyish man in the family. He took after Wad in his teasing, but he was gentler, Christie thought. Alma's older boys—Thurman and Arch—were all eyes, and Alma made them go outside and watch for strangers. Little Bunch worked at the handkerchief knotted around her wrist.

"Is your school class still coming out?" Mama asked Lena.

"I don't reckon they'll want to come just to see four," said the girl.

"Jimmie Lou, your skirt's on hind part before," said Amanda.

"I put it on that way on purpose," said Jimmie Lou, taking a bite of white cake.

John Wilburn and Emily Sue were eating better, holding on to the nipples longer than they had earlier in the day. After they nursed, Christie finished the bread and butter and preserves Alma had fixed for her, along with a piece of ham. The yeast-raised bread was soft and springy and delicate, and the yeast was fresh and fragrant. The strawberries tasted just off the vine.

"I believe I'll have another piece of bread," she said, and Mary Ann jumped up to get it for Christie. "And some of those shelly beans and slaw too," she said. "Just a few shellies."

Now and then various members of the family eyed the remaining babies as if to check whether they were still alive. James's eyes seemed to avoid them. He seemed cold and faraway, as if he were sinking into a deep well. He barely spoke, hardly acknowledged the family. Christie wondered if he was secretly glad he had fewer mouths to feed and if he dreaded, as she did, the slow wasting away of the other babies. She imagined them drying out like Mrs. Pritchard's apples, stored in a dry place that robbed their moisture. She thought of turnips and potatoes in straw.

After the meal, most of the family left. Alma built up the fire to heat bricks for Christie and the babies. Everyone would have stayed up all night if Minnie's body had been there.

"It's too hot for bricks," Christie said.

"It'll cool down directly," Alma said. "The mercury's falling right quick out there."

"The doctor said keep 'em warm," Amanda reminded Christie.

When Alma started to wrap up the brick in an old newspaper, MRS. WHEELER IS BLESSED WITH FIVE QUINTUPLETS leaped out at Christie.

"Boone wanted to save that," she said to Alma. The news seemed ancient.

Amanda cut the article out of the paper. Then Alma wrapped the brick with the remaining pages. The brick was too hot to be set next to the babies. Alma put it under the outing cover at one end and fluffed the cover, making a little hot tent. The babies didn't stir.

In the night, Christie listened to James sleeping, and to the babies' soft huff. She heard a sniffle begin, a tiny bird sniffle—a choked little cry. She was afraid to take the baby up, afraid of learning which one and how bad. She couldn't let James wake up. He needed his sleep, and she didn't want to face his worry. She wanted to chase Mr. Mullins's somber tone of voice out of her head. It clashed with that song Mittens hummed. As soon as the babies were born, Dr. Foote had said they couldn't last.

She realized by the sound that it was Emily Sue sniffling. Her little throat sounded raspy. The brick was probably cold by now. Listening to the baby's rough breathing, Christie realized she hadn't cried all day.

Remembering the family there at supper, she didn't recall seeing anyone cry. They didn't say much about Minnie. They must have thought
losing the runt was not worth fussing over. But that was what could
make her cry—that they thought of Minnie that way.

She couldn't afford to cry. It would take her fluid, her milk, and
she would dry up like an old apple herself.

Emily Sue was the one so much like Susan. Christie eased out of
bed and touched the little face. It was hot. The baby's breathing was
tight and short. Christie could hear Mama snoring on the children's
feather bed in the north bedroom. The kitchen smelled of green beans
and ham hocks, and there was pie sitting out, which Christie snatched
up, hungry again. She had to eat. She wanted milk to drink. But since
the weather had warmed up, all the milk was out in the springhouse.

Christie found her wrapper and a shawl and a bonnet. On the
back porch she slipped into some clip-claps and walked down the path
to the springhouse. The moon had traveled a good distance over the
sky since the family left last evening, and it was beginning the second
half of its night's journey. By morning, it would be low on the horizon, on the other side of the railroad. It was a growing crescent.

The springhouse door had a wooden button that wanted to stick,
but she jerked the door loose. It was chilly inside, but it smelled musty.
They had kept cabbages and turnips here, and when it began to thaw
the turnip tops sprouted. The cabbage leaves rotted, then froze. She
found the milk jug set in the cool flowing stream that backed up into a
pool. Her baby would have been safe here the previous night. No animals would swim in that cold current underwater into the springhouse. They had found a fish in there once, though. And frogs,
salamanders, toads. But they had kept meat in here for weeks at a time,
and only once had raccoons gotten in. Minnie Sophia was gone, as if
she had been taken by something wild. It was possible to imagine that.
It seemed no worse than the way she was yanked away by illness and
then trundled off by Mr. Mullins in that little wicker buggy. Shivering,
Christie grabbed the handle of the milk jug, stepped outside, and
closed the door. She fastened the button, and when she got back to
the house James was up, wondering where she was.

22

By Friday all of the babies were sick. They were feverish and hot, with wrinkled, red faces and feeble, screaking cries. Their little whimpers again reminded Christie of kittens seeking a nipple. She drank the warm milk James brought in early, because sweet-milk was more nourishing before it cooled. Neighbors continued to bring milk to the springhouse, and somebody was always churning, but Christie had now given up trying to get the babies to suck from the hard rubber nipples. Mittens stayed longer each visit, trying to coax the babies to take her breast. She rocked and sang, her songs more plaintive and urgent now. Mama cut a piece out of a new diaper cloth to make more sucky rags, and she and Amanda and Mrs. Willy tried by the hour to squeeze drops of sweetened milk into the babies. Mama kept up her baby talk as she cuddled the babies one by one. Mrs. Willy kept saying, "It's a pity." Alma stormed around, barking orders. She stationed her older children at the doors, and two or three of the men stayed out front at all times. The yard was still full of people. The weather remained cool, and Alma kept the fire going. Christie wanted to pound something to pieces. Sometimes, seeing James outdoors splitting kindling, she could imagine taking hold of the ax and chopping viciously into a stump.

Dr. Foote brought his daughter, Chancey, to sit with the babies on Saturday. He had confidence in his daughter's observations, he said. She was to let him know of any significant deterioration in the babies' health. Chancey was a plain girl with a habit of praying spontaneously, the way some people might comment on the temperature or the direction of the wind. "Lord, have mercy on the little souls," she would say in the middle of a conversation, aiming her eyes at the loft. Christie paid little attention to her. She wished she could walk back through the fields. She paced across the floor, looking out the window, as if she expected someone to come and tell her what to do, or tell the future, or take the babies away. Brother Jones hadn't taken much particular interest in the babies, but he told James he would hold Minnie's service whenever they were ready.

Boone came down, bundled in a scarf and earmuffs. He gazed at the four struggling little forms and said something under his breath. Then he said to Christie, "Nannie's been keeping house for me. Nannie's going to make somebody a good little wife someday."

"Nannie?" For a split second Christie didn't know who Nannie was. "You take care of Nannie," she said to Boone then. "I need my Nannie." A spark of fear burned through her. "What will you do to her?"

"Now, Christie, don't you worry none about Nannie. She's already learning to cook. She fixed me a biscuit, with three peas and a gumdrop on it. I told her it was larruping."

Where was James? She saw Mama scalding the churn. Christie thought Dr. Foote had gone home, but here he was again, pulling those ear tubes out of his satchel. His daughter folded and unfolded her harsh white hands. When she wasn't praying, she was writing in a book.

"Are they going to live?" Mama asked Dr. Foote.

He listened to the babies' chests. He lifted their long dresses the way he had moved up Christie's skirt in his office, looking for those fibroids. The memory enraged her, as if the touch of this man had jinxed her body and now was working its poison on these little bodies. She wanted to shout. She saw Boone leaving, his neck ducked down into his coat, his earmuffs sticking out like a cow's velvet ears.

Dr. Foote removed the tubes from his ears. "It's a spring cold," he said. "They might get over it, but their lungs are weak. If we can keep the right temperature—cool them off when they're fevered and warm them up when they're chilled—they could get over it. But they need nourishment."

Christie was holding the butter mold in her hand. She turned it over and traced her finger on the design carved into the wood—buttercups.

"It's all my fault," she said. "My milk wasn't good."

"Now don't talk that-a-way, Christie," said Mama soothingly. "I believe they was handled too much. It wasn't your milk."

"I gained all that weight," Christie cried. "Why wasn't it enough to feed them with? I'm still big. I'm big as a cow. A cow could give enough." She dropped the butter mold on the table.

"Be still, Christie," Mama said, throwing an arm around her. "You'll strain what milk you've got."

Christie snatched the recent newspaper with the happy story about her and the babies. "Look at us," she said, in tears.

"I'm awful sorry, Mrs. Wheeler," the doctor said, as he put away his tools. "I'd give anything to help these babies live."

"Well, do it! They've got to live!" Christie threw the newspaper toward the fire, and it landed, spread, on the hearth.

"He's doing what he can, hon," Mama said, stepping forward to pick up the paper.

"Tell me what to do!" Christie begged the doctor. "Just tell me what to do."

Shaking his head wearily, Dr. Foote searched his bag as if he might find a magic cure that he had misplaced. He left Christie with instructions for keeping the babies' fevers down, and he told Chancey to stay there till dark, then ride back with Mittens and Sam.

"They might pull through," he said to Christie. "As long as you can get some milk down them."

Through the south window, Christie could see him walking toward his buggy, weaving through the group of Wheelers and strangers out in the yard. Everyone seemed to be waiting.

As Dr. Foote drove away, Amanda brought Little Bunch and Lena down. "There wasn't any school today, on account of planting," she said. "Wad says they've got to be out helping, but Bunch goes along and digs up the seeds like a crow in a cornfield. Bunch-Bean, now set still and behave. We've got to cheer Christie up."

Little Bunch was wearing an indigo dress and white pinafore, with high-top brown boots and gray cotton stockings. The child was tugging at the knot in her scarf and mumbling. She walked around the room, dancing off nervous energy. Then she stopped beside Chancey, and her shadow fell over the babies in the baby bed. Suddenly, before anyone could stop her, Little Bunch began poking at the doubled feather bolster that was their mattress. She pummeled it, feeling it as if she were looking for a ring or a tooth hidden inside.

Amanda jerked Little Bunch away. "Stop aggravating those babies, Little Bunch! Go help Lena wash the dishes."

"Lord, help these precious little ones," said Chancey.

"Where's your mama, Christie?" Amanda asked.

"Out in the garden, I expect." Christie heard the train whistle.

"You know, I miss the train." Amanda sighed and sat down on the bed, facing Christie in the rocker. Amanda said, "What a thing to happen to us. I've had more society in the last two weeks than I've had most of my life. I think when it's all over with, we'll feel like we've been through that earthquake after all. We'll think it happened right here."

"When what's all over with?" said Christie.

"Oh, excuse me, Christie. Oh, I'm such a eejit!" Amanda stood up, flustered. She touched Christie's hair, smoothing back a stray lock. "I mean when we get back to the way we'd been a-being, before all this happened."

"Do you think that will ever be?"

"Well, sometime, I imagine," Amanda said, picking up James Lake.

"I don't care if the train does stop," said Christie with bitterness. "Let 'em all in. Let 'em see. They need to see. Somebody said it was like showing off Jesus in the manger. I feel like I've been living in a manger. Or a hog trough, one."

"Shh, Christie. Don't scare this littlun."

Amanda enclosed James Lake in her arms and stood by the window, rocking him gently. Christie could hear her singing softly.

Chancey beamed her eyes ceilingward and said, "Dear Lord, show us the way, for the way seems crooked and the path strown with temptations and marked with mislabeled signposts."

"Does it really?" said Christie sarcastically. "Signposts? Why, my stars." She wanted to hit this dumb girl.

Christie dashed outside toward the outhouse. She felt breathless and light-headed. Amanda's voice trailed behind her. "Christie, don't be mad!"

As she approached the outhouse, she saw that Thomas Hunt was just emerging. A dog she'd never seen walked up to him, a small brown-and-white dog with a curled tail. Thomas stooped to pet him, then spotted Christie.

"Why, Christie, are you out-of-doors a'ready?"

"Go on in and see the babies. Mandy's there."

"Alma's up at the house scouring pans. She was scouring like she was going to scour plumb through the bottom." Thomas snapped a gallus in place and headed toward the porch, the dog following. "Come on, you good-for-nothing," he said to the dog. "You wait for me out here by the steps."

The seat in the outhouse felt warm. She drew in the smells that mingled from the springhouse, the barn, the bale of straw. Wad claimed filling up the outhouse hole with straw was a waste because it had to be shoveled out more often and used up precious straw. But the Wilburns had always used straw in their outhouse in Dundee, and after moving to Hopewell Christie had begged James for a bale of straw now and then.

She was still bleeding, but not so much since she had been out of bed. She barely had any infection now. She hadn't paid much attention to her own body since Minnie died. Physical sensations seemed to whirl around outside of her, the way the babies were outside of her now. Occasionally, for a few moments, she forgot her situation altogether, and her mind went back to Dundee—she was a young girl, sewing underclothes and piecing quilt blocks; or, younger still, following her Aunt Zulah out to the henhouse to gather eggs when they visited Mama's folks in Tennessee. Even now, Christie could sense the warm underside of a hen she called Mollie, a hen who always let her take the egg without protest. Aunt Zulah protested, though, that you didn't give hens names. It made them persnickety, she said. Aunt Zulah Rhodes was gone now. She died of brain trouble the year Christie married.

Christie felt calmer. She threw straw down behind her. Outside, she encountered the strange dog, who lowered his head to her and wagged his tail. On the back porch she found a scrap of meat and threw it out to him. Now he would stay, she thought, hoping James wouldn't mind that she had fed meat to the dog.

"We thought you fell in," said Amanda when Christie returned.

"Are the babies awake?"

"Just one of them, that little blond one."

"Mollie Lee," said Christie impatiently.

"I still can't tell 'em apart," Amanda wailed. "Christie, Thomas here's been telling what they're saying all along his drumming route. Tell her, Thomas."

Thomas needed no encouragement. Christie took up Mollie and walked with her, rocking her in her arms and humming to her while Thomas talked. Chancey was still sitting in a chair by the bed, dull as a stump.

Thomas cleared his throat and started. "Everywhere I go, when they hear where I'm from, they all want to know, Do you know them Hopewell quintuplets? Of course at first I play like I don't know what they're saying and then string 'em along. And when they find out who I am and how I'm related, why, they all want a souvenir! Or they want me to sign my name! Christie, what you done has gone far and wide! Why, I was down in Mississippi, and they told me it was in the Jackson paper. And I been through Tennessee, and over in Arkansas just a little ways, and back up here, and I tell you *ever*'where they know. I say Hopewell and they say the babies. It's the beatin'est thing I've ever run across in all my drumming days."

"Tell about the one down in Tupelo," urged Amanda. She was busy molding the butter Mrs. Willy had churned earlier.

"This was in a little store. This feller always gives me a big order, and when he found out about the Hopewell quints—I refer to them as the Hopewell quints now—he decided to double his order of baby powder. He was going to paste a special label on the baby powder and make it a souvenir—because it come from me, you see. It's that kind of baby powder the drugstore sent you? With him doubling his order, I made over five dollars right then and there. I tell you, I shot home on wings. But I'm setting out again right soon, soon as I get these orders in. I'm pushing this baby powder idea."

"There's four, not five," said Christie, pausing before the fireplace.

Thomas nodded in the direction of the baby bed, shifted his feet uncomfortably, then changed the subject. He asked Amanda if she needed any complexion cream. He had brought some samples of Dr. Ayer's Peerless Violet Cream. Christie wondered if Thomas thought they had merely dug a little hole in the yard for Minnie, like burying a dead cat. She sat down on the far side of the bed, turning her back to both Thomas and Chancey, and brought Mollie to her breast. Christie hugged her close, as if she could squeeze milk into her. The little face was hot against her skin. Nervously, Thomas and Amanda kept chattering. Christie didn't know where her mother was. She knew Amanda was trying to be cheerful for her, but she wished she could be alone with the babies. Distractedly, she called to Lena and Little Bunch to open the packages Mr. Letcher had dumped in a box by the door.

"Oh, goody," said Lena, wiping her hands on her apron.

"Thomas, you'll be amazed," Amanda said. "We've been getting so many letters." She laid down her butter paddle and picked up a letter at random. "Listen to this." She read aloud, "'Dear Mrs. Wheeler, I had a dream that you would have quintups. In my dream, I was talking to a woman I'd never met. She was big and about to have a baby. I said I hope it's twins and she said I hope I hope. I realize now the dream meant Hopewell and it was you. I read you got very big. Yours truly, Mrs. Raymond Sears.'"

Amanda folded the letter and slipped it back into its envelope. "That's all the way from Georgia," she said.

Lena had opened one of the packages, and she held up a baby dress—blue with pale blue edging and buttons at the bottom, with openings for the baby's legs.

"That trimming is tatted!" cried Amanda. "How pretty. There's a letter with it." She snatched the letter eagerly and read to herself. Then she said, softly, "Oh, this dress belonged to this woman's little dead baby. And she wanted you to have it, Christie." Amanda spread the dress on the bed. "That's the sweetest thing," she said. "This woman says her baby had typhoid fever."

"All five babies would fit in that," said Christie. "Four." She covered her breast and walked around the foot of the bed to the baby bed. She laid down Mollie and picked up James Lake. His mouth screwed around and a bubble of spit popped out, simultaneously with a bubble from his nose. She dabbed at his face and held him upright. He opened his eyes and gazed vacantly.

"Itty bitty bitty!" said Thomas awkwardly to the baby, reaching his hand to touch him. "Itsy bitsy."

Christie stopped short. She had forgotten what to say to babies. Had she been talking baby talk in front of the multitude for two weeks? Had she spoken to any of those strangers, or had she lain there deaf and dumb like a rock, like an exhibit for them to witness? She didn't have a clear sense of herself anymore. She recalled the murmurs, the oohs, the goo-goos they made, the faces. How odd that grown people would babble to babies. Babies couldn't speak at all. She regarded Thomas Hunt, who was grinning foolishly. He still had his hat on, along with his striped shirt, watch chain, vest, traveling trousers, but no coat. The life of a drummer was a mystery. A man lived like a Gypsy, going off on a train with several trunks, to a strange town where he hired a wagon and drove around to the stores and sat around jawboning with rough men. Christie knew he brought the store owners whiskey to loosen their tongues and their pocketbooks. Alma said he even got shaved in barber shops, where men talked filth in dirty back rooms. Christie had heard him curse many times when he thought no women were around. He liked to say, "Goddamn that and a rabbit in the pea patch."

Mama swooped in from the closed-off north room then to see the little blue dress.

"Is that trimming really tatted, Mandy?" Mama asked, reaching for the dress. "Why, it is. Such fine thread." She squinted and held the dress at arm's length.

"Look what I found," said Lena, who had opened another package. "Baby bracelets."

"Why, somebody's knotted some baby bracelets out of colored thread and then embroidered on the names." Amanda held up the bracelets admiringly.

Christie fingered the bracelets, wondering why anybody would take the time and care to fashion the bracelets so carefully as a gift for someone she didn't know. James, John, Emma, Molly, Sophie.

"The names ain't right," she said.

"It won't make no difference," Mama said. "They're close enough."

"There's a stray dog out there," Amanda said, glancing out the window.

"He followed me all the way from the depot," said Thomas. He kept a horse and wagon at a farm near the station in Cross Plains. "He trotted along behind so long I thought he'd never make it back to where he started, so I let him ride in the wagon with me awhile, and he trotted awhile, and then he rode awhile. He seemed bound and determined to come home with me."

"Alma will say it was just like you, to dump another dog on her," Amanda said. "You can go off drumming and then she'll have to feed it."

Thomas grinned. "You don't think Alma'll be tickled to get another dog?"

"Alma's liable to send you *and* the dog back out on the road," said Amanda, grinning back.

Christie couldn't get James Lake to take her breast. She moved from the bed to the rocking chair. She loosened his bonnet and felt his damp wisp of hair. Closing her eyes and listening to Thomas and Amanda bantering, she thought about the time she saw them come out of the smokehouse, one after the other. She had wondered if they had been in there together, and now she decided they probably had. Ordinarily, it would have shocked her to think this, but now the surprise seemed so distant, like something observed on the horizon, the silhouettes of cattle plodding along.

She felt as though she were running after something she couldn't catch. She couldn't keep up with what went on in the smokehouse—or anywhere. She didn't even care. For all she knew, some of the children might be out in the smokehouse now, sinfully exploring each other, or playing around in the hayloft or the stable or the shed that was some distance down the lane, where Wad kept some tools. Jimmie Lou already had boys hanging around on Sundays after church. Christie couldn't stop any of it. Her own sins were more than she could face. She felt stiff and tired and heavy. Back when she was light and limber, she used to fairly run down the lane to the men in the field—to take them a jug of water, or a bucket of dinner. She would run through the morning dew to work in the field herself. She had stopped in that shed on the lane once to get out of a pouring rain. She longed for the simple pleasure of going with James to look out over the fields. Just going to the henhouse to gather eggs would be a great satisfaction. She wanted to return to life. She felt the babies slipping away from her. If she lost them, she would bury them away, plant them like seeds, and they would grow into fruit trees or bountiful grapevines or tall stalks of corn, fat with milky kernels.

"Ain't no sign of that wagonload of presents from town?" Thomas was asking Amanda.

"They're probably waiting to see if the babies going to make it," said Christie sharply. "That's what Alma said."

But Thomas wasn't listening to her—or thinking about the babies. He was drinking in Amanda's words as she told about Wad collecting admission in his cigar box. Amanda had a flair for telling even the most ordinary detail and making it fascinating. It was the way she moved her hands, Christie realized. Her slender, white hands moved like doves, fluttering and soaring. And it was her youthful air too. Christie felt old. She leaned back in the rocker, clutching her sick child against her.

Thomas and Amanda faded away. Outside, some dogs barked. Someone was arriving. Christie wasn't going to move from the chair, no matter who it was, or with what news. Lena disappeared into the kitchen. Immediately, Little Bunch was into the bolster again.

"Get out of there," said Amanda, jerking Little Bunch away from the babies. "What are you after—snakes? We're not helping Christie out one bit. You get out too, Thomas. Christie don't need you down here. Christie, I'm carrying these younguns home, and I'll bring Nannie and the boys down later. Dulcie's got 'em out sweeping the yard since it's warmed up."

Christie closed her eyes. She heard Amanda and Thomas and the girls leave. In a while she heard other people arrive, then tiptoe past the stairway to murmur and squeal at the babies. She wouldn't face them. She heard her mother talking to the people on the porch. "Poor little things . . . drafts . . . baby bracelets . . . tatted dress." Christie heard Mollie whimper. She had no sense of how long the babies could hold on like this. She had made a dreadful mistake. She should have nursed the largest and healthiest one and saved him. James Lake. Her favorite. James Lake and Emily Sue, who was like Susan. She could have saved them both.

She would not let herself cry in front of all those strangers. She wouldn't tell anyone how she felt, even if the Lord took all of her babies. Chancey Foote had been talking to the Lord about whether He meant to take them. Christie envisioned them flying through the room and out the window, up to Heaven. She had lost track of the strange girl and thought she had left. Christie opened her eyes. The girl was there after all, murmuring and writing something in her ledger.

"Dear Lord, have mercy on these dear babies," said Chancey to the loft.

"Mollie needs changing," Christie said, starting to rise from the rocker. She was relieved to know some fluid was going through the infant.

"I'll do it, Mrs. Wheeler," Chancey said. "Don't stir."

Christie did as she was told. All she had to do was utter a word—milk, biscuit, diaper—and someone would leap up and get it for her. She was a queen. Nobody could claim to know the mind of a queen, she thought.

The next day was Sunday. James went out at daylight with his rifle, taking Clint along. When they came back two hours later, Christie was rocking the two boys. They were barely nursing now, and she felt her breasts leaking through her clothes.

"Looky here, Chrissie," said James with an awkward smile as he held up a fresh squirrel.

"It's a fat one—for this time of year."

"I get to have the tail," said Clint, rubbing his hand down the fur.

Excitedly, he reported how the new dog had treed the squirrel and how he had stayed perfectly still while James took aim and killed it. With exaggerated motions of his arms, Clint imitated shooting the rifle.

"You're making my arms tired," said Christie, who had been in one position too long. Clint aimed his finger at each of the four babies in turn.

"Come on, Whistle-britches," James said to Clint, steering him toward the back door, using the squirrel tail to swish the child's head as they passed Christie. "Let's get your grandmama to dress this squirrel."

"The babies can't eat squirrel," Clint said to Christie.

"No, sugar. They're too little to eat meat." She wanted to reach out and hold Clint's face still, to look into it deeply, but her arms were full with the two babies. She thought John Wilburn was interested in sucking.

"Go help Grandmama dress the squirrel," she said to Clint.

"The baby needs to have his titty," James said to him.

Christie and James shared a glance. Her breasts were bared, and the two little boys nestled against them.

By noon, Mama had a pot of squirrel-and-dumplings ready. She brought a bowl of it to the table for Christie.

"When I was dressing the squirrel, I pinched a nerve in my finger, and I can't get the feeling back," Mama complained, wiggling her fore-finger. "Come on to the table, Christie."

"I ain't hungry." She was gazing out the front window. Several dozen people loitered in the yard, in their Sunday clothes. The red oak was swelling with color.

"Ain't none of us going to eat any of this," Mama said. "It's all for you, since James went out and killed it for you."

"I ain't hungry."

"You need your strength. James got this to build up your strength. He went out looking for it jest for you."

"Clint helped," said James, who was at the kitchen washstand.

"I didn't even breathe in," Clint said. "I was so quiet!"

"Ain't nothing as nourishing for a sick child or a new mother as a bird stew or a squirrel stew," said Alma, who had just come in through the back with a bucket of water. "A dove or a patteridge makes a right good stew, but I believe squirrel is superior."

Christie sat down at the kitchen table and lifted the large spoon. The broth was thickened by the dumplings, which Mama had made with long, thick strips of dough. Christie took a bite. It was rich with pepper. She dipped the spoon in the broth again. The tiny head of the squirrel rose to the top, and where the bone was broken she could see the dark filaments of the veins over the brain, little threads making a fragile net cap.

"Eat it," said Alma.

"I can't."

"Eat it or you'll die," warned Alma.

23

OVER THE NEXT FIVE DAYS, THE REMAINING FOUR BABIES DIED. Christie watched in rigid silence, knowing which one would go next. Their fevers seemed coordinated, as if drifting from one baby's last breath into the next baby, like the tones of a xylophone. Their lungs filled, and the babies fought to breathe. Dr. Foote came often and worked with them, but his daughter had some missionary work to do for the church and couldn't return. Emily Sue, the first one to die after Minnie, died during the night as everyone slept. A dozen family members were there when Mollie died. When John Wilburn stopped breathing, the afternoon train was approaching. Christie imagined the crowd from the train swooping in just in time to witness the event, but with its three long mournful notes the train steamed on past. Only one of the four babies died in Christie's arms—James Lake, the strongest of them all, the last to go. The clock had just struck five, and James was still asleep, when the baby began fighting for air. The reverberations of the clock had masked the baby's gasps at first. Christie realized she wanted to be alone with her last dying baby in peace. She didn't wake James up.

Christie sat in the rocking chair, rocking in time with the pendulum of the clock and humming Mittens Dowdy's tune under her breath. The strength in the little body ebbed gradually. She held him until he was perfectly quiet and limp and his only movement came from the force of her own exhaled breath. She held her breath for as long as she could, then, and saw that he did not move again. She sat with him until the clock pinged the half hour.

When James saw the still baby placed under the outing flannel on the pillow beside him, like a gift, he eased himself up slowly and placed his hand on the form to see how warm it was. Christie looked away and began dressing. When she turned back, she saw James clutching the bedpost, his head down. She went to him and wrapped her arms around his shoulders. They could not speak for some time.

"It's all over," he mumbled.

"I've cried so much this week I can't cry anymore," she said finally, breaking away from him. She searched for a handkerchief.

"The worst thing that hurts is to see you hurt," he said, his back to her. He pulled on the heavy britches she had stitched from jeans cloth. "I'll go out to feed before breakfast," he said.

He laid the back log in the fireplace and built up the fire. Then he went out to the barn to feed the livestock. It was first light. Christie began building the fire in the stove, using a tin of coals from the fireplace. She poured water from the oak bucket into the large kettle and set it on to warm. Then, because the day was so chilly, she pulled on her long drawers. Her mother, who had been sleeping badly of late, slept on in the cold bedroom.

Christie had to wash the baby before she fixed James's breakfast. The water was slow. Impatiently she mixed up biscuit dough, taking flour from the bin in handfuls, without measuring. As Christie was rolling biscuits, Amanda arrived with her daughters, her hair frowzy and her buttons done up wrong. The girls' hair hung down without ribbons.

Amanda stared at the little form on the bed. The outing covered it entirely, like a napkin-covered dish on a table. Amanda held Christie and sobbed, but Christie couldn't respond. She felt used up, like a dish of butter. She pulled away from Amanda and methodically punched out a row of biscuits with her biscuit cutter. She greased the pan.

Without warning, Little Bunch, seeing that the baby bed was empty, jerked off the wrinkled oilcloth and went tearing into the folded-over bolster, kneading it—her face contorting and rigid and questioning until she found what she was looking for and her face brightened with the fervor of discovery. Before Amanda could stop her, Little Bunch had torn into a small hole in the bolster with her teeth. She ripped the ticking and went rummaging into the feathers, like a man sticking his arm up inside a cow to free a struggling calf. Her arm came out, feathers drifting in the air and clinging to her sleeve. She clutched a large wad of feathers.

"I knew it!" she said triumphantly, dropping the mass of feathers. A bird-nest shape landed on the floor. Her fist delved again into the bolster, tunneling like a mole. She pulled out another nest woven of feathers, even larger than the first.

"Feather crowns!" cried Amanda. "I should have known."

Christie felt the blood draining from her face and the room went dim. She started across the room to see the feather crowns, but her knees gave way.

"It's all right, Christie," Amanda said soothingly. "It means the babies are in Heaven."

24

Amanda fixed a black wreath with pine cones and dark-pink buckberries and a black bow with five tails hanging down. Lena stitched each baby's name in red on the loose tails, a color Amanda protested was too loud. She fastened the wreath to Christie and James's front door. Christie wouldn't go through the front door. She couldn't look at the wreath. One afternoon, she left through the back door and walked out through the fields, drinking in the spring air with its smells of growth and decay. Spring had trotted ahead of her, and now the first daisies were blooming, and the wind had blown the dandelion fluff about. The white clover was lusher than she had ever seen. She counted the new calves, their legs and tails still clean. The calves scampered curiously up to the fence to study her, then tore away in panic. Her breasts still ached, but she felt stronger, and far back in the fields alone, along fencerows she rarely visited, it was peaceful. Out here, she could cry as much as she wanted to and nobody would see.

The train didn't stop anymore. Now the train whistle was one long, mournful, unbroken note. Only a few curiosity seekers showed up now and again. For several days, neighbors had come to the house with food, and crowds of strangers arrived to pay their respects. Someone from town sent a wreath similar to Amanda's, and Mrs. Blankenship sent a bouquet of geraniums and snowballs that Amanda said must have been raised in a hothouse. Now Mr. Letcher brought Christie the letters from Dundee and left the piles of baby mail, as they called it, with Boone for his scrapbooks. James wouldn't look at the letters. Christie thought it pained him even more than it did her to know what people wrote. Mama went home to Dundee, her heart broken, she said.

The Wheelers were so behind in the spring work that Wad kept on the hired hands to help break new-ground and make other fields ready to set tobacco. When Christie ventured beyond the barn and saw the white canvas-covered beds of tobacco seedlings, she thought of marriage beds. Aunt Sophie's warning had turned out to be true. "You oughter go back to bed and build up your strength, gal," Wad told her. James said Christie didn't have to work out-of-doors. But she stayed out, avoiding the house. She worked in the garden, preferring to work alone, or with Nannie, although sometimes she did not hear Nannie babbling to her or notice the child's inquisitive face staring up at her. The boys followed the men out to the fields. Clint and Jewell were growing brown and hard and tall. She hardly knew them.

She planted beans—one, two, three, four, five. She planted a row of five hills, each with five seeds; five rows of tomatoes; five squash hills. She stared down at her fingers and counted them again and again, until she felt like cutting one off with the hatchet. A flower with five petals, a pink of some kind, was blooming behind the smokehouse, hiding there to trap her. She wouldn't tell James. He was lost in his work, spreading manure on the cornfield and plowing and planting. He came in and shoveled down his food, sank into deep, short naps, gave Nannie an absentminded pat on the head, hustled the boys off to the fields, stared into the fire on those nights that still held a chill. Occasionally he'd mutter "Goddamn," a word that shocked Christie as deep as her womb. But her own buoyancy met his curse with defiance.

"It was nigger milk," James said one night. He was cleaning out ashes from the fireplace, and the children were playing ball in the late spring light. "Nigger milk and cow's milk."

"I'm not listening to that," Christie said.

"It ain't natural."

"Well, I made all the milk I could."

"We oughter have picked two," James said. "And give 'em a chance."

"Which two?"

"You know which two."

"I made all the milk I could," she said.

"Everything was all or nothing," James said disgustedly. "Everybody wanted it to be the 'quintuplets.'" He said the word mockingly, emphasizing its oddness. Christie realized neither of them ever used the word. James went on, "People wasn't interested unless it was five. It was like something in the circus—something that had a name to it, like Siamese twins. We oughter kept two that very first day and sent the others out somewhere. Then none of this would have happened.

There wouldn't have been five all in one place, and nobody would have noticed them." He scraped the last of the ashes into the ash bucket. "I never oughter brought you here in the first place," he said, straightening up. "We needn't have left Dundee. Everything would have been different."

"No. It's my fault. I didn't take care of them good enough. Maybe I deserved to lose them."

She was full of sin. She and James had sinned, with their lusty and reckless indulgence. And as if that weren't enough, her desire had reached out to that absurd, cavorting Brother Cornett, who prattled about the earthquake as though it were a grand show that would entertain them. She had not been faithful. The Lord punished her for her lack of faith, her doubts, her blasphemy. She accepted her sin. She walked around with it. It kept her separate.

Christie couldn't explain the queer lightsomeness inside her. When she went out through the newly planted fields with the children and saw the newborn calves frisking after their mothers, she felt a surge of air lifting her. The throb in her breasts was beginning to subside, but there was a bursting feeling in her, something alive trying to get out. It wasn't like the frightfulness of having those babies inside her. It wasn't like Boone's tale about the woman who swallowed the tiny snake that grew big in her belly. It wasn't physical. It was an outlook, something directing her eyes so that they didn't miss anything. She searched out the coming irises and the blackberry lilies and the ubiquitous wild blackberries and gooseberries. She found little brown jugs, jack-in-the-pulpits, lady's slippers, buttercups, five different kinds of violets—some of them yellow and some white, not violet at all. She looked at everything in a new way. A sunset was like a theater curtain, all multi-colored with glorious lights. She noticed the slant of sun through the cracks in the barn planks, striping the stanchions and feed bins with gold paint. And in a certain light the canvas-covered tobacco beds seemed to be white fire.

And she saw things that seemed funny: Mr. Letcher sitting under the canopy of his new mail buggy like a preacher at a brush-arbor; Mrs. Willy ambling up the lane in that threadbare gingham dress and those falling-down stockings; the old bull in the pasture coming in Christie's direction, his baggage swinging—aiming at her, as though he were about to devour her with love.

IV

Dark-Fire

Summer 1900

1

ALMA BATTLED WEEDS ALONG THE GARDEN FENCEROW, SICKLING DOWN the burdock and jimson weed and sumac, daring any cat or dog to come near. The snakes scooted, double-S-ing into the thicket. Alma's wide feet were planted firmly on the ground in her new spring brogans—her "spreadin'-adder shoes," Wad called them. Once Alma had killed a spreading adder, thinking it was a copperhead, and Wad laughed at her for getting so scared. "A snake is a snake," Alma said.

Christie observed Alma's furious strength—the way she hauled water, or hoed the garden, or hitched up the mule, or shoveled manure into the spreader. Alma beat rugs as if she wanted to murder them.

"There ain't no time to set around for sorrow," she told Christie.

Determined to follow Alma's example, Christie worked steadily. Sometimes she didn't see James all day. She didn't miss him. She served his supper, washed his clothes, sent his dinner to him in the field at midday. She washed the children and brushed their teeth with frayed black-gum twigs, collected eggs from fussy hens, baked pies and bread, put out a wash on clear Mondays. She worked automatically through long mornings in the garden, hoeing vigorously and not even noticing the heat. She churned clabber into butter with a rhythm too fast for any song, sometimes too fast for the butter to gather properly. Often at the end of a day she was astonished to realize the hours had gone. Other times it seemed the day was lasting forever. But whenever a train went by, it jolted her memory and told the time for her. When the teakettle whistled, she held her ears, anticipating the train. She watched each train sauntering past, slowing down as it approached Hopewell. The noon express, though, rumbled straight through, with a single long, chilling note. One morning a freight train passed, and she saw a Negro standing on the coal car, tossing off coal. The black chunks tumbled down the embankment into the weeds. She saw the man the next morning walking along the bank with a scuttle, picking up the lumps of coal.

Christie welcomed the ripening blackberries, the baby-chick sound of bats in the barn beams when she opened the barn door, the carpet of white clover in the pasture, the daisies everywhere. Everything was a new wonder to her. She observed a pair of ducks settling on the pond; a pair of bluejays nesting above the wash-house; a turtle laying eggs in a dirt hole on the lane; a snakeskin stretched on the doorstep like a fine necklace left as a present. The dogwood was spread out through the woods, like thousands of lighted candles. With Nannie, she made a sweat garden—a hole lined with moss where they placed a clump of tiny blue flowers, a sprig of clover, and a row of minuscule seashells picked from the grit James bought for the chickens. Christie covered the little garden with a clear glass bowl that was broken on one edge. The garden looked like the candy garden inside the paperweight her father gave her mother one Christmas, the year Susan was born. In the mornings, Christie and Nannie watched the steam clear inside the glass bowl and reveal the greening moss, which had sent up little shoots with red seeds on the ends. Christie and Nannie made a pond garden, too, in another clear bowl. They filled the bowl with pond water and set it beside the wash-house. They watched mosquitoes hatch, then tadpoles. The tadpoles slowly grew frog feet. Little green plants like lilies, the size of pinheads, sprouted on the surface of the water. Christie dropped a blue button into the water and it sank to the bottom. Nannie said, "The button drowneded."

Nannie begged Christie to make new clothes for her doll, Miss Laney Bright. The doll was ugly and worn. "She needs a new dress," Nannie said, pulling at the tattered calico.

"No, ask Aunt Mandy. I ain't in a sewing frame of mind," Christie said. "And besides, that doll never sets still for me. She's too gigglesome."

Nannie splattered the air with giggles then. "Miss Laney Bright always sets still," she gasped. Nannie ran around the yard, so full of vigor that Christie thought her own amazed breath would fly out after her.

Boone made furniture for Nannie's dollhouse from candy wrappings the older children brought back from town. He made tables and chifforobes from the cardboard, and Amanda fashioned rugs from little scraps of wool and curtains from bits of lace. She made doll-bed covers from feed-sacks, and Boone made several clothes-pin dolls with painted faces. He had whittled the clothes-pins and then turned them into dolls. Christie wondered why he didn't whittle more realistic dolls instead of creating the clothes-pins first. A strange image came to mind: it was as though people were fashioned as trees and then got twisted and bent into believing they were human, with souls. Maybe that's what it was, she thought. We just have human features painted on us. But what are we to start with? she kept wondering. She clung to Nannie and Clint and Jewell. Laughing obliviously in their play, they seemed so fragile—like dry, rustling leaves that might burst into flames.

Nannie dressed kittens in doll clothes. She kept asking what had become of the five babies. Dead, they had looked like dolls to her. Arch told Nannie that her mama and papa were hiding the doll-babies until Christmas. He told Clint and Jewell their mama was crazy. Christie herself felt as though her mind were simply somewhere else, away from what concerned the men and women around her. She was comfortable charging through the season, letting the hard necessity of daily work carry her along. She didn't listen to the clatter around her: Alma and Amanda fussing; Alma yelling at Wad or the children; Wad teasing and growling; Thomas, when he was home, spouting his news of the people he'd seen. The glory that had rubbed off on him had not abated with the loss of the babies. After adding a line of teething powder and a line of nursing bottles to his wares, he had persuaded the manufacturers to print special tags, identifying them as the kind used by the Hopewell Quintuplets. "How do your customers know the bottles didn't kill the babies?" James asked Thomas angrily. "And they didn't live long enough to cut teeth, so where does this teething powder come in?"

Mostly, though, James was silent. He went about his work dutifully, with good sense. He treated the boys and Nannie with affection and humor, as if nothing had happened. Most of the time he treated Christie that way, too. She suspected he was suffering deep inside, but she didn't want to drive the hurt in further by mentioning it.

One June day he came in from working the corn—mad at the mule, mad at the bent tine on the cultivator, mad at the dogs. He said to Christie, while the children were still out finishing their night work, "They're saying we're glad those babies are gone."

"Who's saying that?"

"People at church, at the store. They saw how you didn't hardly cry at the funeral. They're saying we thought we were too good to have the funeral at our own church."

"Don't listen to talk like that," she said.

James sat on the hassock, opening and closing his pocketknife blade. He said, "When my daddy died, the women took care of the body, and Mack Pritchard's daddy built Daddy's coffin, and old Mrs. Culpepper fixed his clothes and helped Mammy line his coffin with sheets. But now Joseph said he heard 'em talking at the square about how we wouldn't bury our own babies—we had to go to a fancy funeral parlor."

"Jealousy," Christie said.

He shook his head and put away his knife. He went to the wash-stand in the kitchen and poured water in the wash pan. He started to splash water on his arms.

"Gossip," she said.

"Well, I've got to hold my head up in this place," he said, drying himself on the kitchen towel. Then he took her elbow and pulled her around to face him. "Remember what we promised when we moved here, how we were going to get along with all kinds?"

She squirmed, cringing from the dirt on his clothes, hating his sour breath, wishing for a moment she had never met him.

"It's still true," he said. "Don't you forget it."

"What do you want me to do, go bawling around the courthouse square? They'd say I was crazy. Or had hydrophobie. They'd go find me a madstone then!" She blurted out her words in rapid bursts, like spitting, the way she always did when he was mad at her.

"Don't you get sassy," said James, letting go.

She knew she should not talk back to her husband this way. But her bitterness at his authority drove deep in her, into a place where she saved such emotions, a place where they could grow into something useful. Abruptly, she went out the door, leaving him standing in the kitchen, waiting to be fed. She headed down the lane. The sun was low and would be setting clear.

She hadn't cried much at the funeral, it was true. Her grief was too deep. And it was hidden under the strange exhilaration she often felt—now, for instance, seeing the late evening light darken the line of cedar trees between the tobacco and the corn, turning them into a foreboding forest. At this time of day, everything in sight seemed so precious and fleeting, every flower head and grass stem on the ground and every bird soaring over the vast sky.

She could hardly believe the babies were dead. But then it was unbelievable that they had been born in the first place, and that so many people had come to see them, from so far away. The funeral was at the Central Methodist Church in Hopewell. Wad and Alma both wanted an additional service at their own, smaller church, saying it wasn't fair to Brother Jones for them to switch churches on him, but

Amanda and Boone both pointed out that Christie and James had been through enough and they should get this over with in one big service that everybody could attend.

At first Christie hadn't wanted to go to the funeral parlor at all. She was afraid of what Mr. Mullins had planned. She dreaded seeing the babies treated by his unusual methods. She was afraid they wouldn't seem dead. They might look so alive she wouldn't be able to bear it. But Mama, understanding more than anyone else what Christie was going through, gathered all her resources and took charge. She fixed up Christie's clothes and sewed on some buttons, and she assigned tasks to the children. Dulcie blacked Christie's boots. The older girls draped the furniture—the beds, the chairs, the safe, the chifforobes—all in clean sheets, and they stopped the clocks at both houses. More food arrived. Mama complained that it was wrong not to have the bodies at home to sit up with all night.

"They took those babies away from us," she said.

After being looked after for so long, Christie seemed to have forgotten her own direction. Things went on around her all that week. Her papa and brothers and sisters arrived on the train during the night. Luther and Jack were nearly grown. Eunice and Emily were taller and more alike. But Papa still had his hacking cough. It worked its way into the familiar household sounds—the clock, the rocking chair, the stove. Christie could hardly bear to look at Amanda, whose own sorrow had subdued her. Amanda herded the small children out of the way, promising them pieces of damson pie if they wouldn't eat it point first, which was bad luck. Her eyes were swollen and her hair unkempt.

The Mullins establishment, with its ornate, expensive furnishings, Persian carpets, and dark woodwork, swallowed up the family. They had never been in such a place. Walking on a rich rug patterned with peacocks and yellow trees made them all self-conscious. The babies, sealed inside a small glass case, were on display on a table in the large front parlor, which Mr. Mullins called the Slumber Room. He had draped the whole room in curtains the color of dried blood. Behind the case, like the box a present came in, was a brass-handled oak chest, the receptacle for the glass case.

Seeing the babies for the first time shocked her into stillness; they no longer seemed to be her flesh and blood. They were objects, painted pink, in identical dresses, white with lace and tatting—fine handiwork. Christie could not recall who had made the dresses. She and James had seen dead people before, and always there was a lifelessness in them that was restful. The faces always seemed angelic, as if they were about to smile, as if all effort used in frowning and confronting life had relaxed and left only peace. But the babies looked tight and contorted, their little features frozen like knots on fence posts. Their expressions were painted in place. Boone said later the babies looked like something petrified.

"And they'll stay that-a-way?" James asked Mr. Mullins incredulously.

"Yes, Mr. Wheeler. They're preserved from decay. And as long as they're in that glass case they'll always be as you see them, your precious babes. If the air doesn't hit them, they can't go back to dust. They'll be that way till the end of time, or till the air hits them."

"I never saw the like," James said, fumbling at his cuff links.

Christie pitied her husband. He seemed uncomfortable in his best suit and collar. She felt like a bird perched on a tree outside, looking in the window. Those weren't her babies plopped on that tatted pillow in the Slumber Room.

"I hope you understand why I insisted on keeping the little angels here," said Mr. Mullins. "Everybody will be able to come here, and it will be the most convenience for you." He turned to leave the room. "I'll leave you two for a little while, before I open the doors to the rest of the family."

When they were alone with the babies, James and Christie stood quietly for a moment, staring. James held her closely and they both cried then. She was aware they were standing as stiff as if they were posed for a photograph. Outside, they heard roaring, the noise of an enormous crowd.

"They don't look right without their bonnets," Christie said. "And Minnie's not in the middle. She's on the outside. She's supposed to be in the middle."

Mr. Mullins had apparently left them bonnetless to show off his undertaking skills. The babies' heads were like carved wood. Their sleeves were pulled up to show their wrists, like peeled sticks. They still wore their bracelets. Their little fingers curved like bug legs.

"Why?" Christie sobbed. "Why did they have to die?"

In the two and a half days before the funeral service, the register album was signed by almost everybody in town. But their signatures were mingled among those of a much larger force of strangers. The train brought people from Louisville, St. Louis, Memphis, and from places even farther away. Someone from California signed the album, and several people traveled in a group from Texas. People still wanted to say they had seen the babies—dead or alive, it seemed not to matter.

Mr. Mullins provided a curtained room off to the side of the

Slumber Room, where the family could retreat, but Christie kept pulling back the curtain to face the people—wanting to see who was there, wanting to see the babies through their curious eyes. She was on display then, too, like a criminal waiting to be hanged. Amanda had washed and ironed Christie's handkerchiefs, but she hardly used them.

Each day at dinnertime Wad drove Christie and James home, where they sat down to the feast neighbors had left. Members of the family took turns being with Christie and James and taking care of the children. The smaller children ran down the corridors and up the stairways of the funeral parlor, sprung loose with glee at their unusual surroundings.

Everyone in the family was dressed up in their dark winter clothes, even though spring was coming on. All the Wheeler men appeared awkward in their suits, and Christie knew they worried about neglecting their work. They stayed out on the street talking much of the time. Crops, no doubt, Christie thought. Wad and his sons traveled back and forth to the farm, tending to the livestock or to Mammy Dove. Boone made two brief trips in, and both he and Mammy Dove attended the funeral.

At night, Wad took Alma and the children home, leaving Amanda to stay through the night with James and Christie at the Mullins establishment. But Christie wanted to go home to sleep.

"Somebody needs to stay," Christie's father argued. "Ye don't have them in your own house to watch over, and something might happen to them here." He was hacking more, and his face had a pallor.

"The Bible says never to leave the corpse untended," said Mama.

"Where does it say that?" asked Christie.

"That was Jesus," Mama said. "He busted out and went right up to heaven when nobody was looking."

"Well, wouldn't that be the finest thing that could happen?" Christie wanted to know.

"Hush, Christie," said James. "We'll stay."

"What if the Devil got them instead?" said Papa. "Or what if somebody was to steal them?" Later he said, "That fancy casket they ordered from Memphis must have cost a fortune. We could have cut one out of pine. I could have made ye some nice brass handles. Or wrought iron. Or we could have made five caskets for what that one cost."

"It's free," Christie said.

Mama said she would have lined the inside with some bleached domestic and trimmed it on the outside with balls of fringe held down by leaden rose-beaded tacks. "A paper of tacks and a couple of yards of domestic is all you'd need to outfit a baby casket." Mama studied the babies for the hundredth time. "I believe they're a-laying antigodling," she said. "They ain't lined up straight."

"I can't see it," said Christie. "But Minnie oughter be in the middle."

"I never heard of a thing like this a-going on so long," Papa said with characteristic exasperation. "Won't they rot?"

"Hush, Lake," said Mama.

"Go on back to Dundee, Papa," said Christie wearily.

She thought she would fly to pieces. Strangers approached her with awe, but her parents found fault at every opportunity. And she thought the Wheelers had to have something to fuss about all the time. That week, Alma had other troubles, for Jimmie Lou had taken up with Herschel Long, a young man from town who hung around the funeral parlor as if he couldn't pay enough respects to the family.

"Courting at a time like this!" Wad hissed to Alma.

"Jimmie Lou ain't none of your business," Alma told him. "If Thomas wants to do something about it, he can."

"Why, Herschel's a short feller, and he's got little-bitty ears and he's already losing his hair," said Wad. "I bet he can't work a lick."

"Well, I expect not," said Alma. "A feller with little-bitty ears couldn't hear you tell him what to do."

Amanda said, "He's a nice-looking boy, Wad. And he's got manners."

"I don't know how she's going to please a town boy," said Alma with a sigh. "He'll be wanting his fine shirts boiled and starched, and no telling what he'll be wanting to eat. Those town folks want things rich, with a lot of oysters and too much meat."

Christie felt as powerless as she had in the winter, struggling against her cumbersome weight. She was heavy and tired. Her breasts hurt. She still felt a misery place deep inside, where the babies had been. Now under that glass, undisturbed, they lay rigidly on their backs, their arms bowed stiffly at their sides. In life, they had lain in varied positions, heads turned in any direction, arms working, their noises soft and pulsating. Mr. Mullins had accentuated the babies' smallness. The dresses were pulled tight, and the babies' necks were bare and red. Their heads were lacquered like the simulated hair on a bisque doll, the shine of their scalps seeping through like light through a lace curtain. Without the bonnets, they looked cold, and more than once Christie had the impulse to cover them up. She could not comprehend her grief. She thought of Nannie lining up her clothes-pin dolls. There was a connection, she thought, as if life were a simple circle, with events occurring and recurring, and when you encountered an event the second time you had learned to feel its pain—as though when you were grown, events might be unbearable, while for a child they meant nothing at all; they were just hollow rehearsals.

On the morning of the funeral, Mr. Mullins located Christie in the reception room. He seemed agitated by some news.

"I have somebody that wants to see you, Mrs. Wheeler," he said.

"Bring them on in," she said. "If I've talked to one, I've talked to five thousand."

"I'm afraid I can't do that, ma'am. You'll have to come with me."

"Who is it?"

"It's a nigger that said she worked for you."

"Mittens!" Christie was so overwhelmed, imagining the woman's sweet, sympathetic face, that she had to sit down. "Can't you bring her here?"

"It wouldn't do, Mrs. Wheeler."

Christie felt the clarity of anger for the first time since she lost the babies. Mittens was more her friend than any of these strangers, any of the townfolks—even some of her family, she thought, as her eyes lit on Wad and Boone and Joseph. But she stifled these thoughts and followed Mr. Mullins.

Mittens was waiting in a little storeroom in the back of the immense house. She was sitting on a wooden bench with her legs crossed and her arms folded. She wore a felt hat with a faded ribbon tied around the crown. And she had on a good, freshly ironed, figured dress. When Mr. Mullins left them alone in the storeroom, Christie burst into tears, remembering her babies at this woman's breasts. When Mittens stood up to hug Christie, Christie could feel how Mittens' breasts were smaller now. The two women both seemed aware that their breasts touched as they hugged.

"I wanted to see them so bad," Mittens said, as they moved apart. "But that white man, he said there was so many peoples he couldn't allow a time for the colored to come in. He say there was peoples from all over the world."

"It don't look like them," Christie sobbed. "It's not my babies."

"I needs to see them if I pays my respects," Mittens said. "I's so sorry, Miz Christie." She dabbed at Christie's face with a rag.

Mittens picked up a napkin-covered plate from the floor. "I brought you some of them angel biscuits like you like. And a bit of cake."

Christie couldn't speak. Mittens said, "I'll tell you what was going through my mind these last two days. I was thinking how the Lord is unfair sometimes, and they'll try to tell you it's not so, but it *is* so, and the thing is, Miz Christie, is what you say back to the Lord finally. Do you say, That's all right, Jesus, I deserve to lose my babies? Or do you straighten up and rare back and say, Lord, you won't get me down that easy—jest watch? You'll get by, Miz Christie. I know you will."

"That's the kindest thing anybody's said to me, Mittens," said Christie. Impulsively, she took Mittens' arm. "Come on," she said.

Carrying the plate of biscuits and cake, she led Mittens through the hall, through a room that opened into the Slumber Room from the back, and before Mittens could realize what was happening, Christie had taken her right into the Slumber Room, which was full of visitors. She led Mittens straight to the glass case. Mittens began sobbing and wailing, and Mama and Amanda rushed to her.

"Here's Mittens!" cried Mama. "Oh, we missed you!"

The loud, happy greetings Mittens got from Mama and Amanda silenced the rest of the room. Everybody stopped talking and stared at the women's mingled sorrow and joy.

"What does she think she's doing?" Christie heard Wad say. Did he mean her or Mittens? She didn't care. Mittens' black cheeks, shining and wet, glistened like exposed hearts.

Later that day, during the singing at the end of the service, one man's voice was noticeable above the rest. He sang as though he were a heifer being led by a rope. "That's one of those men that tromped on your March flowers," Amanda whispered into Christie's ear.

So many of the people greeting Christie after the service were familiar. Mrs. Blankenship passed the casket and made a beeline toward Christie, grabbing her in a sisterly hug. Mrs. Blankenship's face was warm and wet. Her hat had several tiers of ruffles and feathers on it, like an elaborate nest made by a buzzard. The neighbors seemed awkward and bashful, as they mumbled "We're real sorry" or "They look so natural."

"They look so real," Mrs. Willy said. "They look like they might pucker up and commence to bawling any minute."

Mrs. Willy blubbered, lingering so long over the babies that her daughter, visiting from Maple Grove, came forward to usher her away.

For more than three hours after the service, people filed past the sealed-glass case to view the little bodies. The congregation spilled out of the large uptown church. The crowds extended all around the courthouse square. What Christie remembered later was how cloudy it had been that day. And she remembered James standing with Nannie beneath a dogwood tree. He leaned over and lifted Nannie up to his shoulders so she could reach the flowers on the tree. And Christie remembered Amanda marveling to everyone at the supper table that night, as if they hadn't been at the funeral, "Why, that church was so fine, they turned on all their electric lights right in the middle of the day. They just had to show them off, I reckon."

When those electric lights flickered on, Christie had had the impression that the deaths of her children were a grand show at an opera house. Amidst all the sorrow and tears surrounding her, she noticed the little beam of happiness on Thomas's face. And then she thought she saw it on everyone's face—a faint little tinge of excitement and wonder and privilege, as the town shared in a tragic drama. They were all thrilled by the shudder of death and giddily aware of the glow of national attention. Later, at home, she realized she had felt it too.

At home, there was food everywhere. Christie had never seen such a fine assortment of food, more bountiful than any church dinner. Townspeople and neighbors brought what Alma later said amounted to a wagonload of food—watermelon-rind pickles, chess pie, boiled custard, angel-food cake, coconut cake, chicken salad, fried chicken, ham, dried mutton, fruit salad, poached pears, spiced plums, cold slaw, gooseberry jam, tongue sandwiches, sweet-potato pie, banana pudding, blackberry pie, guinea hen, quail, dressed eggs, salt-rising bread, pickled souse, egg bread, soda biscuits, chicken-and-dumplings, damson pies, peach pies, fried pies. The chess pie and the salt-rising bread had been sent by Mrs. Crittenden, from Crittenden's Inn, where the St. Louis newspaperman had eaten dinner.

Now, a month later, as Christie walked back in the fields, leaving James waiting for his supper, she thought about all that food. So much of it had ruined. The fruit pies and the meat kept the longest, but the banana pudding soured and the chess pie dried out. The waste was heartbreaking. She didn't want to think about the funeral. But parts of that week stole back to her from time to time, and somehow they fit into a whole like pieces of Nannie's jigsaw puzzle. Those stiff, lifeless, inhuman things in their glass case—maybe, after all, they had come from the Devil. It had slowly grown on her that perhaps her original intuition had been right—that the Devil had been at work, entering her, disguising himself as innocent, sweet babies, using her mother love to promote his evil. It was as though Mr. Mullins's art had laid bare the Devil's intention, by making the babies look so hard and dry. Her thoughts were hard, she knew, but it was easier to let go of her babies if she thought this way. Yet the babies were her own. She had been blessed as well as cursed with them. But maybe it had been best to lose them, just as it might be better to run from their memory, out into the fields where she could release some of the poison that afflicted her.

The last of the sunlight made yellow blankets on the far field, the one that sloped slightly toward the South. She descended into the creekbed, where a few patches of water from the spring runoff remained in the yellow gravel. She picked a flower from a bank of red honeysuckle, snipped off the end with her teeth, and sucked out the honey. She noticed an elderberry bush in full bloom, a young one that had not bloomed last year. She intended to gather its berries for jelly later in the summer.

She climbed out of the creek and headed out through a field of timothy. Suddenly a fox went trotting through the ankle-high grass. She froze. The fox didn't see her, but his bushy white-tipped tail waved like a greeting. He lowered his tail and moved slowly, his gaze on some slight movement in the thick grass. She watched, breathlessly, for a long time as the fox slowly stalked a mouse or some other small creature in the grass. He pounced quickly and missed. Like a cat, the fox seemed to pretend he was only playing then, as though he knew someone was watching and he didn't want to seem to have failed. She realized that she wasn't afraid, and that she was creeping toward him, to see how close she could get. She had never done such a thing with a wild animal before, but she felt an unaccustomed boldness. She crept so quietly, like a fox herself. The fox made several comical leaps, high and long, snouted the grass, then continued on his way. His path described a broken crescent on the hill, as he disappeared at times into a furrow or depression, then reappeared farther along. She continued following. If she could get close enough to touch him, she would reach to pet his head, stroke his thick fur. She longed to touch him.

The fox was red, with a new glistening summer-gray coat sprouting through the shedding red. His nose was sharp and delicate, his throat and bib white, his front legs dark. Shadows of stripes lurked in his tail. The backs of his ears were dark triangles. She imagined him going to his den, carrying a rabbit or mouse to the little ones. Or was the fox a mother? Somehow, she thought he behaved like a man.

Suddenly someone shouted from behind her. She jumped, and the fox streaked across the pasture and bounded straight through the fence.

"Why didn't you run?" cried Wad. "Law, girl, you'll be chewed to pieces if you go around fooling with wild varmints! If I'd had my gun I'd 'a' got him."

Wad had come out of nowhere. The fox had disappeared, like the sun over the horizon.

2

CHRISTIE HUNG THE FEATHER BEDS OUTSIDE, INCLUDING THE BOLSTER the babies had slept on. She washed all the floors and aired the house out. The spring breeze cleared out the weeks of sour smells that had settled in the house. She washed the quilts. She washed the lace curtains and stretched them across frames studded with sharp, tiny pins. She retrieved the family's summer clothes from barrels stored in the stable and washed and starched and ironed them. She washed and folded all the diapers and blankets to save for Maggie's baby, which was due soon.

She ate little and started to thin out. A spring tonic of sassafras tea purified her blood, and she felt stronger. She helped James replant two acres of corn that had washed out in a hard rain. They worked silently, as if they were both afraid their grief would come pouring out and flood the field.

But she felt she had been drained of every fluid and couldn't produce more tears, just as she hadn't been able to make enough milk for all five babies. She woke up in the night sometimes, feeling them again, trying to identify which one was tugging at her breast and which ones were squirming nearby, blindly crawling over her belly. In another dream, she was covered with writhing snakes.

Everyone blamed the changeable weather for the babies' illness. Alma blamed Dr. Foote as well, saying he didn't care for them as closely as Hattie Hurt would have. Mama declared the five little ones just couldn't live; there was too much against them. They were handled too much—just loved to death, she said. Christie kept thinking she shouldn't have let so many strangers pick them up. She should have let that woman in Ulster who had lost her baby take one of them. She should have given away three of them and nursed the two strongest ones. She had paid too much attention to the visitors. The excitement strained her milk.

Her mind refused to give her peace. Why had they been born to her? Why had they been taken from her? The newspaperman from St. Louis said it had never happened before that a woman had five babies, at least not in America. But Boone said it had happened in other countries—Africa and India. What was she to make of that? If it had never happened here before, then it must be a token of some kind, as people had been saying all along. She had been chosen as a vessel, they said. She heard that preachers were talking about her babies, just as all those preachers at Reelfoot had rambled on about the coming earthquake. At church, Brother Jones talked about the hand of God removing the babies and how they were called home for a higher purpose. And how it had to be. And how it was for the best. People had to make something out of the unusual, she thought; it had to mean something.

If they were a sign of something, she thought, then their deaths did not necessarily mean the story was over, or that the event they foretold had yet occurred. Maybe something was still about to happen. The thought hit her from time to time like a fresh nightmare.

"What do you make of all this tongue-wagging?" she asked Amanda.

Lately, Christie and Amanda seemed to watch each other from a distance, as if they couldn't bear to come closer and speak because they would collapse from sorrow. Amanda seemed agitated, as though she believed somehow the fate of the babies was her fault. But at the same time, she blamed her husband for meddling.

"Well?" Christie asked. "What are the babies a sign of?"

They were standing near Alma's garden, and Amanda's face was shaded by a lilac bush. The blooms had faded to brown.

"I'm afraid to say," Amanda said. Her egg basket was at her hip. Nannie was squatting next to a chicken.

"What is it?" cried Christie. "Is it those feather crowns?"

"I don't know." Amanda's body seemed to have a light tremor. "My Aunt Puss used to beat her pillers ever morning so they wouldn't form death crowns."

"Do you believe the babies were evil? Tell me."

"No, Christie. Heavens, no. Don't you think that." Amanda touched Christie's shoulder. She was shorter than Christie and she had to reach up. "Those crowns are a good sign. It means they're in Heaven."

Amanda set down her egg basket and embraced her. When Christie saw Nannie peering up at them curiously, she moved away from Amanda. Nannie went on playing, jingling a leather string of metal doodads her grandpapa had made in his blacksmith shop. Amanda continued, in a low voice, "Whatever it means, you just be proud, Christie."

"I do feel proud. That's the trouble." She turned aside, loosening herself from Amanda's hand.

Christie's mother wrote from Dundee that a neighbor had found an egg with a perfect cross etched on it. "I know it means something," Mama wrote. "Your papa don't believe in signs. But he was impressed by that hen egg."

James was skeptical. "I've heard of calves born with their tails tied in knots," he said. "And I've heard of madstones found in the stomachs of deer. And people are all the time finding signs on eggs. But I don't think we know what signs mean."

"But why did all this happen to us?" she repeated. "Why were the babies taken from us?"

"I don't know. I've tried to figure it out, but I don't think we're meant to know."

"You don't think having five babies at once means anything?"

"If it does, we don't know what, and maybe we're not supposed to."

"Then why would God even write out a sign if He doesn't want us to know?" she asked. "Why would He even bother?"

"It's a test," said James. "He wants us to trust in Him and stop trying to figure everything out."

"It plagues my mind," said Christie. "Everything is a question."

"It's better just to let it be," he said.

"Anything Brother Jones can't explain, he lays it onto God's 'mysterious ways,'" Christie said angrily. "But I believe God gives us credit for more intelligence than that."

"That always was the trouble with you, Christianna Wilburn," James said teasingly. "The way you always ask questions. But that's why I married you, I reckon. I never knew what I might learn." He grinned, but his grin had a twist that made it seem about to curve into a heavy frown.

They were in bed, and he turned the light out then. He rolled toward her, running his hand down her arm. She pushed her feet up against his shins. She felt tired. He held his hand there against her elbow, and she grew relaxed. When her side became uncomfortable, she turned away from him but readjusted her feet so they touched his. They went to sleep that way, night after night, neither making more than a tentative, half-hearted effort to reach out, a gesture that died in the middle. Still, lying there together was comforting, and she thought it was a small but strong link between them. That little touch at night was their acknowledgment of each other's pain and their substitute for talking. She felt no desire for him. The urge was dead in her, like a worn-out spider in the fall that prepares to dry up and die when the winter cold hits.

But despite her grief, she did feel grateful to be herself, and to have James and their three remaining children. When she sat in church and listened to Brother Jones preach (he mentioned the babies every Sunday), she felt important. She dressed somberly for church and tried not to smile. It was a contradiction, she knew, that she should feel so empty with sorrow, yet so keenly alive that every speck of creation jumped out at her with a brilliant vividness. She didn't know if James felt anything like this. She watched him from the yard, working with the animals—loading up piglets to sell at the stockyard, or turning the muley cow out to pasture, or pouring a pan of milk for the barn cats. She'd see him with Luke, the collie dog—his mouth moving, talking to the dog in earnest conversation. He didn't stalk around on his tom-walkers anymore.

The tobacco came along. The fragile seedlings sprang up beneath the yards of canvas, drank in the trapped moisture like thirsty babies, and took off in a open-armed stretch toward the light. In the field, she helped set the plants in the carefully cultivated hills—mounds like breasts. Everywhere Christie saw mistaken reflections. Sometimes in a chance arrangement of objects, she could see those searching mouths, a bubble forming in the corner of one. When she happened upon a nest of gaping baby robins in the red-haw tree at the corner of the smokehouse, for an instant she saw five of them, in bonnets and long dresses.

One day in early summer, the men cut hay all morning and raked it into windrows in the afternoon. Threatening clouds forced them to work frantically to get the hay in before it rained. After supper, the children went to bed, and James left with a lantern to finish hauling in the hay. Christie got the clabber ready for the next day's churning. She checked the supply of wood for tomorrow's cooking, and she made a trip to the outhouse in the moonlight. The moon and a star near it were shining, but clouds were rolling in. The moon seemed to race behind the clouds, popping out intermittently in a game of hide-and-go-seek. The grass was wet. A cat sat crouched on a rock near the outhouse. Christie missed the dog that had been hanging around since spring, the dog Thomas had brought home. One of Alma's boys had found him on the creek bank, behind some rocks, where he had crawled off to die. He had always been there to greet her when she went out the door. He had been eager to see her and happy to get scraps, but he didn't ask anything more of her. Why did the dog have to die too? For a moment, a hot fountain of rage spewed up in her. She fought it down.

A misty rain was beginning, but she knew the men would keep working. She saw their lanterns in the far field, moving occasionally as the wagons wobbled down the lane to new positions. She could see lamplight up at Wad's house. On the surface, everything seemed so normal, just the way it had always been—children sleeping, women cleaning up and doing night work, men working late in the fields.

Back indoors, she cleaned a lamp and filled it with coal oil. It was full dark now and she needed the light. She set the lamp on the table next to the bed, in their old bedroom. The front room was open now only on Sundays. Impulsively, she opened the chifforobe and began searching behind James's Sunday hat for the knotted scarf she had hidden. She unknotted it and spread it out. The two crowns seemed smaller than before. A few feathers had loosened, but the weaving was unmistakably tight, like bird nests. She had heard of feather crowns in the old days. Granny Wilburn had spoken of feather crowns, but Christie had not been old enough to pay attention. Before her mother left for Dundee, she told Christie she hadn't seen any feather crowns since she was a little girl herself. If they were in a person's pillow, it was a sign the person was going to die, Mama said. But Amanda had told Christie that when a crown was found after death, it meant the person had gone to Heaven. Christie had the impression the crowns were something celestial, from the Bible. The angels had feather wings, but she could not remember any pictures of angels who wore crowns of any sort. Sometimes they had halos. Sometimes Jesus had a halo. Probably the feather crowns of Heaven were made of angel wing-feathers— the downiest, softest feathers closest to the skin. Feather crowns had to mean something good, from Heaven. They had to mean her babies were in Heaven. An angel had left the crowns, she thought, the way a fairy would leave a nickel for a child's tooth.

She recalled Little Bunch's wild eyes when she dug into the bolster. Where had she seen that child's wild eyes before? She braced herself against the bedpost as she remembered Little Bunch's tantrum at Reelfoot. Everybody thought she had been seized with the spirit of the Lord, for so many people that day were falling over, overcome with the spirit, writhing in their rapture, as if their bodies could hardly bear the ecstasy. And that day, a fellow had said something about a crown. Christie remembered a man on a platform, a curtain behind him parting. She remembered Little Bunch's eyes going wild—then or earlier that day?

James couldn't stop her asking questions. He wanted to trust blindly, close his eyes to the past, go forward without reference to the babies. But she wanted to know where they fit in, where the phenomenon belonged in the catalogue of the world's wonders. It still puzzled her deeply that a person such as she—only a farmer's wife, in a place virtually unknown—could produce a phenomenon that could be of significance to the entire world, like a star shining with such brilliance that people could see it everywhere. But if it were so special, so rare, then her blame for having lost the babies was profoundly greater.

She thought she heard a voice calling her. She quickly knotted the scarf over the feathers and hid the bundle in the chifforobe.

3

One morning in June, Henry's wife, Maggie, went into labor with their second child. Christie was in front of the wash-house stirring sheets in the wash kettle when Amanda came to tell her that Maggie's water had broken. Henry had gone to get Hattie Hurt, and Mrs. Willy was already there. That woman could smell a birth coming a mile off, Christie thought.

"Maggie had a hard time with her first one," Amanda said. She had on a new bonnet made of scraps Christie recognized from one of Alma's everyday dresses. The material was dull gray shepherd checks, but Amanda had trimmed it with yellow rickrack.

"I'll be on directly," said Christie. "Soon as I finish this washing."

"You don't want to go, do you?" asked Amanda.

"Well, I oughter. They expect me, after all everybody done for me."

"You don't have to, Christie. We'll manage."

Christie didn't reply, and Amanda left. Outside the door, Nannie was playing with some little rubber animals Thomas had brought her—a cat, dog, snake, horse, and bird. She was floating them in a bowl of water. Her doll clothes were in another bowl of water—soaking, she had explained. "My younguns just get filthy," she said.

Christie carried more buckets of water to the wash kettle and built up the fire. She boiled sheets and punched them down and stirred them angrily, then lifted them dripping into the wash-house, where she whipped them through two bluing-tinged rinse waters before wringing them out. Her heart felt as heavy as the sopping sheets. As she wrestled a wet sheet through the wringer, she glanced up to see Dulcie and Jimmie Lou standing in the doorway. Dulcie was barefooted, and Jimmie Lou had a daisy pinned to the side of her head.

"Mama told us to watch Nannie," said Dulcie. "Mama said you might forget to watch her."

"She said you was to go up to Maggie's with some baby clothes," said Jimmie Lou.

The daisy clung to Jimmie Lou's dark hair like a spider. Dulcie had the same fat nose as her sister, but she was fair-haired, with lighter eyes.

"You girls go on home. Nannie and me are doing all right." Christie tugged the sheet while cranking the wringer handle.

"I wanted to carry Nannie to the creek to look for crawfish," said Dulcie, bending over to hug Nannie. "Mama won't let us watch a baby be borned."

"She said if we ever saw it, we wouldn't never want to have a baby," said Jimmie Lou. She had carefully tightened her blouse into her skirt to accentuate her youthful figure, Christie noticed. Jimmie Lou's eyes were shaped like peach seeds, and her top teeth stuck out in front.

Somewhere inside the wash-house a cricket was chirping—a sign of good luck, Christie thought. It was true that she was forgetful. Last week she had left Nannie playing with stick dolls beside the wash kettle while she went behind the house to hang out the wash. When she remembered and tore around the corner of the house to see if Nannie was all right, the child wasn't there. After a frantic minute, she found her behind the henhouse, pulling up her drawers.

"Don't you get out of my sight!" Christie cried.

"I had to river." Nannie wriggled out of her reach.

Now, as Nannie swished her hands in one of the rinse tubs, Christie said to Dulcie, "Nannie's helping me wash." Clint and Jewell were setting tobacco with the men. She had Nannie. She couldn't be without Nannie. "Both of you girls oughter be out hoeing tobaccer," said Christie sharply. "If it wasn't washday I'd be in the tobaccer patch myself."

"I ain't working tobaccer today," said Jimmie Lou. "Besides, they're nearly done."

"Jimmie Lou's sweetheart's coming," Dulcie said. "And it ain't even Sunday."

"You better be careful, Miss Priss," Christie said, her voice faltering. "You better watch out who you're slipping off with."

"I don't reckon it's up to you," Jimmie Lou said with a smirk.

Christie took hold of Jimmie Lou. "Don't you talk back to me, young lady." She shook Jimmie Lou's shoulders. "What is it? What's the matter with everybody?"

"Quit grabbing me! That hurts."

Christie felt like slapping Jimmie Lou, but she let go. She noticed a hen scratching in the hard dirt in the side yard, and she thought she heard it crow like a rooster. She looked around for a stick, ready to thrash it. But the hen hadn't crowed, she decided, when a rooster sauntered into view.

"That rooster's begging for a place on the dinner table," she mumbled. She'd pluck those fine feathers gladly.

As the sisters walked away, Christie threw a rock at another pesky chicken in the petunia bed. The flowers had had showy heads all month. Sometimes strangers still came by and helped themselves to flowers or such souvenirs as they could find. With Nannie following, she started hanging out the sheets. Nannie flung dishrags and the children's underwear onto the thorny bushes. The sun was growing hot, and Christie needed her pale blue sunbonnet with the deep brim, but it was in the dirty clothes. She loosened the dark bonnet she had on. Her hair was damp and oily. Nannie's hair was fine as spider threads and growing long. Months ago, Christie had wanted it to grow long enough to plait, so she could twist the plaits around and pin them up in a little crown on Nannie's head, but now she didn't want to see any crowns. Nannie's hair was almost the same color as Mollie's. Mollie's hair was straight, but Emily's hair had a slight curl to it, a little wave that would have been easy to fix when she grew older.

Christie squeezed a pair of blue-jeans britches till her knuckles were white. She finished three washings of jeans britches and had dinner ready when James and the boys came in to eat. They were hot and hungry, and the little boys ate intently, like their father. She gave them all more chicken and biscuits. They didn't notice that she didn't eat. A fly had drowned in the milk gravy, and at first she thought it was a raisin. She dipped it out with a spoon and flung it out the back door.

"Hurry, boys," James said. "We got to get back to work."

"My old bones is weary," Clint said, in a manly way that made Christie hoot abruptly.

"We ain't got time to take a nap today," James said, draining the last of his buttermilk.

He went out the door with an arm on the shoulders of each son, herding them back to the field. Using a white tablecloth, Christie covered the chicken and potatoes and beans to keep for supper.

Outside, she dumped the rinse water from the wash onto the flower beds. As she was gathering in the sheets that were dry, Alma appeared. Alma might have been a lot like Jimmie Lou when she was younger, Christie realized. She could see Jimmie Lou's haughtiness reflected in Alma's practical authoritativeness.

"Maggie's doing good," Alma said. "It's a little girl. She's got a mark on her head, but Hattie says it'll leave. I'm glad old Foote didn't get in on this one."

When Christie didn't reply, Alma continued, reporting the details of the delivery. Christie nodded, as if Alma were talking about a load of stovewood. Alma caught the edge of the sheet Christie was trying to fold over. Together they folded it and matched the edges, then folded it again.

"You're thinning out," Alma said to her. "You don't want to lose that weight too fast, or you'll have low blood."

"I'm strong. I've always been stout as a mule." What did Alma care? And how did she know how much Christie ate? Christie slapped the folded sheet down in her basket and yanked at the next one on the line.

Alma removed her bonnet and aired out her hair for a moment, then clapped the bonnet back on. She said, "When I had my second one, I thought to my soul I never was going to get back to feeling like I oughter. I think I got up too quick."

"I thought I heard you say Jimmie Lou was an easy baby."

"No, Jimmie Lou was the third one. There was one between Thurman and her that died."

"I didn't know that."

"Oh, it was born dead. It didn't take on no personality. We didn't even put its name in the graveyard. It didn't have a name."

"I didn't know about that."

"It was a long time back. I got right up and went on back to work. I didn't feel good, and I wasn't much 'count, but I had to keep from thinking."

"No use thinking—that's what James says," said Christie, reaching for a pair of James's drawers. They were still damp, so she left them hanging. "He says worry is time throwed away."

Alma shook her head and stared in the direction of the smoke-house. "Thomas ain't never said one word about that baby since it happened. He goes off and forgets everything here." She touched her bonnet. "Well, I can't stand here all day, working up the past. I've got enough younguns to keep up with. And Thomas don't care if the boys get in trouble. Thurman's going to turn out bad. I declare to my time, this whole country—all the way from here to the Mississippi River and back—is gone plumb crazy. My old mammy laying in her bed and missing the pot and won't eat what's put before her, and Boone's so trifling he decides he ain't going out-of-doors because it makes him sneeze, and Mandy claiming she's too good to get out in the fields because the sun might hurt her complexion, and Wad carrying her around on a piller." Alma sighed.

"Did Thomas give Thurman a whipping?" Christie asked. She knew that last Saturday night Thurman had got ahold of some whiskey. He and a bunch of other boys went to town and got loud and wild.

Alma snorted. She said, "Thomas is just about as useful as a stinkbug when it comes to handling the chillern." She stomped in her big shoes along the uneven brick steps of the path. "Jimmie Lou's been a-fooling around with that town boy that started to come out here in March when you had the babies. Herschel Long. He's up there now. I had to hurry off to Maggie's, so I don't know what they've been up to. He brought her a box of taffy." Alma laughed, a loud scoff. "On a Wednesday, setting on the porch eating taffy."

Wad appeared before Christie and Alma with an ax and a bucket, his mouth hanging open as if pretending to be intensely interested in their talk. Then his narrow lips lifted slowly into a grin.

"What do you want?" Alma demanded. "And what are you a-doing with that ax and that-there bucket?"

Her brother didn't answer. He leaned the ax against the house and set the bucket on a step. He cleared his throat and hitched up his galluses. He turned away from Alma like a pitchman in an exaggerated prelude to saying something important.

"Speak, Butt!" she said to his back side. "Mouth won't."

"Jimmie Lou's gone off with that town boy," he said, turning.

"Herschel Long? Why, I was just telling Christie about him. Gone off in the middle of a workday? Where'd they go?"

Wad shook his head and ran his hand up and down the ax handle. "They went to town. I saw her run in the house and get a basket or something, and then they was off."

"Are you going after him with that ax?"

"Shoot, no. Mandy sent me out to kill that hen that's been strutting around a-crowing like a rooster."

Christie felt faint. "I heard that this morning," she said.

"Mandy said ain't no hen's supposed to crow like a rooster," said Wad.

"Oh, pshaw!" said Alma. "I ain't aim to dress no hen for supper. We're still eating on that pork shoulder."

"I reckoned that hen a-crowing might bother Christie. It bothers Mandy. She says it means somebody's going to die."

Christie dropped a clothes-pin.

Alma said, "Well, if Mandy wants to dress a chicken, you can kill it for her, but I don't imagine she wants to."

"Jimmie Lou was dressed up—in some blue getup," Wad said.

"Why, she can't go running off in her good clothes in the middle of the week!"

"Thomas oughter get a shotgun after that boy, if you ask me," said Wad.

"A town boy tickles Thomas pink," said Alma. She felt of her hair under her bonnet. "I've a good mind to go after 'em myself."

Wad said, "If she was mine, I'd carry a shotgun."

Christie bent to pick up the clothes-pin, which had fallen into a clump of high grass. Alma glanced at her quizzically as she straightened up.

"I got an idie," said Alma, untying her apron. "Wad, hitch me up the buggy. Christie needs to go to town, I expect. We'll take Dark-Fire. Come on, Christie. And bring Nannie. It'll do you some good to get out."

"Come on, Nannie, we're going to ride to town," Christie said, without hesitation. She lifted Nannie and ran inside to grab a washrag and dab it at the child's face. After finding a clean pinafore for Nannie, Christie slipped on a clean skirt and waist and a good bonnet and was ready by the time Alma drove up with Dark-Fire. It was a chance to go to town, and she could pretend she had no choice but to go along with Alma in this emergency. She felt an eagerness all the time now— a busy current hurrying her along without her consent. Sometimes it was anger. Sometimes it was grief. Sometimes it was just as empty and simple as boiling water. It had an ease to it, and she didn't have to stop to figure the meaning.

"I'll brain that girl," said Alma, setting the whip to Dark-Fire, as if practicing to use it on Jimmie Lou. She had cleaned up, except for her shoes.

They drove out to the lane and toward the railroad track, and by the time they hit the road north toward town, they were flying. The roadbed was dry and in good condition. The horse streaked along. When they met a buggy heading south, Alma lifted her whip in a greeting, and the men inside stared, surprised to see two women and a child rushing toward town so fast.

As they neared the stockyard, Christie recalled with a shiver the time last winter when she went to town with James. She was lying virtually flat in the wagon, and there was snow on the ground. Every move of the mules made her feel that her insides were jarring loose. She remembered Dr. Foote poking inside her so clumsily, in the strangest way—not painful, more like a mole tunneling. Fibroids, he said.

"I don't think Jimmie Lou will be able to please a man with high notions," said Alma. "She ain't been raised that way. She's impatient, and she always was the type to get hurt easy if she couldn't do something right and you picked on her or laughed at her. I never will forget that ice cream she churned one time. She turned the crank so fast it wouldn't freeze. It was purely whipped cream! Thomas told her she was going to get butter out of it before long. He teased her about that for the longest time. When Thomas sees me with the churn out, he'll say, 'Where's Jimmie Lou? That gal was born to churn.'" Alma rared back and laughed, then shook her head. "Nosir, I don't think she'll be satisfied trying to put on airs."

"She's plainspoken," said Christie. "With a lot of wants."

"I told her to get what she could out of this Herschel now. When the new's worn off of his idie that he's going with somebody important, he's liable to drop her. That's what he likes about her now, but it won't last."

Christie wondered if Jimmie Lou felt special because she was related to the babies, the way Christie felt proud and important—as if the babies had left a glowing coal inside her that wouldn't go out.

Alma slowed down at the stockyard to pass through a throng of farmers at a livestock auction. A man was trying to force a Holstein heifer into the back of a crosstie wagon with flimsy sideboards.

"That wagon ain't going to hold that heifer," Alma commented as she guided Dark-Fire through the mules and dogs and donkeys crowding the road.

Breaking free of the commotion, Alma headed over the bridge above the railroad. The boards of the roadway rattled dangerously. Christie held Nannie tight, afraid she would bounce out of the buggy. She could feel her own excitement run through the child's body. Nannie's gaze took in all the new sights hungrily. She didn't seem frightened by anything they saw: the high bridge, a drove of mules that bucked and snorted toward them, or a large brush fire on a street corner.

At the square, the traffic was light. Most of the stores seemed lively, though, with several traders going in and out. The courthouse square looked clean, the result of a new law prohibiting people from eating watermelon or setting out their dinner there. Now grass was growing.

Alma drove slowly around the square. The streets were dusty. Most of the hitching racks were vacant. Herschel Long's buggy was not at Long's Hardware, his father's store. Christie noticed a new selection of calico in the window of Madison's Dry Goods, on the corner where she had fainted last summer. She remembered Mrs. Blankenship standing over her in that flower-garden hat. Now in the window of Mrs. Sassoon's millinery shop was a hat made of bunched white ruffles, suggesting the froth of egg whites floating in boiled custard. Alma paused at the drugstore for a moment, her eyes searching.

"I thought shore he'd take her there for some cream," she said. There was a sign for ice cream in the drugstore window.

Dr. Foote's name was written in bold black lettering on a window above the drugstore. Glimpsing a woman standing with her back to the window, Christie remembered how she had thought the doctor was violating her. But later, after Dr. Foote became so familiar to the household, she came to regard his work as impersonal; it was like fixing broken buggy axles or shoeing horses.

Alma stopped Dark-Fire alongside a peddler in a large canvas-covered wagon that was pulled up at a drinking trough. Christie recognized the man, an Irishman in a ragged felt hat. She had bought thread and spoons from him at her house last summer, as well as the colored ribbons she had used to identify her babies. He was wearing the same shirt of blue-jeans cloth with calico patches on the shoulders and pockets.

Alma called out, "Hey, mister peddler man. You seen a young gal about so high with brown hair, dressed up in a blue suit, with a boy in a buggy? Good-looking buggy. Ugly boy, a little too fine for his britches. She might have had a straw hat with gobs of ribbons."

"What's the matter, ladies?" the peddler asked in his Irish brogue. "You lost her?"

"She's my girl, and she's slipped off with this town boy. I'm going to tan her hide when I get ahold of her."

The peddler grinned, his yellow teeth sticking out at several angles. "She ain't been this way. If she had, she would have stopped and bought some of my pots. Look at these—cast-arn, reliable, lifetime service, hard enough to kill a man with if you was to need to hit him on the head. A good investment for a young woman starting out on the crooked, uphill road of married life, 'cause one thing is for certain—she'll have to be a-feeding her family."

"Ha," said Alma. "She can't cook nothing fitten to eat."

Alma turned the horse and they rode slowly around the square. Several men came out of the courthouse and lit up cigars.

"I thought they'd be at the drugstore having cream," said Alma.

"Don't suck your thumb, Nannie," said Christie, pulling the child's hand from her face.

"There's the Crittenden Inn," Alma said. "That St. Louis feller eat there but didn't tarry long enough to spend the night." Alma halted the horse for a moment to stare at the inn. "Law," she said. "I still can't get over it—all that's happened."

Mrs. Crittenden's chess pie, Christie thought.

They drove north of the square for two blocks and turned right onto Walnut Street, Alma sizing up each house along the way.

"Jimmie Lou said it had black shutters, a fine old house," said Alma. "I bet that's it up yonder on the corner, with them two big black-walnut trees out front—just like she said. When she come here to meet his family that Sunday, she said she'd never seen such a mansion. I believe she was scared to death, scared she'd say the wrong thing or not know any manners. She always was a girl for getting in over her head."

"The buggy's not there," Christie said.

"Ain't that old Mrs. Humphreys?" Alma asked as they passed an old woman in black plodding along with a cane. "I saw her at the funeral."

Christie hadn't often gotten glimpses of the nice houses in town, which were a few blocks off the square. When she and James came to town, it was to trade, so they stayed at the square. Hopewell had a number of large houses, most of them on Walnut Street, where there was an abundance of the magnificent trees. Most of the houses were painted white, and a few of them had tall, white columns holding up the second-story porches and shading the entryways below. Christie tried to imagine the fine workmanship inside—exquisite woodwork, oak stairs, molded banisters, embossed-tin ceilings, polished wood floors, elaborately carved furniture.

"I believe the mayor lives along here," said Alma. "What if he was to see us?"

"Would he know us?"

Christie was agitated and excited. She realized someone might recognize her. Soon they passed more modest dwellings, small frame houses—unpainted or with fading whitewash. Alma pointed to a tumbledown house and said it was a blind tiger, where whiskey was sold illegally. She turned the horse northward, away from the courthouse, and they passed a grain company, a tobacco warehouse, a crowd of men, some ragged boys playing stickball. They crossed a creek, and then the buildings ran out and cornfields began. Alma turned back toward the courthouse. Christie was beginning to feel her mind jumble up like socks in a wash kettle. What had Dr. Foote done that day he probed her in his office above the drugstore? Maybe he had touched with his fingers what he thought was a monster with five heads, or innumerable feet, and he was afraid to tell her. She had often wondered if sleeping in that dormitory tent down at Reelfoot had caused something noxious to enter into her, the way Brother Cornett had entered her in that dream. So many strangers were there, some of them not at all balanced or healthful, some she could imagine with poisonous minds. Amanda still wouldn't talk to her about Reelfoot. Not long ago, Boone had told Christie the story about the formation of Reelfoot Lake. Reelfoot was a young Indian with a crippled foot who loved the maiden Laughing Eyes. But her father wouldn't let her marry someone deformed, so Reelfoot stole her and carried her home. In punishment, the Great Spirit stomped his foot so angrily it caused the earth to roll and reel as the Mississippi River flowed into the new lake. Christie imagined the deformed Indian limping through Hopewell with his bride, the earthquake cracking open the street behind him.

It was broad daylight. They were amongst friendly townsfolk near the square. But the streets they were searching now, to the east of town, were mostly unfamiliar to her. A few of the houses they passed were large and formidable looking. Some of the people who had crowded into her own small farmhouse back in the spring lived here. Yet she couldn't go up to their doors and drop in—even if Dark-Fire lost a shoe or Nannie needed a drink of water. If she knocked on one of these doors, grand oak doors with brass knockers, would they remember who she was? Weren't her babies still the most talked-of subject in town? So why not walk into someone's home?

She was looking for a grove of trees, a place to hide while she relieved herself, when suddenly Mr. Mullins's establishment appeared before her. She hadn't been sure of the location, for she had paid no attention to the route when she had been carried there in the spring. She hadn't imagined she would want to return, although Mr. Mullins had said to visit anytime. The small sign in the grass—SAMUEL MULLINS, FUNERAL PARLOR—was fashioned from wrought iron, like a road marker. Christie didn't realize she was gripping Nannie so hard until Nannie squealed.

"I'm sorry, sugar," said Christie, feeling strongly the need to relieve herself. The funeral parlor had a special room for that, with pipes carrying water, but she could not go in.

"Why don't you go on in?" Alma asked, stopping the horse. "It's about time."

"No, that ain't what we come for," Christie said.

"Mullins said to come anytime you could."

"I don't want to go in there."

"I brought you along on this wild goose chase to get you out a-stirring," said Alma. "I thought it was time you went back."

"But why?" Christie asked in a voice that seemed to come from someone else.

"Go on in there, Christie—and make up your mind."

"No! What are you doing to me, woman?"

"Go see them babies again and then bury 'em—you and James."

"I can't. I can't think about it yet."

"It's about time y'all got 'em in the ground."

"No," Christie said. "I can't look at 'em now. Not yet."

"But we come all this way," said Alma. "Might as well go in."

"No. I'm not presentable."

"Dad-burn," said Alma. Abruptly, she turned back toward the square, driving Dark-Fire smartly toward the main intersection.

Christie rode along grimly, her eyes on the horse. She wouldn't let Alma tell her what to do, or what to believe, or what to feel. She didn't want Alma to intrude on her specialness or have anything to do with lifting the blame Christie pulled over herself like a heavy quilt.

"Well, knock me down and call me Tootsie May," said Alma when they reached the square. "There they are."

Herschel's horse and buggy were hitched near the drinking trough for horses directly across the street from the peddler's wagon. The horse, a dark, glistening stallion, pulled and stretched his neck against the rope. He exercised his lean legs in place, as if he felt so exuberant he couldn't stay still. The buggy was a fine one, a shifting top with shiny black leather rigging. The wheels and the trim were painted a startling yellow, and the hood was a rich black like the horse. The leather seats were shiny as the backs of doodlebugs.

"It would take a heap of cold biscuits to shine up that-there leather," Alma said.

Jimmie Lou and Herschel were just entering the drugstore when Jimmie Lou spotted her mother.

"She's got on that blue taffeta suit I made her," said Alma. "Wad got that right." Alma hopped down from the buggy, pushing the reins into Christie's hands. "Hold on, Christie."

Because of all the noise in town—horses and shouts and the tinker's gibberish of the Irish peddler nearby—Christie could scarcely hear Alma and the wayward pair. A few words drifted to her occasionally. Christie watched Jimmie Lou's abashed look at meeting her mother like this; she saw Herschel's embarrassment, his nervous grin lifting the droopy ends of his mustache; she could see Jimmie Lou twisting her hands together behind her back, as if she were hiding something. She could hear what Alma was saying now. "I didn't raise you to go slipping off like this. Who do you think you are?"

"We're right in the middle of town," Christie, judging by her gestures, imagined Jimmie Lou saying. "In front of everybody."

Christie felt peculiar, sitting there behind Dark-Fire, who had raised his tail and was dumping several blond clods onto the well-fertilized street.

Alma turned back to the buggy, muttering, "Should've let Wad kill that chicken."

Herschel's face beamed up at Christie and Nannie then, as he came forward and invited them into the drugstore for ice cream.

"I want to do something special for our famous little mother," he said with a smile that seemed as big as the half-moon of a fried pie.

4

THE FOLLOWING WEEK, JIMMIE LOU AND HERSCHEL ANNOUNCED THEIR engagement. The wedding, within the month, was a simple ceremony at the church, unremarkable compared to the shivaree Herschel's friends and Jimmie Lou's brothers perpetrated afterward. Amanda told Christie that on the wedding night, Herschel carried Jimmie Lou to the Longs' house in town, and his parents and uncles and grandmother and several children kept them up late, showing them albums and telling family histories—even serving some fortified wine called sherry. Amanda was wide-eyed as she told about the wine. She said, "And then Herschel's friends come by in a big carriage and carried him off and stranded him out on the Ulster Road without his britches—till nearly midnight—leaving Jimmie Lou in this nest of strangers! She said they all set around her, all stiff and straight as cow prods, talking at her and asking questions till she thought she'd cry. She said they wanted to know all about your babies, Christie—like they were crops that failed."

Amanda paused for Christie to say something, but Christie was staring above the wash-house at a patch of sky between two walnut trees and thinking how empty and pale it looked, like a drained milk bucket.

"And then," Amanda went on, "about one o'clock in the morning, the Wheeler boys did *their* dirty work. Thurman and some cousins made a dumb-bull noisemaker. They stuck it underneath the weatherboard near the bedroom window where Jimmie Lou and Herschel had finally gotten together. The boys said it made the most ungodly noise! It must have scared Jimmie Lou right out of her clothes, if nothing else got her out of them."

Amanda's face had not been so animated since the first time the train stopped and the passengers charged across the field to see the babies. She looked so young when she had something to tell. Her skin, with its faint dusting of freckles, was rosy and fresh. Christie imagined Amanda growing old, still watching out the window for somebody interesting to come by.

"Jimmie Lou found out one thing for sure that night," Amanda continued. "Herschel has a scar from here to here—all up and down his stomach and chest. It must be two foot long! He got it from shooting anvils one Christmas. He hadn't made the fuse long enough, and when he lit that fuse the black powder he'd jammed down in the holes wasn't packed in good, and some of it was scattered out between the two stacked-up anvils. And that went shooting out and caught a stick that went flying right at him. Jimmie Lou talked about that scar like she was right proud of it, like it was something to pet!"

Christie felt indifferent to Jimmie Lou's future, to Maggie's new baby, even to Amanda's cheerfulness. She felt betrayed by the way Alma dragged her to the funeral parlor, when she had been drawn to town by her own desire to go somewhere, to get away from the sad reminders at home. Sometimes at the Wheelers' Sunday dinners, she felt like jumping up and screaming so they would notice her anguish, but she was not sure she would get their attention even then. And she was not sure she wanted it. Most of the time, she wanted her isolation.

After church on the first Sunday following the wedding, the family gathered at Wad's for dinner, as usual—everybody except Jimmie Lou and Herschel. Alma declared that Jimmie Lou must believe she was too good for them now. Maggie and the new baby were there, and the whole family seemed surprised by how large the little girl was, after being used to the five tiny creatures Christie had borne.

"She's stout already," said Amanda, lifting the infant and blowing playfully into her face.

"Jimmie Lou'll be back by Christmas with her tail between her legs," said Alma. "Mark my words. But she's made her bed and she can lay in it."

"I'd allow she done right good," said Thomas, who had come home late the night before. He never went to church. "Jimmie Lou never even had no luck at a box supper, and now she's hitched to a fine young man with a family business." Thomas turned to Christie, then James. "If it hadn't been for you good folks and what you did, Jimmie Lou would have ended up with some farm boy that couldn't spell his way out of a buttermilk jug and thought chess was just a kind of pie. Now she's got somebody that can teach her things."

"But Jimmie Lou likes to get out in the fields," Alma said. "She likes to pick berries. She likes to pitch horseshoes. Can you feature her a-throwing a oyster supper?"

"Where's my cake?" Arch demanded in a whining voice.

"What cake?" Alma said innocently.

It was Arch's tenth birthday, and Alma had kept him in a state of misery all morning by pretending she had forgotten about his special ten-year cake. For a child to live to his tenth year was always a cause of celebration. Christie recalled when her brother Luther turned ten and got his cake.

Arch began to cry, and Thomas shook his head sadly. "Ten year old and still a-crying like a baby."

"He wants his cake," Amanda said, patting the boy gently on the head.

"Shut up that sniveling, Arch," said Wad, as some of Alma's blackberry cobbler landed with a splat on his plate. "Did I ever tell you about old Inch Burke?"

"Naw." The boy kicked at the rungs of his chair.

Wad leaned back in his chair, balancing on the two hind legs. "One day the Lord told Inch either to kill one of his chillern or cut off a hand. So Inch took a ax and chopped his hand off. He laid his arm down on a stump like he was fixing to kill a chicken and just whacked his hand off."

"Plumb off?" Arch's mouth hung open and his nose was running.

"The Lord said be snappy about it, so Inch, he just went for the ax. Then he got lockjaw and couldn't open his mouth, so he had to eat soup. And one day his teeth got to bothering him. So he went to town and the dentist said, 'I can't pull them teeth if you can't get your mouth open!' So Inch went back to the creek and set on a rock and took a knife and prized his mouth open and gouged out his own teeth. Wellsir, that finished him!"

"Imagine doing that one-handed," Joseph said, winking at Arch.

All the men laughed, and then Henry said, "I remember Maddie Burke, his widder. She was a sight full of aggervation."

"Now, Arch, that just goes to show what some folks will do for their chillern," Wad said. "But don't count on it."

"In the Bible, Abraham had to sacrifice Isaac, and the Lord didn't say nothing about no hand," said Alma.

Suddenly Amanda, holding an empty gravy bowl, marched over to her husband at the head of the table and said in a shrill voice, "I'd be ashamed!" She turned to Alma, who was collecting dirty plates. "It's the boy's birthday," Amanda said.

Glaring at Amanda, Alma grabbed Thomas's empty plate. She carried the plates into the kitchen and returned with Arch's cake. Arch jumped up with a shout. The beam on his face could have sliced the cake.

"A little cake that's all yours!" Amanda said lovingly to Arch. "A ten-year cake is the most special thing there is."

Alma had made two layers in her smallest pans and covered the little cake with boiled white icing that glistened like iced-over snow. Arch grabbed the red candied cherry on top and ate it.

"Reckon you're old enough to start cutting tobaccer this year, little man?" said Wad, rising from the table.

"Tobaccer's the nastiest thing I know of," Amanda said, as she set a tea pitcher on the table.

Wad laughed, and the others joined in. Amanda went outside, slamming the front door. Christie could see her on the porch with the old bird dog, Buford. She thought the laughter seemed awkward and fearful. Joseph and Henry laughed loudly, their laughter siding with their father's. James looked up at Christie, as if asking her apology for joining in with the men's humor. Christie turned away. Dove, eating in her corner, dug around in her mashed potatoes as though she were hunting for something. Christie gave Nannie a piece of chicken wing and then went to the porch where Amanda was petting the dog.

"Come on in and eat, Mandy," Christie said.

"When Wad chews, it's like a cow and her cud," Amanda said. "But at least a cow's chewing sweet grass. Tobaccer's plumb nasty." She spoke to the dog. "Reckon you'd ever take up chewing, Buford?" The dog lay down with a groan.

"James finds a heap of satisfaction in working tobaccer," Christie said. "But it's right toilsome."

"Oh, it's toilsome," Amanda said with a shudder. "I purely dread cutting time."

"Come on in, Mandy. Dinner's getting cold."

When the women sat down to eat, Boone talked about the album he was making, with the clippings and letters Christie had let him have. The men had finished eating and had scattered into the parlor, except for Boone, who ate slowly. He rose from his place so that Alma could sit down.

"You spent all day yesterday a-making on that book," said Alma.

"He got glue all over the floor," said Dulcie.

"I cleaned it up," protested Boone.

"When can we see the album?" asked Lena.

"Not till it's done with," Boone said. "But I got something else to show you."

He took something from his pocket and hid it behind his back, then held out his fists to Nannie, who bashfully picked one. Slowly, he opened his fist. Inside was a little bed with five tiny dolls in it, all between sheets. The bed was made of wood, and the dolls were rubber. They were covered with a rectangle of calico.

"It's for your dollhouse," Boone told Nannie.

The girls crowded around to look. "Did you make it?" Lena asked.

"A feller give it to me the other day. Said he got it at the funeral."

"I seen somebody a-selling them," said Wad, as the men drifted back toward the table to look at Boone's surprise. "I seen several folks shell out fifty cents for one of those."

"You're wishing you'd thought of it, Daddy," said Joseph.

"It's a souvenir," said Mary Ann, holding the little object up to the light.

Christie saw James gazing out the window, his face like a hollowed gourd. She speared a chicken liver and cut it up in small pieces for Nannie. On Sundays, Amanda always set up a small table so the children wouldn't have to wait till last.

"Eat your dinner, Nannie," Christie said. She started collecting chicken bones for the cats.

The family had spoken little about the babies. Now the subject dropped like a bucket down a well. The men, still standing around, turned to tobacco talk. Wad said he didn't expect to come out ahead on tobacco this year. Henry, with the new baby, needed the cash crop, but Wad wanted to hold it off the market for a year until prices went up.

"They ain't gonna give nothing for it," said Joseph, as he rolled a cigarette. "I go along with Daddy to hold back on it this year."

"If we don't make a good yield and they don't want to pay us nothing for it, then we won't get much anyhow," Wad said. "We're just as well to hold on to it till they need it."

"Folks will always need tobaccer," said Joseph to Henry.

"There's too much of it as it is," said Wad, pulling out his own plug. He sold his tobacco crop loose-leaf, unpressed, but he bought chewing tobacco at the store because it had sweetening in it.

"James, you're better off without five extra younguns to feed," said Henry, nodding toward his own new baby.

Maggie laughed in a girlish manner that made Christie want to strangle her. Maggie wasn't holding the new baby right, and she didn't see how it was fretting. Maybe it would die.

Christie dumped scrapings into the slop bucket. Then she took the scraps out to the dogs. From the side of the house, she saw Wad come out to the porch and spit into a snowball bush. She wondered what it would be like to chew tobacco. Tobacco plugs smelled sweet but made such a vile liquor of spittle. She couldn't imagine kissing anybody who chewed. James didn't chew, but still she wouldn't kiss him now. She hoped Clint and Jewell would never chew. Already Thurman had his own cigarettes, which he rolled and smoked in town or behind the barn.

Today the talk of tobacco and the smell of burnt onions and the sight of congealed bacon grease on a bowl of wilted lettuce all ran together, coalescing into a particular memory she'd forever associate with this moment. She prized each sensation. Everything was of equal importance, nothing favored, the way each baby grabbed her and wouldn't let her choose one over the other. As she went back indoors, she heard the word "feathers." The men were still standing around, while the women worked in the kitchen.

"Why, a feather bed is one of the most valuable possessions in a house," said Thomas.

"Red meat and feathers," said Henry.

Thomas said, "Little Bunch, wasn't you the one that found them things?"

Little Bunch nodded sullenly and gouged out a chunk of black-berry cobbler from the pan with her fingers. She sucked on it.

Thomas said, "I never did see 'em. What'd they look like?"

"Bird nests," Little Bunch said, making a circle with both hands. "Big birds."

Thomas sat back in his straight chair, leaning at a precarious angle. He said, "I've got people down at this little store in Nutbush that say they've seen 'em big as a hornet's nest."

"How would you sleep on a piller with that in it?" demanded Alma.

"They was going to die," said Little Bunch.

Lena slapped her sister's hand. "No, it means they're in Heaven. Mama said."

"I've heard it's a sign of death," said Boone. "But why would there be just two? That's the why of it."

"The weather was so changeable, they took the pneumony," Maggie said knowingly.

"Them babies was wooled to death," said Alma. "Just like a old dog got aholt of 'em and wooled 'em. I saw one of the dogs a-shaking a possum out by the corncrib the other day. That's what all that han-dling did."

Christie finished drying the platter that had held the roast hen. She carried the platter into the parlor to the china safe. She set it inside, upright in the back, behind where the Sunday plates and glasses would go. She closed the glass door of the safe and walked out the front door, leaving behind the tobacco talk, the idle gossip, Thomas Hunt's bragging, old Dove's moans, Boone's wheezes. Christie walked out of the house and down the porch steps and down the lane. She didn't even think to take Nannie with her. She felt unattached, unburdened by anyone pulling at her. She walked all the way to the railroad before she remembered that she had simply been headed home.

She turned back, and James caught up with her at the fence by the tobacco patch. The dogs scampered around him eagerly. The bird dog, Buford, hung back to sniff at something dead, and Luke, the collie, halted, waiting for him to catch up.

"Go on, boys," James said to the dogs. He laid his hands on Christie's shoulders. "I didn't know about that doll bed," he said. "Nobody meant to hurt your feelings, Chrissie. They don't know they're doing that."

"Well, they must be stupid," she said. "How has Mandy lived with them all these years?"

"That's just the way they all are," James said. "They're hard-hearted and hard-headed, but I know they don't mean it."

"But what Alma said is true—the babies *were* wooled to death."

"We couldn't stop it, though," James said. "People would have busted in."

"I don't want to be here," she said. The hound, Zeke, sauntered up and collapsed lazily at James's feet.

"I'm so sorry, Chrissie," he said, drawing nearer. "But I've been thinking out there in the fields, all these long days. And I don't believe God means for us to keep blaming ourselves. I don't believe He meant for us just to dry up inside and blow away. I think He wants us to keep on."

"What do you mean?"

"Maybe He means for us to try again—have another one."

She shook her head no. She remembered her mother saying to do what James asked when they were married. But somehow that no longer applied. She didn't really believe he meant what he was suggesting. They couldn't ever replace those babies. She said, "We didn't do a good job. How could He trust us again?"

James pulled a long stem of timothy and absently rolled it between his fingers. "Do you want us to go back to Dundee?" he asked.

"No. I wish we could, but our place is here."

She spied a tobacco worm on a leaf and reached down to pluck it. The fat thing wiggled between her fingers; its head waved, searching.

Last week James had sent Clint and Jewell out with buckets to pick the tobacco worms. They thought killing worms was a great amusement. The green worms were hard to see, hidden on plants and mimicking tobacco leaves. Now Christie wondered what it would be like to be a tobacco worm, hiding and disappearing in the obvious, like a blue quilt-piece against the blue sky, an exact match. What would a tobacco worm see? Would the worm know pain when a little boy pinched its head off? She dropped the worm onto the hard dirt and flattened it beneath her shoe.

"Wad's worried about the crop," James said. "I'm afraid if we hold the tobaccer off the market the other farmers will make trouble for us. But I don't see how I can go against Wad." He gazed out over the tobacco patch. Some of the leaves were already turning yellow, the dust settling through a haze of hot sun. "I feel so bad," he said. "The tobaccer didn't work out, and I counted so much on this dark-fire when we moved here."

"But it's pretty," she said.

The tobacco was beautiful in the fields, dark as night in some lights. Sometimes it was like the skin of a dark green watermelon. James, it seemed to her, didn't see it the way she did, his mind was so full of what had to be done. But when she saw it in the mornings, in the first sunlight, the sight was breathtaking. The rows led off into the distance, the plants lined up perfectly like soldiers. When they planted the slips in the pegged holes, setting them on the check, James was insistent that they be lined up perfectly straight, and spaced so precisely.

5

By mid-July, the men were sowing Hungarian grass, buck-wheat, and cowpeas. The last rain had been in late June—an unusual rain that lasted for several days. Some of the wheat sprouted right in the chaff. The crop was hurt by rust and smut, but they saved most of it. Now the wheat and oats were in. The tobacco was looking dry.

Christie worked long afternoons alone putting up green beans and tomatoes, scalding the jars in the steamy kitchen. She was not even aware of the heat. When she churned, her mind was restful. She liked to hear the swishing sound of the clabber change in texture as the but-ter slowly separated. Waiting for the butter to gather while she churned so steadily made everything seem suspended in eternity. She still felt a strange ebullience at times like this, a feeling as high as her sudden plunges into despair were deep. Mama wrote that she had set down the babies' names in the Wilburn Bible. Christie hadn't written their names in her Bible. She didn't know where their handprints and footprints were. She thought Dr. Foote had taken them. She and James went along in their work without saying much. Sometimes she thought James looked at her as though she were a diseased calf isolated in a pen.

On July 14, the first roasting ears were ripe, and Christie picked turnip greens to take to Alma's the next day for Sunday dinner. Jimmie Lou was coming with Herschel.

"Shoo that hen out of the garden, Nannie. We don't want chicken mess on the turnip greens."

Waving her apron, Nannie tumbled forward down the border of the patch toward the chicken. The child was growing fast, her shape slimming and her movements becoming more and more sure. She was high-spirited, but she always minded, except when her brothers tried to boss her.

"Shoo, shoo," Nannie said. "Don't mess on the turnip greens."

The next day, Jimmie Lou and Herschel arrived at her mother's in the yellow-trimmed buggy, bringing a lady cake Jimmie Lou had made. Under the large post-oak tree out front, the whole family crowded around Jimmie Lou, who was wearing a new Japanese-lawn dress of deep green, with a yellow-pansy figure in it. Alma was so flustered she stepped into the petunia bed. The children gaped at the newlyweds, and Boone crept down from his loft to get a look at them. Christie sat on a stump, making a clover chain with Nannie.

Jimmie Lou's cake squatted unevenly on a cake plate with a clear glass cover. Amanda took it from her and held it steady, out of reach of the dogs. Christie thought about the twin cake-stands James had brought her one day, so long ago. One of them was chipped now, and she didn't use it anymore. The first cakes she set on those stands were coconut cakes. She could still remember cracking the coconut, drinking the milk, and grating the white of the coconut until she had a pile like snow.

"Jimmie Lou's been feeding me real good," said Herschel, beaming at his wife proudly. He was stocky and thick-waisted, with straight yellow hair, while Jimmie Lou was slender and long-waisted. Her dark hair was piled and fluffed high above her forehead. Together, they resembled salt-and-pepper shakers, Christie thought.

"I don't know who learnt her to cook," said Alma, reaching down to straighten the flowers she had stepped on.

"Oh, Mama, you mashed your petunies," Jimmie Lou wailed.

"Does your pappy do right well with that store?" Wad asked Herschel.

"He does during the fall and the spring—when everybody's either stocking up for winter or getting ready to plant. We used to stock groceries, but they were hard to keep. Once, we had a hogshead of cheese to ruin and a whole shipment of flour we had to send back on account of weevils." He laughed and clapped his hands.

"Weevils won't hurt you none," Alma said, taking the lady cake from Amanda. She started indoors with it.

Herschel grinned at Christie and gave Jimmie Lou a puppy pat on the head. "I tell you, Mrs. Wheeler, it ain't been the same at the store since the big commotion back in the spring. Everybody says, 'How does it feel to marry into a famous family?'" He laughed. "It's sure been good for business."

Herschel admired the farm, waving his hand to take it all in—the topped tobacco, the cows grazing, the garden drying up, chickens running through the dirt yard, and the smooth, worn stumps where the menfolks sat of an evening.

"Farm's looking good," he said.

"The tobaccer looks good, but it won't bring nothing," Wad said. "These chillern's as well to forget about new shoes for school."

Thomas Hunt seized Herschel's hand and gave it a vigorous shake. "Those Deere gang plows moving good this year?" he asked.

"Can't say anybody wants those," said Herschel. "They all believe nobody will ever improve on the Brinley turning plow or the Avery batwing middle buster. I tell 'em they're just afraid to try anything new."

"I'm with you there," Thomas said. "Some of these old fellers just won't take to anything they wasn't raised on."

Men always had to talk business of some sort, Christie thought as she went indoors. But when men were alone together, James had told her, their talk often turned to women—about their persons. The notion disgusted Christie. Yet she—and her person—had been a subject of discussion all across the nation. When she was working she could forget that. The days seemed so regular and ordinary then. But now, on a Sunday—the day of the Lord, when they stopped working and neighbors came visiting—she was reminded once again, and it came at her with a heavy rush, like a wind that could blow her over.

The cuckoo bird cuckooed twelve times, and the men sat down to eat. The long oak dining table had heavy legs and a dozen ladderback chairs. On the table was a glass preserve stand, a vinegar bottle with a cracked stopper, salt-and-pepper boxes, and a dish of butter, its molded round shape flattened and gouged. Christie saw all this through Jimmie Lou's eyes, but Herschel acted as though he were in the finest home in the county.

"The whole town's still stirred up over you, Mrs. Wheeler," he said, as he helped himself to the platter of chicken.

Her cheeks burned. She finished serving some green beans dotted with tiny new potatoes and carried the empty bowl back to the kitchen. She heard Joseph saying the cat had got her tongue. People had been saying that to her since she was Nannie's size. She carried out her bowl of fresh turnip greens and a platter of roasting ears. As she passed the children's table, Nannie cried out, "I don't want no turnip greens. They got chicken mess on 'em."

Everybody burst out laughing, and Jimmie Lou covered her face in embarrassment.

"Now, no need to act above your raising, Jimmie Lou," Wad said cheerfully. "Herschel will just have to get used to us Wheelers."

"All of our messing and gauming," Alma said with a grunt.

In the middle of dinner, Boone abruptly left the table and went to get some of the baby mail. When he returned, he began reading the letters aloud to the others. Christie escaped to the kitchen and started slicing Jimmie Lou's lady cake. She could still hear Boone reading the letters.

"Here's a good one. A woman writes all the way from Jamestown, New York, that she believes our little mother here—where'd Christie go to?—should be a heroine, with a plaque, and her likeness put in the Capitol as a great American woman."

"The letters are still coming," said Amanda. "People can't get over it."

"Christie, get over here," called Thomas. "You ought to be right proud."

Christie cut the cake, running the knife underneath to lift a slice onto the platter. The cake was dry and pale. It seemed to be made with old eggs.

"There's been a lot of sympathy postcards," said Boone. "And people send pictures of their own chillern."

"A lot of them's dead," said Lena. "Pictures of dead chillern."

"You can tell they're dead," Dulcie said. "The way they're laying there all dressed up, with their eyes closed."

"And flowers in their hands," said Little Bunch. "You never lay down with flowers in your hands unless you're dead."

"Have you girls been playing funeral again?" Jimmie Lou asked suspiciously.

They shook their heads no.

"When Lena and Little Bunch here played funeral, they kept burying the cat," Jimmie Lou explained to Herschel. "That poor cat got so tired of being buried, he finally run off to the woods, and we didn't see him for two or three days!" She squealed with laughter.

"Here's a picture of a little girl," said Boone, passing around a picture. "Look at how they've got her setting up like she's still alive."

Christie brought out the platter of sliced cake. She slid a slice onto James's plate, and he bent over it. He sat rigidly, like a plank fence that a bull couldn't break. He ate his cake in two bites.

"What do you make out of all of this, Mrs. Wheeler?" Herschel asked Christie.

"I don't have anything to say to any of those people."

"Still, you might oughter write back and say thank you," said Jimmie Lou.

"Is that what I oughter say?" Christie asked, holding out a piece of cake to Herschel.

Herschel said, "Well, people mean kindly, ma'am."

"She don't have time to write no letters," James said loudly. He rose from the table and went out to the porch.

Christie started gathering up corncobs for the pigs. Boone had cut all his corn off of the cob with his pocketknife. "I don't know what to write," she said.

"I'd just write them thank you," said Jimmie Lou in a teacher voice. "And how I appreciated their taking the time to write, and how I hope they'll have good luck and happiness."

"That kind of talk don't amount to a hill of beans," said Alma, stomping into the kitchen with an armload of dishes.

"People like that come in my house and just wooled my babies to death," Christie said, in a voice so small no one even noticed.

"Who'd pay for that many stamps to answer all them letters?" asked Wad.

The men drifted to the parlor and porch to smoke or chew. The parlor got a good breeze. Boone returned to his loft with a cough and a loud belch. Christie picked up the letter he had left lying on the table and read it to herself. It was from a woman who had lost her baby in childbirth. *You're lucky your babies lived as long as they did,* the woman wrote. *Some people don't even get five minutes of the precious soul's time on earth.* Christie folded the letter and placed it in its envelope. Amanda took it from her and thrust it into her apron pocket.

"Let's eat, Christie," she said cheerily. "Why, Alma, you set two forks at my place. I must be going to New York!"

Everybody laughed. Christie and Amanda exchanged glances, like old friends meeting in a crowd.

While the women ate, they talked about canning green beans and cream corn. They sucked the chicken bones clean and relished the giblets. They scraped the bowls, not wanting to throw out a smidgin. The vegetables were cold enough for the grease to thicken. The men had eaten all of the turnip greens. The women moved up and down, eating and clearing dishes and sorting scraps. They inspected the children's plates for waste. Christie didn't say a word. She ate the gizzard bits left on Nannie's plate.

Alma, sampling her daughter's lady cake, said, "It don't have enough eggs in it. Did you beat them half an hour?"

"I tried to."

"It would be better with some pineapple in it," said Dulcie. "Or oranges. Not just plain."

"You don't make lady cake that way," said Jimmie Lou.

"I like flavored cakes better," said Dulcie.

"Well, this is a lady cake," said Jimmie Lou.

"Listen to Miss Priss," Alma said.

Later, as the women were cleaning up, the dogs began barking. Everyone crowded into the living room to see who was passing. Through the front window, they could see two buggies stopping in front of the house.

"Is that the preacher?" Alma gasped. "Good Lord 'a' mercy, we eat up all three of them chickens."

"No, it ain't the preacher," said Wad, adjusting his galluses. "It's somebody from town."

"That ain't none of your people, is it, Herschel?" asked Alma.

Herschel moved closer to get a view through the window. "No. Why, there's Mr. Redmon from the paper and George Blankenship."

Wad went outside, along with James and Henry. Christie watched from the window. Mrs. Blankenship was there too. And a man she recognized from the drugstore. A rigor ran up her spine, turned, and dived into her stomach. She recognized the small man with the black hair and mustache, wearing the striped pants and string tie and that tall, dark hat she had seen before—Mr. Mullins. One of the horses dropped a horse turd right beside him. Her heart beat fast. She saw James talking to Mr. Redmon. She saw Wad waving at the fields. So far, they were talking crops.

"Are they coming in?" Alma asked nervously. She and the older girls were clearing away the table. Christie was rooted at the window, the small children gathered around her. Alma swatted a dish towel in their direction and ordered them out back to play. "Go on now, get out from underfoot. You too, Arch. Thurman, get those younguns out of here."

"You mean me too, Mama?" said Jimmie Lou teasingly. "Am I still a youngun underfoot?"

"You and Herschel's behind this whole thing, I'd allow."

"We didn't know they were coming," Jimmie Lou protested. "Honest, Mama."

"They're probably just out for a drive," said Herschel. "But I need to go out and say howdy-do to Mr. Redmon and them." To Alma, he said, "Excuse me, ma'am. That was a mighty fine dinner."

"I bet that feller in the stovepipe and striped britches is hot as a firecracker," said Alma. "That's that Mr. Mullins, ain't it?"

Christie had an impulse to carry Nannie out the back door and run home. But she couldn't move. Everything outside seemed so dusty. A haze hovered above the group of visitors. And then a cat strolled toward the horses and paused to rub against one horse's leg. The horse's tail twitched, and the cat leaped at it playfully.

"I thought we were shed of those people," Christie said to Amanda.

"What could they want?" Amanda said, one hand shaping her hair and the other wadding her apron nervously.

"They didn't stop by just to say howdy," said Alma. "They're a-wanting something, shore's you're born."

6

AT THE END OF THE DAY, AFTER CHRISTIE HAD DONE UP HER NIGHT work and the boys had fed the hogs and James had milked, Wad came down to the house. They were finishing supper—just ham and cold cornbread and some of Jimmie Lou's lady cake—when he appeared in the kitchen, his face clouded. Christie rushed the children outside to play in the last light. The sun was setting fair, which meant a clear day tomorrow.

"It looks like we're going to have to do what they say," said Wad, dropping his hat on the table and sitting down with a grunt.

"How do you figure that?" said James, with a sharpness in his voice that Christie had never heard him use toward his uncle.

"Look at the way things are going. My boys want to go ahead and sell the tobaccer, but if we do, it won't bring enough to get through the winter on." Wad's mobile features danced in mingled anticipation and worry. "But if we do what Mullins and them was talking about, then we might could hold the tobaccer off till next year and get a better price."

"You mean if James and me do it," said Christie. "Not you."

"You could pay Blankenship and finish paying off what you owe me," Wad said. "I could settle up with the feed mill and what I owe my boys. Why, you're liable to come out ahead, the way they're talking, James. We could buy more stock—some heifers." He didn't look at Christie. He seemed to be speaking to the calendar on the wall. She stood at the stove, waiting for water to boil.

"I'll have to know more about that McCain feller they brought out here," said James. "I need to know what's behind it."

"Well, you've got a point there," said Wad, leaning back in the kitchen chair, so far back Christie could imagine him toppling and breaking into pieces like a porcelain doll. She had a new sense of power, because the Sunday visitors had come to her, needing her. She felt a cold clarity inside her, like a crystal gazing ball.

"I don't see no way out," said Wad. "The wheat didn't make much, the tobaccer's bad with them worms, and them pinhookers that come around won't offer the price it takes to raise it. Why, even the cabbages is puny."

"Well, Uncle Wad, I reckon your farm was running good till we come along and ruint things for you," said James bitterly.

"Now, James, don't think like that," said Wad, reaching into his pocket for his barlow knife. "I always thought of you like my own son because you was John's boy, and John was the best brother to me. He would've done anything for me. But I ain't just thinking of my own self. I have to think about my new grandbaby and what might happen if the tobaccer prices hit bottom. Looky here, if a feller comes by and offers you a hundred dollars a week, then I reckon you'd be a fool not to jump to it. A hundred dollars a week!"

"It might be like that wagon of presents," said James. "We might never see it."

"But you sign a piece of writing. If he don't pay, you can go to the law." Wad played with his knife, scraping bread crumbs on the table into a little pile, then scattering them.

James swabbed the grease from his plate, working his cornbread down to the last bit.

"It's with Christie," he said. "I won't make her do it."

Christie set a chunk of lady cake into his vacated plate and grimly began washing the dishes. She glimpsed herself as a young girl, marrying James. They started out together laughing, like Jimmie Lou and Herschel. No one could have expected what had happened. And now what lay before them could not be imagined either. The thought hit hard, yet far down inside her was a pang of joy. She wanted to go away—anywhere. She felt a strong desire to get away and start over again, with James. If they accepted Mr. McCain's offer, they could satisfy Wad yet defy him at the same time. She didn't want to consent to the proposal for Wad's sake. She wanted to do it for her own sake—to declare her independence of Wad, to get away from him, far away. And she wanted him to know it.

As she wiped a plate dry, she said, in a hard, slow voice, as if she were a piece of kindling about to catch fire, "Well, I'll do it. But not for you and not for your tobaccer crop."

"What's got into you, Christie?" said James, rising from the table in surprise.

"I think I want to take that feller's offer," she said quietly.

"I reckoned you'd see it my way," Wad said, a smile breaking across his tired face.

"But I'm not seeing it your way," Christie said with a clatter of plates. She turned to the kitchen window, with its view of the side yard, where the children were playing leapfrog, with Nannie huddled down beneath flying feet. She would have to leave the children behind.

"I don't know what she means by that," Wad said to James.

"Think on it," said Christie, slapping a dishrag angrily at the table.

According to the account Mr. Jenkins wrote in the *Hopewell Chronicle* two days later, the visitors to the Wheeler farm that Sunday had first attended church and then they had dined at the Crittendens' establishment on Main Street. Christie, reading aloud to James from the paper Boone brought down, recalled the white tablecloths and the candlesticks she had seen through the windows when she went to town with Alma.

Boone waited, out of breath and leaning on the door facing, while Christie finished reading the article aloud. In a detached voice, as if she were merely reading the crop reports, she read, "'It was a fine day and on the way they had lifted their voices together in a song— "Flow Gently, Sweet Afton." During the previous week, Mr. Mullins had laid to rest three good Hopewell citizens, and the growing reliance on his services, as the city becomes too crowded to deal with burials in the traditional family way, had caused him to take thought. Mr. W. Greenberry McCain appeared, as if in response to Mr. Mullins's musings. He had been seen in town before, back in the spring, when so many visitors arrived in Hopewell, but nobody saw him drive in this week. They supposed he came in on the train and walked from the depot to the newspaper office, where he consulted with our editor, Mr. Redmon.

"'From there, he and Mr. Redmon sallied forth to Mr. Mullins's establishment, and after Mr. Mullins had listened to Mr. McCain's offer, they proceeded to enlist the persuasive powers of Mr. and Mrs. Blankenship, whose position in the community is well known. Nobody could take a step without the advice and sanction of Mr. and Mrs. Blankenship, said our newspaperman. Mr. McCain had not sought out the Wheelers directly because he feared he would be intruding. He wanted his plan, as he said, to be a "civic endeavor," one which would glorify the name of the town, bringing it prestige (as if it hadn't garnered enough already, considering the events of the spring) and be carried out in the most decorous way possible. Mr. and Mrs. Blankenship readily consented to the project and agreed to try to enlist the cooperation of the Wheelers, without whose good graces the town would not have received the recent honors that have been bestowed upon it. Mr. and Mrs. Wheeler have been kind enough to allow the community to claim as its own the famous Wheeler Quintuplets, whose names will live in history and song throughout America.

"'Thus, Mr. McCain tarried two nights at Crittenden's Inn, partaking of Mrs. Crittenden's fine cooking, including her immortal sweet-potato pie, and meeting with quite a number of our local citizenry, most prominently the merchants on the square. As it happened, Mrs. Blankenship was just completing a memory book that she was about to present to Mrs. Wheeler on a propitious occasion, so she bestowed the last few touches on the attractive album and carried it with her when the small group from town traveled forth to call upon the Wheelers. Mrs. Blankenship had pressed some flowers and commissioned some hand lettering to be done on the album. Inside she had collected likenesses and newspaper cutouts of the Hopewell Quintuplets, including the first reports in the *St. Louis Dispatch,* written by Mr. Roberts, who had journeyed to Hopewell by train to get a first-hand glimpse of the quintuplets. Mrs. Blankenship also collected mail that had been sent to the *Hopewell Chronicle*—inquiries, reprints of news about the quintuplets from other periodicals, including several magazines, and telegrams. She collected all these into a fairly sizable memory album and presented it to Mrs. Wheeler on Sunday last.

"'The committee had finished dining early and traveled on out to the Wheelers, finding the Wheelers still rejoicing over a lady cake made by the former Miss Jimmie Lou Hunt, now Mrs. Long, this young miss having won the heart of one of our finest young men, Herschel Long, son of Mr. Long of Long's on the court square. The courtship was an expeditious one, Mr. Long having pursued his bride after hearing about the quintuplets and going out to see for himself, his attention alighting instead on Jimmie Lou, a niece of our James and Christianna Wheeler. The happy couple was at Sunday dinner when the party arrived.

"'The Wheelers respectfully listened to the proposal carried by Mr. McCain (who is of Alabama and formerly traveled for the Phillips Music Co., in New York) and discussed the situation with Mr. Mullins. Mr. McCain proposes that Mr. and Mrs. Wheeler travel with the Fair Day Exhibition Series, an educational series of lectures and diversions, for the purpose of educating the generally curious and concerned public about the Hopewell Quintuplets and the miraculous event that ended so unfortunately for the Wheelers. It is thought that there is a great amount of general public interest in the matter of quintuplets. Mr. and Mrs. Wheeler readily and with good nature agreed that it would be for the public good if they could present the truth to the audiences in their own words, so that if such an event should happen again the world would know what to expect.'"

"I never said I'd give no talk," said Christie.

"Me neither," said James.

"But if people come up to me I might give 'em a piece of mind," she said.

"He said he'd do the talking," James said. "I ain't giving no speech. Are you through? Does it tell about the rest of what we're going to do? Or is it just more words?"

"They said Jimmie Lou was a niece, but she's your cousin."

"Nobody will know the difference."

Christie went on reading aloud. The feather crowns came up in the last paragraph. "'Two feather crowns the size of birds' nests were discovered in the feather bed the Wheeler babies slept on. The little bed is vacant now, wept over by the grieving parents on their tobacco farm south of Hopewell.'"

Mr. McCain had told her he wanted to display the feather crowns in a small glass case that Mr. Mullins would provide. Christie had examined the crowns again, knotted inside the scarf. The feathers were unmistakably entwined together, making little hats.

"Are you sure we're doing the right thing?" James asked when she finished reading the newspaper.

"Wad said you have to on account of the tobaccer," Boone put in.

"No, we *don't* have to," Christie told him. "I said I *wanted* to go. *I'm* the one that decided." Through the window, she could see the boys out in the tobacco patch, suckering tobacco plants. "Here's what I'm going to do," she said. "I'm going to show people what they done to my babies."

"Well, you'd be a fool not to go," said Boone. "This is the chance of a lifetime."

"You didn't hear me," Christie said, her voice rising. "You and Mrs. Blankenship don't know the first thing about it. You're just alike. You both just want pretty pictures."

Boone shrank from her, like a threatened puppy. She started to feel something boiling inside her, like the bubbling foam that rose on jelly when it smoked its pipes—the moment the liquid had cooked down. She knew she was smoking her pipes too.

Boone had kept Mrs. Blankenship's memory album. Christie didn't even open it. She recalled Mrs. Blankenship handing her the album on Sunday as if it were alive, a replacement for the babies. Mrs. Blankenship had said, "I wrote you twice and never could hear from you, and finally I decided I had to come by and give you this surprise I'd been making for you."

"I didn't see any letters from you," said Christie.

Mrs. Blankenship glanced around impatiently at the Wheeler farm. She said, "I can't tell you how life is changed now that we have the telephone service. If you had the telephone, you could talk to anybody in town without ever having to feed a horse or hitch up a buggy."

Christie stared dully at the rich plum-red leather album, with its gold filigree.

Mrs. Blankenship smiled. "I thought you'd enjoy having a book with all the newspaper accounts and the cabinet card from the funeral and several likenesses. I hope you'll treasure it as you look back in years to come."

Christie's head buzzed. She wouldn't embarrass herself in front of Mrs. Blankenship again. She was determined not to faint. Her head cleared.

"I'm much obliged," she said simply.

Christie knew the woman was dying to get a look at the feather crowns, and Christie felt a little lift of gladness at keeping them for herself. But now the newspaper was reporting that Mr. McCain would take the feather crowns on the lecture trip and that Mr. Mullins was making a special display case for them.

She folded the newspaper and handed it back to Boone. Boone had sunk down into a soft chair, exhausted and nearly speechless with the excitement of the news.

"The paper didn't tell about the babies," he gasped. "It didn't tell how you're taking the babies with you."

Christie charged outside into the blazing sun. She felt as if a thundercloud had lifted from her head and drawn out all her thoughts. A longing for escape pulsated through her like warm rain. She wanted to go.

7

AUGUST CONTINUED DRY AND HOT, WITH ONE GENTLE SHOWER THAT did little good. The tobacco was yellowing, and the tomato vines were burning up. Christie and James had promised Greenberry McCain they could leave soon after the tobacco was cut and the other crops were laid by. And he said they would be back home before the last of pea time. Wad assured James that he and his sons would be able to gather James's corn crop; so much of it had been damaged by ant cattle sucking out the roots the job wouldn't take them long.

Mr. McCain had been out visiting. In his Sunday clothes, he had walked over the fields, admiring the tobacco. He wore polished shoes made of leather so thin his toe knuckles showed. He brought presents for the children—a clown doll for Nannie, two softballs and a ball bat for the boys. The boys batted at the new, clean, sweet-smelling balls until they lost them both somewhere in the tobacco patch. Mr. McCain said his mother ("now gone to her heavenly rest") used to have a cast-iron range just like Christie's, and he remembered with great pleasure her canned tomato juice and pickled peaches. He had been raised on a farm, but he was a city man now, making his head-quarters in Montgomery, where he lived with his wife and four children. He traveled widely through the South country. "Just seeing this great land of ours is the supreme satisfaction," he said. He had started out selling sheet music, a fact that interested the Wheelers because Thomas Hunt had once been in the same line.

"I got out of sheet music right before rags got so popular, and I keep threatening to get back in," said Mr. McCain to Christie, as he pulled a handkerchief from his pocket and held it out to Nannie.

A penny was knotted loosely in the corner of the handkerchief.

When the shy little girl finally got the penny out, she dropped it on the ground and started to cry.

"Here it is, Punkin," said Christie, picking up the penny and shielding Nannie in her apron. "What do you say to the nice man? Say 'Thank ye.'"

"What's that man's nose so big for?" Nannie asked Christie in a loud whisper.

Mr. McCain laughed heartily. "Because I keep it out of other folks' business and let it *grow!*"

Mr. McCain treated them courteously, always with respect for their wishes, Christie wrote to her mother. *He said he knows how we'll miss Nannie and the boys, but we'll never be so far away from home that we can't get back real quick if one of the children is sick. Lena is in such a fret to go along, and Jimmie Lou now says she wishes she hadn't got married and set- tled down to being an old lady because she wants to go! But I think Mandy, secretly, is the most envious. I believe she wishes she could just run away from home. She and Wad used to tease each other so lovingly, but now there's a bushel of hard feelings between them. I hate to see Mandy in such despair. She's my best friend in the whole world.*

One morning Christie and Amanda speculated about the trip as they peeled peaches on Christie's front porch. Amanda said cheerfully, "Now, Christie, you just go on out there and enjoy the sights and write back what you're doing. And don't worry none about Nannie and the boys. Dulcie and Lena and me will watch them every minute and they won't be ne'er a bit of trouble."

"I'm afraid the boys will be a burden," said Christie.

"No, they won't. They'll be out with the men. Christie, this is a lifetime opportunity! Now you go on out there and have a elephant time."

"I'm not scared," said Christie.

"I wouldn't expect you to be," Amanda said. She tossed a peach seed at a chicken venturing into the petunias. "But oh, Christie, what they want you to do—do you think you can bear it?"

"Yes, I can," Christie said, reaching for a peach in the bucket on the floor. "I'm going to let the whole world see. I'm going to show them what they done to us."

Amanda touched Christie's cheek, pinching off a speck of some- thing that had landed on her. She said, "Christie, just don't lose your faith."

"Oh, I've got faith," Christie said. She peeled the peach without a break in the spiral. "And I've got that lock of hair you asked me for. It's in my pocket."

"I wanted it for a keepsake."

Christie cut her peach in half and gouged out the seed. She wished Amanda were going with her on the trip. She said, "Don't you think I'll come back?"

"I wouldn't if I was you. Oh, I know you'd have to come back and get the chillern, but if you could just keep going, wouldn't you?"

"I believe I might," Christie said, gazing toward the railroad tracks.

At dinner on Sunday, Christie and Amanda huddled in the kitchen corner by the stove. They weren't talking about anything in particular. They just seemed to be keeping close company. Alma spooned up a bowl of shelly beans from the kettle. Christie and Amanda followed her to the table with bowls of squash and mashed potatoes.

Alma said, "The paper said James and Christie owed it to everybody to get out there and meet the public. Is that a fact?"

"That's what they're saying in town, Mama," said Thurman, reaching for the beans.

"Everybody oughter mind their own business," said Alma. "The very idie, sending James and Christie out to kingdom come when there's so much work to be done."

"They ain't doing this job for free," said Wad, with his mouth full.

"The preacher believes it's a good idie," said Henry. "That's what he meant this morning about not hiding your light under a bushel basket. I'd allow he was talking about you, Christie."

"Oh, reckon he meant Christie?" said Maggie, who was in a corner nursing her baby, a little girl with a saucer face and a stupid look.

"Christie's too bashful about her talents," said Boone. "That makes me recollect the woman that walked a tightrope over Niagara Falls—with her feet in bushel baskets. She wasn't bashful."

Alma set the bowl of beans down and roared. Thomas had brought that story back for Boone once from some paper he picked up.

"Well, Christie's been too peaked to get out and strut lately," Alma said. "Why, she ain't said boo to Maggie's little baby here. She's just lost the will to make over a baby, I reckon."

"I feel stout as a horse," Christie said, glaring at Alma. "I'm working as hard as I ever did." She changed the topic, remembering to tell Thomas what Mr. McCain had said about sheet music. "He said the big thing now is rags," she said.

"I didn't know people peddled rags nowadays," Alma said. "Most everybody here hangs on to their rags."

"He meant they make the paper out of rags," Amanda said.

"That's not what he meant," said Thomas. "He meant a kind of music they call rags. It's everywhere."

"There you go, making me out a ignorant country woman," Alma said, stalking off into the kitchen.

"Oh, I feel so dumb," wailed Amanda. "I didn't know rags was music either."

"A hundred dollars a week," Wad said incredulously as he emerged from the stupor that often accompanied his feeding. "Christie and James go off for part of September, October, November. Ten weeks," he said, spreading out his fingers. "A thousand dollars. That's more'n we'd all get from the whole tobaccer crop and wheat and corn put together."

"And all the traveling expenses is paid," said Joseph, reaching for the salt. "Meals and hotels."

"Wonder what they'll feed you," said Amanda.

"It won't be as good as home cooking," said Alma, showing her face again. "What you eat out ain't fitten to eat."

"Sometimes it is," Thomas said. "I've been fed good on the road."

"I wish I could go out and eat somebody else's cooking," Amanda said as she dumped a ladle of mashed squash onto her husband's plate. "I wonder what those rags sound like."

Alma said, "Law, I'd feel plumb helpless if I had to depend on strangers for my grub, not knowing who growed it or how it was put up."

Amanda said, "Alma, now don't talk Christie out of going!"

"Oh, I ain't worried about Christie," said Alma. "I know she'll go even if she has to live on jerky and dried 'simmons. She'll do ever-what she's of a mind to do."

"Yes, that's true," said Christie, calmly forking tomato slices onto the men's plates. "It used to not be true, but now it is."

James looked at her oddly but stayed quiet. She felt lighter and stronger every day. Only Nannie pulled her apron strings, anchoring her to the ground. What stirred inside her nowadays felt like ripe peaches splitting their skins.

By the end of August, the tobacco was ready to cut. Clint and Jewell had been playing Master and Slave with tobacco sticks, wanting to be allowed to help cut tobacco. The sticks were sharp and dangerous. The boys pretended they were tobacco knives.

"Can I have a knife like yours when I'm big enough to cut?" asked Clint, whacking at a clod of clay in the yard.

"If you show me you can use it and not cut yourself, you can," said James. "But if you're not going to take care of it and treat it with respect, then you ain't ready."

Clint hit his tobacco stick repeatedly against the porch rail. "I can cut good. I could cut right now."

"Yes, and you'd cut your big toe off," said James.

The next morning, Christie tromped out to the patch in a pair of Alma's spreadin'-adder shoes and a pair of James's britches to protect against the sticky tobacco gum. Women never dared to wear britches, but she didn't care what anybody thought now. As soon as she reached the patch, a bug found its way up the britches leg and tickled her skin. She slapped at it.

"Watch out you don't get a snake up in them britches," Wad said.

Joseph, who was cutting in the row ahead, said, "Like that time that necktie creeped out of your britches leg and you thought it was a snake?" Joseph laughed.

"It was in church," Wad said, laughing at himself.

"He almost joined the Lord, he jumped so high," Joseph called to Christie.

She hated tobacco cutting. There was an art to it, and she hadn't mastered it. She had cut only two seasons in the past. Now she was determined to cut this dark-fired tobacco with a vengeance.

The plant had to be split down the stalk, then cut off near the base so that it could be flipped upside down and hung on a long stick. Splitting the stalk required careful aim—the stalks were never quite straight. At first her aim was off. It was like trying to kill a fish flopping in the mud. Tobacco gum coated her hands, stinging a sore on her knuckle. Already the day was blazing hot, and she steamed inside James's heavy britches. The knife blade glinted in the sun. Follow the seam of the stalk, try to get it in one go—that was the rule. She hacked three times on one stalk. Some leaves fell off. She tried to steady the plant, holding the tip of a leaf that she didn't dare pull too hard for fear of damaging it. She couldn't stand too close to the plant or touch its stem or she might cut herself. Each plant, though its stem was hard as a young tree, wavered. From a distance, James watched her, as though waiting to see what she might do. Farther down the field, Joseph's wife, Mary Ann, split and whacked. She had been cutting for years.

"Oh, bedad!" Wad cried out, at some bug or thought. He split and whacked, split and whacked.

Christie listened to the men talk—laughing and telling stories about farmers whose tobacco barns had burned or who had cut off their toes with their tobacco knives, stories that were funny only in retelling. Now and then the men would stop at the end of a row and sharpen their knives. "No time lost in whetting," they would say, looking lazy. Christie was intent on the work, absorbing the details—the way the bugs stuck in the gum on her sleeves, the way the tobacco began to droop almost as soon as it was cut. From where she was working, she could see the white of the curtains in her house and the pink of the petunias that the chickens hadn't scratched up yet.

Christie worked slowly, studying each plant, looking for the center of the stem—the heart, the line down its center—and trying to line up her knife and her swing precisely.

"We ain't hiring you to make kraut," Wad yelled at her when she mangled one plant.

"Be careful," James called to Christie. He had on old boots with rags stuffed in the toes.

In Alma's shoes she felt as sturdy as the tough tobacco stalks. The rhythm grew smooth. Bend, grab, slide, slip, whack, let fall, bend, grab. Her hands grew gummy. The britches were sticky. With increasing ease, she worked steadily, thinking only about the tobacco plants, each one an individual, having its own requirement for splitting and cutting. The insects drowned on her gummy skin. Her face was darkened with gum and sun, and the sweat running through the sticky residue burned in her eyes till tears washed them out.

For a long while the whole patch was quiet—no one talking, just the grunts and whacks and mutters. Then the men would burst into idle talk for a while, mostly addressing the tobacco plants—"steady there" and "I got you good, damn you" and "Hold still, you cotton-picking bastard."

Christie still felt exhilarated. Cutting dark-fire was like cutting her shallow roots to this place. She was freeing herself, so she could leave. Three whacks in a row, three perfect cuts. She wondered if old Mammy Dove missed working tobacco—if there was something about it so familiar and ingrained that she couldn't bear to give up—or whether she was glad to be free of the blisters and burns, the steaming heat, and sticky gum in her eyes. If learning to die was learning to let go of things, would Dove find it easy to let go of something that burned into a person's skin and eyes and heart?

Christie wasn't ready to let go of her babies. If the world killed her babies and wanted to see them dead to draw some lessons from them, then she would show people more than they bargained for. She'd show them, with spite burning in her eyes. She could imagine curious faces staring hard enough to bore a hole through her. But she would be ready. She would be master of the scene. She imagined the spectators being unable to depart until each of them had heard the full story, with all the details. They would not leave until they had absorbed her indignation, until she had fully faced them with her babies—fragile, faded leaves. Her eyes would shout at the people. All of the audience would be pinned to the spot as if caught by a bolt of lightning—as if the Lord Almighty had held them hard by the shoulders in a moment of terrifying knowledge and not let them move from the spot until they fully knew her pain and wrath. Then they would slink off, carrying her sickness away from her, never to forget what had happened to her, Christianna Wheeler. They would carry the memory of her like a warming stone a child carries in a pocket to school. The stone would grow cold, yet they would never be able to throw it away or warm it up again.

She swung her knife hard. She envisioned the steady seasons of tobacco: the beating sun, the tobacco curing above the hickory fires in the barns, growing richer and richer in its smell and dark texture, until one damp day it would come "in case"—that particular moment when it was flexible enough to be stripped. After the stripping, it would be prized into hogsheads and sold. But she would be gone. For several weeks, she would be outside that cycle—going off at a tangent, like the stick that drives a child's hoop.

For a week, they cut tobacco and filled the barns: first Wad's, then James's and Henry's and Joseph's. After they cut the tobacco, they had to let it wilt in the sun until it could be hung without the leaves breaking. They hung the plants upside down on long sticks that they heaved onto the wagon Henry drove through the field. Although Alma said it was too soon for her to exert herself so, Christie insisted on housing tobacco alongside the men, lifting the heavy, loaded sticks above her shoulders and up to the rafters. The work strengthened her and made her feel more prepared for what was to come.

The sun coming through the cracks in the planks of the barn walls made geometric shafts of light and dust. Tittering sparrows flew through them, gleaming white. The barn seemed like a church. But the beams were random. Nothing important was illuminated. Outside the barn, just visible through the cracks, was a bank of whitetop, the weed farmers hated but that Christie secretly thought was pretty. It was a tiny daisy, hundreds of blooms on a single stalk. This year, the whitetop grew in profusion, as delicate as baby's-breath.

When the firing began, a few days after they finished housing, Boone had a spell of coughing and took to his bed. The hickory smoke that cured the tobacco leaf always seized up his lungs, and he wouldn't go outside as long as the fires smoldered beneath the tobacco hanging from the rafters.

The first night of the firing, the neighbors set out on a round of night visiting, keeping watch over the fires and staying up long past dark. Mack Pritchard brought new apples and the Culpeppers brought sorghum molasses. The Wheelers provided watermelons and hens. The children played with frantic energy, as though some spirit were operating them like those electric churns Christie had heard about.

"Growing the dark-fire is toilsome work, but it's worth it just to do it," James said to Christie. They were behind their barn, looking out into the hayfield where the boys were playing in the near dark. Henry had found one of their balls in the tobacco patch. James said, "If the farmers don't stick together, the price will just keep going down." He ran his hand across his forehead. "But maybe it was a mistake to come to the western country here to grow dark-fire," he said. "If we'd stayed in Dundee, none of this would have happened."

"You can't make a hog go backwards," said Christie.

"All that fuss from all over the whole world, and we ain't no better off," said James.

"We'll see what happens," said Christie impatiently. She longed to be traveling, learning about new places. It was true—it was a lifetime opportunity.

The girls were playing drop-the-handkerchief at the edge of the pasture. The boys were still playing ball. Christie could hear them calling to each other, yelling insults and warnings. Mr. Mullins would be coming by in the morning for the feather crowns in order to fit them in the glass case he had devised. Greenberry McCain wanted Mrs. Blankenship's album taken along, as well as the feather crowns and the funeral register. Mr. McCain would have signs and handbills printed up. His lecture would be informative and inspirational, he promised. Christie had thought of all these details over and over, picturing the program in her mind until it stopped shifting shape.

"I have to put out a wash tomorrow and get our clothes together," Christie said.

"Are you ready to do this?" James asked.

"Except for leaving the children," she said. "But we have to do it, so we'll do it. They'll get by. Mandy will take good care of them. Nobody's as good with children as Mandy. You know that."

They could see Amanda moving out toward the girls, her soft, lilting voice meeting theirs. She joined their play, taking her place in the ring, and they all started to move, hand-in-hand, picking up speed until Dulcie, outside the circle, dropped the handkerchief. Christie saw

Wad and Henry leave the barn, in serious conversation. They turned up the path to Wad's house, and on the way they joined the neighbors who were packing up their wagons to leave. Mack Pritchard seemed to have lost his hat, and Ethel Pritchard was getting her clean pie plate back from Alma. Christie felt as if she and James were just watching a scene in a drama. Already, they were far away, looking back.

"Don't forget this was my idea," Christie said to James. "I want to do it."

The sounds of the children playing—a throng of them with their high, trilling shrieks—traveled out through the air, crossing each other and colliding. Joseph was in James's barn watching the fire, in case a fragment of leaf dropped into the fire and sent the barn up in flames. Anything could happen, Christie thought. But probably nothing would ever happen in their lives that compared to what had already happened to them. That thought made her bold now, as if she had been granted as much power as was necessary or possible. She was ready to confront the world, with all her anger and curiosity and urgency. Then Christie heard Nannie calling her, and she went around the side of the barn.

Bats were flying out of the barn, dipping and whirling like swallows. They had been smoked out by the fires. They would have to find another home during firing season. Christie felt like the bats, having to leave her home for a period until the fires were over. She heard Nannie calling her again, and she hurried into the dark.

V

The Journey

Fall 1900

1

THE DAY THEY LEFT WAS SUNNY AND CLEAR. MR. W. GREENBERRY
McCain drove out from Crittenden's Inn in a hired carriage to fetch
the Wheelers. Christie thought James appeared distinguished in the
new suit they had ordered from Sears, Roebuck & Co., although she
knew he felt awkward in it. They had spent forty dollars to equip
themselves for the trip with carpetbags, a large imitation-leather case,
and traveling clothes. Christie had on a new navy suit trimmed with
black braid. She had never bought a ready-made suit of clothes before,
and she had to let out the hem a little and take some tucks in the
jacket.

Samuel Mullins was waiting for them in the front parlor of his
funeral home, his small, limp hands pawing the air nervously. Christie
held herself back, behind the men, fearing the sight of her babies. She
was determined to feel nothing, no more than if they were a set of
porcelain figurines. But she was spared the sight. The glass case had
already been fastened into the oak chest and locked inside a large
trunk, which was resting in a corner as if it were an innocent feature of
the furnishings.

"Now I must entrust you to take good care of the precious cargo,"
Mr. Mullins said to Greenberry McCain in his thin, jittery voice. "I
know it means everything to these good Wheelers, and it means considerable to me, with so much work invested in them."

"You can count on me, Mullins," said Greenberry confidently. "I
have a good deal invested as well. I've just been assuring James and
Christie that I'll do everything in my power to take care of what right-
fully belongs to them."

"This is going to be worth so much to the people of America," Mr. Mullins said, almost whispering. "I can't express my appreciation deeply enough."

"Don't even try," said Greenberry. "I take heart at your attempt."

"You must relay back to me what people are saying," Mr. Mullins said, touching Greenberry's sleeve anxiously. "Not many people around here are used to these new techniques. So I really want very much to know what impression my work makes and if they have any quarrels with it. And of course you must let me know if the work doesn't hold up."

Christie and James stared at the brass-trimmed trunk, buckled with leather straps. The top was rounded, so nothing could be set on it. It seemed hard and sturdy, built for rough handling.

"I've got the glass casket packed with pillows inside the chest," explained Mr. Mullins. "If you pack it back the same way, those little lambs will still be resting on their eternal bed just like they were."

"Won't they jar loose?" James asked.

Mr. Mullins smiled and caressed the trunk. "They're held in by straps around their little middles beneath their clothes, so even if the trunk gets turned upsy-daisy they won't move. Don't you worry about your precious angels. And there's more pillows holding the chest into the trunk."

The room was dim, with the morning light peeping from behind the heavy damask curtains. A strangely dark painting of the Resurrection, with Jesus flying above the mouth of the cave where he had been entombed, hung over the mantel. He was reaching upward into a small, brilliant shaft of light in the sky, his hands extended so that each finger was splayed out like a spider leg. The picture foretold her journey, Christie thought.

Mr. Mullins smiled at her and said something in farewell. Then he squeezed her arm and said, "It would please me so much to have these precious babies returned here, so that we can show them indefinitely."

At the station, Greenberry McCain handled the baggage, personally locating a safe place in the baggage car for the trunk. Then he paid a porter a quarter to ride with it and keep watch over it. On board, Christie and James hunted chairs on the left side of the train, so they could get a good view when they passed by their home. They sat near a starved-looking couple with four children, a woman with a squalling baby and two little boys, and several jovial men who loudly made it known that they were going to Nashville to a grain-company seminar about improved seed strains. Almost as soon as they were seated, the train began to move out, with a flourish of steam and an accelerating hum of wheels. Within a few minutes, they were approaching the farm. Christie was accustomed to the whistle and roar of the train, but now she was on the train and not at the house. First the barn came into view, floating toward them, and then she could see her house clearly—the view all those travelers had had, all those visitors who stopped back in the spring. She gasped.

"The chillern!" she cried, punching James's leg, then immediately felt embarrassed that she had touched her husband so familiarly in public.

Lined up against the fence were the children—Amanda's and Alma's and her own. There were eight of them, all the children but Thurman, who thought he was too big to do anything with the younger ones. Christie thrust her arm out the window and waved.

"Look at Nannie. She's got her sunbonnet on."

"Look at Jewell wave," said James. "I think he sees us."

Greenberry McCain sat across the aisle reading a St. Louis newspaper he had bought from the conductor. He seemed to think it very ordinary to be reading a morning paper brought all the way from St. Louis. He hardly looked up, but James and Christie waved to their family until the receding figures were out of sight.

Christie felt she had to have a steady mind during this trip. She was much more excited by the prospect of the journey than she had let James know. A rumble of expectation had been growing inside her. She badly needed to get away from the place that had held her a prisoner. If she could go to new places, she had been thinking, she might get over her grief. But the sight of Nannie waving and waving stayed with her. Nannie had been up in the night with a sore throat, and Christie gave her a teaspoon of coal oil and sugar. By morning her throat seemed all right, and she sucked on a piece of Boone's horehound. Amanda declared that it was impossible for the Lord to take another one of Christie's children from her.

Early that morning, Amanda had cornered Christie in the bedroom, where she was looking for her hairbrush. Amanda's wispy hair was falling into her face and her eyes were red. She said, "Now, Christie, I may be clumsy and I can't cook perfect, but one thing I can do, and you know I can—I can take care of little boys and girls. Alma may not like the way I do it, but I'll give the littluns a lot of loving, and Lena and Dulcie will help, so don't you worry none."

"I wish you could go." Christie found the brush in a pile of sewing.

"I don't have to go, I reckon. You'll tell me everything." Amanda began pulling the sheets from the bed. "I'll wash these today."

"I hope people don't look down on us."

"Don't you be ashamed of who you are, Christie."

"Will they think we're hicks and live like animals, dropping a lit-ter?" Christie had not dwelled on that thought in some time, but now her nervousness seemed to flutter around for something to alight on.

"Don't think such a thing, Christie! You're just as good as anybody out there, and there'll be thousands of people who will admire you. Remember nobody's done what you have."

It was true that she still felt the glow of her fame. It lingered, like mist in the morning. But she had an urgent purpose—to get out there and face the public, to show them her pain. She wanted to get revenge on them, on people she didn't even know. She thought her love for her babies would carry her through the coming weeks. She wasn't going to let people forget them easily.

As the train moved beyond the familiar landscapes, Christie drank in every detail she could see, imagining how she would report it all back to Amanda. The trees were still green, but the fields were gold and empty like cleaned-out rooms. Now and then they passed farmers gathering corn or Negroes hauling wagonloads of tobacco covered with old quilts. At crossings, people waiting in buggies and wagons waved at the train. Christie thought back to her journey from Dundee to Hopewell four years before, when she had been so optimistic and high-spirited. That journey had been cold, with clouds threatening rain. She had felt homesick briefly, but as they ventured into unfamiliar country, her excitement overcame her, and she felt like one of those early explorers she had read about in history. Clint and Jewell couldn't sit still, and James, busy driving the team, spoke little. Christie held on to the big bundle of a baby in her lap and sang song after song.

> *My sugar lump, and won't give her up,*
> *My sugar lump, and won't give her up,*
> *My sugar lump, and won't give her up,*
> *Oh, turn, cinnamon, turn.*

Nannie smiled, and the wagon bumped a rock, startling hiccups out of her.

Later that day, Christie remembered, a muddy road slowed them down, and the horses struggled to keep the wagon from miring up. She taught Clint his letters from a little cloth book she had sewed together from remnants; *A* for Ant, *B* for Bee, *C* for Cat, *D* for Dog. She and James sang "The Brown Girl" and "A Woman Lived in a Far

Country." The wagon jounced through a thick forest, and Nannie cried. Christie sang and rocked.

Now, on the train, James stared straight ahead, looking stiff and hot in his new clothes. His large, thick hands were unaccustomed to resting idly there on his knees. They resembled worn tools.

"We're in Tennessee," Greenberry sang out a while later. "Tennessee used to be part of North Carolina."

"You learn something new ever day," said James, in a listless tone.

"I used to be quite a scholar of history," said Greenberry, folding his newspaper carefully. "I contemplated going to the seminary but knew I couldn't stick to that much study."

He took out his plug of tobacco and carved off a small piece with an ivory-handled pocketknife. He offered the piece to James, but James said, "No, I don't believe I care for a chaw of tobaccer."

"I'm giving up chewing after I get done with this plug," Greenberry said. "Cigarettes are so much more satisfying."

The train passed cleared tobacco fields, faded green pastures, flat bottomland. Then it entered wilderness, where the trees were close enough to touch through the window. Branches slapped the side of the car. It was warm, and Christie fanned herself with a fan Mr. Mullins had given her. The fan had his advertisement and a picture of Jesus with a halo on it. The halo was a little off center, like a lopsided daisy-chain crown.

By the time Greenberry McCain got his tobacco chewed up well, the train was on a trestle bridge. Christie glimpsed the brown liquid in his mouth. Below her window, she could see nothing but water. After crossing the river, the train plunged into thick woods. Christie's great-aunt on her mother's side, Hatt Rhodes, had traveled across the Great Plains and over the Rocky Mountains, looking for gold. The wagon party lost several oxen and were forced to leave their furniture and other possessions along the trail. Christie always imagined a nice what-not or a chifforobe sitting out in the desert. Aunt Hatt gave birth while on the trail. Her diary, which Aunt Sophie had, stated the event in a simple sentence. *Woke up yesterday with a fine baby girl, whose breath soon stopped, had to leave her under a pile of rocks.* Aunt Hatt's husband disappeared a year after they reached California, and Hatt took in washing in the mining camps. After a while no one heard from her anymore, but somehow Aunt Sophie got the diary. Christie wondered if she should keep a diary, now that she was leaving home.

"Your fore-parents came up this river to Hopewell, James," Christie said.

"What good are fore-parents?" said James. "They're all dead."

"They'll say that about you one of these days," said Greenberry, removing a little silver spittoon from his coat pocket. He spat into it and snapped the lid to.

"I've got to take care of who's coming after," said James. "I ain't got time to worry about who went before." He cracked his knuckles.

"Well, I always thought history was instructive," said Greenberry.

"James means we can't take time to worry about our ancestors, since we don't have to sew for them or feed them," said Christie, as she reached into her sewing bag. "But I think it's interesting to know about your ancestors." She decided not to say anything more, knowing James would feel jealous if she sided with Greenberry McCain.

She worked some buttonholes for a while, but she couldn't keep her eyes off the scenery. It was getting hillier—pretty, rolling land, with clusters of harvesters here and there. Seen from this distance, the landscape was like a picture, as if the people in it were only decorations.

The train stopped several times, letting people off and on. A quiet, hatless man reminded Christie of her Uncle Willis—his broad forehead and drooping mustache. A woman's round, sad eyes and straight, fine hair evoked her Aunt Dora on her father's side. She counted eight redheads in the car.

At noon, Christie and James ate the dinner Alma had fixed for them—fried chicken, ham, cold slaw, potatoes in their jackets, green beans, biscuits, fried pies. Greenberry McCain had brought his dinner from Mrs. Crittenden's—ham, cornbread, potato cakes, corn, and sweet-potato pie.

"We'll be eating high on the hog everywhere we go," Greenberry said. "But I'm sure going to miss Mrs. Crittenden's fare. This morning she made me her special corn pone with damson preserves."

"What are we going to do with Alma's dishes?" James asked Christie.

"We'll use them to get dinners put up for us to carry on the train," said Christie impatiently. Alma had also sent along jars of plum butter and peach pickles and kraut, even though she knew James hated kraut.

Christie thought she could ride this train indefinitely, savoring each town and field and mule they passed, as long as she never had to look inside that trunk. Dread began gnawing at her, like a mouse somewhere in the walls of her house. When a child in a chair up ahead tried to play peep-eye with her, she turned her face away.

In Milan, Tennessee, they waited at the depot three hours for the Louisville & Nashville to Nashville. The train was late, and Greenberry was afraid they would not get to Nashville in time for their program that evening. Christie sat on a bench and sewed, feeling a reprieve in the delay. James, restless, walked up and down the street, now and then checking with the baggage room to make sure the trunk was still there. Greenberry paced along the platform and smoked. He had bought a package of factory-rolled cigarettes.

"Thank heaven," he said when the whistle sounded.

On the Nashville train, Christie couldn't concentrate. She put away her sewing, thrusting her workbox down into her carry-bag. Her chair was unsteady, with soiled upholstery. She stared out the window. All summer, she had tried not to think about the babies. The promise of being with them away from the painful reminders at home had seemed good—something saved for a special occasion. But now that she would actually see them again, she dreaded it even more than she had dreaded their funeral. A knot gathered in the pit of her stomach as Nashville drew near. The train slowed down, inching past long warehouses and grain companies and stockyards.

"Hurry, hurry, hurry," Greenberry said when the train stopped. "James, let's run to the baggage car."

The station was crowded. As they rushed across an expansive waiting room, Christie glimpsed oak and rich gold and a deep green like the dark-tobacco leaf. Above her, several enormous depictions of women in loose robes hovered over the high arches that anchored the high ceiling. The women seemed to be emerging from the walls, with vegetables in their hands, but there was no opportunity for her to study them. The passengers plunged into the stream of moving humanity—like cattle at a stockyard, Christie thought. The rush was unsettling, and she felt unable to grasp all that was happening around her in the moments it took to get through the station. They couldn't tarry, Greenberry McCain said. There was no time to go to their hotel first. They had to go straight to the exhibition hall. He ordered the baggage to a carriage and hustled them along. All of this occurred in just minutes. She saw James stumble as they rushed to the street. Inside the carriage, she was conscious of the brassbound trunk in the compartment at the rear. It was like a caboose, following them.

"This is the worst day of my life," James said, staring at his lap.

"No, it's not," said Christie, clutching her carry-bag to her knees. She wished he weren't so ill at ease in strange places, but she didn't want him to know of her own fear.

The horses wove through streets jammed with nightlife. Throngs of people were out walking by the light of gas lamps. The streets were lined with brick structures, some with white columns and cornices. Soon the carriage halted in front of a tall, yellow-trimmed building. A blue-striped awning stretched over the entrance.

"Is this it?" James said. "It sure is big."

"The Nashville Opera House," said Christie, reading the name engraved above the double doors. A cluster of people obstructed the entrance.

"The finest," said Greenberry, bounding down from the carriage. He directed the driver to unload the trunk and one of the bags and to deliver the rest of the baggage to their hotel. The driver was to return for them at nine o'clock. Christie saw Greenberry give him a dollar.

"Come on," Greenberry said to Christie and James. "We're right on time. Let's get going."

She paused to read the large bill out front. It was set in a black frame.

The Greatest Wonder of Nature in the Last 500 Yrs.
THE WHEELER QUINTUPLETS
Five Babies
Born of One Mother in One Night

SEE the Babies the Whole World Is Talking About
SEE the Mother and Father in the Flesh
HEAR the Renowned Educator and Lecturer,
Mr. W. Greenberry McCain,
Discourse on the Phenomenon of the Quintuplets
7 P.M. sharp September 20, 1900

Christie remembered the Amazing Frog-Girl from a carnival back in Dundee when she was a child. She had expected to see a little girl with skin like a frog and webbed feet. Instead, inside the sideshow tent, she saw something preserved in liquid in a jar. It was very small, with a curious resemblance to a fish, like a large tadpole that had begun to turn to a frog. It was possibly a frog whose development had gone awry. The liquid gave it a pale, bleached appearance. Christie had been relieved that it wasn't an actual girl, but what stuck vividly in her memory was what she had imagined—an ugly little girl with frog feet.

"You don't need to read it out to me," said James when Christie began to read the bill aloud. "I can read that."

Greenberry McCain ushered them into a side door. He and the carriage driver had set the trunk inside. "What a crowd!" he said. "Nashville is a coming place. I knew they'd want to see."

"I don't want to see," said Christie.

James snapped, "We agreed to come on this thing."

"I won't look."

"Well, don't then."

Greenberry McCain didn't seem to notice what they said. They were walking briskly down a dark, narrow corridor, and he was pulling the trunk along on wheels by a leather strap knotted on its handle. Christie hadn't realized the trunk had wheels. That did not seem possible. She thought of her boys pulling Nannie across the yard in the little wagon that James had made.

A hefty man with a broad face appeared from a dark doorway and greeted Greenberry with relief. "We were afraid you weren't going to get here, Mr. McCain," he said.

"This here's the manager, Mr. Rankin," Greenberry said to James and Christie.

Hastily, Mr. Rankin shook James's hand and showed them into a small room next to the stage, where they could wait until time for the program. From the doorway of the room, they could see two Negroes going through a door marked STAGE DOOR. One of them propped the door open. The stage was arranged with two tables, a lectern, and three wicker armchairs. The curtain was closed, its thick folds fluttering slightly.

"Y'all just wait right here till we get everything set up," Mr. Rankin said to James.

He helped Greenberry pull the trunk to the stage. The trunk was sitting on a rolling wooden platform that Greenberry had strapped to it when he checked it onto the train, Christie learned. She and James stood in the little room, their eyes on the stage.

James dug out his pocket watch. "Wonder if Thurman got the cows milked," he said.

The room was dingy and dim, with oily rags piled on a table and a broom and mop standing together in a corner like shy sweethearts. The wood floor had just been oiled. Some men deep in conversation walked by the door, and a little boy sped past, wailing after a woman who warned him that he would fall on the oily floor.

"I'm hungry," James said glumly.

Christie gave him some cold chicken left in their dinner bucket. She wasn't hungry. James got cranky when he couldn't eat on time, and she had always prided herself on having his meals ready. Now his appetite made her angry.

"Do you want this jar of kraut?" she said, pulling Alma's jar out of her bag.

"No. Who ever heard of eating kraut right out of the jar, without no pork?" He sucked on a chicken bone and dropped it in the dinner bucket.

She saw Greenberry McCain on the stage. The trunk lid had been flung back, and she could see white pillows. She watched him lift out the oak chest. It was covered with carvings of lambs, birds, vines, fruit, and berries—the Garden of Eden, she realized. She turned her head. In a few moments one of the Negroes on the stage brought the trunk into the room with them and set it down, its lid still yawning. Christie and James stared at it. The insides were papered with a pink floral design.

"We're ready for you," Greenberry said, popping into the room. "Don't worry, I'll do all the talking." His hand patted the air; then he rushed away with a little skip.

A sheet covered the glass case containing the babies. The table supporting it was set to the left of the lectern. The other table held Mrs. Blankenship's album, the little glass box of feather crowns, and some smaller objects: the five nursing bottles with black nipples, some pieces of cloth that Christie recognized as diapers and outing blankets, a set of baby dresses, and some of the gifts they had received from the public. She recalled the silver feeding spoons and cups. She hadn't realized that so many souvenirs of their babies' short lives had been assembled. She couldn't remember how Greenberry McCain had obtained them. She watched him drape a sheet over that table too.

"All you have to do is set here," he said, indicating two wicker chairs, one on each side of the table that held the babies. Christie could hear voices from the audience, on the other side of the curtain. The stage floor was polished oak.

"Wonder how many people are out there," said James. He belched.

"I feel sick," Christie whispered to James. "Let's ask him if we can wait in that room. I didn't expect all this—"

"It was your idea to come," he said, his voice hard as a stone. "You wanted to be with the babies. So now you are. And you'll have to go through with it."

As they took their chairs, Christie resolved not to reveal her feelings again to James throughout the rest of the trip. She didn't care if they never spoke again. The stage was hot and dark. When the curtain parted, a flood of light hit her face. Dimly, she could make out the audience, shrouded in darkness. Electric lights flickered along the side walls and above the stage. It felt so strange, to be in a windowless room, full of people, at night, with false lights beaming all over her. James was sitting far away from her, the babies a barrier between them.

Christie could make out the first few rows of people. Surprisingly, many in the audience were dressed up, as if for church.

"Ladies and gentlemen," Greenberry McCain began in a somber tone. "I'm part of a lecture-tour company that sends out representatives to speak to the public about educational matters. Every season brings a new subject. In the past, the Fair Day Company has sponsored the Funkhouser lectures and lantern-slide programs on the Nation's Capital, the Natives of Africa (with two missionaries lecturing with me), and the wonders of science—electricity, the telephone, and the talking graphophone, with demonstrations.

"Today we have for you one of the most wondrous occurrences in the history of mankind. A year ago, a young woman called Christianna Wheeler, mother of three small children, was living simply on a tobacco farm in the region of the Jackson Purchase in Kentucky, with her hard-working husband, James. Today Mrs. James Wheeler is one of the most notable and most admired women in the United States. What has she done? Let me tell you."

Greenberry went on and on, in a low, even voice, quietly presenting their story, dragging it out for savored detail and suspense. His manner was more compelling than Christie would have imagined. The talk was entertaining but restrained—not exaggerated like a medicine man hawking Indian oil from the back of a buggy. Christie heard James's stomach growl. Her own stomach clenched. For all the grief she felt for her babies, petrified under that sheet, her overwhelming sorrow suddenly was for her husband, dragged away from his work and made to sit on display like a prize turnip at the fair. She regretted snapping at him. She could feel his loathing of the situation and his fear of strangers. He was still sucking chicken out of his teeth.

After going on for some time, his pitch rising and falling like a preacher's, Greenberry McCain turned his attention to the stage displays. "We want to show you this admirable collection," he said, removing the sheet from the table of mementos. "Here we have the five little nursing bottles used to feed the babies milk from cows, a sized-down diaper cloth to show how small they were, a chart of statistics recorded by their doctor, who devoted the energies of his practice to caring for the little mites, miscellaneous likenesses of the precious babies, and a display of cuttings and letters of good wishes from all over the world—even from the Queen of England and the President of our United States."

Greenberry spun on his heel suddenly to face Christie directly. He said, "And last but not least—and most important—are the real live flesh-and-blood parents, Christianna and James Wheeler, here as proof that this really happened. You'll see their likenesses in some of the photographs with the babies."

Finally, Greenberry invited the audience to come forward and view the quintuplets, restored to a lifelike appearance for the enlightenment of the general public.

"There's much to see, ladies and gentlemen, but please form a line and take time-about."

He lifted the sheet covering the babies. The crowd, on its feet, applauded spontaneously and began to form a line. An usher stood at the end of each row while the people filed forward expectantly, as if they were coming to the altar to be saved. Mr. Rankin, the manager, directed people along as they reached the stage.

Christie stared straight ahead at the crowd. She did not let her eyes fall on the glass case. She did not know if James was looking. The people came forward, their eyes aimed at the babies.

The people drifted past. Their casual utterances and their eagerness seemed so familiar. Christie was thrown back into the spring, when a multitude of strangers crowded around her bed, train passengers smothering her with their attention. She felt light-headed.

"They look like they're about to cry."

"They're all just alike."

"Why, they ain't no bigger'n puppies."

"Wonder how they fed all these."

"They look so real."

"I bet they sure made a racket when they commenced to cry all at once."

"It's too bad they couldn't save ne'er a one of 'em."

A man tipped his hat wordlessly to Christie and James. Some people shyly muttered to them, and Christie had an impulse to talk about her babies, as any proud mother would dote on her offspring. But, instead, her anger revived.

"Get your eyes full," she said.

"Look at 'em," she said to a man with large ears that stuck out like funguses from a log. "But you can't touch 'em."

Most of the people stood in awe, too dumbstruck to speak to the babies' parents. Christie heard one man whisper to another, "Look at the pappy—bet he didn't figure on five. He must have hit the bull's-eye."

A redheaded woman spoke to Christie. "I 'magine your heart is just broke to pieces." The woman's freckles were sprinkled across her cheeks like measles.

"My babies was wooled to death—pure and simple," Christie said. "By people just like you. But now nobody can touch 'em."

She lost track of time, and the people blurred together. She never glanced toward the babies. She sat at an angle, turned away from the display. She couldn't see James. She couldn't see the table of souvenirs. She saw Greenberry bustling around, talking to first one spectator, then another. She heard not a word from James.

Finally, it was over. The glass case was safely locked away. They were in the carriage again. The trunk was in the compartment behind them, with the wheels still strapped on.

"Well, I thought it was just splendid," Greenberry murmured. Christie and James remained silent.

"Are you sure you need us along?" James asked Greenberry later, as they drove down a dark street. "All we done was set there."

"Absolutely. They want to see you. You're a big part of the whole attraction. You see, for them to believe those babies are real and not just dolls painted up pretty, they need to see the real flesh-and-blood live parents. You add drama. These folks want a story. Believe me, your service is indispensable." Greenberry seemed to throb with good spirits.

"We have to be along," Christie whispered to her husband, while Greenberry spoke with the carriage driver. "So we can get the payment and so the babies don't get lost."

"They're liable to get away from us real easy," James muttered.

"Did you look?" she asked him.

"Yeah."

"I didn't."

"I couldn't help it," he said.

"Had they changed?"

"No. Not a bit."

The hotel was a spacious brick building, with four stories and a large lobby with electric lights in a chandelier. People in the lobby were dressed fashionably, and there was a hush in the air, as if they were afraid to speak up. It was because of the soft carpets and the lights, Christie decided.

"I'll go out and round us up some grub," Greenberry said after he had made arrangements at the hotel desk. "The dining room's closed—too bad, because they're famous for their barbecued goat and their ambrosia."

"I could eat a goat, I believe," said James.

"I'll see what I can locate," said Greenberry, handing James a key. "Y'all go on up. Your room is number two-oh-three. They already sent your big case up, and that good man at the desk is going to take care of the trunk. He's going to keep it in the storeroom. It's like a bank vault."

"I'm not sure about leaving it," James said worriedly.

Greenberry laughed. "Let me show you the vault. I don't think even Jesse James could break it open."

James followed him to the storeroom behind the desk. Christie watched them talking with a man in a uniform. James, returning to Christie's side, seemed to be satisfied.

Greenberry left. They could see him out on the sidewalk looking up and down and finally deciding on an easterly direction.

"Let's go," said James, picking up their carpetbags.

Christie followed, with her small carry-bag. Her foot hurt, and she was more tired than she had realized. She was hungry now.

2

A WELL-DRESSED MAN WITH A BEARD STOPPED THEM BY THE STAIRS. "Aren't you the couple with the quintuplets?" he asked politely.

"Yeah, we are," said James, setting down the bags. "Why?"

"My name is Dr. Graham Johnson. I wonder if I could talk to you about the quintuplets? I was at the lecture and take a great scientific interest in such matters. Here's my card." He pressed a small card into James's hand. James handed it over to Christie. "I understand that you are now on a lecture tour, but I wonder if when you finish I might help you."

"How could you help us?" James asked.

Christie glanced at the card, catching the words "Institute of Man, Washington."

James picked up the bags again. "Mr. Johnson, we've had about enough help from just about everybody you could name, and we're tired."

"He growls when he's tired," said Christie apologetically.

The man had a narrow forehead, straight brown hair, and small ears. He spoke with a Northern brogue. He said, "I don't mean to interfere, but I thought maybe you might be considering what to do with the babies' remains when you're finished with your tour."

"What are you talking about?" James asked suspiciously.

"I represent an institute that studies scientific curiosities, and I can assure you the infants would be in good hands if you were to deposit them there. Our institution is devoted to the advancement of science, not to public entertainment. If you should ever find that you need somewhere to deposit the remains—a place where they would be kept permanently and safe from the curious eyes of the public—then I can be of service."

"I reckon they'll go back to Hopewell," James said uneasily.

"They oughter be buried," said Christie, dropping the card into her carry-bag.

"What are you doing all the way down here from Washington?" James asked the man.

"I was here on a research trip, when I saw the lecture advertised in the newspaper."

Christie thought she recognized the man now. He had been sitting on the aisle near the front. She remembered the lights on his spectacles. Her head throbbed.

"Thank ye kindly, sir," said James, starting up the stairs. "Excuse us. We're a long way from home and we ain't never been in a hotel before."

"Don't let me hurry you," Dr. Johnson said, smiling politely. "I'll be in touch again, if you don't mind."

Going up the stairs, James said to Christie, "I didn't believe they would stay like that, but they're just like when we saw them the last time. It's like you canning green beans. They stayed exactly the same. I didn't believe that."

"I was afraid to look," she said.

"Well, you don't have to be. There ain't nothing new. I guess they'll stay that way forever."

Christie shivered. "What do you think that man wanted with them?"

"A lot of people would like to have those babies."

Their gas-lighted room was pleasant, with several chairs and a rose-patterned carpet. The wallpaper was blue, with little wreaths of forget-me-nots in the design. Beside the washstand was a breakfast announcement. The washstand had hot and cold faucets and a porcelain sink, and in a closet there was an indoor commode, with a sign on the wall: PULL CHAIN.

Christie sank into a soft chair. "Well, here we are," she said.

"I was afraid your nerves might go off," James said.

She waved away the suggestion. "Don't worry about my nerves."

The gas light on the wall blinked. She felt her nerves were like the heavy thread she used on blue-jeans britches. She got up and washed her face and brushed her hair. She stared out the window at the crowd of people and horses on the street. The smell of horse manure drifted into the open window. It was a welcome reminder of home—the smell of wet straw and warm animals.

A while later, Greenberry McCain rapped on the door and handed them a grease-soaked sack of fried potatoes and sausage and two bottles of sarsaparilla.

"It was all I could find," he said.

3

To the *Hopewell Chronicle,*

Dear Editor,

Here is the news of our travels. In this first ten days we have had a
variety of settings for our exhibition with the Fair Day Co. The first was a
sizable opera house in Nashville, and a large crowd was attracted. It was at
night, and the theater was lighted with electric bulbs. After stopping in
Nashville for three days, we traveled to some smaller cities in the state of
Tennessee, where we appeared at a grange, another opera house (where
they play melodramas), and an exhibition hall. Yesterday we arrived in
Alabama, where we sat with our exhibit all day in a fairgrounds building,
while the public passed through to see the babies. We stop here for three
days, with Mr. W. Greenberry McCain offering his lecture five times a
day. Mr. McCain presents the whole story of the babies, and he recounts
many scientific facts about unusual births, going all the way back to Julius
Caesar. Mr. McCain has worked out the chances of quintuplets happening
and says that the chances of five babies being born at once, and all normal
and not premature, are forty-six million to one.

Down here they draw their words out so long it's like pulling molasses
taffy. It's pleasant to listen to, if you have the time. The Southland is of a
fair climate but filled with far more poor folks than we are used to seeing.
The results of the War are everywhere, and the evidence of defeat is wide-
spread, even so many years later. At the train stations in the larger towns
there are sometimes beggars. And the Negroes are still living in the same
quarters accorded to the slaves in pre-War times, but now their families

have multiplied and there is sure to be less space for all. Occasionally we see from the train an old plantation house, somewhat weatherbeaten, and behind it the old slave cabins small as corncribs.

A sight unusual to our eyes is that of cotton fields. The picking is going on now, and it is quite remarkable to see the fields full of white fluffs, contrasted with the colorful attire of the field hands. We notice wagons with wire-mesh sides filled to the brim with fresh cotton. The weeds on the roadsides have caught stray cotton fluffs blown about by the wind so that sometimes you think it has snowed. This domestic plant, so useful in daily life, is grown with a great amount of toil.

The new train station in Nashville opened in September, and it is as magnificent as a palace. It is constructed of marble and stone, with grand columns, and is full of immense statues of handsome women. The train, too, is a memorable experience. The screaming and pulling of the brakes and the noise of the cars jostling each other are difficult to get accustomed to, but there is much to see and learn. Not only the sights out the window, but so many kinds of people you see on the train, dressed in all manner of ways, from formal and stylish to modest and plain. Many passengers bring dinner baskets from home—a good many corncakes and fried chickens and biscuits and ham. At train stops Negro women meet the train, with sack lunches for sale. The boardinghouses offer a plain, hearty fare much enjoyed by tired travelers. Sometimes a carriage meets us at the station and we board in a private home, in a town where Mr. McCain has contacts. In Nashville we stopped at a large hotel with piped water, where they serve ambrosia.

Yours,
Mrs. James Wheeler

Christie read the letter aloud to James on the vine-shaded porch of their rooming house. He was rolling a cigarette, catching the crumbs on his britches. He didn't smoke often. At home he smoked behind the barn, because the smell made her sick.

"Do you think they'll print it?" Christie asked.

"They told you they'd print anything you send 'em."

"I don't know about the words. They'll want it to be of a high tone."

"You were good in school. It sounded pretty high-tone to me."

Her handwriting had a flourish and a forward slant that looked as though the letters were running, bent forward by a fierce wind. She folded the letter.

"They might not print that part about the niggers," James said.

"But it's true."

"They won't be interested."

"Well, I found it interesting."

James licked the cigarette paper and twisted the ends. "That's the way you are with everything," he said. "You'd find a white-oak crosstie interesting."

"As long as we're out gallivanting, we may as well take note of what's out here," she said sharply. "I don't understand anybody who won't try to learn something."

She had asked two innkeepers if they knew anything about the Institute of Man, but she could learn nothing. She was reluctant to ask Greenberry about it.

"You didn't tell about that house with the leak in the ceiling," James said. "And you said the food was good—the food ain't been that good."

She unfolded the letter. "I forgot to tell about the crowds."

"Tell them next time."

Christie and James were accustomed to court day and mule day at home, with throngs of a thousand or more around the square, but the crowds in Nashville had seemed endless. The morning they left Nashville, it almost seemed that the crowd would push forward onto the tracks in front of the train.

She read her letter over again. She knew it was too simple, but she couldn't set down what was really in her heart. As she had determined to do, she faced the people squarely, with her anger sharpened and aimed. She felt pride and anguish and resentment—and desire for revenge—all mingled together. Her eyes burned fire. The public's greedy curiosity was just the same, whether the babies were alive or dead. But she hadn't expected so many people to bring their own grief to her. Every day, amid the curious stares, she met someone who told her of losing a baby, or pressed upon her a photograph of some dead child lying in a heap of flowers or sitting in a straight chair as if still alive. Just yesterday, a woman gave her a likeness of a little girl with curled hair and a large hair bow, lying with her doll on a bed. The woman's sorrow crashed into Christie's own like trains head on. Christie had no words to offer the woman. She didn't know what solace the sight of the five lifeless babies could give. Could her babies' deaths really have been a greater gift to the world than their lives might have been? She had never believed that, but everybody from the preacher on down had urged the idea upon her. Greenberry McCain argued in his talk that the fate of the babies served a higher purpose, and he called on his knowledge of Scripture to bolster his point. But most of his analogies didn't make sense. He seemed to snatch a Bible quotation out of thin air, whatever came to him, and work it into his talk. He was especially fond of Psalms 94:8. "Understand, ye brutish among the people: and ye fools, when will ye be wise?"

Two days ago, in Pulaski, Tennessee, Christie had finally looked directly at the babies. Greenberry had left her and James for almost half an hour while he went to get a late dinner. Before going, he apologized for hurrying them along on the tour without allowing them a moment alone with their babies.

"I realize I oughter let you be with them before, and I feel mortified about it," he said. "I feel such a fool that I rushed you into the show that first night. But we were running late." He sighed. "I just didn't think. But don't blame me, please. I'm eager to do right by you. To show you my good faith, I'm giving you the second week's payment in advance."

The glass case was covered by the sheet. Slowly, James inched it back, and Christie expected fresh grief to surge forth from her heart. But she restrained herself. The forms inside the case were dolls, as Nannie had thought. They hadn't changed. Christie had already memorized the painted, changeless features back in the spring. There was nothing more to be gained from staring into the babies' faces now. They held no lost meanings or fresh messages. She stoppered up her feelings the way her mother bottled grape juice with her mail-order bottle-capper.

4

DAY AFTER DAY, A MOB OF STRANGERS BUNCHED AROUND THE GLASS box. They pawed at the bottles and dresses and pictures on display. Women ogled James. Christie stared them down. She and James learned to slide their chairs slightly forward during the program, so the babies were not in their line of vision. Christie told James that, although she didn't want to look at them, it steadied her to know the babies were right there. But at the end of each program, when Greenberry McCain packed the glass case back into the oak chest and then lowered it among the feather pillows and buckled up the trunk, uncertainty returned. The trunk made its journey by porter, dray, horse-drawn streetcar, coach, or train to its next destination—to be stored in railway baggage rooms and baggage cars and basements or the back rooms of hotels and inns and rooming houses. Greenberry always seemed to be a step ahead of Christie and James—up in the morning before they were, already finished with breakfast and greeting them with news of their next destination. He outfitted himself smartly in a boiled shirt, high-standing collar, black necktie, gray-striped trousers, vest, black coat, gloves, and a broad-brimmed black western hat. Somehow he found a fresh newspaper every morning, from Memphis or Nashville. Occasionally, he got the St. Louis paper. He preferred the St. Louis paper because he was following a sensational court case there (a doctor accused of murdering his wife and faking her kidnapping).

As promised, he paid all the expenses, and he gave them a hundred dollars each week, which they sent home promptly by money order at the train depot's express office. They knew the travel schedule a week or two in advance, so they were able to send word of their where-abouts to Amanda. When they arrived in a new city, Greenberry usually dropped Christie and James at a rooming house and then disappeared for hours at a time. He often said he had business to attend to, involving the management of their tour and other lecture tours he was organizing. The silver flask he carried in his coat pocket had not escaped the Wheelers' notice, but he never appeared drunk. Rot-gut whiskey, James allowed to Christie.

Without an atlas, it was hard for Christie and James to get a sense of direction, but Greenberry seemed to know the travel schedules by heart, and he knew where the depots and coach stops were. Christie had thought they would go to large cities only, across greater distances, but Greenberry said he expected to journey slowly through the small cities of Tennessee, Alabama, Mississippi—and possibly Arkansas—before heading east to Atlanta, eventually circling back to Hopewell. Traveling was tiring, but the effort seemed to absorb some of Christie's grief. The continual uprooting had a compelling rhythm, and her mind grabbed eagerly at anything new. At times, the memory of the babies as live, sucking, squirming beings at her breasts renewed itself and kept her on edge, anxious that the trunk remain in her presence, but she was determined to be strong. She knew she had to be. She forced her attention onto the new landscapes. She observed the traffic, the roads, the hawks sitting on the fence posts, the lay of the land. The grinding and routine clacking of the wheels and the thunder-roll of the train's engine replaced all other natural rhythms—the seasons of work in the fields, the ceaseless canning and preserving, or babies feeding and crying. She had escaped from toil. She felt strung by a thread, hanging above normal life—a taut string that would break if it were touched.

She could hardly bear to be with James all the time. The trip threw them together in a way she couldn't get accustomed to. The cramped quarters—whether they were traveling, spending the night, or sitting with the babies in an exhibition room—made them acutely conscious of each other and embarrassed by each other. She recalled uncomfortable Sunday afternoons when they courted in her parents' parlor. She remembered James back then, his hands reaching for her, his legs and elbows—even his grin—groping in her direction. Now they were close together at all hours. But they didn't want to touch. Increasingly, James irritated her. He used to be so easygoing, but now he was moody and argumentative. Greenberry McCain's fussiness and casually superior air bothered him. James reminded Christie of a spirited stallion penned up at the stockyard. He had nothing to do and he was desperate, she realized, whereas she had plenty of sewing to focus her mind. She made several shirts for Clint and Jewell and a dress for Nannie. She worked buttonholes while they sat through Greenberry's talks, which varied in tone and length according to the audience. Every day Greenberry laid out the display of lifeless souvenirs. The feather crowns resembled a boy's bird-nest collection. The babies in their glass prison were as rigid and unchanging as the clothes-pin dolls Boone had made for Nannie.

As they traveled farther south, they visited smaller towns, appearing at courthouses and churches and exhibition halls. The babies drew crowds from miles around, but there was a sad, dispirited air about many of these people, like mules broken to the plow. Their mouths gaped in silence; they seemed afraid to speak to Christie or James. They lowered their heads, abashed. Christie felt awkward at thrusting her babies in front of them. Many had pale, blotched complexions, and some of the women were enormous, their breasts and hips bulging grotesquely through drab calico dresses. Christie saw a woman with a knot the size of an orange on her neck.

The effects of the War were everywhere. The War was like the Reelfoot earthquake, Christie thought, except it showed less in the features of the land than in the defeated faces of the people and in the dilapidated buildings. Some of the houses where Christie and James stayed had once been quite fine, but now they had a faded air about them. Most of the smaller rooming houses were modest, with plain, unappetizing food. Many times as they traveled, Christie and James found their noon dinners at a crossroads general store—a dime's worth of cheese and a can of sardines, with crackers and maybe a pickle from a barrel.

One day in northern Mississippi they waited outside a general store for a farrier to treat a mare that was having trouble with her shoe. The horse had begun to limp. Christie was eating a fried dried-peach pie. She longed for a good fried pie, with a sweet, dark filling crimped in a crisp, fat half-moon. This one was soggy and tasted stale.

"When are we going to Memphis?" Christie asked Greenberry. She wished she could see that nice couple from Memphis she had met.

"I'm trying to work that out now." Greenberry was eating soda crackers, with a bottle of sarsaparilla.

"What's in Memphis?" James asked.

"Memphis has a fine opry house," Greenberry said. "You'll like it."

"I know some people in Memphis," Christie said. "I'd like to let them know when we're coming."

"Oh, they'll know by the advertising dodgers," said Greenberry, turning his attention to the farrier, who was having to gouge out a nail from the mare's hoof.

Her father wouldn't have shod a horse so badly, Christie thought.

The mare, a chestnut with a white diamond on her forehead, was in pain from the nail, which had gone into the quick.

James was sitting on the edge of the store's porch with a fried pie. Christie saw him take a bite and then pitch the end piece into a patch of weeds. He was studying the horse, one of a team of four that pulled their hired coach.

"That horse don't need to be going nowhere," James called to the driver, who was beneath a tree playing a game of checkers with a drummer. "That horse needs to rest." James turned to Greenberry and said, "We was going to travel in style, you said. 'We'll go by train,' you said. But here we are out in the middle of nowhere with a broke-down horse. See how that mare's a-suffering?"

"I believe that mare has got thumps," Greenberry said. Then the mare hiccupped loudly, causing the farrier to jump. Greenberry dropped his handful of crackers. "Goddamn it!" he cried. "That-there was my dinner!"

James jumped off the edge of the porch. For a moment, Christie was afraid he was going to threaten Greenberry for cussing in front of her. Instead, James grabbed the mare's reins and began working with her, calming her. The horse was the color of James's hair.

"Easy now, girl," James said, running his hand alongside the mare's neck.

They traveled past cotton fields that day. The dry plants were bursting with white fluff, like popped corn. Negroes, bent double, were stuffing the ripe cotton into long canvas sacks. The land was flat as a pond, and it was covered with cotton for miles. The sky was white, too, like an enveloping bedsheet. It was vast and hovering. The coach swerved around a dead brown dog and almost slid into the ditch. They passed railroad work gangs, all Negroes, swinging sledgehammers in unison. They passed tawdry shacks, burned-out brick buildings, churches identifiable only by crude, weathered wooden crosses. Along the road, groups of Negroes in rags trudged barefooted, their skin grayed by the dust. Some rode on cotton wagons, wobbling with the movement of the wagons. Against the cotton, their dark skin stood out like coal. Gazing across the endless fields, Christie thought she had never seen such desolation.

As the carriage entered the town—little more than a few clusters of shacks and a brick church—James tapped Greenberry's knee. He was sitting across from them and staring out at the fields.

"Ain't no opry house to talk in around here, I'd allow," James said.

"I reckon not," Greenberry said, tossing the burnt stump of his cigarette out the side of the carriage.

A yellow cur ran beside the coach, barking.

"I expect folks here are too busy picking cotton to go to shows at the opry," James said sarcastically. "Where are we, anyhow?"

"It don't matter, James," Christie said, elbowing him.

"This is a good fair we're going to, one that draws from five counties," Greenberry said, swatting at a fly. "There'll be a good crowd."

The coach drove into the fairgrounds—a hayfield, with temporarily constructed pavilions and several tents. The fair was small, with no horse races, plowing contests, or mule pulls that Christie could see. She saw pens of donkeys, dogs, chickens, ponies, hogs, and sheep. The ponies and the donkeys were lying on their sides in the hot sun. The sheep all held the same position—heads down, grazing. They were so still they might have been statues. The coach drove past a large tent with a sign out front:

SHENOBA COUNTY FAIR AND AGRICULTURAL EXPOSITION

Their destination was a small canvas tent, in a row of tents at the edge of the field. The driver stopped the horses and climbed down from the spring seat. Greenberry hopped out to speak with him.

"What's he got us in now, a carnival?" James grumbled as he helped Christie down from the carriage. He had been fuming since they left the store.

"We're here," Greenberry said, with a cheery laugh. "The driver's going to carry our baggage to Mrs. Burns's house over in Shenoba."

"Are you going to show my babies in this little tent?" Christie demanded.

"Look here, McCain," James said. "This place don't seem like much. You've been dragging us down ever pig path."

"Give me a hand, James," said Greenberry, reaching for the trunk, which was strapped on the rear.

James helped Greenberry roll the trunk into the tent. The wheels jerked along the bumpy ground. Christie followed, her hand on the trunk protectively. When it came to rest inside the tent, Greenberry started to unbuckle it, but James placed his hands on the lid, preventing Greenberry from lifting it.

"This tent's mighty little," James said, glowering at him.

"Now, James. It'll be all right," Greenberry said, straightening up and plucking a bit of cotton fluff from his trousers. "I meant to tell you earlier. The Hart Brothers' traveling wagon-show has let me sign on with them. They provide the tent and a boy to help out—sell tickets and so on. It's a good thing for us, because they follow the fairs, and that draws the people. It's a wholesome show. People need it." Greenberry gave James a broad smile. "The Hart Brothers are personal friends of mine," he said. "You couldn't ask for finer people."

"A wagon-show? Are they going to haul us in a wagon from place to place?" Christie asked, with disgust.

"You're not hauling my wife around in no wagon," James said.

"Oh, no. We'll take the cars or hire a coach, as usual," Greenberry said. "Don't be disturbed, Christie. I know we ain't been stopping at the finest places, but I promise to do better. Mrs. Burns runs a good house—clean and pleasant."

"I'm getting tired of your promises," said James. "I thought this whole trip was supposed to be for education. But it's turning out mighty sorry."

"Why, we're just taking advantage of the greater audiences that come to the fairs. Being with the Hart Brothers don't change the educational value of our presentation one bit! In fact, it improves it!" Greenberry paused thoughtfully. "You were right, James," he said. "Down here it's harder to find any big opry house."

Greenberry pushed aside the tent flap and swept his arm across the view of the grounds. His face was red. "I'm telling you, James, back when we started out three weeks ago, I could tell you were as out of place at the opry house as a frog in Sunday school. But ordinary citizens such as you and me attend the fairs and the traveling shows. I say, Why deny our common humanity? Why set ourselves up in an opry house and start cutting didos for the mayor up in a box on the wall, all dressed up fancy and afraid to spit?"

Greenberry fidgeted with his watch key. "There's going to be a good crowd here," he said. "If they have any quarters in their pockets all year it's right now, when the crops are coming in, so they're looking to spend." He studied the straw on the ground, then looked up into James's eyes. "We lost the War—remember? People don't have much down here, James. And they need something to uplift their souls! You don't want to keep them from seeing your little treasures, now, do you?"

"How many do you aim to cram in this-here tent?" James asked. The tent was half the size of Christie's front room.

"Don't worry, James," Greenberry said, taking a machine-rolled cigarette from his package. "We'll let people in just a bunch at a time, maybe two or three times an hour." He lit his cigarette and blew the smoke out the open tent flap. "People will come to a show at the fair that ain't used to going to a lecture. They don't want to dress up, and there ain't no place to hold the lecture anyway. But we'll reach more people this way."

"But we'll have to set here all day for that," James argued.

"Don't act so ill, James," Christie said, dropping her carry-bag. "We'll make do."

Greenberry puffed on his cigarette. James stepped outside the tent to study the surroundings, and Christie followed him to the opening. The trunk was behind her. Nearby, a man was pitching colored balls at bottles on a board. Christie looked around at the common folks Greenberry spoke of. Did they really need to see her babies in order to uplift their souls? She noticed a white man angrily ordering a Negro out of his path. Apparently, the Negro had brushed against him. She still couldn't get used to seeing so many Negroes. She saw a little Negro boy with some spun sugar on a stick. Several of his friends were pulling at it, laughing as they devoured the flimsy stuff. It was odd to see them snatching after cotton that way, as if they were dreaming and the cotton bolls in the fields had suddenly turned to candy. There was so much going on right in front of her eyes, she had no idea how to make sense of it all.

"We'll be all right," she said to James in a small voice.

"I don't expect there's a thing we can do about it anyhow," James said.

She ducked back into the tent, and James came in behind her. The trunk sat there, like a stone.

Greenberry flicked ash from his cigarette into the straw on the ground. He shook his head and grinned. "Why, you'll see a lot of educational happenings here," Greenberry said brightly. "There's a woman that handles snakes here!"

He mashed out his cigarette in a clod of dirt, then began fussing with some stools and a folding table he carried strapped to his bag.

"I don't want you setting those babies on that flimsy contraption," James said. "The whole mess is liable to fall down and break."

"Oh, I'll make it steady." Greenberry opened the table and tried to anchor the legs, but the ground was uneven and the table wobbled precariously.

"Set them on the ground!" Christie cried. "Back in the corner here, where we don't have to look."

Greenberry collapsed the table and placed it where Christie pointed. "I'll set them on top of this," he said reassuringly. "Christie, I know you don't want your little babes setting right smack on the ground."

During the show, Christie glumly watched Greenberry's flamboyant manner as he displayed her babies once again to a new batch of curiosity seekers. He had exchanged his black western hat for his top hat, which made him stand out more. He cut his lecture short and got quickly to the business of revealing the mementos and the babies. The tent was hot. People munched popped corn as they passed through the tent. They dropped peanut hulls on the ground. The smaller locales made her babies less special, Christie thought angrily. Greenberry pushed the people in and out rapidly. Several groups passed through. Someone asked, "Are they all brothers and sisters?" and someone else compared the glass casket to a cake-stand. James whittled a stick with his pocketknife. Christie sat rigidly on her stool with her sewing, but she didn't sew. She picked at a hangnail. She thought about all the money these people were spending, on their peanuts and bottles of dope and tickets. She was taking their nickels and dimes and quarters, and it was adding up to an unheard-of amount of money. It was going to set her free.

After the last group left, Greenberry spit on his handkerchief and wiped the fingerprints and smudges from the glass case. He reached for the sheet to cover it, but Christie grabbed the sheet from him and laid it over her babies, careful to tuck under the edges so no one would trip over it. She flung her sewing into her bag. She put away her spectacles and brushed straw from her bag and set it inside the trunk.

"I'm going to go see that snake woman," she said.

"I'll watch things here if you both want to go," Greenberry said amiably. "I'm going to let the niggers in at four o'clock."

"What do you want to see a snake woman for?" James asked Christie. He removed his hat, smoothed his hair, and replaced the hat.

"Just to see."

"You oughtn't to go see a woman like that," James said.

"I ain't afraid of snakes—are you?"

"I don't need to see no snakes."

"Look at the world, James," she snapped. "You might learn something."

She fled from the tent. She had to get out. James sat there like a bug on a stump. During the show she had heard him muttering under his breath, mocking Greenberry. She had never expected to sit in a tent while people tromped through to gawk at her babies. She had always enjoyed traveling shows when they came to Dundee or Hopewell, but being in one seemed wrong, like drinking liquor at church. It made her heartsick. Some people had giggled and pointed at her babies, and when she spoke to them they ignored her. She didn't know now what to do with all the spite she had brought with her on the trip. Her resolution to get even with the public seemed futile. People didn't really want to know about her babies.

She passed by a young couple who had won a dish set and a red velvet pillow at a pitching game. She glanced into the large exposition tent and saw a row of shiny new plows, crop displays with prize ribbons for the tallest corn, the fullest cotton bolls. She stared at a long table of pies.

She found the snake woman's tent just beyond the agricultural display. Christie paused at the advertising bill hanging between two poles. On it, several brightly colored pythons and boa constrictors entwined themselves around a scarcely clothed woman—The Snake Woman from Borneo. Her naked legs showed.

The Snake Woman's tent was noisy. Christie made her way through a knot of people. She had to peek through the bent elbow of a heavy, smelly man. Then he moved aside so she could see. The Snake Woman from Borneo was thin and dirty-faced, with long, tangled hair resembling dozens of baby snakes. Bare-legged, dressed in a short, gray tunic roped at the middle, she sat in a pit about two feet deep, surrounded by small, dark, wriggling snakes. The crowd shrank back, squealing, but Christie stood still. The woman played with the snakes like a child playing with kittens.

Christie couldn't count the snakes. She thought there must be a hundred. They were crawling over each other, writhing in slow embraces. But they weren't the huge jungle snakes pictured outside. Most of them were little gray rat snakes or black racers, and some had a yellow stripe down the back. Some had intricate brown mosaic patterns on their bellies. None of them were fat or very long.

"Somebody get a hoe!" a man and a woman yelled, almost simultaneously.

"A copperhead will bust a man's heart," the man said.

Christie didn't see any copperheads. Perversely, she wished Alma could see all these snakes. One was crawling up the side of the pit, and the Snake Woman grabbed it and shook it, spouting out some gibberish, as if she were giving it a talking-to. Suddenly, with her other hand, she snatched up a snake and hurled it at the audience with a shrill cry.

A man ducked. "Watch out!" he yelled. Others ran from the tent. A scream of fear rippled through the crowd, but the snake turned out to be only a piece of rope. It landed against the front of the tent. The crowd's shrieks turned to nervous laughs. Christie was silent. She shivered, but she wasn't afraid. She stared at the Snake Woman from Borneo admiringly, wondering what kind of courage it would take to handle snakes.

5

GREENBERRY LEFT THEM AT MRS. BURNS'S HOUSE LATER AND ARRANGED to pick them up the next morning. He was going out that night with the Hart Brothers, Joe and Bob.

After supper, Christie worked on her embroidery, and James lay on the bed in his drawers fanning himself with one of the Jesus fans from Mullins's funeral parlor. Christie could imagine Mrs. Burns's house as a funeral parlor. It was a large old house with dark, faded furnishings. The room was clean, though. A balmy breeze made the paper window shade flutter.

James stood up and stretched. The strings of his drawers hung loose.

"Where do you reckon there is to go of a night around here?" he asked. "He dumps us here, and they all act like they're going out to have a good time." James began to pace across the room. He said, "Them Hart Brothers don't even look like brothers—one fat and one skinny."

"I ain't wasting my time worrying about Greenberry McCain," said Christie, drawing her needle through a daisy petal. "I don't care if they go out and rob banks."

"He's nothing but a horse trader," James said. "I know his kind. The kind that'll file a horse's teeth down so you can't tell he's old. I oughter known before. I wouldn't trust him no further than I can spit."

"I don't care," Christie said. "I don't care what he says or what he does. He can't do anything worse to us than what we've already been through." She ran her needle through several tiny stitches on the flower's stem. Then she said, "If we have to go wherever he takes us, then I aim to sew, whether I have to set in a tent all day or ride on a mule or whatever he dreams up next. I don't have my machine, and I can't sew as good by hand, but that's what I aim to do. Anyhow, it's a chance to get some embroidery done."

James paced nervously between the washstand and the bed.

"What's wrong with you? What are you worried about?" Christie said impatiently. Her thimble flew off her thumb and James picked it up.

"Everything's all dried up around here. It ain't hardly rained since we started out. I hope we've had rain at home."

"Maybe there's floods at home. You can't go by what it's doing here."

"What are you working on?" James asked, handing her the thimble.

"A pinafore for Nannie."

He stuck his palm out the window, as if he might catch a drop of rain. The dim lamplight made enormous shadows on the wall. He was a giant on the wall.

That night, sleeping fitfully in a sagging, creaking bed in which James occupied the center valley, Christie remembered how much she had feared dying in childbirth. James rolled over, and the cotton mattress shifted with him. She thought about the feather bed she had brought to their marriage; somehow, it had seemed important in drawing them together. She could hardly believe that at one time she had desired James so much; now she was repulsed by his smells and sounds. She pulled a frayed quilt around her face to block his breath. She could see herself and James far into the future, coming toward each other and then backing off, unsure of each other. She and James would be like neighbors who would visit awkwardly and silently in the front room on Sundays and carry pies to funerals.

In a scrambled dream she relived the births, remembering her feeling of peace at getting out the demons and her puzzlement that they were actually babies. She dreamed she was at home in bed with the babies when the train stopped and the passengers raced across the field to the house. A man in a bow tie promised her a new machine. She dreamed she was sewing baby clothes on the machine—long dresses and bonnets edged with yellow rickrack. She sewed miles of rickrack. A phrase rolled over and over through her mind, "the place where the lion roareth and the wang-doodle mourneth for his first-born," like words that had come straight from the Lord. Awaking, with the rickrack streaming through her mind like train tracks, she thought touring the Southland with her dead babies was much like being in bed with the babies alive. Back home, strangers came to her to see the babies, but now she took them out in search of strangers to show them to. In either case it seemed necessary for people to see the babies. Even if they had lived, they would always draw attention, she thought. Five little ones—all alike, trudging down the road with their schoolbooks and dinner buckets—would be a remarkable sight.

6

THE HART BROTHERS RAN A SMALL, LOOSELY ORGANIZED WAGON-SHOW. The entertainments included a magician, ball-pitching games, a trained dog, some Shetland ponies, and several extravagant though brief melodramas. The juggler, the Snake Woman from Borneo, and a fat-lady named Miss Fairy May Turnbow were regulars, while other acts came and went. Three or four medicine men tagged along with the show, selling worm-syrup, nerve-food powders, sluggish-liver remedies, and purifying tonics. The show set up alongside agricultural fairs, staying a few days at each one. Since it was festival season, the crowds were enormous. Greenberry let groups into the tent every fifteen minutes. He had changed his remarks to fit these crowds, leaving out the medical details and the historical comparisons.

Christie tried to be indifferent to the chomps and gapes of the curiosity seekers trailing past her babies. She pretended to be invisible. She stared right through people, or she sewed while they swarmed in. Or she sat nonchalantly reading one of Greenberry's newspapers. That was what she liked to do best, she decided. She told James this was his big chance to improve his reading, but he just grunted when she passed him the paper.

They traveled slowly through Mississippi and Arkansas towns. Greenberry paid their room and board, so they did not need much spending money. Christie kept five dollars sewn inside her waist, and they had some spare change. The accommodations varied in quality. Greenberry insisted he was doing all he could for them, but one time they lodged with a shopkeeper above his store, and another night they had to sleep in the same room with an old woman dying from stomach trouble. Their meals were plain and often tasteless, when the cooks were too saving with meat. Christie and James ate fat-soaked greens and boiled cabbage, potatoes, and turnips, with hard cornbread and meager bits of pork. On several days they could not get any pork at all, and James declared he felt weak without it. Even though his impatience with Greenberry McCain grew, James did enjoy talking crops with farmers at the fairs. He learned a great amount about cotton and peanuts, which folks at home didn't raise. And he befriended a black-and-white spotted dog who followed the wagons. He called the dog Jubers.

The news from home whirled through Christie's mind like leaves scattering in the wind. Amanda wrote that Christie's letter in the Hopewell paper caused a stir—everybody was still proud; James Culpepper's barn burned with all his tobacco; Arch broke his foot falling off the porch, playing too rough; Nannie was so smart she was learning the letters in Jewell's blueback speller.

In a village in the Ozarks, Greenberry joined them on the porch of their boardinghouse. He blew cigarette smoke out at a peaceful lake view. They had just eaten supper, and James had his feet propped up on the porch railing. He grunted when Greenberry sat down, but he didn't speak. Christie didn't want to talk to Greenberry either. He was always pretending something was much better than it was, and he didn't seem to notice the things that were actually good—like the pretty lake held by the hills as if it were a giant handful of water. He had just praised the boardinghouse cook for her home cooking (burnt cornbread, pie that wasn't sweet enough). Christie concentrated on her embroidery.

"Believe I'll head on out to the revival," Greenberry said.

"Good," James said. "I can tell you need some religion." He was teasing, but with a cutting note in his voice.

Greenberry said, "They're already stomping and shouting down there."

Christie could hear the singing from a tent-revival meeting down the road, and she wondered fleetingly if Brother Cornett might, by chance, be preaching there. She hadn't heard any preaching on their travels, but she hadn't missed it.

"Did I ever tell you I could have made a preacher?" Greenberry said.

James grunted. Christie said, "No." She remembered what he had said early in the trip about his inclination toward the seminary.

He puffed on his cigarette and blew the smoke out slowly, as if calculating his words. "Funny. I was called to preach. I was cutting timber one spring when I was a boy—oh, I was a big boy, not married yet, but not a man either—and I sawed down this big old tree, and just as it was about to fall I heard the voice of the Lord coming out of it."

He paused for a moment, waiting for Christie and James to ask him what the voice said. When they remained silent, he went on. "It said, 'Greenberry, what are you cutting down this-here tree for?' I looked up and all I could see was light. It seemed to take an awful long time for that tree to fall, and in that time I felt every question and every doubt I ever had. My mind went through my whole life in those few seconds, the way they say a person's whole life passes before his eyes at the moment of death? By the time that tree landed, I had been through every question. It was like the Lord was questioning me, pinning me to the ground. And I didn't have a good answer for why I was cutting down that tree. I'd cut down hundreds of trees in my life. There wasn't nothing to it. Trees are in the way. You have to cut them down before you can farm a lick, so why He asked me, that was a mystery. I thought He meant for it to mean something, and I keep looking for the answer, but I still haven't found what I'm looking for."

"It must mean something," said James. "The Lord wouldn't ask a stupid question."

Christie wondered whether the Lord might have been teasing Greenberry. Or maybe somebody was playing a joke on him, she thought, remembering the family story about her great-grandfather Thomas Wilburn's call to preach. "So did you start preaching when you heard the call?" Christie asked.

"I thought about it. I thought I would, but things got in the way."

"What things?"

"Temptations."

He laughed, then grew serious. He said, "I must tell you, James and Christie both, that I have never in all my days of traveling been so proud to associate with anybody as I have with you fine people. It's just the saddest thing to see, and you can tell how people feel about those darling little babies. They come in with tears in their eyes. Christie, you have done a valuable service. It chokes me up to have to show those little babies, and I can't even imagine what you folks went through."

On the lake some geese were landing, honking loudly. The sun was setting. James stood up and stretched, turning his back on Greenberry. Christie snipped her thread and put away her needle. She had finished embroidering Nannie's pinafore.

7

THE WEATHER CONTINUED MILD AND DRY. AT A COTTON FESTIVAL IN Little Rock, a crowd of a thousand watched a hot-air balloon float almost out of sight, carrying six passengers in its wicker basket. The people waving from the basket were just specks. Some pickpockets went to work when everybody had their eyes on the sky. Rowdies carried their brown jugs of alcohol in plain view, and several fights broke out. A Jesse James show, staged with a bank robbery and assassination, drew hundreds. A handsome woman known as the Queen of the Nile gave a dramatic reading from a popular melodrama, *The Wayward Heart of Tuscaloosa*. She dressed in a flowing blue-and-silver robe and wore a tall black wig and black eye lines. A man walked a tightrope strung above a street.

Christie wandered through the crowd along the riverbank. She pushed past large, slow families and church groups. She wanted to walk as fast as the river was flowing. Nobody pointed to her in recognition—the famous mother. She kept walking, looking.

In Conway, later that week, a new act joined the wagon-show—a medicine man named Colonel Happy Tucker, peddling his Lovebird Liniment. While James remained in the tent with the trunk, Christie went to watch the medicine show. Someone said he had some good singers with him. By now James was used to the way Christie fled the tent at every opportunity.

A crowd had gathered near a small creek that divided the fairgrounds. Some brightly dyed feathers and bits of colored banners fluttered from a rope strung between two black-gum trees. The medicine man, in a glossy black top hat like Greenberry's, had stretched out a canvas awning from the back of his buggy, and he was fussily arranging

Indian artifacts on a table—some arrowheads and bones—in an effort to draw his audience in. Christie carefully examined the graceful arrowheads. She had always wondered about how people had lived in Indian times, before trains and brick buildings. She used to see an old Indian back in Dundee selling fried pies on a street corner. He wore a blanket around his shoulders and could sign his name.

When the musical show began, she found a shady spot under a shagbark hickory. A trio of women known as the Wiggins Sisters performed. The tallest of the three played a guitar, and all three sang— skillfully and fervently, as if their lives depended on what they were doing at that moment. Christie recognized the old ballads; she remembered her mother singing some of them to her when she was little. Leaning against the tree, she listened to song after song: "Lila Lee," "The Cambric Shirt," "Barbry Ellen," "Lord Thomas and Fair Ellender." Amanda would love to hear these sisters sing, Christie thought. They had pretty voices. They harmonized so easily, and they didn't seem nervous. They were attractively dressed, too, in gored skirts of a rich, deep green, and white waists with billowy sleeves and layers of lace and rows of multiple tucks. The ribbons around the lace collars matched the color of their skirts. All three had on enormous palmetto-straw hats, with large plaid bows tied jauntily around the crowns. Each of them wore a chrysanthemum flower, freshly cut, and carried a lace-edged handkerchief. The guitar player had poked her handkerchief up her sleeve.

When Colonel Happy Tucker began pitching his Lovebird Liniment ("It makes even heartache disappear"), the sisters—red-haired and big-boned—headed toward the lemonade stand. Christie followed them. They were discussing whether to split one lemonade or two, but when the tall one found some extra pennies she had hidden in her pocket, they decided to buy three.

"If Colonel Happy don't pay us soon, we'll be down to eating the feet off of the chicken," the smallest one said. Her freckles danced across her cheeks like chicken grit scattered on the ground.

All three stared unself-consciously at Christie when she moved nearer to hear what they were saying.

"I liked your singing," she said, embarrassed. "My mama used to sing that last song when she patted a baby to sleep."

"Hit's 'Old Aunt Matilda,'" said the tall one. She was even taller than Christie and had a long-waisted figure.

"How did you know the song?" Christie asked.

The sisters looked at each other blankly and shrugged. "Hit's something we always knowed," said the smallest one.

"Then your mama must have sung it to you," said Christie. She remembered her mother singing Susan to sleep. It seemed years ago.

"I reckon that's how we got all our songs," said the middle one. "Big, did Mama sang that last song we sanged?"

The tall one said, "I reckon. She was always a-sanging." The woman studied Christie, peering directly into her eyes, and then she said, "I'm Big and this-here's Little. And that one's Evelyn. We're the Wiggins sisters."

"I'm Mrs. James Wheeler."

"We're proud to know you," said Big, with a broad smile.

Little nudged Big. "She's the one with them dead babies."

"I know that! I knowed it right off."

Their quaint speech sounded like Granny Wilburn's, Christie realized. Listening to them was like hearing news from back home in Dundee.

Later, the sisters came to see the babies, staring at them in astonishment. Evelyn whispered to Christie, "That song you wanted to know? Colonel Happy said if you sanged it to a newborned baby, the baby will die. Reckon that's what happened to you?"

"No."

"Well, I thought it might be, and I thought I'd tell you if-and you didn't know." Evelyn was using a peacock feather for a fly-shoo.

Little said, "Colonel Happy, he just made that up. He don't know his ass from a hollered-out punkin."

"Little, I've told you not to talk that-a-way," Big said sternly. "Law, them babies is so pitiful. Our Mama had fifteen chillern and five of them's dead."

"Not all at oncet, though," said Little. "That would be grievesome." She wore a brooch with a photograph of a child on it.

"You could still have some more, honey," Big said kindly to Christie. "Look at those little-bitty baby bibs," she said, pointing to the display.

"Them's the littlest babies I ever seen," said Evelyn. "Does their eyelashers and fingernails keep on a-growing?"

"Hair, too," said Little, bouncing on her toes.

Christie shook her head. "They're preserved the way they was," she said. "For all of eternity." A wave of despair hit her, but she fought it.

"I thought maybe their hair might grow," Evelyn said.

"I told you it didn't grow none," Big said to Evelyn, elbowing her sister in the ribs. Big said to Christie, "Your man over there—he must've been as proud as a bull without his britches on." She and Evelyn grinned at each other.

During the next two weeks, with the Wiggins sisters around, Christie began to relax. She enjoyed their company at meals in the boardinghouses. She walked with them around the fairgrounds the wagon-show visited. She played hearts with them. The sisters were genuine people emerging from the crushing crowds of faceless strangers who made Christie feel so exposed. She found the sisters' directness refreshing. They said things that would have been hurtful except for their kindliness in other ways. They took a lively interest in everything Christie could tell them about her babies and the attention they had attracted back in the spring. They even wanted to know the babies' names. Christie told them all about the train stopping and how the women had hovered over her in her dark front room back in the winter. She told them about Amanda. They wanted to know all about the tobacco farm. And they were curious about Clint and Jewell and Nannie. Greenberry McCain never mentioned the children.

When they weren't performing, the sisters wore plain clothes like Christie's—calico and domestic skirts, with simple waists. They had brought their sewing along too. Little was embroidering a pillow slip, and the others were piecing quilts. Christie noticed that they said "patch" instead of "piece," just as Granny Wilburn always did.

The medicine show went on several times a day, and Christie could hear it from her tent, but whenever she had a chance, she went out to watch the sisters sing. Their voices blended like birds singing at dawn. Christie loved Big's deep voice, with Evelyn's harmony, and Little's soprano sailing above the others. Big plunked her guitar with a hickory-nut shell.

But James said their songs were too sad to listen to. When the Wiggins sisters heard he had said that, they laughed. Somehow, they thought everything James said was funny.

8

IT RAINED. FOR THREE WEEKS, DURING CONTINUOUSLY RAINY WEATHER, Christie and James traveled through Arkansas, the coaches frequently miring up in the mud. A cool spell accompanied the rain. The rain splattered the tent, and occasionally the wind shook the tent loose from its moorings. Once, the rain turned to hail. The sound of the hard balls of ice striking against the tent made Christie think of her father driving holes in hot metal with a punch tool. Amidst the unceasing swirl of strangers, she depended on the companionship of the Wiggins sisters, and she found a comforting regularity in the sight of certain familiar faces such as those of the Queen of the Nile (a clever poker player with a good eye for racing horses, Christie learned) and the fat-lady, Miss Fairy May Turnbow, who rode grimly in a flatbed wagon. The Snake Woman was from Pennsylvania, not Borneo, and she had been to college, Christie learned. One Wednesday, the Wiggins sisters abruptly quit Colonel Happy Tucker, but they turned up again by Friday, and Christie was relieved to see them. Colonel Tucker had sweet-talked them back, Big said. He bought them new sailor-style outfits, but they still wore their straw hats with the plaid bows.

On a cool, cloudy afternoon in Hot Springs, Greenberry went off to manage a cockfight. He had stored the trunk at the depot, ready for the trip to the next town. James and Christie rode to the fairgrounds—James wanted to watch the races, and Christie wanted to be with the Wiggins sisters. While Evelyn and Little went out in search of some throat drops, Big and Christie sat in a pavilion away from the wind. Christie was finishing some britches for Clint, and Big was piecing a churn-dasher quilt for her mother.

"Look at those younguns over yonder," Christie said, pointing toward the fat-lady's tent, where some girls with thin yellow hair stood scratching their heads. "You can tell they've got lice." She shuddered. "Some of these people look plumb wormy."

Big worked her needle fast and evenly. "They better buy them some Wonderful Worm-Syrup from Colonel Happy," she said. She laughed without humor. "Of course it ain't nothing but sorghum and water and a smidgin of alkyhol. Colonel Happy's awful bad to drank, hisself. I tell you, some men do things women wouldn't believe." Big creased the seam in her quilt block. "Colonel Happy tried to get Little in his room one night—he had her backed up in a corner. But she screamed and we come a-running."

"Is that why you quit the other day?" Christie asked.

"Yeah, but we can't get a-loose of him." Big gnawed off her thread. "We hadn't never been out of the holler till Colonel Happy come through. First it was Evelyn he had his eyes on, and now Little. If he tries anything with me—well, he knows better than to mess with me. Mammy don't have no idea what-all goes on out here. Hit would kill her to know. But it ain't a bad life." She smoothed out her quilt block and held it up. "But I couldn't never go around with my babies like you're a-doing. I don't know how you bear it, Christie."

Christie jammed her needle through a heavy pocket seam. She said, "Those poor chillern over there scratching their heads look hungry. But I've seen women down here that are pert-near as fat as Miss Fairy May Turnbow."

"Did you know Miss Turnbow has a sweetheart?"

"No." Christie couldn't even imagine that.

"I used to see them together in Birmingham, Alabama. That's where she was raised. He's a drummer—and he ain't near as fat as her." Big whisked a bug off her bonnet.

Christie said, "All these people come and look at her, and they come and stare at my babies. I'd shovel manure right in their faces."

Big touched Christie's hand. "Don't blame them, Christie," she said kindly. "People need something to lighten their day."

"But why don't they listen?" Christie demanded. "Yesterday Greenberry McCain was trying to tell one bunch that come through about what happened to the babies and why they died, but nobody was paying any attention to a word he said. They just wanted to gawk at the babies. After-while, Greenberry pointed to me and James and started telling about us, but there were these two women swapping their recipes for dream cakes, and they got in an argument over what to decorate them with. Sometimes people look at the babies like they weren't ever real. I know they don't look real now, but they used to be. Why don't people understand what I went through?"

"I don't know," Big said quietly. "I feel like that sometimes, when we're up there a-sanging. Sometimes we sang and sang and nobody even hears. But that don't mean the song ain't pretty." She laid her quilt block on her pile of finished blocks. "What will you do with them babies, Christie, when the season's over?" she asked.

Christie couldn't answer. The stringy-haired children trudged away from the fat-lady's tent. They moved so slowly, as if they had on weighted shoes. But they were barefooted.

9

AT MOMENTS—WHEN SHE WAS BEING ESPECIALLY PATIENT WITH JAMES, or washing out their underclothes with Alma's lye soap, or brushing James's suit—Christie felt that her situation was almost normal. But at other times, the odd and intolerable reality of the babies' presence struck her afresh. They were still with her, unchanging, a permanent reminder—but more than just a chromo likeness on photographic glass. They were the actual bodies, her own flesh.

She had never inquired into Samuel Mullins's process, but as the trip wore on, she wondered about it more and more. She thought if she could touch the babies, they might feel like porcelain dolls. Mr. Mullins might have baked a finish on them. But they looked somewhat softer than that. James Lake seemed the most real—with the most flesh on him, because he was the largest—and Minnie seemed the hardest. It grieved Christie that they hadn't been laid in the right order. She was certain she had told Mr. Mullins how they went. It seemed unbearable to see Minnie at the far right instead of in the middle. Her new position on the edge of the pillow close to the glass seemed to emphasize her smallness, as if she might disappear into the crack.

Christie studied the babies for signs of change, but even the white of their tatted pillow remained pure, with no specks of dirt or lint, no spots or stains, and no trapped bugs.

James caught her gazing at the babies one day before the crowd came into the tent. He had just entered with some lemonade. He wore a hickory-striped shirt that had lost a button.

"If you keep on looking at them, your eyes are going to bore a hole through them," he said.

"I can look at 'em if I want to. They're mine."

"You look at 'em like you expect them to soften up, like cookies in a cookie jar. You can take 'em home and set 'em on the bed and look at 'em ever day for the rest of your life if you want to. They won't come back to life. But is that anything to do?" He pulled the sheet over the case.

She could hear the Wiggins sisters singing.

Go away, go away, darling Cory,
Stop running around my bed.
Bad whiskey's done killed my body,
Pretty women's gone to my head.

What a gift to be able to sing, she thought. If her babies had lived, maybe some of them would have had a talent for music.

"What *will* we do with them, James?" she asked.

"I tell you one thing we ain't going to do. We ain't going to go traipsing off again with no more damned shows."

"Well, I know that. You don't have to cuss to make that plain."

"I'll keep on cussing as long as we're in this mess. I can't help it."

She drank some lemonade from the glass he offered her. It was warm and watery. The Wigginses' voices drifted through the tent like sweet cooking smells.

Don't you hear the bluebirds a-singing?
Don't you hear that mournful sound?
They're a-preaching Cory's funeral
In some lonesome graveyard ground.

She turned to face James directly. She said, "We have to figure what to do with them when this is over."

"I 'magine you'll be sorry then," James said mockingly. "I believe you're having a fine old time. You like all that singing and that Gypsy fortune-teller and all them medicine shows—and them snakes."

"I can name times when you wanted to go see a show more than anything," she said sharply. "That time you cut hay so fast your arms were raw, just to get done in time to go to the carnival."

"Going to one and being in one is two different things."

James positioned his chair so that the display was visible only out of the corner of his eye. He took some lemonade, washed it through his mouth, and spit it out onto the hay that carpeted the ground under their tent. He said, "Old Gooseberry's just in it for the money. He's a-raking in them nickels and dimes."

It was almost time for the people to come in. James drained the glass of lemonade and set the empty glass down in the hay beside his chair.

"Don't forget to take the glass back to the lemonade stand," Christie said irritably. She arranged her folding chair so that she wasn't sitting at a slant. Drawing her shawl around her, she said, "What *do* you think we oughter do with the babies, James?"

"Mullins wants them," James said. "He believes people are going to want to see them for years to come. He's awful proud of his preserve job he done."

Christie badly wanted to sew a button on James's shirt. Some chest hair peeped out at her. She could hear Greenberry outside rounding up a herd of the curious. His manner—urgent, quick, and exaggerated—had grown lately more like a pitchman's than a lecturer's. She heard him promise the crowd the eighth wonder of the world, a miracle that confounded natural science. "You won't believe your eyes!" he virtually shouted. The people charged in then with Greenberry, who ground out his cigarette under his shiny leather shoe and then whipped the sheet away from the babies. People crowded around the glass case, then stared at Christie and James, bug-eyed. Christie felt like throwing her scissors at them.

"They look so natural," said a snaggle-toothed woman, who averted her face from Christie. But Christie saw the woman's hungry smile when her eyes alighted on James.

At the end of the week, the show headed back into Mississippi. In the city of Jackson, there was high excitement on the streets. Two men had been shot at a baseball game the day before. And a circus was coming. The Hart Brothers would be setting up within the circus grounds for a one-day extravaganza.

Christie and James watched the circus parade from the veranda of their rooming house. The calliope steamed out its whistling notes, garish like the colors of its gilt paint. Four clowns rode by in an electric horseless carriage. A camel and some ponies followed them. Several cages of sleeping animals rolled past on wagons. Christie saw the black panther yawn and wished he would let out a cry, but he settled back into his sleep. She had heard that a panther sounded like a woman screaming. An elephant followed the wagons, his long, comical snout unfurling like a leaf. The bareback riders, young women in scanty costumes of loud colors, cavorted and turned somersets atop their horses. James lit up over the circus girls, Christie noticed. In a way, she was relieved, not jealous. At least he was interested in something; it had been sad to see him languish. Last night he hadn't slept well. The tavern below their room had been noisy until long past midnight. The revelers, in town for the circus, sang "A Hot Time in the Old Town Tonight" over and over. And she heard a piano playing loud, fast ragtime. During their travels, she had heard a number of rags drifting out of dark doorways. The pianos were loud and rumbling, and the sound thumped through the walls. The music had a rough edge of danger.

Now, as the bareback riders disappeared from view, Christie said, "Remember, James, when we were sparking, we went to the circus in Dundee? You bought me lemonade and a box of taffy, and we went to all the sideshows, and the drama show, and the concert music. You didn't leave out anything. I remember how you were growing a mustache and you were so stiff in your high collar and new shoes."

James spit a persimmon seed over the railing into a clump of weeds. Christie remembered Wad spitting into Amanda's hollyhocks.

She continued, "There was a parade, with beautiful girls in golden chariots. I'd never seen anything so grand. And we saw a lion!"

"That thing opened up and roared and liked to scared me to death!" James said, breaking into a grin.

"And remember when that circus went on to the next town and some fool shot it?"

"Yeah."

"I cried when I heard about that."

She wished she and James could enjoy a circus once again the way they had when they were sparking. What would be different if she could go back and start over as a young girl? Would she have a different choice? Would she marry James?

This circus seemed much different from that dazzling one from her younger days, she realized a few hours later, as she watched the performance. The striped big top was smelly and stifling. The barker didn't fool her when he sold boxes of candy for a dollar, promising a fabulous prize in each one. A man on the front row found a string of pearls in his box, and a girl pulled out a diamond ring. Christie knew now that the people with the prizes were planted; the other boxes might contain a penny or a worthless trinket. The barker's spiel sounded hollow. The clowns pulled a small spotted dog around on a rope, jerking it roughly. There was no lion.

Before the show ended, James went to meet Greenberry at their tent. Christie slipped off alone. She was looking for the Wiggins sisters. She hadn't seen them all day. A cluster of bareback riders, still in their glittery costumes, passed her. One of the women said, "The Devil take him! If he does me that way again, I'll tell him to shit fire."

Walking carefully because of all the mud and manure, Christie went to the midway of sideshows. Large colorful banners advertised the tattooed lady and the strong man and a family of dwarfs. The sword swallower was life-sized in his picture—a nearly naked man in a head-rag, ramming a three-foot sword down his gullet. She had never seen a man swallow a sword, but she had heard that sword swallowers really did poke swords all the way down to their stomachs. When she and James went to the circus in Dundee, they had seen a woman sliced up in a box. The box with the knife blades reminded her of her mother's kraut knife, a blade set in a long board over a tub.

Beyond the midway, at the far end of the grounds, Christie saw banners for the three-horned, three-eyed bovine and some biblical animals: the behemoth in Job, the lion of Judea (the panther), the prodigal's swine (a wart hog, she overheard), the hind that calved, and the sacred ship of the desert (the camel). She could see the animals in a pen behind the row of cages, which had biblical paintings hanging on them—fanciful representations of fabled beasts. The behemoth in Job turned out to be a hippopotamus.

Christie paused in front of a picture of what appeared to be a bearded man wearing a red sateen gown cut low to show voluptuous breasts.

HALF-MAN, HALF-WOMAN
Charley Lou Pickles

A smaller sign said MEN ONLY ADMITTED.

Christie had heard of people like Charley Lou Pickles. She looked around for the Wiggins sisters, but she didn't see anyone she knew. James wouldn't come looking for her—he wouldn't leave the babies alone. She saw the pitchman speaking to a cluster of women. She edged her way into the group.

"Ladies, I'll let you go around behind the tent and get yourselves a good look," the pitchman said, pointing with a tobacco-stained finger. "I won't tell on you."

The women were buying tickets. Christie dug into her pocket for a quarter. The pitchman, babbling rapidly, grabbed her quarter, snapped off a ticket, and rushed her with the other women around the little tent into the back entrance. As they waited in a partitioned area, the women smirked and giggled, but Christie stayed silent. She felt she was doing something wrong—slipping off from James to see something she shouldn't.

"We had a morphodite in Blytheville," a woman beside her said. "He dressed like a man, but he had tits."

"What if you don't know and then you marry one of them?" her companion asked in a loud whisper. She was a short, scraggledy-haired woman in a straw hat and brown-stained gingham dress.

"They can't get married."

"I heard they could."

"They can have babies."

"Here it comes. Ooh!"

Christie could not tell if Charley Lou Pickles was a man or a woman. The pitchman referred to the person as "it." The hermaphrodite—tall, with long hair tied back with a white bow—had smooth but sallow skin and appeared to be middle-aged. Silently, Charley Lou Pickles pulled apart a loose Oriental gown to reveal small, tight breasts, like a young girl's.

"It's hairy!" a woman squealed. Christie recognized her as a woman who had been hovering around James that morning, grinning at him invitingly.

Charley Lou Pickles opened the robe below the waist. A dark-pink tobacco worm hung against mysterious flaps of skin, loose folds above a crack like a woman's. Several women gasped.

Christie felt a twinge of nausea. She could not imagine how Charley Lou Pickles felt. She had never heard a person referred to as "it." Charley Lou Pickles had a hard, unemotional stare but didn't seem mean. He or she seemed like a prisoner. Charley Lou Pickles turned indifferently, moving the gown this way and that at the direction of the pitchman. The women, in splint bonnets and shapeless checked dresses, were agog, studying the strange double person the same way the crowds stared at Christie's babies. She realized how greedily she was looking too. She backed out of the tent, disappointed in herself.

But her babies weren't freaks of nature. Her babies were normal. They were only little babies. Her children. She felt weak-kneed as she made her way through the heavy throng. She passed a man whose medicated-scarlet underwear showed beneath his shirt cuffs. She brushed against some cotton candy. A man yelled at her, something ugly she couldn't understand. The women in the sunbonnets and drab dresses who had shared her view of Charley Lou Pickles were burned in her mind almost as clearly as the hermaphrodite was. She had been doing the same thing they did. She would go see a madwoman play with snakes. Or a frog-girl. Or a woman getting sliced up by a kraut knife.

Christie stood still and the people flowed around her. They were celebrating the end of a year of hard labor in the fields. They chopped cotton. She had chopped tobacco. She spotted Fairy May Turnbow being carried on her hammock chair by four men and heaving such a sigh of despair it seemed she didn't want to go on living.

Christie reached her tent, with its blue-and-red sign, THE AMAZING FIVE BABIES. Greenberry was standing outside with a cigarette. People were lining up, and a boy was selling tickets.

"We're having a grand turnout today!" he cried. "I reckon on a thousand or more before the day's out." He lifted his top hat to feel his scalp. He had found a bloated tick on his head the day before.

She couldn't speak. He didn't notice how she was trembling. He replaced his hat and picked up the box at his feet.

"Look at this, Christie. I just got this from the depot."

He pulled out a miniature baby bed like the one that had appeared at the funeral. It was a little wooden bed about an inch and a half wide with five tiny dolls, each wrapped in a bit of thin outing. The dolls were identical, the outing cheap, the bedding a little pad of cotton. Horrified, Christie darted into the tent without a word.

"Where've you been?" James asked.

"Did you see them things he's got?"

James nodded. "He had a company in St. Louis to make them." James was sitting on a stool, cutting a slice from an apple with his barlow knife. He said, "I've already had it out with him. He's selling 'em for a quarter, and there ain't a thing we can do about it. That paper we signed didn't say he couldn't do it." He dropped the peeling and poked the apple slice into his mouth.

"How does anybody think up something like that?" She removed her hat, which was causing pressure on her head. "Who would want it?"

"Where did you go?" James asked.

She knew he was changing the subject deliberately so that she wouldn't be so upset. His head was down and he was working laboriously on his apple. She sat down on a stool and swept her skirts out of the hay.

"I just walked around," she said. "There's a sword swallerer."

"I'd like to see McCain swaller one," James said bitterly. "I could help him get it down."

"What can we do about them things?"

"Ain't nothing we can do. We signed that paper."

Christie hid her head in her hands for a moment. Then she said, "Mama always said I looked on the bright side. I always thought I could take just about anything. But not this."

James stood up and was about to come to her when Greenberry entered the tent carrying the box. Reaching inside it, he grabbed a handful of the baby-bed souvenirs and tossed them onto an empty fold-ing chair. "Here, have some of these," he said with a large gesture of generosity. "Take some of them home to the children." He tucked sev-eral of the things down into Christie's carry-bag. Somehow, the baby figures were tied together into the little bed so they didn't fall out.

James stepped forward, facing Greenberry. He wiped his knife with his handkerchief, then closed the blade. "Christie don't want you selling them things," he said. He slid the knife into his pocket.

"Oh, don't worry, James," Greenberry said, closing the box. "I didn't order many, and I don't know how they'll go over. It might not be what people want. You never know." He grinned and hugged the box.

"Well, *I* know, and I don't want to see any of these anywhere—ever." James punched the box lightly with his fist.

"Oh, James, James, James," Greenberry said, like a father berating a silly, stubborn boy. "If people don't want them, well, we won't make 'em buy the things. You can't push something off on folks. But per-sonally I believe they're going to want a pretty little memory, a sou-venir of this sweet scene."

"I believe Christie's been through enough," James said furiously.

"If you had any idea what that does to me, you wouldn't pull a trick like that," Christie said to Greenberry. "If my babies are the mir-acle of the century, like you claim, then nobody's going to forget 'em that easy." He was grinning at her. She looked away.

"You don't believe they're a miracle," James said to Greenberry. "You just believe they're something to make money off of."

Christie turned her back to the men and began adjusting her hat band. It was too tight. She slapped the hat on her head again, hard. She heard Greenberry mutter something and walk out of the tent.

"Damn him," James said. "He always runs off. He don't want to be pinned down."

"He ain't thinking about us," Christie said as she searched through her things for a handkerchief.

When she found it, James stared at her uncomprehendingly, as if she were a magician who plucked scarves from the air. For a moment, they regarded each other silently. "Did you go see that man swaller the sword?" he asked her finally.

"No, I was looking for the Wigginses."

"Big was just in here. Her and the other two have up and quit again."

"Oh, no! Have they already gone?"

James nodded. "She said tell you they'd find us in Birmingham,

Alabama, when we get there next week. I tried to make her wait, but they was in a hurry, trying to get away from Colonel Happy."

"Oh, I'm going to miss those girls," Christie said, deeply disappointed.

"She said not to worry, they'd be sure to find us again."

"I'll miss their singing. I need them." Christie needed Big's strong arms and her sympathy. She was afraid Colonel Happy had mistreated Little again.

The tent was stifling, so warm she almost expected the babies to sweat. But they stayed the same, like turtle shells. Her heart was like a piece of hot metal in her father's forge, so hot and hard it would shatter if it were dropped in water. Something had shifted inside her. Back when the babies were throbbing with life, it had been natural for her to open up and share them with the world. She shouldn't have done that. But she could never change what had happened. Nor would she ever be able to punish the world for the wrong done to her. There was no point trying. The wrong was much bigger—and deeper—than she had thought. She remembered the camp meeting at Reelfoot. These sideshows and medicine men and pitchmen reminded her of those preachers standing behind their stumps and screeching and squawking like jaybirds, ranting about the earthquake that never came. The preachers were medicine men, hawking their concoctions for saving the soul from damnation. She remembered the man who was going to escape to the moon.

She and James sat side by side in the sweltering tent with their gruesome display. A long time afterward, she saw a photograph taken of her and James that day—their eyes frightened, assaulted by the crowd of onlookers.

10

AT BREAKFAST IN MRS. CUNNINGHAM'S LODGINGS IN VICKSBURG TWO days later, Christie and James were so absorbed in a letter from Amanda that they didn't notice Greenberry leave. They hadn't been speaking to him much. He had brought them the letter from the depot and dropped it on the table. Christie thought he went to read his newspaper in the parlor then, but when they left the dining room, they saw that he had gone.

Mrs. Cunningham stopped them. She was carrying a fly swatter. "Wasn't you aiming to go with him?" she asked. "He slipped off from here like he was scared of something. And he ain't paid the bill yet."

"Did he have the trunk with him?" Christie asked, alarmed.

"Where's the trunk?" James asked, lurching toward the storeroom near the stairs.

"Oh, it's right where you left it," the woman said, rattling the keys in her apron pocket. "The door's still locked."

At James's insistence, she unlocked the door, and he inspected the trunk to his satisfaction. "Did he say where he was going?" he asked.

"I believe he said he was going to Tupelo."

"That's where we're going next, but the train's not till one o'clock," James said.

"He's always got some business somewhere to tend to," Christie explained to Mrs. Cunningham. "He'll have to come back and pay the bill."

"I was kindly surprised at him up so early," Mrs. Cunningham said, aiming her fly swatter at the door facing, which was scarred with bullet holes from the War. "He didn't go up to his room till nearly midnight." She drifted off to the kitchen.

"I wonder what he's up to now," James muttered to Christie. "I 'magine he's out peddling them things on the street."

Since the circus, they had not seen the box of souvenirs, and Greenberry had not mentioned it. They were used to his absences and were generally glad of them, but since he showed them the souvenirs, they had been wary of his intentions. Christie's rage at him had collapsed and sunk in her like a hard ball of dough, ready to rise again. She wished she could see the Wiggins sisters.

Christie sat down in a rocking chair in the parlor to mend a sock, while James went outside to the garden house. Mrs. Cunningham's place was a run-down, two-story brick house with high windows and scarred woodwork. It had once been a fine house belonging to a cotton merchant. Christie gazed out the window at the Spanish moss hanging from the trees. It resembled the gray-green moss that grew like mushrooms in the woods at home—the kind that bloomed with lines of tiny red soldiers. Here, the hanging moss filtered the sunlight and gave a gauzy feel to the atmosphere. Mrs. Cunningham had called the trees live oaks, but they were unlike the oak trees at home. She said the trees with the shiny leaves were magnolias, and she called the bright-flowering vines on the porch "boogerville flowers."

Christie had read Amanda's letter aloud to James, and now she read it again to herself, finding fresh angles to each bit of news. Amanda's handwriting was dainty, as carefully formed as her quilt stitches. Amanda wrote:

Wad wanted me to tell you your corn crop made good. The crib is full, with thirty-six wagonloads. The boys started stripping tobacco yesterday and Clint and Jewell are stripping like little men. Clint's pile yesterday weighed fifty-four pounds!

Nannie is so sweet, helping me with everything, and I take her out in the yard and swing her in a swing Wad made for her. He notched out a board for a seat. She was afraid at first but now she goes high. Little Bunch and Lena have been fussing over who gets to look after her. Bunch had some fits, but I truly believe she's growing out of them. They were just little chicken fits, one at the supper table and one when I was fixing her hair. Wad had a fit too when he found out Lena had been talking to the Price boy down the road! Wad says the Prices are all deadbeats, not worth killing, and of course Lena is too young to be talking to boys. Dulcie, on the other hand, was a popular gal at a box supper at church last Saturday. Bryce Palmer is sweet on her, and he bid a dollar for her box. But Dulcie said later her lemon pie turned out as soggy as a cow pile!

William Jennings Bryan was through here, giving a stirring talk, they say. All of Hopewell was in a whoop. And the revival came and went. A Brother Peevy from Alabama, a little man with a rough face like the skin of a pickle. Christie, did you realize it was nearly a year ago we went to Reelfoot? So much has gone on since then. If we had known then what was going to happen, would it have changed anything?

Jimmie Lou is growing a baby, we all believe. She hasn't said anything, but she's filling out. Well, Christie, I keep thinking how life goes on, and there's always a crop of new babies, just like the new calves and the kittens in the spring. And some of them thrive and some of them are too weak. I guess we have to accept that, for it's the way of our Creator. I know I can never walk in your shoes, but I know it's been hard for you, Christie. It must be hard now to look at their little still faces day after day and know they will never pucker up and cry or reach their little arms out to you.

We're all well, except for Boone. He coughs so much now and wakes up strangled. I asked him your question about the Institute of Man, and he thinks it's a big place up in the government. He's heard tell of it and asks why you want to know. He is almost done with his memory book, Alma and me and the girls are all sewing on winter shirts, and I'm making you a surprise. Mammy Dove is still piecing on that quilt. It's getting dark earlier. Wad and his boys are working till dark. He said tell you he needed your strong hands, James, but not to rush on home and give up that hundred dollars a week. He won't even spare ten dollars for new shoes for us all this season. How did I marry such a tightwad? You know that's where he gets his name, I don't care what he says about any wad of chewing tobacco. Alma said he didn't know any more about loving than a dead horse does about Sunday. But you should see how proud he is of his new grandbaby. He's strutting his onions these days!

I miss you and all the fuss you stirred up, and I pray you'll get home safe again. Have you found that nice couple from Memphis yet? Tell James his dogs are lonesome without him.

> Your loving
> Amanda

Christie hadn't read Amanda's P.S. aloud to James. Amanda wrote:

P.S. Christie, I try to be good and patient, but you'll never know the sickness in my heart. I wish I could be there with you, so that we could hold each other up. Sometimes I can't quite hold myself up straight and I don't know where to turn.

Christie folded the letter, intending to reread it on the train later. The sorrow underlying Amanda's normally cheerful innocence made Christie feel a sour homesickness she hadn't felt before.

"Mandy didn't say what Wad's aiming to do about the tobaccer," James said. He had just returned from the garden house, and Christie was working up the courage to visit that filthy little enclosure, which was shrouded with gourd vines.

"Mandy's got the best heart," Christie said, forcing the letter down into her pocket. "But she hurts too easy."

"She don't ever give herself enough credit," said James, touching Christie's shoulder. He was standing and she was sitting. A river of memories flooded her mind: Nannie dressing a kitten up in doll clothes; the boys catching lizards with grass loops; Jewell playing horsey on a limber branch of a hickory tree.

Mrs. Cunningham interrupted them then. She had hard, sunken features that seemed to belie her funny, high voice. "I'm so proud to have a famous personage under my roof," she said. "Mr. McCain told me all about you. I didn't get to see the traveling show. I had fourteen to cook for last night and then had to get up before light to raise the bread this morning. I hope you enjoyed your breakfast. Did it suit you?"

James said, "The sausages was hard, and the biscuits was cold."

"Them sausages has been drying out ever since my stove started acting up on me. It won't draw good. But I saw you et yours. The light-bread went so fast I had to turn in and whip up some biscuits."

When Mrs. Cunningham left, Christie said angrily to James, "Why can't you be more polite?"

"Well, she asked, and I told her. That grub wasn't fitten to eat."

"It's better to be friendly," said Christie. "Ain't that what you always tell me? You never want *me* to say what *I* think."

"If her sausages is hard and she asks me, I aim to tell her. It don't matter what she thinks about me. She ain't my neighbor."

Christie said no more. Since the day of the circus, she sometimes contradicted James for no good reason, as though a spirit had suddenly possessed her. On occasion out in public, she took the lead in a conversation, although she knew that made him look bad.

"I've a good mind to go out looking for McCain," James said.

"Suits me," Christie said, closing her workbox.

"You stay here and I'll go look for him. If he's selling them things, I'm going to put a stop to it."

After reassuring himself again that the trunk was safe, he left. He went in the direction of the public square, where some traders had congregated. Christie put away her workbox, and after visiting the outhouse she wandered off in the opposite direction, away from the businesses. James wouldn't know. Maybe she would even run into Greenberry.

She walked for a few blocks, into an area that was dusty and poor, scattered with piles of bricks, probably from buildings that had been toppled in the War. She passed tarpaper shacks and burned-out foundations. A barrel on a corner signified a tavern. The smell of horse manure seemed to come in waves down the street. She was glad to be alone. Amanda's letter gave her an uneasy feeling, for something unmentioned seemed to be disturbing her. Amanda had taken the fate of the babies to heart. Her grief seemed like an offering of friendship, Christie thought. Amanda would appreciate this trip so much more than James could. She would enjoy the privilege of being let loose from labor for a spell. Christie glanced down at her hands, which were softening in their idleness. It made her sad to think of Amanda scouring and washing, spoiling her fine, slender hands.

It was well over a year since they went to Reelfoot. Why did Amanda think it had been less than a year? Had she been as confused as Christie herself had been since that time? At Reelfoot, everybody believed the Lord was on His way, and then when the babies came, there seemed to be a connection. Thousands believed there was a significance to the wondrous births. But she had learned that her precious gift to the world actually meant very little to anyone but herself and James, and possibly Amanda. The audiences took pleasure from seeing her petrified babies, but they didn't learn anything. Their interest in the babies would vanish as soon as they entered another tent and saw the hippopotamus or the similarly built fat-lady. They might remember her babies from time to time, vaguely, the way Christie remembered the lion roaring at the first circus she and James had attended together. But nobody would remember any significant particulars, such as the way Emily Sue's hair curled. They wouldn't realize what they had seen. Why hadn't she understood this months ago, when all those people landed at her bedside like buzzards? She felt so innocent, as if she had had to learn every basic lesson of life the hard way, and by the long route. There had been no one to guide her, no precedents, nobody to look to except Brother Jones.

But Brother Jones wouldn't recognize Jesus Himself, walking down the street with a halo on, she thought bitterly. For a man of the church, he had remarkably little vision about anything. She remembered a time when he preached from Deuteronomy and used it to forecast the tobacco crop. That had sounded questionable to her then, and now it struck her as absurd. For a long time, during her pregnancy, she had believed that the excitement Brother Cornett stirred up at Reelfoot had entered her so profoundly that the creatures inside her were like a manifestation of her sinful thoughts. And then when the babies were born, she knew her own mind had multiplied her hopes and fears. And afterward, she had listened to too many people try to make something out of the babies' brief lives. It was just more babble from Reelfoot, she thought. Now her head seemed to be clearing, the babble fading to murmurs.

Christie turned down a boardwalk that paralleled the river. If she were to run into Greenberry with those baby-bed souvenirs, she would wrench them all from him and throw them from the bluff into the river. Gleefully, she pictured the surprise on his face, his features jumping around as if disconnected.

The boardwalk ended, and a dirt path continued past some small houses. She could feel the steaminess of the river, but she couldn't yet see the water. Somewhere far ahead someone was singing. She strained to hear. The song was bursts of hollering, with a quieter refrain. It sounded like a Negro sundown holler—that long, loud collective sigh of relief she had been hearing every night when the field workers quit. But this voice seemed to echo and reverberate, and when it had surely died out, it started up again, a little louder, then louder still. Again it grew softer, repeating the pattern. The sound rose out of the trees the way a bird's song would, although the notes resembled no bird's song Christie had ever heard—except maybe that of the rain crow, or certain owls at night. Unafraid, she followed the sound into the woods, keeping to a narrow deer path. The hollering was strangely beautiful, reminding her of Mittens' song. It wasn't exactly the same melody, but it belonged in the same family—if music had families of sounds.

The vegetation was dying back, and walking was not difficult. Stickers clung to her dress. She watched for snakes. Eventually, she spotted the singer leaning against a tree, his back to her. He had on a straw hat and ragged blue clothing. She saw now that he had a guitar, and she could see his brown hands working the instrument. He had a bottle in his right hand, and he rubbed the bottleneck along the strings of the guitar to make the whining note she had heard; the guitar seemed to have a voice, answering his song. He was singing about a woman who lived alone, a large woman in a house by the cotton fields, where he worked. She was large and soft and dark as the river at night. The song didn't have any regular rhyme or rhythm; he seemed to be making up the words as he went along, the way Mittens did. But Christie began to see the woman in the song, the mighty woman coming at night to warm him in his cold bed. The memory of her carried him through the day, working in the cotton fields to get his hundred. As he sang, the woman became the voice of the guitar, answering him, as if she were a spirit inside that bottle. He might have been leaning onto the tree for the strength to create the extraordinary sounds. It was as if the man's mouth and windpipe were an instrument for emitting a feeling so deep down it was painful to let out. Christie crept backward. She hid behind a pecan tree and listened to the tortured song. It gave her a glow inside like an electrical bulb.

The song continued. The Negro sang about trying to find the woman in the daytime, for he was too weak to pick cotton and he needed her like medicine. He managed to stagger to her cabin, but no one was home. It seemed that no one had lived there for many years. Exhausted, he lay under a bush and waited for night to bring her back.

When the song ended, Christie stole away. Finding the path, she rushed out of the woods, propelled by a desire awakened in her by the music. Her heart beat fast. Something was moving in her, like the desire she felt when she first journeyed to Hopewell—a longing for something new and surprising. And she had felt it when she went down to Reelfoot—that desire swelling when she listened to Brother Cornett. And then her excessive desire seemed to manifest itself in her five babies. Then, losing them had shattered her desire. But now she felt as though her mind were gathering its scattered, aimless longings and rolling them together into one.

She remembered something Big Wiggins had said: "If you can sing a song, a body can see straight into your heart." She felt that the singer in the woods had sung her song for her; in his song she had heard her own accumulated rage and sorrow, coming out in deep, clear notes. It was a song she thought would stick in her mind, repeating, the way Mittens' song had. Already, it played through her head, as if it were reorganizing her memories, sharpening them and shaping them for some new purpose.

Quickly, she stooped to gather some pecans scattered across the walkway, and then she hurried back to Mrs. Cunningham's, arriving just ahead of James.

"Did you find him?" she asked.

"No. I looked all around at the depot and the main street," James said. "I saw some good horses, but the traders down here are slick as owl grease. I figured Gooseberry would be right there with them."

He didn't notice the stickers on her skirt, and she hid the hem she had torn on a greenbrier. James would be disturbed if he knew she followed a Negro man's voice into the woods. And she didn't know how to tell him the nature of the song she had heard. She could almost visualize that immense, dark woman coming to the singer at night, giving him the strength to get through the day's labor.

Upstairs, Christie changed clothes. Mrs. Cunningham brought her some warm water and a dirty-looking towel. Mrs. Cunningham lingered, beaming still about Christie's fame. "I'm so proud y'all stopped with me," she said. "And I want you to be sure to come back again. Make Mr. McCain bring you back through our way."

"We won't be back," Christie said, holding the dirty towel by one corner. Mrs. Cunningham's admiration was of no significance to her. This scrawny landlady was nothing like the woman in the song.

Later, Christie and James waited downstairs with their baggage, but there was no sign of Greenberry. Mrs. Cunningham was setting the table for the noon meal.

"Are y'all eating with us?" she asked.

"When McCain gets here," said James. "He's paying."

"Well, he must be coming back," Mrs. Cunningham said. "He ain't taken care of the bill yet."

"What if he don't come back?" said Christie.

"Well, I'm afraid I'd have to ask you fine folks to pay the bill."

"We'll just wait here till he turns up, ma'am," said James.

Mrs. Cunningham darted into the kitchen, and James rammed his fist against the door, then cradled the pain. "He was supposed to pay us today," he said. "If he don't come back, we don't even have enough money to get home. And I wouldn't know how to find the way anyhow."

"Now don't get worked up, James," said Christie calmly. "We can't let him run our lives."

She wished she could just get on the train and go to Memphis, or New Orleans, or anywhere by herself. She was still churned up by the song she had heard. She had never heard such an earnest cry from the heart.

"I expect Greenberry will come back," Christie said to James. "He's always going off somewhere."

"I've been calculating how much he's taking in," James said, flexing his fingers. "All week, I've been counting the people. He stands there and wags his tongue, and I count the people in my head. Last night, he had about three hundred and fifty. And during the day, I estimate a thousand. He's running 'em through like a dose of salts. And they paid twenty-five cents apiece. Say it was twelve hundred people. That's close to three hundred dollars—ever day! Besides them souvenirs. You *know* he never throwed 'em away." James shook his head and began pacing. "If Uncle Wad knew how this was going, he'd be fit to be tied."

"Well, Greenberry's paid us what he agreed to," Christie said.

"He's liable to sell them souvenirs by mail order. He could do that for years." James lowered his head and said quietly, "We oughter knowed ever'body in the world would want to see the babies. We knowed that." He squatted to tie his shoe.

He went out again, walking down the street. Christie took her sewing to the long verandah so she could see the mossy trees and the boogerville flowers. Several carriages pulled up, and a vegetable wagon. A man in a horse-drawn dray delivered some baggage from the depot. Greenberry had said the train was at one o'clock. Christie closed her eyes, trying to bring back every note of the song she had heard. She had to remember it.

At twelve, Mrs. Cunningham came out and asked her if she wanted some dinner.

"I can't pay for it," said Christie.

"I'll put it on your bill, if you're sure he's coming back."

"I reckon we'll do without."

Her stomach grumbled. Restlessly, she went inside and sat in the parlor. The dining room smelled inviting—ham and potatoes and gravy and green beans. The apple cobbler on the sideboard was bubbling hot. Even though James had complained about the breakfast, Mrs. Cunningham's cooking was better than most of the food they had encountered in their travels. It was odd that Mrs. Cunningham was so impressed with who Christie was, yet wouldn't give her a morsel to eat. The woman probably believed they were rich, Christie thought. She touched the five dollars hidden inside her waist. Stubbornly, she refused to take it out.

She saw James outside and went out to greet him on the verandah.

"Mrs. Cunningham offered us dinner," she said when he walked up the steps. "But I said we couldn't pay for it."

"I'm ready to eat. Can't we go ahead and eat?"

"Well, what if Greenberry don't come? You were afraid he'd gone off."

He began to clean mud from his shoes on a wrought-iron boot scraper at the top of the steps.

"James, you were right," she said when he finished. "We oughtn't to have sent all the money home to Wad. We might need to buy a train ticket."

They went inside and waited. James watched out the window. At twenty to one, he said, "Here comes old Gooseberry."

"Hello, folks!" said Greenberry with a large smile, as he shut the front door and removed his hat. "Are you good folks ready to go?"

"We've been waiting on you," said James, scowling. "We didn't know what you were up to."

"I got tied up with some of my wife's kinfolks. Talk, talk, talk," he said, shaking his head. "I couldn't get a word in to say I had to leave! They made me set down with them to eat. Lottie's sister can cook like an angel—she had fried rabbit and chicken salad and wilted greens and corn and berry cobbler. I eat till I thought I'd bust. I guess y'all eat one of Mrs. Cunningham's fine dinners."

"No, we didn't," said Christie.

"Oh, that's too bad. Well, let me settle this bill and we'll have to get on out of here." Greenberry patted his pocket and strode to the desk.

Christie and James glared at him. Mrs. Cunningham and Greenberry jabbered like old friends. Greenberry's face was red. It glowed like foxfire.

11

FROM THEN ON, THE TRIP WAS LIKE CHARGING AHEAD ON A HIGH-spirited, headstrong horse. Since she heard the man singing in Vicksburg, Christie felt she had turned a corner into brilliant sunlight. A deep need was growing in her, an urge to be free of the burdens she had carried for months. During the trip, James's spirit had dulled, and he plodded through the days like a mule at a plow, his blinders preventing surprise. He seemed worn down, like the singer in the woods when he lost the woman whose power he needed so that he could go on with his labor. James spent hours whittling. Christie tried to get him to make some playthings for the children, but he just worked sticks down to nubs.

For weeks they had spent all their time together idly. That had never happened before in their married life. Now she was used to seeing James take out his things from his bag and try awkwardly to adjust to an unfamiliar room. He stropped his razor, lathered his shaving brush, splashed water for yards. It irritated her that he wouldn't hang up the towels or request more hot water when there was too little. His clothes smelled of tobacco, soaked up from the atmosphere of the trains and crowds, and no amount of brushing would remove the harsh smell. She washed his shirts with lye soap and wrung them out as hard as she could.

She was restless and alert. As they ventured northward, the weather cooled off, and the sky turned gray. It rained. Their room in Tupelo, Mississippi, was in a private home with an iron rooster on a weather vane and two calico cats who came indoors. The room was small but pleasant, with yellow-flowered wallpaper and a soft cabbage-rose carpet and embroidered coverlets. It was clean.

"This room ain't big enough to cuss a cat in!" Christie said with a laugh when James bumped against the chifforobe.

James moved the lamp so the light hit her sewing more directly. The movement made large shadows across the yellow-flowered wall. He sank onto the bed. It was too early to go to sleep.

"Gooseberry McPain," he said, staring at the ceiling.

"I don't pay no attention to him anymore," said Christie, who was darning James's socks. She didn't have a darning egg, so she was using a goose egg she had borrowed from Mrs. Holmes, the owner of the house.

"Goddamn horse trader," James said. "At least he pays on time."

After being almost stranded in Vicksburg, James had decided to keep out some cash for emergencies.

Christie wove her needle through the sock deliberately.

"Look at this egg," she said when she removed it from the sock. "When I was ten years old, Mama give me a setting of goose eggs— I've told you this before. Remember? She give me a dozen eggs. Ten of them hatched and eight lived to grow up. She told me if I kept my geese going year after year, by the time I married I'd have enough feathers for a fine feather bed and two pillers. And I did. What's funny now is thinking about that little ten-year-old girl I used to be. What did I know of marrying? What did I think I was saving feathers for?" She shuddered. "Some of those very feathers are in them feather crowns."

"If you hadn't saved them feathers, all of this might not have happened," he said.

Ignoring his foolish objection, the kind of thing he'd said too often, Christie said, "I remember one goose. I called her Fanny. Law, she was mean; she gouged a plug out of my arm once."

"I heard a feller say last week he found a feather crown in his mama's piller after she died," James said, raising up on his elbow. "He called it a death crown. And then he told about a dream he had where she come back after her crown. He wanted it to remember her by, but she chewed him out and stole it from him. He woke up scared, but the crown was still on the mantel."

"You'd probably find them in any piller if you looked," Christie said. She removed the egg from the sock. "The person don't have to be dead."

"You don't believe they're a sign of anything?"

"I don't know what I believe anymore." She jabbed her needle into the strawberry emery on her pincushion and shoved her sewing spectacles into a blue sock she kept them in. "You can put the light out," she said. "I'm going to carry Mrs. Holmes her egg back."

Mrs. Holmes was cleaning up the parlor. She was brushing cat hair from the brocaded seat of a roundabout chair. The mingledy-spotted cats sat on another chair washing each other's faces.

"Honey, if you want to keep that egg to use in your traveling trip, you go right ahead," said Mrs. Holmes, a dumpy woman with a kindly face.

"No, I'd just break it," said Christie. "Thank ye kindly anyway."

As she warmed herself by the fire, she studied the family pictures on the mantel, serious-looking adults staring out from the frames as if observing the visitors. Some of the men wore uniforms.

"That one was my husband," said Mrs. Holmes, touching a portrait of a wide-eyed young man with wavy hair and a thick beard. His uniform had a row of shiny buttons the size of quarters. He was seated, with a pistol tucked into his belt. His right hand clutched the handle of a sword, which was pointed straight up. Mrs. Holmes said, "He was killed at Fort Donelson. He was twenty-four year old."

"Were these his books?" Christie asked. Above a heavy sideboard was a shelf of books. She had noticed them earlier. Some of the titles intrigued her: *Conquering the Humours, The Encyclopedia of Animal Life, An Almanac of the Body.*

"No. A feller left them here five year ago, said he'd be back through, but he never did come," Mrs. Holmes explained as she stooped to pet a cat. "He was a doctor, I believe."

"Have you read them?"

"No, I ain't even opened into 'em. I don't read nothing but the Good Book." The woman began dusting her pictures. "But you go right ahead and read in them, if you're of a mind to," she said. "They ain't doing me any good, collecting dust."

The next morning, Mrs. Holmes returned the goose egg to Christie—on her plate, fried with the yellow eye open, and a good piece of back bacon. It was as though the woman thought Christie still needed extra nourishment, for her babies. Christie took two cups of coffee, for she had stayed up late in the parlor, reading from the books. The medical books were over her head, but *The Encyclopedia of Animal Life* was all about the science of life—not only mammals but lower forms, such as worms and insects. For a long time in the night she read about strange creatures she hadn't known existed, tiny beings that could not be seen with the bare eye but had to be studied with a microscope. There were creatures made of a single cell, and transparent, with eyes and mouths and innards, and even feet. They weren't germs, and they weren't the tiny beginnings of a larger life. They were complete in themselves. Some of them reproduced by dividing in two. One was called a slipper animalcule, or paramecium. It lived in ponds, and it swam by waving a fringe of hairs resembling eyelashes. Christie wished she could hear James's mother try to say "paramecium." Or "slipper animalcule." The words swirled around in her head like fringe-edged creatures themselves.

"Are you losing your mind?" James said, when she tried to explain at breakfast what she had been reading.

Her eyes were tired, and learning about the little creatures only raised more questions. Where were these tiny things? Were they everywhere? Why had their existence been such a secret? How would you know where they were if you couldn't see them? What was their purpose? She thought of the pond at home, and the pond garden she had made with Nannie. Did the pond have those little animalcules in it?

As she finished her egg and biscuits, she said to James, "About those feather crowns—I've been wondering about them. I believe there's a bug that eats on the feathers and gets them all twisted up. A real teensy bug you can't see. Littler than a chicken mite. Some kind of feather bug."

James laughed. "I believe I felt some of them in the bed with me last night." He scratched an itch on his arm.

She said, "There's so much in the world that nobody understands, or even notices."

12

THEY SPENT TWO DAYS IN TUSCALOOSA, AWARE THAT ONLY THREE weeks remained of their obligation. They spoke little to Greenberry McCain, who seemed flustered in their presence. James said the man was a coward—he was trying too hard to please them. The Hart Brothers show had gone ahead to Birmingham, but the Wheelers did not expect to rejoin it until Saturday. Christie had been impatient to find the Wiggins sisters in Birmingham, but Greenberry had added the extra engagement in Tuscaloosa, where they sat on a stage in a small theater. She embroidered a dresser scarf and James whittled.

Saturday afternoon they boarded the train to Birmingham, which was just a short distance away. The train was packed and noisy. Several men were drinking from brown jugs. They whooped and yelled.

"There's a hanging in Birmingham," Greenberry explained to them as they found their chairs. "People are already celebrating, I'd allow."

"It's like a bunch of the faithful going to a camp meeting," Christie said. Greenberry stared at her quizzically. She didn't elaborate.

The train was approaching the outskirts of Birmingham when a commotion occurred in the next car. Christie heard noises like boards clapping, and two men burst into their car, yelling and cussing. The men—young, in traveling suits—appeared frightened, and one of them had a smudge of dirt on his cheek.

"They's a fight up ahead," the shorter one gasped.

"Are they robbers?" someone asked. Half the passengers were standing.

"Everybody be quiet. We're liable to get our heads blowed off," said the other, enjoying his prominence as the bringer of news.

All the passengers talked at once. The two young men passed

through the car. James grasped Christie's hand. Greenberry, sitting across the aisle, glanced at them and confidently patted his coat. He carried a pistol.

"Just set still," he said to James, as if he had been through such events a hundred times before. "A hanging always gets people's blood up."

A straw-haired man staggered down the aisle, and Christie heard a man behind her comment, "That whiskey's so strong, they must of been a dead hog in it."

"I have to go," Christie said to James. The sudden anxiety set her insides in motion, and she badly needed to relieve herself. The ladies' wash-room was at the rear of the car ahead.

"No, stay right here," James said, restraining her by the elbow.

"But I'll be safer in the wash-room. I can lock the door."

"Let's just stay away from any fights. You don't want to get hurt."

A hush settled over the passengers, as they waited to see what would happen. A child screamed out, and a baby cried. Christie was miserable.

"We'll get into Birmingham in twenty minutes," Greenberry said.

"You can wait," James said to Christie.

The quiet lifted. The passengers resumed whooping and passing around their jugs. The train pulled into the station without further incident, and Christie dashed into the ladies' waiting room at the station. The filth of the place was worse than a henhouse; through the walls the noise of the crowd was a steady roar. When she emerged, she spotted James waiting nearby with their small carpetbags. The station was so crowded he had to hunch up against the wall.

"Did you find out what happened on the train?" she asked.

"Somebody said it was two fellers arguing over a horse. That's all I know."

"Where's Greenberry?"

"There he comes."

Greenberry was struggling through the crowd, trying not to get his fine clothes dirty. The crowd was aimless and sweaty. People elbowed their way along, some eating from folded sandwich papers or dragging bawling children.

"The hanging's done over with," Greenberry reported when he reached them. "A lot of folks here missed it."

"You should always go early to a hanging," James said sarcastically.

"Get Christie on to the hotel," Greenberry said briskly to James. "I'll wait for the trunk and our cases and be on directly. I'll get you a carriage."

Christie tried to move forward with her carry-bag. James had her by the arm, guiding her toward the street. Greenberry was behind them, and he signaled a driver.

"There's our boy with the trunk right now," James said.

Greenberry turned around. "Go on, James. I'll get the trunk and our baggage and be right behind you. There ain't room for us all—and the trunk—in this carriage."

He whirled away and started into the crowd. Christie could see the trunk about fifty feet away. A porter was pulling it by its strap and it was rolling through the crowd as if it had a life of its own. She saw Greenberry grab the strap.

The rickety carriage with two balky horses and an indifferent driver sauntered to the hotel with Christie and James and their carpet-bags. Greenberry followed in another carriage. The streets were filled with celebrating crowds, and now and then someone fired off a pistol. Men clustered along the sidewalks, their brown corn-liquor jugs drained and tossed onto the streets among the litter of advertising dodgers and horse manure. Christie saw a number of dogs nosing into the trash for scraps. She heard firecrackers.

The driver said, "Everybody sleep good tonight." He tried to tell about the hanging, but it was so noisy Christie couldn't hear, and James wasn't paying attention. He had lost sight of Greenberry.

Hundreds of horses, many harnessed to wagons and buggies, waited outside the courthouse. The hanging had taken place in front of the courthouse. Their hotel was on the same street. Four stories high, the hotel was made of bright, new red brick and looked clean outside, but inside it was dingy and dark, heavy with the smells of grease and cigars. A man near the door handed James a postal card with a picture of a large, baby-faced man on it.

"That's the one," the man said with pride. "He raped and murdered and stole. And he done his mama dirty—before he shot her. And he probably raped his mama too. Look at him. Don't he look like nothing but a big old baby?"

Christie and James examined the card. James was enraged by the man's language in front of her. But she didn't mind it. Men made so little effort to please women with their manners and behavior; bad language was the least of their offenses. She'd rather hear ugly words than see tobacco spit or breathe cigar smoke.

The registration desk was unattended. James set their carpetbags in a corner out of the way. The parlor was filled with men drinking whiskey and smoking. They all seemed eager to tell Christie and James about the day's doings.

"Fats Fortenberry," volunteered one of the men. "He sold them-there postcards to buy tobaccer and liquor his last day."

"He give a purty speech," said a hunched-over man in a straw hat. "Music to my ears. If he'd been running for office, everybody would have voted for him. Oh, he repented and bent down and kissed the ground and talked sweet about his dear old mama in heaven. I believe if he'd kept up that kind of talk, he'd of been set free by night."

The men all laughed uproariously. "Too bad his 'dear old mama' what he plowed with a Smith and Wesson couldn't of seen how he went out in style," said somebody.

"He was just like a preacher a-preaching a wedding," said a man in a brown suit so large on him that he had the cuffs and sleeves rolled.

"They had him tied to his coffin, and they hauled him to the gallows on it, and after the deed was done they cut the rope so he fell right smack in the coffin. They straightened him out and hauled him right on down the street."

"I expect he broke a leg or two."

"It was a most satisfactory hanging."

The group of men, telling their juicy news, all beamed at Christie and James. Christie felt tired and wanted to get to a room so she could wash and rest. She heard a pistol shot, out on the street. A dog ran through the parlor.

"Where's Greenberry?" Christie asked her husband.

"He oughter be here by now."

"He's got the trunk."

"He'll be on directly."

James paced between the front window and the door, looking out for Greenberry.

A man in the parlor said to them, "I expect there ain't no rooms left. The train done brought five cars in from Montgomery for the hanging." He turned to his companions and said, "I've got a souvenir from a swell little necktie party last fall—a man hung for killing four people in a bank over in Tuscaloosa."

"What d'you get?"

"A button and a little scrap of blue-jeans material."

"Have you been to a lynching?"

"You don't need to be hearing all this," James said to Christie, turning back toward the hotel reception desk. A squat, gray-haired man appeared then. "I'm George Murphy," he said. "The proprietor. Did you folks have any baggage?"

"Our friend, Mr. Greenberry McCain, is bringing it in a wagon from the depot," James explained.

"Our carpetbags are there in the corner," said Christie, embarrassed that the hotel proprietor might think they were checking in without baggage.

James glanced at her with warning eyes. She should have known to leave this business to him, but sometimes her frustration forced her forward.

Instead of showing them to their room, the proprietor asked them to wait in a corner of the parlor for Greenberry and the baggage to arrive. The cigar smoke and the sour smell of corn liquor pervaded the air. They sat there a long while, their ears unavoidably picking up more gossip about the criminal—he stole his brother's cotton crop (already baled and graded); he shot his sweetheart on their wedding day (at the time this was believed to be an accident, but a few years later when he shot his second wife for going to town without his permission, his ways started to seem suspicious); Fats wasn't always fat, and his real name was Percy; he won a fortune gambling on the river and ate up his profits; his weight sank a boat once; he had a faithful old dog named Delbert who finally turned against him.

"Where's Greenberry?" Christie muttered.

"Don't fret, Christie," said James. "He'll be along directly."

"I'm not fretting. I'm mad. I'm tired of worrying about where he is."

But when Greenberry hadn't come in an hour, Christie and James were both sick with worry. It seemed clear either that Greenberry had absconded with the precious trunk or that some ruthless person in the crowd had stolen it. Stealing a trunk would be easier than stealing a cotton crop. Christie couldn't imagine how Fats Fortenberry had done that. Her eyes watered from the smoke.

"Oughtn't you to go look for him?" Christie implored.

"I can't leave you here by yourself," said James.

"Maybe we could ask again for our room."

"I'll get you some tea."

"Sarsaparilla or a dope."

James stood around at the desk trying to catch the proprietor's attention. The man was engaged in spirited conversation with three of the men in the lobby. They were taking bets on what day a spider in the dining-room window was going to quit operating its web before packing up for the winter. Finally, James got the key to their room. He said to Christie, "I'll go see if I can locate Greenberry. I told Mr. Murphy our bags was delayed, so he'll keep an eye out for them if they turn up. He's going to send you up a Co'-Cola."

"Be careful, James," she said, touching his arm.

13

THE ROOM WAS *L*-SHAPED, WITH DIRTY LACE CURTAINS AND A HEAVY, dark bedspread. Christie arranged her sewing on the bed. The bottled dope a Negro girl brought up was invigorating, and Christie felt improved. It was ice cold and burned her throat pleasantly. She unpacked her carry-bag and settled herself in the tiny, dark room. She could hear occasional pistol fire and shouting outside, and in the distance someone was playing a fiddle.

She suspected that the wagon-show and the hanging had been scheduled together on purpose, so the weekend could be a holiday festival, with increased profits. Hangings and entertainment shows alike attracted so many farm people, who brought in their hard-earned dollars for such celebrations. Right now she had more feeling for Fats Fortenberry than she did for Greenberry McCain. She was tired of Greenberry's disappearing acts.

She wished the Wiggins sisters would turn up. They weren't registered at the hotel, she had learned. They had said they would find her in Birmingham. She sat on the bed without her shoes and tried to concentrate on hemming a skirt.

More than an hour passed. The longer James was gone the more she feared the trunk was lost or stolen. But why was James so long? Could he be following Greenberry? Could he have fallen in with a dangerous crowd who offered him the irresistible temptation of a brown jug? That seemed preposterous, but she was learning so much about the world she felt like writing the raw truth to the *Hopewell Chronicle* and daring Mr. Redmon to print her opinions of the duplicity of men. She had not written to the paper again after her first letter.

The duplicity of women, too. She loved the Wiggins girls, but she had seen Evelyn drinking something mysterious—and it wasn't Colonel Happy Tucker's Wonderful Worm-Syrup. She knew the Queen of the Nile smoked hashish. She had seen Greenberry and Colonel Tucker hobnobbing in the casual company of some of the circus showgirls; they had entered a tent—not one of the show tents, but a private one.

She had always thought of herself as level-headed. She had been through what no woman ever had endured, and she had done it with a poise and hardened nerve that sometimes perplexed James. But her suffering wasn't the worst a person could go through. That Negro man singing in the woods sounded a note of suffering so deep she couldn't reach it to compare. Ever since they began their trip, the sight of so many poor Negroes had bothered her. She kept wondering why God allowed such injustice. Why did the colored folks have to be slaves? Had God been punishing them for something? Why would a loving God punish anybody so harshly? Or why would He make a person like Charley Lou Pickles? She could hear Brother Jones reaching for his familiar answer, "God's mysterious ways." That meant you were supposed to accept what you couldn't understand.

That didn't suit her. It never had.

She had been thinking hard thoughts about God lately. He hadn't been fair. Why would He punish her for having lustful thoughts about a dark-haired preacher with a rousing way of expressing himself? Why would He extend His punishment to her babies, and to James, and to Amanda? Brother Jones once said a wicked woman fouls all around her, but now Christie doubted that. She wasn't truly a wicked woman, was she? Her sin seemed so small now. All she did was dream. There was a lot God hadn't punished, and a lot He hadn't punished enough. It was as though He punished randomly, for fun, or as though He couldn't keep up with all the misdeeds of the human race. Maybe after He created people, they multiplied so fast, they were out of control—like germs.

Like the germs that killed her babies.

For a cold moment she contemplated the possibility that she was stranded in this bleak city in Alabama—far from home, without family—and that the gruesome, frail shells of her precious babies had been stolen away for some wicked purpose. What would someone do with them? If the thief used them in a public show, the babies would be recognized. So he probably wanted to possess the babies for his own, to keep them in the recesses of his home, known only to his closest friends and family. His? She thought back to the many women who had written her, women desperate for a baby—even *one* baby; plenty of greedy, conniving women would like to get their hands on something as unusual and precious as the famous Wheeler Quintuplets. She imagined the private glee of one of those women, perverted in thought and spirit, who would stoop to snatching the stiff, painted little bodies.

That woman wouldn't be able to resist opening the glass casket, and the babies would all crumble to dust.

Or, a kidnapping. With a note to follow, demanding money. James might at this moment be tracking down the stolen infants. There were women who would even kidnap James at gunpoint, in hopes he could plant a set of babies in them. Usually kidnap victims were persons of wealth. But it was likely, she reasoned, that people might assume the Wheelers had gotten rich from all the gifts and opportunities they had received.

That wagonload of presents from town had never come.

She lay on the bed, her stomach turning and snarling.

There was a knock at the door, and Christie jumped off the bed. A Negro maid in a pink cap told her supper would be in the dining room at half past six. The courthouse clock had just struck five, and there was no sign of James. He had been gone two hours.

"By all means," said Christie, shaking. "My husband oughter be here by then."

"I'll lay a place for y'all, ma'am. We have so many people with us tonight on account of the carnival and them that come in for the hanging."

"Much obliged," said Christie, closing the door.

The streets were quieter, with only occasional whoops and rebel yells. Then she heard someone in the hall say, "Wonder how Fats Fortenberry enjoyed his little send-off party."

"Bet he's hot now!"

The two men guffawed drunkenly. Christie flung open the door and yelled, "I hope when it's your turn you burn in Hell!"

The men's mouths dropped. "Why, ma'am—"

"Fats Fortenberry's a better man than either one of you!"

Christie slammed the door shut and bolted it. She immediately felt better, as if the knot in her stomach had unraveled and left her calm. James, if he heard about what she said, would have a conniption fit. She enjoyed the thought. If he learned that she had said "Hell," she would just smile. She ached with worry for him—but as with all bouts of worry, there came a point at which she burst through into serenity, by relinquishing all claim to concern. Having explored the pit of worry and having imagined and played out all the worst scenes possible, she couldn't be surprised by anything. Actual news could not possibly be worse than her fears.

If God had been paying attention, maybe He had chosen her to bear five babies and then to bear their loss because she *could* bear it. Someone like Amanda could not. But often Christie thought she was on the verge of learning why it had happened to her, when a fresh question appeared. What if it *had* happened to Amanda? And losing five babies was not unheard of. The diphtheria that took Susan had taken all six children of a couple in Dundee. It was the unusual circumstances of five infants born at once that made Christie's pain unique. But was it any worse? she wondered. What made it *seem* worse was also what made it better, she thought. The way the people came, the way everyone praised her, the way she had been so proud of her babies.

When James finally returned at a quarter past six, with their large imitation-leather case, she felt she was just getting over some silly spell.

"It was a breakdown of the carriage," he said, still standing in the open doorway. "Gooseberry had to transfer to another one and wait for a fresh team of horses. So he dawdled around at the depot. I should have known he'd get mixed up in the whooping and hollering and carrying on. I tell you, there was more noise at the depot than ninety-nine cows and a bobtailed bull. I thought I'd never find him."

He stepped out into the hall. Two young Negroes came through the door with the brassbound trunk. James gave them each a nickel and shut the door.

"What's the trunk doing up here?" Christie asked.

"I told Gooseberry we wanted to be with it, and not have it in the hotel downstairs because of all the commotion going on this weekend."

"Good. But I thought we had to go be in the show tonight."

"No. It turns out we're not. I don't know what's going on. I think he's on the outs with the Hart Brothers and now he has to root around for a place to show the babies. If I know him, he'll have 'em out on the sidewalk and collecting money. But we don't have a place at the show now."

James opened his carpetbag and pulled out a shirt that seemed clean. He pulled off his shirt and began to wash. The hotel had piped water.

"I didn't even argue with him," James said. "I don't care. I thought we'd just try to get through these last few weeks."

"Well, I'm glad we don't have to go out tonight. We can go eat. The hotel has supper for us at half past six," she said.

"I know. The feller at the desk said we're having ribs and Irish taters boiled in their jackets and butter beans. And hominy, too. And greens-with-hog-jaws. I'm purely starved."

James seemed so relieved, as though he had just finished hauling in a load of hay before a downpour began.

Downstairs, the desk clerk gave James a note, and Christie read it. Greenberry had decided not to stay in the hotel. His message said he would see them the next morning at ten. He was working out a deal to show the quintuplets in Asheville, North Carolina, and Atlanta, Georgia, at proper exhibition halls.

"Well," said James. "We'll see what kind of outhouses he's got us lined up for."

A dog wandered through the dining room, sniffing for crumbs. Christie saw a spider outside the window, a night orb-weaver. She saw some men pointing to the spider and laughing. The spider wouldn't be closing up for the winter yet, she thought. The outside air that flooded through the door was balmy, like spring.

Christie and James sat silently at one end of the long table, passing the bowls of greasy food down the line of men, who for the duration of the meal recounted the last hours of Fats Fortenberry. "What were Fats Fortenberry's last words to his mother before she died?" "Hello, Mother. It's cotton-chopping time. Whoopsy, daisy! I was aiming at 'at-'ere cotton stem. Good-bye, Mother."

That night, Christie couldn't sleep, and her tossing woke James.

"Are the witches bothering you?" he said.

"No. I think that Co'-Cola's keeping me awake. It was mighty powerful."

She wanted to go home. She had believed there must be something that was better than putting up with the day-to-day hardship of a routine life, and she had been eager to leave home and travel into the unknown, with her precious babies. But the trip had provided few memories to treasure. She would remember the Negro man singing in the woods, and the Wiggins girls—the way they talked and sang, especially the haunting way they sang the lullaby "Old Aunt Matilda." And she'd remember Mrs. Holmes, with her calico cats and her picture of her young husband, killed in the War. And she would remember the live-oak trees and the boogerville vines, and how the South was so warm and dusty. But she would also remember how listless and broken everyone seemed.

"I need some liniment on my back," she said to James.

"I'll turn on the lamp," he said, sitting up.

She searched through her carpetbag for a liniment she had bought from a medicine man in Tennessee, early in the trip, when she believed what medicine men said. In the dim light from the gas lamp, she saw something flutter out of the bag to the floor. She picked it up. It was the card from the Institute of Man. She had stuck it in the crevice behind the inside pocket of the carpetbag. She felt a little shiver. She wondered if she should mention the card to James. She handed him the liniment.

"Rub this on my back," she said.

He poured a little in his hand. It was strong-smelling, like chocolate and mint. She pulled up her shift and lay on her stomach.

"What is this stuff?" he asked. "Can you drink it?"

"I think you can do anything with it," she said with sudden abandon. "You can shine brass or clean buggy rigging. It cures piles."

"Reckon it'll unstop the gut? Or clean sores?"

"It polishes furniture. Anything you're of a mind to do with it." She laughed, and she could see he was grinning.

"Well, it must be a miracle."

He rubbed her back and the liniment soaked in, but it was the warmth of his hands that soothed the ache. His hands had lost their rough calluses.

"This potion made a Negro man's toe feel better right through his boot," she said. "The Negro said his toe was sore, and the medicine man just poured it on his boot." She lifted herself up on her elbows and gazed toward the street lamp through the lacy curtain. "James," she said. "Where's the money Greenberry paid you this week?"

"Right there in my pocket. I had a time hanging on to it in town this evening," he said. "Why?"

"Just wondering." She punched up her pillow and rested her head again. She said, "I've had enough of this."

"At least let me rub your shoulders."

"I meant I've had enough of all of this."

"Well, as you said, we can't just go home. We signed that paper."

"But that piece of writing asked too much from us. We didn't know what we were getting into." She paused and groaned pleasurably as he worked her shoulders loose. "We could just go," she said. "We have the trunk. We could get to the train—before he even knows we're gone."

"Do you want to carry the trunk back to Mullins?" James asked, pausing in the back rub.

"No. Mr. Mullins wants to keep them."

"I don't want him to have them," said James. "He ain't got no right."

"What do you want to do with them, James? Take them home and set 'em by the fireplace?"

"We oughter bury them."

"I used to believe that," said Christie. "But now I don't think we oughter bury them." She turned over and pulled down her shift.

"We oughter get 'em in the ground where they belong. I thought you said you wanted to bury them."

"You know what would happen?" Christie said, sitting up, next to James. Her feet brushed the wool rug. "If we bury them, somebody will come along and dig them up and take them off and put them in a freak show."

"I don't want to keep them in the house. Right now they're in the same room with us, and we can't sleep. It's like the room is haunted."

James seemed close to tears. She had not seen him like this on the trip. He bent his head into his hands.

"I want to see Nannie," said Christie.

"Well, let's go home," James said, decisively. He lifted his head. "Let's stop all this foolishness and go home where we belong."

He stood up and marched over to the trunk in the corner.

"I'm going to open it, and we're going to take a good look at what's there. They're just like dead cats, dead dogs, dead anything. They're not real anymore. They ain't nothing but hulls, like locust shells. We could throw them away, in the trash buckets out behind the hotel here. We could burn 'em. What Mullins did to them wasn't right."

James paced around the trunk. He was speaking calmly, although his voice was rising. His hair was rumpled, sticking out in all directions like a dried burdock weed.

"Hush, James. The people trying to sleep will hear you. They won't have the slightest idea what you're talking about."

"That Fats Fortenberry. All day I heard about what a criminal he was, but ever'body loved him. He put on a good show. Gooseberry McPain would have made good in charge of him. Maybe Gooseberry can specialize in hangings next. He could line up a series of them with the Hart Brothers and rake in a fortune. There's a fortune in hangings! And souvenirs. He could have little ropes and nooses and dolls like this." James rummaged into her carry-bag and found one of the souvenir baby beds Greenberry had put there. He took each tiny doll and snapped it in half. The fragments flew all over the carpet.

Christie was growing alarmed.

James started unbuckling the trunk. "Look at this," he said. "Look what we've done. It was witches in us. Or that earthquake, like they said."

"Be quiet, they'll hear you."

"Who, these babies? These babies can't hear." He flung back the lid of the trunk and threw aside the top pillows. The pink floral paper inside the lid of the trunk had curled on one edge. The oak chest was nestled down inside the other pillows. He yanked the chest out by its handles and set it on the floor. He opened the chest and lifted the glass casket out. He set it on a table at the foot of the bed, so that the babies faced them. "Now, what would happen if I was to take this apart?" he said.

"Don't do it, James."

"What if the hotel manager was to come up and find out what we've got here? They'd probably arrest us."

Christie jumped off the bed and grabbed his arm. "What are you doing, James?"

"I'm gonna open this up and put 'em in the right order so you'll stop complaining about Minnie being on the edge," he said.

"No, don't open it!"

"Why not?"

"They might crumble."

"Like the Bible says—we go back to dust."

"Mr. Mullins said if the air hits them, they'll turn brown and crumble. It's like canning peaches," she said, snatching at words. "Peaches turn brown in the air." She reached for her wrapper and pulled it around her. She stoppered the liniment. "Here, turn that lamp up. I've got a notion."

He turned up the lamp, and they were suddenly transfixed by the babies in the case on the table, lying there before them, mute observers. James stopped speaking, and they both seemed to halt in the middle of a step, as if realizing they shouldn't argue like this in front of the children. Christie felt they were in the presence of the babies, or rather their memories of the babies; they were imposing their memories of the babies onto the still forms under glass. For the first time on the trip, she felt a surge of grief she couldn't keep in, and when she started crying James did too, sobbing more quietly, and their cries weren't just for the babies but for themselves, and what they had endured, and especially what they hadn't known. They wept for their innocence. They had made such a muddle of their lives, and now they had ended up in a hotel in Birmingham, Alabama, site of a hanging, far from home. None of this should have happened. Their lives should have been so simple, she realized. The little ones were just babies. People had been having babies forever.

They heard a knock at the door. A man said, "Is somebody dying in there?"

"It's all right. Go away," said James. "Thank ye anyway."

James hunted through his clothes and found a handkerchief for her. In the lamplight, the babies seemed imbued with looks of wisdom, as if they had understood everything all along.

"They were sent for a purpose," James said.

"What's that?"

"I don't know. Something. To teach us."

She hadn't cried for many weeks. It was as though she had been waiting for some illumination to loosen her tears. There were still so many questions hanging. But now she felt she could see how the babies had come between her and James, and she knew they would always be between them in some basic way. But she and James were closer now too. They were tied together in a knot, the babies their bond.

"Come here, Chrissie," James said, reaching for her. They sat on the edge of the bed, and he held her in his arms until her sniffling quieted down. He held her close, breathing on her neck. "What we did wasn't wrong, Chrissie. We never did anything wrong."

"I know."

"I was awful scared when you were carrying those littluns. I didn't let on, but I was so afraid I'd lose you."

"I didn't tell you how scared I was, either," she said, rolling his handkerchief in her hand. She leaned back against the pillow, pulling him down with her.

"Wait just a minute," he said, getting up.

He walked over to pull down the shade. She raised her shift over her head, removed it, and placed it over the glass case on the table at the foot of the bed. He turned out the light and came to her. For the first time in many months, she relaxed in his arms and let her body dissolve in his, her need rising and falling like grief. But the grief turned to pleasure, as they grabbed and rolled and—finally—plowed, their passion like something free they had forgotten to claim.

Only a short spell later, calm and drained, she turned on the gas lamp and searched in her bag. In the dim lamplight, she showed James the card.

"This is what we have to do, James," she said.

14

CHRISTIE HAD KEPT A TRAIN TIMETABLE, AND SHE DISCOVERED A TRAIN to Atlanta at six-thirty in the morning. Immediately after breakfast, a Negro man from the hotel drove them to the depot with their bags and the trunk. The streets were quiet now. The litter of papers and brown jugs seemed to have been strown by a fierce storm. In the early light, Christie noticed a picture of Fats Fortenberry on a crumpled handbill.

At the depot, they bought tickets to Atlanta and made reservations on the Washington cars. James paid for the tickets with a crisp new bill.

In the past, Greenberry McCain had bustled around, making reservations, buying tickets, arranging for hotels and meals, managing the brassbound trunk. But now Christie believed she and James could take care of themselves. All they had to do was ask questions and pay attention. She was proud of James for making inquiries and getting the trunk tagged. While she waited on a bench, James followed the porter to the place on the platform where the baggage would be loaded. She watched him as he hired one of the baggage hands to ride with the trunk. James behaved with confidence, just as though he were harnessing horses or driving a team of mules through a creek bottom.

When James had said in the early hours of the morning, "We'll take a flying trip to Washington, and then we're going home, and we're never going to go off again," she felt relieved. His words gave a direction to their journey now. Indirectly, he was standing up to his uncle, giving up the last three weeks' worth of earnings on the tour in exchange for their peace of mind. Now that they were going home, he had a glow and fire about him. He had even hummed a little song that morning while he was shaving. They were still young, she thought.

The train chugged out of the station, flinging cinders in a storm of noise and smoke. The day was dry and calm, with a yellow glow in the East. Christie took out her sewing, then put it back when she remembered this was Sunday. She gazed out the window for a while. The Southern scene was burned into her brain by now: the bunches of dusty Negro children ("ash cats," she heard someone call them) watching the train go by; old women lugging buckets; brown-and-white dogs slinking through refuse; dusty mules loafing or pulling loads; shacks by the train tracks; the bare, hard dirt of the roads.

"Look how red the dirt is here," Christie said to James.

"I'm surprised anything would grow in it," he said. He grinned and slapped his knee. "I like to think about old Gooseberry wondering what went with us. Let him wonder."

"He might come after us and try to make us pay for the three weeks we owe him."

"When we get to Atlanta, we might oughter send a telegram to Wad and them and let them know we're coming home," James mused. "Or we could telephone to Mrs. Blankenship."

"I don't want to telephone out to her! She got us into this mess with Greenberry in the first place. She'd find him right off."

The train swayed and rocked. The cough of the engine, the spin of the wheels, the churning rhythm, would stay with her all her life. She decided to sew even if it was Sunday. She began hemming a shirt sleeve. Clint might have outgrown the shirt in the time she had been away. James did not seem to realize she was sewing on the Lord's day. Her mother would be horrified if she knew. Once, Aunt Sophie had washed drawers on a Sunday and the next day come down with a dreadful cold. Christie suppressed a giggle, thinking of Aunt Sophie's pinched old face squeezing out one of her admonitions.

"I hope that boy's watching out after the trunk," James said fretfully. "What if he takes a notion to hop off at one of these pig paths we're stopping at?"

"Well, I guess worse things have happened in the world," said Christie. "Seems like all we've done all fall is chase after that thing."

"Read me that card again."

Christie showed him the card and read out the words.

> Dr. Graham Johnson
> The Institute of Man
> — B Street
> Washington, The District of Columbia

"I wonder where that's at," he said. "How will we find it?"

Last night James had argued that the babies belonged in Hopewell, not in some distant city, but she had persuaded him that the babies would make a contribution to science and knowledge if they were in an official institution. Now she cringed as she realized Greenberry McCain had used the same argument to get them out on the tour. The lecture series would be so educational, he had blithely promised. She wondered if James was feeling that Washington was one more place she was dragging him to. And if Wad found out they were giving the babies away free, he would never let them forget it. But just before falling asleep, James had said finally that he wanted to be finished with the babies and go on with life. If they took them home, there would always be painful reminders, he admitted. And strangers would still come to Hopewell to find them.

Now, as the train flew through a pinewoods, he said, "I've been studying on that new-ground Wad and me broke before we left. I've a good mind to plant corn in it in the spring. I can just see them pretty rows of corn coming up where there used to be nothing but berry briers and thistles."

Christie imagined herself at home—feeding her family, sewing pinafores for Nannie, washing James's blue-jeans, lowering a bucket into the cistern to draw water, building a fire under the wash kettle, hoeing the garden, splitting tobacco stalks clean down the center without a waver, saving scraps for a stray dog, watching a cat washing her kittens. She thought about the winter ice coating all the bushes and trees, an oak torn by lightning, the spring calves, dew on moss like a soaked sponge.

As they approached Atlanta, James went to the baggage car to check on the trunk and the boy he had hired. When he returned, he said excitedly, "Guess who I saw in the last car?"

"Greenberry?"

"No—the Wiggins girls!"

"Oh, they must have left Colonel Tucker again. Did you speak?"

"No. I sighted them, but they didn't see me to speak. They were at the far end of the car."

"I'll have to find them when we stop." Christie began to gather her things, eager to catch the sisters.

At the Atlanta station, James ran forward to locate their baggage, leaving Christie on the platform with the carpetbags. Christie spotted the Wiggins sisters as they left the train. She waved and they flew toward her with loud whoops. They weren't dressed alike today. They had on plain, worn clothes with the look of hand-me-downs. Each of them carried a tattered carpetbag, and Evelyn's guitar hung from her shoulder like a hunter's kill.

"Well, if it ain't the little lady that had all the babies," cried Evelyn, when they reached Christie. "Hi-dy, Christie. Let me hug you."

"Hi-dy," she said, and they all greeted and hugged.

"Where's James?"

Christie pointed. "Over yonder after our trunk."

"I heard Greenberry quit the Harts," said Big, her eyes lowering so that her eyelids showed pink with a rash. "Where are y'all off to now?"

"Up to Washington," said Christie, realizing the instant she said it that she shouldn't have revealed her destination. If the Wiggins sisters ran into Greenberry, he would dig it out of them. She knew how they loved to talk.

"Have you got them babies with you?" Evelyn asked.

Christie nodded. "We nearly lost them yesterday, but we've got 'em." She said, "I missed y'all. I was afraid Colonel Happy was being mean to you again."

"Oh, we've got our troubles with him," Big said.

"We're going home to see Mama," said Little. "She's old and she's got to have her turkeys killed this time of year."

Thanksgiving. It would be Thanksgiving in a few weeks, Christie thought.

"We usually go home and kill 'em for her," said Evelyn. "She used to manage, but she's got so she can't hardly lift that ax."

"Big made up a song oncet about Mama's turkeys," said Little excitedly. "But we won't sing it. Hit don't make a lick of sense and you have to make gobble-gobble sounds at the end of each line. I think it makes us look undignified." Little laughed.

"Well, Mama don't have just turkeys," said Big defensively. "She's got a peacock and a peahen too. But I think them things really are meaner tempered than turkeys. I'd rather be around turkeys any old day."

The sisters, it turned out, were waiting for a train to Knoxville, where their uncle would meet them and carry them home in his wagon. When James appeared with the porter and the trunk, the sisters stopped talking and snickered. He tipped his hat to acknowledge them—something he had seen Greenberry McCain do. Christie wanted to laugh. The sisters closed up like the blue faces of the four-o'clocks that bloomed beside the wash-house at home.

The Atlanta station, the busiest and largest they had ever been in, had a domed ceiling and pictures painted all over the walls and gigantic columns and statues. Everything in Atlanta had to be rebuilt after the War, Greenberry had told them. Christie learned from the timetable on the wall that the train to Washington left at three o'clock and would arrive at eleven the next morning. James went to buy the tickets, and Christie stayed with the trunk and the bags. The moment he left, the Wiggins sisters burst into gab again.

"You've got the beatin'est man, Christie," said Evelyn.

"He's a gentleman," said Little with a shiver of pleasure.

"Just think, you've got those babies right there in that-there trunk, not two feet from me," Big said. "That gives me chill bumps."

Christie passed the time pleasantly with the Wiggins sisters, while James kept wandering off to look at something or to pace up and down the platform. She thought James seemed more curious about things now, less bored and distraught, and that pleased her. She drank a dope and the sisters gave her some soda crackers. They chattered about their Aunt Bug, who had built her own house. Christie could imagine her ancestors in these women. Her father's people were mountain people, from North Carolina. Ever since she left Dundee she had felt that she didn't belong anywhere, but she sensed a strong kinship with the Wiggins sisters. She wished she could go with them to their holler and meet their mother and see her turkeys. The Wiggins girls were crude, and they didn't know how to say the right things. Yet Mrs. Blankenship, who could say all the proper things, made Christie feel far more uncomfortable. Very few of the people who came to see the babies knew how to say something that didn't cut into Christie's heart. But there wasn't any pretend in the Wiggins sisters, she thought.

Feeling a fire start up in her again, after last night, she sat contentedly in the waiting room, listening to the sisters and their stream of talk and watching the people pass by—so many different faces, people who seemed intent and purposeful, everybody going somewhere, looking forward to something. A group of people in white were headed for a seminary weekend; a bunch of schoolchildren had been to a waterfall; a trio of uniformed men from an old-soldiers' home were on their way to a reunion. She noticed a few women here and there who seemed to be traveling alone, keeping their secrets. Maybe they were on their way to visit maiden aunts or children who had moved away, Christie thought. Possibly they were on the first trip of their lives and they were lonely and afraid. Or maybe some of them had married and followed their husbands to a new home, just as Christie had done, and now they were journeying alone, back to sick or dying parents. She searched their faces for sadness and fear.

After a while, Christie and James ate some biscuits and ham they had brought from the hotel breakfast. They had been the only guests so early at the breakfast table, after the night of revelry, and the server told them to help themselves. Christie had wrapped the food in a piece of calico, and she had plenty to share with the Wiggins sisters.

James ate his biscuits and went to the men's waiting room.

"He don't tarry around us, does he?" said Big.

Evelyn laughed. "Your man's tongue-tied, Christie."

"Y'all are the ones that shut up tight when he's around," Christie said, teasing them.

She knotted a thread. Suddenly a tall, long-necked man bowed before her and began to speak, startling her. James was lounging near the ticket windows on the other side of the room, watching a pair of men play checkers. The man said, "Are you Mrs. Wheeler?"

"What?" She dropped her thimble and Big Wiggins scooped it up.

Evelyn said, with pride, "That's her. That's the one that had all them babies. They was in the show with us."

Several pairs of eyes turned toward Christie, but she was fearless now.

The man said, "I'm Odell Pike? An associate of Greenberry McCain? I spoke with him by the telephone this morning from Birmingham. He asked me to drop into the station to see if I could find you. He was afraid something had happened to you when he didn't see you at the hotel. He heard y'all took the train out this way." The man's watch chain dangled against his vest like a little noose.

Christie saw James hurrying over. "What do you want, mister?" he said.

The man repeated his message. The Wiggins women crowded near.

"And what ought I to tell our friend Greenberry?" Odell Pike asked. He was in a dark suit, with crumbs on his lapel.

"Don't tell him nothing," said James.

"He didn't understand how y'all left without any message," Mr. Pike said in a sorghum-syrup tone of voice.

"We had to leave," said Christie. "We didn't have time—"

"He wanted me to tell you that he's arranged an exhibition at the finest tour hall in Montgomery," Pike went on. "He said there was electric lights and the finest accommodations."

"Tell Mr. McCain we'll be sending a telegram," said Christie, looking up at James but speaking to Mr. Pike. "We're just going to send a telegram now."

"Are y'all waiting for a train?" Mr. Pike asked. "What time's your train?"

The man lingered, asking more questions, but James and Christie wouldn't give him any information.

"I'll be around in the men's smoking room," said Mr. Pike, gesturing with his head. "I told Greenberry you must have had some urgent news from home."

"That's it," said James. "Bad news."

"We're on our way home," said Christie. "Our little boy's sick."

"I'm real sorry, ma'am. I hope he's better by the time you get there."

The fellow lifted his hat and turned toward the smoking room. Christie moved to the other side of the trunk to speak with James. She lowered her voice so the sisters wouldn't hear. They were very quiet, with their heads cocked. Christie said, "I'm afraid Greenberry will telegraph to Wad and them, and he'll find out we're not there, and then they'll be worried over us at home. We need to send word that we ain't lost."

"But if we sent word to Wad, he'd probably spill the story to Gooseberry," said James. "We could wait till we get to Washington."

"How did we get into this mess?"

"Well, this might be a wild goose chase anyway," James said. "What if that doctor in Washington ain't there? What if he's decided he ain't got room for the babies after all?"

"Oh, James, maybe we oughter telegraph *him*. If he says no, we need to go on home right now. I'm glad you thought of this."

"We didn't think it all through," James said disgustedly. "We'll be a-traipsing around all over the country with this trunk and Gooseberry right behind us."

"Well, we've got time to send a telegram to Washington and we can ask for a reply here." She laughed. "I've seen Greenberry—Gooseberry—do that. I'm sure we can manage it. You wait here with the trunk and I'll go do it." She felt good calling him Gooseberry. They were going to outwit him, even if they got in trouble with God, country, and neighbors and had to lie their way home.

"What will you say in the telegram?" asked James.

Pondering the card the man had given her, she said, slowly, "'Mr. Johnson. We accept your offer, will arrive with the babies at train station at eleven-ten A.M. Monday. If agreed, telegraph Atlanta Depot before three P.M. today.' How's that?"

"Say 'quintuplets,'" said James. "So he'll know what you're talking about in case he forgot our name."

"Did y'all have bad news at home?" asked Little Wiggins, moving close.

"We're straightening it out," said James.

"We're not going to Washington after all," Christie told them. "We're going home." What was another lie?

"I told Big that man looked like a detective, and she said she hoped y'all wasn't in any trouble or nothing."

Christie realized that in the past she and James would have told anybody anything they wanted to know; they had let the general public into their house to see their babies, and they had taken their babies around on display. Now they wouldn't let anybody know what they were up to—not even the Wiggins girls, who she thought had such good hearts. She went to the telegraph office in the train station and arranged to have the telegram sent. The man behind the glass said he would find her if there was a reply. It was amazingly simple to send a telegram.

"We'll be right over there." Christie pointed across the station. "That's my husband with the brassbound trunk."

"I'll look for that, then." The man looked inquisitively at the trunk and then again at the words of the telegram.

Christie watched the man click a telegraph machine, little dit-dit-dits as incomprehensible as men playing poker.

"Who are y'all sending a telegram to?" Little Wiggins wanted to know when Christie returned to her seat.

"To my mama," she said quickly. "To let her know where we are."

"We get the rural delivery all the way up in our holler," said Big.

"We got a telegram oncet," said Evelyn. "When Daddy died and Mama was trying to find us. We was in Vicksburg with the man from Lily's Liver Pills and Sass'ras Spring Tonic."

"That tonic never sold a bit," said Little. "Hit was stupid to sell sass'ras in a bottle when anybody in his right mind would just go dig up a sass'ras root and not be out a dollar for a bottle of tonic."

"When we got that telegram, my heart just stopped," said Big. "I knowed what it said before we ever opened it."

"I knowed what it said before we even *got* it," said Evelyn. "I knowed we'd be a-getting it. Hit come to me in the night."

Big squeezed Christie's hand. "I'm glad you're a-going home, Christie," she said. "Get them babies on home."

When the Wiggins sisters left on the Knoxville train, they made Christie promise to write them, and they promised to find her if they ever came to western Kentucky with their medicine man.

"I don't know how long we'll keep on with him, though," said Little. "Mama needs us at home, and we're kindly tired of sanging in medicine shows. You see all kinds, but it grows boresome and we miss church."

"I love to hear y'all sing," said Christie. "I'm going to miss it."

"We need to be a-sanging in church," agreed Evelyn. "Hit's Little that wanted to go off with Colonel Happy."

"Well, he was a help to us," said Big. "Even if he is the biggest flimflam man on the face of the earth. Now bye-bye, Christie, you take care of them babies and don't let that casket break on you."

The Wiggins sisters waved from the window as their train pulled out, and Christie waved until the train disappeared. She had seen so many strangers that day, she knew she'd never remember a single one of them. But she would never forget Big, Little, and Evelyn. She had a vivid picture in her mind of their mother and her turkeys and her small patch of ground in a mountain holler. Christie wondered why none of the sisters had ever married. They seemed older than she was, and they had surely been enough places to meet marriageable men. She suspected they held each other back, the trio of them woven together like a potholder. Any man who tried to break the strands would find himself tangled up in all three, as well as with their mother, Christie thought.

She felt anxious. She had nervously worked buttonholes and hemmed sleeves all day, and she hadn't eaten anything but the ham-biscuits and soda crackers. Some people had stared at her disapprovingly for sewing on Sunday. The Wiggins sisters hadn't commented on it, though. She looked forward to riding on the train and wished they could have paid extra for a Pullman car so they could sleep. They had never been in a Pullman, although they had traveled overnight several times, miserably jolting along in straight-backed coach chairs or wooden benches.

Several trains arrived and departed. Passengers drifted through the station like rain and wind. Christie and James lost track of Odell Pike. A train from Birmingham arrived, and Christie sat up straight and still, watching.

"There he is," James said in a low voice.

Christie wished she could escape with all their baggage to the ladies' waiting room, but James stood up and faced Greenberry McCain. Greenberry sauntered forward and leaned against a large column. He wagged his head in disappointment. He flicked his cigarette ash onto the floor.

"James, James, James. What are we up to now?"

"Wellsir, that's a good question," James said with his most impish grin. "Howdy-do, Greenberry."

Christie kept sewing—a whipstitch, which she thought was appropriate.

"We've got an agreement," Greenberry said.

Christie cut her thread, then threaded her needle again as Greenberry went on talking, begging them to come back. James stood silent, and Christie imagined that his ears were flattened back like a mule's before he kicked.

"Well, Gooseberry McPain," James said. "It's been fun, but we've got to get on home now. It just didn't work out. Can't say it was as much fun as it oughter been. Nosir, the grub didn't suit me, and Christie's tired of sleeping in beds that have been slept in by Lord knows who. And she don't like bedbugs! Not to mention, oh, a few things like not knowing where our next meal is coming from. I hadn't never missed a meal in my life till we come on this trip, and my insides is all bothered by that. It ain't natural."

Greenberry smoked his cigarette down while James spoke. Christie stayed silent, sewing fast, still whipstitching along a hem. She was tickled at the way James was enjoying himself.

James said, "Oh, the show was right fun. Nice to get in free! We used to have to save and save to have a quarter to get in the shows at the fair. Christie and me always loved to go to the carnival. We loved the cotton candy and the fortune-tellers and the pitching balls and the organ grinder. But I reckon we had enough of it, Mr. McPain. It ain't what we started out to do, as I believe you know. And so, I reckon we're just tired of it. Good-bye." James waved his hand in Greenberry McCain's face. Greenberry frowned.

"James, don't forget to thank him for watching out after the trunk," Christie said, not taking her eyes from her stitches. "It's a miracle it didn't get lost. I'm sure ever'body that takes their dead babies out on a trip such as this would want somebody just like Mr. McCain to take care of them. And thank him for that time he bought me a dope when I was so thirsty in Mississippi."

"I had no idea," Greenberry said, fumbling in his pocket for another cigarette.

"And thank him for all those little souvenirs," Christie said. "The babies in their bed? I'll put 'em on the Christmas tree."

James said, "You get the idea, mister."

Greenberry kicked against the column, and he drew on his cigarette and blew the smoke across the waiting room as if he expected to hit something with the force of his breath. "Oh, you good people. You're the best people I've ever worked with. How can I make it up to you?" James and Christie didn't answer. James had one foot on the trunk, and he let Greenberry go on. Greenberry said, "I told Lottie on the telephone I was bringing you home with me. She wanted me to tell you she was so thrilled, she couldn't wait. And she was going to let you have the best bed. And fix you a home-cooked meal. Why, the last time her daddy killed a hog he give her the head and she put up a dozen jars of mincemeat. She said she'd make mincemeat pie."

"You ain't paying attention, Greenberry," James said. "Just think how we feel."

"I always thought about how you feel," he protested. "I've done so much for you folks. I lived up to my end of the bargain, now didn't I? I've got us set up in the finest theater in Montgomery! And after that, Davis Hall in Atlanta. That's the finest opry house in the South."

"I believe this is the end of our talk, Greenberry," James said. He waved in the man's face again. "Bye-bye."

Eventually Greenberry McCain left the train station, saying they hadn't heard the end of him. Christie and James burst into nervous laughter.

"We better watch out, though," James said. "He might get on our train."

The telegram from Dr. Johnson still hadn't come by the time their train was due to board, but James decided they should go ahead to Washington anyway. "We may as well go," Christie agreed, aware that once again she was as eager for the notion of travel itself as she was for the destination, but she was glad James was taking the lead this time. James, who had found a baggage hand to look after the trunk, accompanied the fellow to the baggage car. He rejoined Christie on the platform and they stepped up into their coach, carrying their small baggage and the carpetbags.

"No sign of Gooseberry so far," said James, surveying the platform.

"I don't think he'll chase us. I don't think he has any idea what we're aiming to do. He probably thinks we're going home, because if we were, we'd take this same train and change in Chattanooga."

James touched her elbow. "Well, I hope we ain't going to Washington for nothing."

They situated themselves on the train. Christie rummaged through her scrap bag for her button string. The contents of her carpetbag were jumbled—dirty clothes, unfinished sewing, her workbox, and Alma's empty fruit jars, which she had hauled everywhere. She had sewed her way through a bolt of bleached shirting. She hadn't bought any presents for the children except a supple-sawney for Nannie—a jumping jack made of pasteboard and cotton string to work its arms and legs. She had meant to buy some colored pinwheels for the boys. She picked up the supple-sawney and moved its arms and legs so that it danced. James saw it and grinned.

"It's like you," she said.

She was settling herself in her chair with her sewing, and she was just threading a needle, when suddenly the telegraph clerk rushed into the train. "Your telegram, Mrs. Wheeler," he said.

Christie ripped it open before she remembered to thank the man.

"He wants them," she said, smiling at James.

15

CHRISTIE RECOGNIZED DR. JOHNSON FROM THAT DISTANT NIGHT IN Nashville—before Fats Fortenberry, before the Snake Woman from Borneo, before the Wiggins sisters. She and James were tired, and they said little as they let Dr. Johnson guide them through the bustling train station. It was even larger than the station in Atlanta. Once again, they followed the brassbound trunk, this time carried by two men Dr. Johnson had brought with him. He spoke to them in English, but Christie thought the men spoke a foreign language to each other. They seemed to say, "Donkey, donkey."

"The institute is just a couple of blocks," Dr. Johnson said when they reached the street. "But I have a carriage."

The conductor had warned them that they were entering a northern climate, and Christie and James had searched through their bags for something warm to wear. Outside, it was chilly, although the sun was bright. Dr. Johnson wore a long overcoat and top hat and carried a walking stick. He led them to a waiting carriage. In the carriage, he sat facing them, placing his stick across his knees. Christie did not remember the walking stick in Nashville, and she wondered if he had injured himself. Maybe it was just a style, like the hat, she thought.

The grounds outside the train station were a confusing melee of vendors, beggars, fast-walking pedestrians, horses, and vehicles of all sorts, including bicycles and a horse-drawn streetcar. A few of the new electric cars passed by; they glided along unaided, reminding Christie of children's wagons. On the sidewalks, bunches of well-dressed men hurried along, surrounded by the shouts and hootings of the traffic and the ringing sounds of horseshoes on hard pavement. The street was wide and busy.

"I was surprised to hear from you," Dr. Johnson said pleasantly. His beard was neatly trimmed and his hair cut in a straight line above his ears.

The carriage was waiting for a train to pass before proceeding across a crowded pavement.

"Mr. Johnson, we need to talk first, before we leave you these babies," James said. "We need to hear more about what-all you aim to do with them. And you'll have to show us where you're going to keep them."

"We don't want to leave them if you're going to do anything to them," Christie said nervously. "They have to stay just the way they are."

"I assure you, Mrs. Wheeler, that they'll be treated with the utmost respect," the man said. "Did the lecture tour proceed satisfactorily?"

"It turned into a carnival," James said disgustedly.

"It's a long story," Christie said.

"I can imagine you've been through a terrible ordeal," the man said sympathetically.

"Did you want the other stuff?" James asked. "The feather crowns and the bottles and their bibs and cups?"

"I want to keep the memory book, James," said Christie. She hadn't considered that the memorabilia might be of interest to the institute.

"Oh, no, we're only concerned with the natural phenomenon itself," Dr. Johnson explained. "We're not after the social history."

He seemed to be a kindly man, Christie thought, even though he had a reserved, Northern manner. She tried to imagine him and the Wiggins sisters in the same room.

"How long will you be staying in our city?" he asked.

"Oh, we're going right on home," James said. "We just come to see you about—what's in that trunk."

"That's disappointing. You must stay long enough to take in the sights."

They could get a night train that would take them in the direction of home. They would have to change in Chattanooga and in Nashville, Christie explained.

"Well, you have a whole day ahead of you!" Dr. Johnson said encouragingly. "A great deal can be done in one day."

As they moved clear of the train station they could see the Capitol behind it, rising high on a hill. The dome was like a gigantic cake-cover, Christie thought in amazement. They turned west, and the Washington Monument loomed in front of them, beyond a vast park.

"Imagine that thing raising up out of our tobaccer patch," James said to Christie. "He sure got himself some tombstone."

"He was the father of our country," Christie said.

Her husband was the father of quintuplets, an achievement that was just as remarkable in its own way, she thought. But she knew James wouldn't think he deserved a monument.

"I appreciate your concerns, Mr. and Mrs. Wheeler," said Dr. Johnson when they arrived at the institute.

He escorted them into a side entrance of a long red-brick building and up a steep stairway. The trunk went first, and he guided its ascent.

"Keep it level now and don't let it bump against the railing," he cautioned the men.

The men had straight black hair and blue eyes and strong muscles. They were astonishingly handsome, Christie thought. She would enjoy telling Amanda about them. Brother Cornett's hair, dark as a blackbird, flashed through her mind.

On the third floor, they reached a large room partitioned with tall bookshelves. The men set the trunk in the front of the room and then, with a spurt of unintelligible words, bounded back down the stairs to tend to the horses. Christie and James stared after them, then sat down on a lumpy, dark-green velvet couch. Christie thought James seemed edgy, as if he might snatch the trunk and run if Dr. Johnson said one word he didn't like.

The doctor removed his hat. His straight brown hair was parted and carefully combed to the side. Not a hair seemed to have been disturbed by his hat or by the weather. His short beard had a tinge of rust in it. It was the color of that spotted stray dog Christie had befriended in the spring. Dr. Johnson offered them coffee, but they refused. He sat down behind a desk, facing them as they sat stiffly upright on the backless couch. Christie imagined them in a photograph, sitting motionless for the camera. She remembered a photograph of the babies in which James Lake moved his head. The resulting image was an optical illusion, an enlarged baby with a second face hidden in the folds of his dress.

"What is this place anyhow?" James asked.

"This is where we'll keep the remains of the quintuplets," he said in his carefully enunciated Northern brogue, which Christie found especially stark after hearing the South drawls of Mississippi and Alabama. "We collect unusual medical phenomena for study. We preserve them for the sake of science—and history too."

"I told you," Christie said triumphantly to James. "It's for science, a contribution to knowledge. And history."

"That's true," said Dr. Johnson. "And you can make it possible with your generous—uncommonly generous—gift."

"Does that mean we can't ever get them back?" Christie asked, wondering if later this might all appear a huge mistake.

"That depends on how we draw the papers up," he said. "You could donate them, in which case they would rest here in perpetuity. Or you could deposit them, which would be more like a loan."

"Then we could get them back if we changed our minds?" asked James.

"That's correct."

"Do you hold on to them the way they are, or do you do something to them?" James asked.

"We respect their persons to the utmost degree. I want you to understand the kind of organization this is. It's not a place where the public visits exhibits, like a history museum, let us say. It's a restricted collection, for research students and medical specialists. And I should add that we will respect your privacy. The quintuplets won't be identified, even to our researchers."

"If you take them out from under the glass, they'll crumble and turn into dust," Christie said. "When the air hits them."

The doctor didn't seem to hear her words. "The kind of materials we collect here are devoted purely to scientific purposes," he went on, gesturing toward a corridor behind him. They could see a room with shelves loaded with boxes of various sizes. "That's a small part of our collection, items waiting to be catalogued. We have tissues from murder victims for study and preservation; we have President Lincoln's bloodstains, for example. We have brain tissue from some of the most intelligent people who ever lived as well as from some of the least intelligent, for comparison. We have body organs from victims of cholera and other dread diseases. We have the preserved bodies of several pairs of Siamese twins. We have the organs of a number of hermaphrodites. We have the brain of a white man and the brain of an Indian and the brain of a Negro man, for comparative study. We have the brain of a dwarf. I cannot stress too much that we do not put our collection on display like a lurid sideshow. We just want to study why these differences occur, so we can understand them, for the good of mankind. That's why we're called the Institute of Man. There are so many things we don't understand about mankind—about our strange diversity."

"Mr. Johnson, why *does* such a thing happen?" Christie asked excitedly. "That's exactly the kind of question I've been puzzling over for months now. And nobody seems to have a good answer for why these things happen."

"That's what we're after."

"Well, what causes five babies at once?" Christie cried. "Is it normal? Or is it like a two-headed calf?"

"There was a two-headed calf in Hopewell a few years ago," James explained.

Dr. Johnson nodded and said, "People throughout time have imagined many explanations for such extraordinary occurrences, but instead of relying on the imagination here, we look at the facts. In the case of identical twins, we now know, one egg divides in two; whereas in fraternal twins, two separate eggs develop and the twins are not identical in appearance. In the case of quintuplets, what happens? It's so rare we don't really know. Maybe, Mrs. Wheeler, your experience will shed some light on the question."

"She thought it was from this earthquake," James said, and Christie's cheeks flamed.

"Don't tell that," she said. "I don't believe that anymore."

"Earthquake?"

"That big earthquake they predicted last year got her all stirred up," James said. "She fainted, and she never done that before."

Christie hurriedly changed the subject. "I gained so much weight, I couldn't hardly get out of the bed the last two months," Christie said.

"Tell me everything you can remember," the doctor said, dipping his pen into a silver-rimmed inkwell.

For some time he asked questions, and Christie told him what she knew. He wrote busily. Some of his questions were odd, about her sleep habits and diet. And some of them embarrassed her, and she couldn't answer. He probed her for a long time about family history, asking if twins ran in her family, but she knew of no twins in either her family or James's. The doctor asked if she had eaten anything unusual, like mushrooms.

"I never have eat a mushroom in my life." She paused, looked at James for a moment, then blurted out, "I believe it had to do with the family I moved into. The Wheelers. I was raised in Dundee, and James carried me to Hopewell in 1896 and we settled in with his Uncle Wad. It's such a big clan of people, it's like they're running out in all directions, and they're loud and they fuss at each other, and we had to live under their roof for a year till we got our own house built." She shuddered. "They got me all riled up. It was Wheelers. The Wheeler clan."

James looked at her with hurt eyes. The doctor was not writing down that part of her story, so she stopped, realizing it was of no interest to him. It was her own story, what she'd kept to herself. She felt embarrassed that she had blurted it out now, because it surely wounded James and she did not know how she would make it up to him.

"Do you know why the babies died?" Dr. Johnson asked.

Christie bent her head down. "There was so much going on. Little Minnie was weak, and I think she took the sickness first and passed it on to the rest of them."

"They had to feed on cow's milk," said James. "She couldn't make enough for them."

"The wet nurse helped," Christie said.

"She was colored," said James.

"That didn't make no difference," Christie snapped.

"Is it your feeling they had plenty of milk?" the doctor asked.

"There was enough sweet-milk to feed the whole church congregation," said James. "But they didn't take to it at first."

"It was too rich," said Christie. "It made them colicky, and Mrs. Willy wanted to give them catnip tea, but we couldn't get any."

She was growing agitated. She felt light-headed.

"They were wooled to death," she said in a barely audible voice. "All the people from the train handled them, and they got sick."

A serving maid entered with some cinnamon rolls and a pot of coffee. She poured coffee for Christie and James.

"I'm sorry," Christie said to Dr. Johnson. "I hadn't expected to have to go into all of that again."

"Well, I hadn't expected you either," said Dr. Johnson pleasantly, as he took a cup of coffee from the maid. He held up his cup for her to add cream from a little white pitcher embossed with grapevines. "I almost missed your telegram, since I'm not normally here on Sunday. But the Western Union boy found me at home."

"I didn't think about you not being here," Christie said. "I oughter thought about you being shut on Sunday. I knew it was Sunday." Her eyes were fixed on the grapevines, twining around the cream pitcher.

James took a roll, ate it in two bites, and reached for another one.

Dr. Johnson said, "I'm afraid this short notice has caught me a bit unprepared. Why don't we do this? Please allow me to write more questions to you as they occur to me. Then you may answer at your convenience."

For a few minutes they attended to the rolls and the coffee. The rolls were delicious—yeast-raised and sweet. Christie felt eased by the food. Dr. Johnson chatted about his home in Syracuse, New York. His children were grown, and he had moved to Washington to take this government position.

"What's your wife's name?" asked Christie, warming up to the doctor.

"She passed away many years ago," he said sadly. "Lucy died in childbirth. And now, when you finish your coffee, I would like to unpack the trunk and see what you have brought us."

James knelt to unbuckle the trunk, and as he opened the lid, Dr. Johnson walked around the desk. Christie was afraid she'd throw up. She remembered vomiting on Minnie. It seemed so long ago. The familiar oak chest emerged from the trunk—its ornate carvings of lambs frisking among grapevines, nibbling berries, birds casually flying above them, all a scene of innocence she felt such pity for. And now she realized there was a tiny fawn, lying in the leaves, almost concealed, as though the carver had created a puzzle for the eye. The bright light coming through a glazed patch of the roof revealed the fawn's image.

James said to Christie, "Do you want to see?"

"It's all right." She braced herself. She had thought that she and James had finally said good-bye to the babies Saturday night in Alabama. It did not matter if she saw them again. They were permanently imprinted on her mind's eye. They would always be with her. She thought she could not experience any new grief, yet after the babies were unpacked and Dr. Johnson left the room for a while, Christie began to cry, and her crying swelled until she was crying more than she ever had. She could sense James's grief too. He held her so closely she thought they would have to be chiseled apart.

"I love you," James whispered into her hair.

All her memories of the babies rushed forth—the live, colicky, milky bodies, exuding all their fluids, the heat in the bed, the care she took not to mash the fragile creatures, the way Minnie curled her little fist and could barely summon the strength to cry out loud, the fat fullness of James Lake as he drank so thirstily, the little gurgles Mollie Lee made when she had too much milk in her mouth, the way Emily Sue tended to push away with her fists, the way John Wilburn's face would go red so quickly when he cried. She remembered giving birth to them, each birth distinct in her memory now. She could assign each birth pang to a particular baby.

Christie had been traveling for nearly two months without dwelling on these memories, trying not to remember the sensations of the babies' bodies, without even thinking much about Nannie and Clint and Jewell. Earlier, too, she had denied her memories. Periodically through the spring and summer—hoeing, picking, and canning vegetables, and topping and cutting the dark-fire—she had felt an uncommon elation that she couldn't explain. She had felt glad to be alive; she had felt strong; she had felt the gratification of the attention she had received echoing in her heart, an uplifting feeling that partially offset her grief. Now she thought she must have a strong heart to go through what she had. James had been a stranger, remote and burdened by his work, his youth gone. The babies had driven all desire out of her. But now she and James were together again, saying goodbye to what their passion had brought forth. And she felt as if the dance they had begun long ago was now getting under way again, resuming its long, slow rhythm.

"We'll be home soon," James said, touching her damp cheek.

The doctor returned with some papers for them to sign, including a formal declaration of purpose—an official printed document declaring the "Property" to be in the safekeeping of the Institute of Man. The "Property" was described in a handwritten insertion as *five infants: three females, two males, twenty-three to thirty-three days of age, preserved in airtight glass container.* The Property would be stored in the permanent collection and would not be used for display. The writing said the Wheelers would be informed of anything done with the Property—such as removal to different quarters. It said the institute would be liable for damage or destruction, except in cases of acts of God. Her face still hot from her tears, Christie smiled at James as she read it out to him.

"Does this mean we can have them back if we change our mind?" Christie asked. "We have to make sure."

"Yes, notice the word 'deposit,'" Dr. Johnson said reassuringly. "It's not a donation. You may desire in the future to reconsider it as a donation."

James and Christie hesitated for a long time, but then Christie took up the pen and signed both copies. She signed *Mrs. James Wheeler.* On second thought, she added *Christianna Wilburn Wheeler* in parentheses below.

"Usually, the woman doesn't have to sign," James said.

"This is a special case," Christie said, handing James the pen.

For their trouble, Dr. Johnson provided them with a sumptuous meal at a large hotel. Although Christie loved oysters, she had never eaten them in public. Oysters were said to excite the spirit. But now, daringly, she and James ate a dozen oysters. Christie even tried crab cakes, which James wouldn't eat because they smelled too fishy. And they went out in the carriage, driven by the two handsome foreigners, on a tour of the city. Christie had never seen such enormous buildings, surrounded by such filth and noise. She thought of the littered grounds around the Hopewell courthouse, before the law was passed against watermelon eating and picnics. The entire town of Hopewell could have fit in the yard around the President's palace, which was as white as new teeth. Sheep grazed out front. The Smithsonian Institution was like a red castle. The Library of Congress was heavy gray granite with a green dome.

But the splendid buildings and the historical monuments were too much to take in. Christie sank into herself, cuddling the warm little glow of emptiness she carried with her now. She felt very sleepy. The gleaming buildings shouted at her like a clean wash hanging on the line. James led her up into the Rotunda of the United States Capitol Building, and they peered up at the paintings in the dome.

"Three domes in two days," he commented.

Dr. Johnson arrived at the train station in time to see them off. He had brought the trunk, which still held the empty oak chest and the feather pillows. He had locked the glass casket in a vault at the institute. To their surprise, he insisted on paying for a Pullman compartment for their trip home.

"You came all this way, at your own expense, and you've been through a great deal of pain. It's the least I can do," he said warmly.

"You've been mighty kind," James said, shaking the man's hand. "We're much obliged."

"I'll take care of your little ones," Dr. Johnson said to Christie, clasping her hand.

Christie couldn't speak. Finally she said the cat had her tongue.

The train pulled out of Washington as the sky was fading. The white spire of the Washington Monument seemed like a guidepost, a way of locating her babies forever, Christie thought.

The seats in the Pullman car were upholstered with a plush material that muffled sound. The ride was comfortable, and so private they might have been the only passengers on the train. After an unexpectedly satisfying supper in the dining car, they returned to find their compartment made into berths, and their traveling bags brought from the baggage car.

"I'm so glad we don't have to worry about that trunk anymore," said Christie, as she sorted through her carry-bag for her washing rag.

James grinned. "Gooseberry McPain won't never get his paws on it now."

"James, do you realize nobody ever said what that doctor said—

about keeping the babies out of the public eye, like they were too precious to let just anybody see?"

"Nobody thought of it, I reckon," said James.

"It's just the opposite of what Brother Jones told us to do."

James didn't speak for a moment. "We can't blame Brother Jones," he said.

But she would. She knew what to blame at last. She saw the central flaw in her desire to understand why such an extraordinary thing had happened to her. It wasn't *why* it happened—that couldn't be known; it was what the world made of it that was at issue.

"I want to get out that quilt you brought," said James, as he unbuckled the straps of their large imitation-leather bag. "It's plumb cold in here."

He laid the case on the lower berth and let the halves swing open. Christie caught sight of the black nipples on the familiar nursing bottles, and she remembered Mittens. She thought she would give Mittens one of the bottles, for a keepsake. Mittens had always found the black nipples so funny. Christie loved the way Mittens laughed—a long, drawn-out, skidding hymn.

James said, "You know what?"

"What?"

"I just realized something. The memory book is here and them cups and bibs and bottles, but that glass thing with the feather crowns—it ain't here."

"It's not?"

"It started out in the trunk, but then Greenberry carried it in that big case of his sometimes because he was afraid it'd get broke. And then we started putting it in here with the bottles and things. But it ain't here."

"So he's got the crowns now?"

James looked white. Christie reached out and touched his face. "It's all right," she said. "I don't care anything about them. Let him keep 'em. I never did understand what those things meant anyhow."

The train lurched and jerked steadily through the night. As the night wore on, she found herself thinking ahead to the work to be done: gathering in dried peas and beans, hilling up turnips and cabbages, teaching Nannie her ABC's, killing hogs in the first long cold spell. She felt as light as one of old Dove Wheeler's legendary angel-food cakes.

VI

Royalty

Fall 1937

1

THE TRAIN WAS PICKING UP SPEED, SHOOTING ACROSS THE FLAT, REC-tangular fields, whipping through small northern villages anchored by church spires. Christianna Wheeler readjusted the antimacassar on her headrest. The young woman across from her had dozed off. She had boarded in Chicago, where Christie had had a long layover. The woman, in an expensive cashmere suit, had carefully placed her coat in the overhead rack. It was growing dark, and they seemed to be traveling through heavily wooded areas. Occasionally they burst out into open fields. Far beyond the fields, lights twinkled and receded, as if they were running away from the train's monotonal, businesslike whistle.

The speed put Christie in mind of that flying trip she and James had taken through the South, so many years ago. Everything was so much faster now, but back then it seemed they were hurrying along, tumbling like the bareback riders at the circus in Mississippi.

The young woman, who had said her name was Sarah Jennings, appeared so much less innocent than Christie remembered herself at that age, when she was eager to face the world. In the last hour, Christie had told a great deal about her life to this Mrs. Jennings, but not the whole story. She hadn't told about the babies. She hadn't talked much in years about them. Instead, she told Mrs. Jennings about the farm, what it was like to grow the dark-leaf tobacco. She had to grope for comparisons, for the young woman—just a girl, really—regarded Christie as if she had come from an exotic land, like something pictured in Boone's Museum of Humankind scrapbook. So much required explanation: burning plant beds, setting the seedlings, cutting and housing and curing the plants, then bulking them and stripping the cured leaves, then tying them into hands and prizing them into hogsheads. Mrs. Jennings was traveling to meet her husband in Toronto. He was a surveyor, and they would be living in the North Woods for several months. She said her trunk was full of woolens and furs. Christie felt a little chill, but she was well padded, her weight settling her solidly into her seat.

As the train passed through a small city, Christie looked down at the automobiles gliding along the highway parallel to the train. The train's shadow swooped down over the vehicles and passed them. She had lived through one miracle after another. Were quintuplets any more of a miracle than the automobile? Or the aeroplane? Her babies were born right at the dawn of a new age of miracles, almost as if they had been a signal of what lay ahead.

Mrs. Jennings lurched out of her sleep and straightened up. She said, "It's a good time of year to travel—before the snows begin." She yawned behind her glove. "Autumn is my favorite season," she said. Restlessly, she shifted in her seat and gazed out at a small depot the train was rushing past. "Could I trouble you to borrow your magazine?"

Christie handed the magazine to her, and the woman switched on the reading light. Mrs. Jennings stared at the photograph on the cover for a moment and began to thumb through the pages. Christie didn't know why she had brought that *Life* magazine from home. She didn't want to look at it again. She had tried to read a book but couldn't concentrate. She watched the dark scenery, out the window, beyond its reflections of the train's interior.

She couldn't tell the real story. Once, Christie's story had been known far and wide, but now what had happened to her was so long ago it seemed like a deep secret. How could she tell this stranger about Amanda and James and Mittens and all the others, let alone the events of 1900? It was impossible to tell a life story, she thought. Where would you start?

The train whistled and raced without pausing through another village station. She remembered the train taking her and James home from Washington. It was so slow. In the early morning when it went around a horseshoe bend they could see it almost double back on itself like a hoop snake. She remembered the startling mountains, dark risings of earth and blue ridges, a landscape that might have been shaped by an earthquake.

They never told anybody what they did with the babies. But there were rumors. People said she and James took the babies out of a box once a year, on their birthday; they said the Wheelers held little birthday parties for the babies, and donkey parties; they talked about the Christmas presents the babies received. It gave Christie and James much pleasure to disappoint Samuel Mullins, who wanted to put the babies on display at his funeral parlor. It still made her smile to think of him in his buzzard-black clothing.

Greenberry McCain had come through town about three weeks after they returned, pleading with them to finish out the tour. He kept saying, "If y'all had just told me you were that unhappy—I had no idea!" He left them alone after that and returned to Alabama to build his wife a house. James told Christie he suspected Greenberry hadn't been able to fill out the extra bookings anyway, after the collapse of the agreement with the Hart Brothers. And market season was passing, so folks didn't have the money to blow on shows. "He was just a golly-snorter of a man," James concluded.

Amanda was looking poorly when they returned. She had let her hair go, and her face was thin and pale. Christie was afraid that taking care of the children had been too hard on her. But Amanda's eyes brightened like berries when she brought a present down to the house for Christie.

"It's the surprise I told you I was making," she said eagerly.

It was a small flower wreath made out of human hair. Christie's mother had made one once; they were a craze when she was young.

Amanda's excitement flooded out. "I nearly ruint my eyes working on this," she said. "Look! It's got everybody's hair in it—Alma's and Wad's and all the chillern and yours and James's. I even got some of your mama's. I got the design from a book Thomas brought home last winter."

When she mentioned Thomas, her face reddened and she lowered her eyes. Somehow Christie knew this, even though she wasn't really looking at Amanda. She was transfixed by the effort Amanda had put into the wreath. It was composed of painstakingly woven little flowers of fanciful designs and varying sizes, like a button collection, all arranged in a horseshoe shape and mounted on a piece of brown velvet inside a picture frame. In the center was a cluster brooch shaped from more of the dainty flowers. All of the flowers were formed entirely of hair. The overall effect was of a carefully preserved bouquet of garden posies—sun-faded and drenched of their color. Dead.

"Look in the middle, Christie," Amanda said, touching a tiny flower in the central brooch. "I put little locks of hair from the five babies right smack in the middle. Ever petal is made from one of them. I cut them one day when you were taking a nap and I was washing the babies. I cut the hair from the back, where you wouldn't see. I put each lock in a slip of paper with the initials. I looked at those bracelets to make sure. The top one is Emily Sue, and going around the clock is James Lake, John

Wilburn, Minnie, and Mollie. I put them in by the alphabet, so you'd know. I was so careful. That's the *finest* hair. It was so hard to work, but I wanted something that would last longer in memory than that black wreath I made in the spring." She touched the flower's stem. "This white hair, of course, is from Mammy Dove," she said.

"Then you knew they were going to die."

Amanda looked stricken. "Oh, no. No, no, no, no. I was just going to put the locks of hair in Boone's memory album. That's all. I decided on the wreath later."

The dried-looking shells of the flowers were lifeless and brittle but as intricate as feathers. Christie and Amanda cried in each other's arms for a while then, and later Christie hung the wreath in a corner of the loft, above the brassbound trunk, where she wouldn't have to look at it every day. She explained to Amanda, and at the time she thought Amanda understood.

Christie thought about that wreath so often in later years. No one seemed to notice it up in the loft. For several seasons, life was so hard that nobody had time for reflection. As manufactured cigarettes grew more popular, the dark leaf lost its value. It was almost worthless under the tobacco trust, and farmers tried to withhold their crops from the market. Wad helped organize a group of farmers who would ride out in the night to talk other farmers into joining their association to fight the trust. The truth was that they forced them to join. If any refused to join, the leaders would scrape their plant beds bare. Through the Black Patch Wars, as the conflict during the next few years came to be known, no Wheelers ever burned anybody's tobacco barn, but some barns did get burned. The turmoil grew into a bloody, awful thing, spreading all over that country—from Paducah down as far south as Clarksville, Tennessee. Throughout those hard years, Christie patched and remade clothes, picking through the rag barrel for scraps. She made sheets and even underclothes out of feed-sacks. But the feed-sacks were good quality and made the best-feeling sheets, she thought, although bleaching the ink from the sacks was toilsome. The preachers once again reached for signs of God's grace and called for renewed faith in face of the hard times. She herself was through with that kind of thinking. You could torment yourself into knots trying to figure out where you stood with God.

Christie recalled only one occasion when Wad said something to James about making more money out of the babies. She didn't know what Wad had in mind—he might have thought of selling them out-right—but James didn't let him get the full thought out. James reminded him their debt had been paid and threatened to move to Dundee. After that, Wad never mentioned the babies again. As for

Christie, she no longer had any patience with Wad. She would walk away right in the middle of one of Wad's notions, holding Nannie so tight she'd cry. "You'll smother that youngun," Alma protested. Wad and Alma regarded her aloofness suspiciously.

Christie was actually as clear-eyed and strong as she could imagine ever being. But her calm strength must have been so startling that Wad and Alma couldn't look straight at it. "That gal's plumb crazy," Wad said once when she went back in the fields with Mittens to pick wild greens. She went to Mittens' little shed of a house and ate corn pone with her. She took Nannie to play with Mittens' children. Wad tried to put a stop to it, but he had no power over her. He didn't understand why she went down to the creek or out into the woods by herself. He didn't know why she laughed at him so much. Later on, he and Alma even tried to take Nannie away from her, and eventually they succeeded in poisoning Nannie against her, when Amanda wasn't there to stop them.

Looking back now, Christie realized that the Wheelers were always too busy putting food on the table to take care of each other. They would take care of the sick and dying, and they would carry food to neighbors in trouble, but nobody took time to look down deep at what was bothering a person. When Alma cared for Christie and the babies, she was too busy washing diapers and running two households to pay much attention to what Christie was feeling.

So many of those years ran together in the unrelenting hard work. Christie kept quiet, working alone, bolstered by the strength she had gained from her ordeal. After what she had been through, she thought she could face anything in the world without batting an eye. She clung fiercely to her remaining children. But Nannie got away from her. And then Clint. All but Jewell—a genuine Wheeler, except for an occasional streak of Wilburn imagination. He married a little Sullivan girl with bad nerves and a need for attention.

Christie didn't expect life to be fair. Alma's boy Hub went off to the big war and came back without a mark, but Clint lay now under the shadow of a cross in France. It was still hard to believe, maybe because it seemed so hard to prove. She was told she gave him for her country, but Christie wondered how many times in history mothers had been told that. Any mother would rather have her boy than any country in the world, for the earth would always be here and it did not seem to matter in the long run how the wars turned out. A person could sacrifice all she held dear for a land that didn't return the favor. James said her thought was unpatriotic. He said the nation did hold her dear in its fuss over her accomplishment. She had her doubts about that, but James would probably be gratified now to know how the citizens of Hopewell took up the collection to send her on this trip. He would have been proud, she thought. She didn't want to go at first, but curiosity eventually got the better of her. My life story, she thought.

Jewell carried on the farm, the same acreage James had worked. Jewell was steadfast and practical, sticking with the family homeplace, still wrestling with the demands of the dark tobacco. But he liked the newfangled ideas and had invented a silage shredder that worked on a cable. She thought that was the Wilburn showing in him. Hub and Arch went out to their own farms on the other side of the county. There were enough Wheelers to populate a town. She shuddered to think how many there would be if her babies had lived.

She could see a string of pies—pies at funerals and pies at weddings and pies at birthings. The rhythm of eating something special carried people in and out of life. She saw the women waiting on the men and the sick and the old and the young. The women were constantly in motion. Christie remembered the dutiful way Alma had waited on her old mother, Dove, and her brother, Boone. Not long after they died, Alma had to turn around and wait on Wad. It was pitiful to see him wasting away, his spirit gone after he lost Amanda. His lungs got bad and he wheezed worse than Boone ever did. Alma took care of him as if he were a baby. She didn't have to fool with Thomas Hunt anymore. Thomas had gone off to Texas and never came back. Alma ignored his absence at first, but she finally got the law to look for him. They couldn't turn up a clue to his whereabouts. The company that sent him out on the new sewing-machine venture went bankrupt. James said the outfit must have been crooked. He suspected Thomas had been murdered, but Alma firmly believed Thomas had settled somewhere with a new wife.

Alma's tombstone didn't even mention Thomas Hunt's name. It said ALMA S. WHEELER, 1858–1928. The day she died, she said, "Well, I'm fixing to go now. I ain't waiting on Thomas." There was no room for him beside her in the graveyard, either. She got herself crammed in between Wad and Amanda, just as she had done in life—elbowing them apart. Christie thought Alma got Jimmie Lou to arrange that. When Alma took sick, Christie moved up to the main house for a time to look out after her. "I can never fill your shoes," she told Alma. And Alma had said, astonishingly, "Christie, you're the only woman in this whole family that ever had a head on her."

Alma's boys had all married and brought their wives and children to the farm until they could build their own houses. Then Thurman bought his own land. Arch and Hub waited to divide Wad's land, but

Jewell bought them out. Thurman was a Wheeler through and through, Alma always said. It was the girls, Jimmie Lou and Dulcie, who turned out more like Thomas, eager to leave. Dulcie married late, a boy in town. Amanda and Wad's daughter Lena never married. Nannie went up to the North to work for the same newspaper that St. Louis reporter from so long ago had worked on.

Things shifted, went through phases and new positionings over time, Christie thought. Jewell looked after her—splitting her stovewood, killing the hogs, plowing the fields. He did all the man's work James had taught his boys—most of which she knew how to do herself, except for cutting hogs and birthing stock.

Gazing out the window of the train at the dark fields, Christie let her thoughts drift into the fields back home. She could see James plowing the cornfield with that big gray Fordson tractor Jewell bought. It was so high up in the air James seemed to be riding an elephant. She saw herself driving to town in her car, driving around the square. When she crossed that railroad track under her own direction, she felt a freedom she had never known in her life. But she never drove on down the highway. After she got home from Washington, she didn't have a chance to leave again. Everyone in the county knew her and treated her respectfully and politely and no doubt gossiped behind her back. She held her head high, without shame, still secretly elated by her knowledge of what she had done. As time went on, the babies receded in her consciousness, although now and then she would think of the nursing bottles, or skinny Mittens' plump breasts, or she'd remember the sight of the frolicking, Sunday-dressed train passengers coming toward the house. She'd still see them in her mind's eye every time she went out to embrace the sunset or listen to birds singing. And she would feel a rush of sorrow when she pictured Amanda's thin figure. She could almost hear her voice now, singing some lullaby that sounded more like a song about a broken heart than a song for a baby.

One day in 1903, Christie went out to the crib to shell corn for the chickens. That was Nannie's job, but Nannie had gone to Dundee to see Mama and Papa and all the cousins. It was fall and the work had slacked off temporarily. Christie ran the corn through the corn sheller and started out through the chicken yard with her bucket, scattering corn along as she went. She thought she heard something fall in the smokehouse. She was afraid a rat had gotten in. Just as she opened the door, she heard a little gasp and there was Amanda, pulling down her skirts in a hurry. Christie didn't have to guess who was behind the grain chest, his shadow falling against the hanging pork shoulders and butts. She turned away and shut the door.

Later that evening, Amanda came to see her, in tears. Christie was on the porch shelling beans for seed. James was still in the barn. She was often alone and had time to think and look out over the fields while she broke beans or peeled peaches or churned. The fall weather had turned everything yellow, and the late evening sun highlighted it. The strands of gray in Amanda's hair were shining golden in that light.

"I can't do nothing right, Christie," Amanda sobbed. "If Wad was to find out what I've done, it'd kill him."

Wad was sick in bed with the grippe at the time, and Thomas Hunt had been home for the past week.

She said, "I can't stand to go upstairs and wait on Wad. I can't stand to hear him suck his teeth and slop his grub like a hog. I can't take care of him like Alma can. I can't take care of anybody. I thought I could take care of chillern, but don't ever trust me again, Christie."

"What happened to Little Bunch wasn't your fault," said Christie, reaching up to smooth Amanda's hair out of her face. A few strands stuck to her damp forehead.

"Yes, it was. And Wad blames me too. I didn't believe anything was wrong with her. Wad claimed she was weak in the mind and couldn't keep up at school, but I knew how smart she was. I thought those fits were a way of drawing attention. But the poor child kept on having them fits one after the other all night long. And of course Lena thinks it was her fault, 'cause she couldn't wake up enough to come and tell me."

For weeks, Amanda had repeated this account over and over, as if it were news to Christie each time.

"Well, didn't Wad have Lena out digging taters all day, so she was too tired to get up?" Christie pointed out. "Maybe it was Wad's fault. You can't go on blaming yourself, Mandy. Nobody could have helped Little Bunch."

Amanda didn't seem to be listening. She was twisting her hem into a knot. Christie gathered up her apron and let the dried beans fall from it into a bucket.

"Mandy," said Christie, standing up. "I know you'd like to wring Dr. Foote's neck, and so would I, on general principle. But there ain't no cure for fits. Some people just have 'em. And they can get bad. That's just a fact."

"What will become of me?"

Christie took Amanda by the shoulders and shook her gently. "Mandy! You've got to carry on. You can't give up."

"I'm sorry, Christie. I'm so sorry. Why is life like it is?"

"I don't know. I don't know why you were carrying on with Thomas either."

"I'm so ashamed, Christie."

"Do you care for him?"

Amanda shook her head. "It could have been anybody—anybody with some new to them." Amanda started to weep. She drew her apron to her face. "It didn't happen before. Just this one time."

Even now, so many years later, Christie could feel the warmth of Amanda's desire, the longing that seemed to shoot out of her in all directions. She could remember the apron Amanda was wearing that day, a bleached white feed-sack with the blue lettering still faintly visible. Amanda had edged it with a yellow grosgrain ribbon.

Christie remembered James coming toward them from the barn then. He was carrying a bucket of milk. When he saw Amanda in tears, he politely retreated, not wanting to embarrass her. James had been so handsome, but he didn't travel on his face, as the saying went, and Christie had gotten used to his looks. What a hurtful thing they had done by denying each other an intimate touch throughout that terrible time. They had been so afraid that she might hatch out another huge brood. She wondered how many women turned away from their husbands in order to avoid more children. She had always thought husbands were naturally demanding, imposing their urges on women, without regard to the consequences. But during that summer and fall, she saw James freeze, then retreat. Now she could see him as plain as day, sitting on that jerky old train, wearing that Sears-Roebuck suit. His callused hands stuck out awkwardly. As the journey wore on, they grew pale and soft. The sweet hotel soap washed away their strength. She had felt so sorry for him, seeing him sit hour after hour, a blank stare on his face. He looked empty, his spirit sucked out.

The conductor passed through the car, with the news that the dining car was open. Christie went to the ladies' wash-room to wash her hands. She had become so conscious of germs; there had been outbreaks of typhoid fever recently. Long ago, people coming into her home to see her babies would say, "Why, it's so clean!" as though they had expected barnyard filth. But James had the boys out picking up those visitors' trash every day. And Mrs. Willy always had that broom with her. Alma chasing out waspers. Mama's dress hem dragging. James's nose on John Wilburn. The girl with the blond topknot, Mollie Lee. Christie saw herself in the train mirror. Her spirit hadn't died. It was like something enormous in her, like a pregnancy that she had to carry around all her life.

"Here's your magazine," Mrs. Jennings said, handing it back to her as Christie sat down again. "That's a truly remarkable story."

Christie looked at the magazine again—the five figures on the cover, five little children all alike, a world wonder—and her eyes filled with tears. Quickly, she rolled the magazine and stuck it down into her satchel. The train was slowing down. She could feel the wheels grind, as if they were trying to go backwards.

2

THE STYLISH, SHORT-HAIRED WOMAN WHO MET CHRISTIE AT THE STA-tion in Toronto wore a wool coat with a fur collar and cuffs that cir-cled her wrists and neck like sleeping pets snuggling against her. Her eyebrows were brush strokes, painted on like upper rims to her specta-cles. She gushed questions and barely waited for answers.

"Are you tired? You've missed the peak of our spectacular fall scenery," she said. "I'm afraid it will appear to be winter up here."

"I didn't sleep much on the train, but I don't think I could even close my eyes now," Christie said, surveying the fast-moving crowd. "There's too much to see."

She retrieved her suitcase—a new one, presented to her by the cit-izens of Hopewell. The woman greeting her, Mrs. Margaret Shel-burne, insisted that Christie call her by her first name. Her air of enthusiasm reminded Christie fleetingly of Amanda.

"Here's the plan," Margaret said. "We'll start driving and hope to arrive in time for the afternoon play period. We'll stay at a little place nearby for the night, and we'll be able to go back for the little girls' morning playtime tomorrow. And if Madame Dionne can't see us today, then we'll have time tomorrow. I arranged a reservation at a lit-tle hotel as soon as I found out you were coming. In the summer, it's impossible to find accommodations up there, but this time of year there are vacancies. B.D.—Before the Dionnes—there was absolutely nothing, but since the crowds have descended, some places have opened, and some people have even opened their homes for bed-and-breakfast."

"I'm used to just about anything," Christie said, heaving her suit-case into the back seat of the automobile they had just reached. She glimpsed in her memory a horse-drawn dray from a train station somewhere many years ago. It came to her: Vicksburg, Mississippi. A Negro man singing in the woods. A bright purple flower on climbing vines everywhere. Spanish moss on live oaks.

Margaret adjusted her rearview mirror and then her hat. She said, "My husband wanted to drive us, but I talked him out of it. He would have to leave his office, and he's so fortunate to have a good position, he shouldn't risk it. I assured him we'd be perfectly all right. He was afraid if we had a breakdown, some stranger might take advantage of us, but I know how to repair almost everything on this vehicle." She blared the horn a couple of times for emphasis. "The only problem may be the weather, but we'll take care."

Margaret Shelburne was a confident driver. She whipped into the outbound traffic, facing the morning sun, and daringly wove in amongst a thick stream of cars. As soon as they reached the outskirts of the city and turned north, past a lake, she began singing.

"I love the open road," she said, interrupting herself. "There's the old Forsythe home," she said, pointing with her right hand. Her leather-gloved hand emerged from her fur cuff like the timid head of a groundhog.

Christie had no idea who the Forsythes were, but their place was an enormous mansion with several stone turrets and bay windows like potbellied stoves. She kept quiet. Here and there gold-and-red leaves still clung to the trees, but most of the trees were bare. The day was bright but chilly, and she had no gloves. She examined her brown, wrinkled, work-hardened hands. Mrs. Dionne was a farm woman like herself. They would have much in common, she thought. She was nervous, wondering if Mrs. Dionne would have time for her. Maybe the woman was too busy with important visitors. She would have so much to do with five active children.

"I don't want to take all the credit for enticing you up here, but it *was* my idea," said Margaret happily. "When Uncle William wrote me last year from Kentucky and asked if I had seen the Dionne girls, he aroused my curiosity about you. I hadn't even heard of the Hopewell Quints. He used to live in North Bay when he was a child, near where the Dionnes are, and now he's in Kentucky, home of the other quintuplets. It's such a coincidence!"

"Small world," said Christie, nodding.

"This is quite a feather in my cap, to have you here and to escort you up to the North Woods. It's such an honor for me!" She slammed her hand on the horn and swung around a car that had stopped in the road. "Uncle William has told me a great deal about Kentucky over the years. He comes up here every five or six years to shoot. But his heart is in Kentucky, having married a lovely lady down there. He told me all about how famous you were back then. That must have been so exciting."

"It was a long time ago," Christie said.

She drank in the scenery. For so many years, she had been accustomed to seeing not scenery but soil cultivation—the crops that thrived, the pastures for the livestock, the lay of the land. But now land appeared to her like pictures, formed of simple colors and shapes: the rectangles of fields, the ovals of ponds, the triangles of trees. She realized that now she saw places more as she had when she traveled as a young woman, when she loved the surprise of a new configuration of the earth and would imagine herself living there. Here in Canada, the hard blue of the lakes seemed to scream in shock against the deep green of the pine and spruce. She thought the shaggy, dark trees must be spruce. She had read at the Hopewell Library—a little room in the basement of the courthouse—that this section of Canada grew predominantly pine and spruce and maple. There seemed to be little population here, which was a relief.

"Well, we're out on the open road now," Margaret said after a while. "It should be smooth traveling for the next two or three hours. And then the road becomes fairly bumpy as we get nearer Callander, but there's a new road that goes out from Corbeil to the quintuplets' estate. My friend Florence Thistle told me all about it. This is so exciting for me, and I'll be delighted to report back to my ladies' club all about our visit." Margaret sighed with satisfaction. "Florence says the Dionne babies have given Canada an identity, a place in the world," she said. "We don't have to look to England for everything. We can be proud to be Canadian. We have our own royals on our own soil." She laughed giddily. "I'm afraid I'm bubbling over," she said in apology. She turned to gaze at Christie with gray, vacant eyes. "Now," she said. "I want to hear every detail about you and your babies."

The drive took seven hours, with two stops for sandwiches and tea. The tea was hot, not iced, and the sandwiches were potted meat spread thin on light-bread. Christie didn't feel motivated to tell her hostess much about her life. She was nervous. Last night in the sleeping berth, she had been disturbed by her old dream of following the brassbound trunk, a dream she hadn't had in years. Now, as she thought about that dream, she began to dread seeing the little girls and their mother. What would she say to them? She was afraid her envy would cause her to make a fool of herself. She was afraid the pain of her memories would spill out. The memories of her babies were hidden deep in her head. Long ago, she had learned not to look at reminders, such as the albums and the pictures they had collected, for those seemed to spoil the memories—occasional glimpses that surfaced inside her, from behind her eyeballs it seemed, when a little image would float forward and evoke fully some scene from that extraordinary year. She feared that the little Canadian girls would agitate her memories too much, stir them up and make her mourn out loud. But she chided herself. At her age, having seen so much death and hardship, she ought to be able to look at almost anything without going to pieces. Why had she always feared she would go to pieces? She knew she was the least likely person to shatter. She never had broken, yet losing control seemed to be her greatest fear. And after she came home from that trip, many people expected her to lose control. They tried to make sure she lost it. They said she couldn't be trusted. They gossiped. But Christie thought they were only imagining themselves in her situation. They expected a woman to be weak. It made her angry when people judged others by their own limitations. They had done it to Amanda, and she couldn't get out from under it.

Christie rubbed a spot on the window and spied a hawk sitting on a dead branch. The landscape and the sky had faded to pale tones of blue, yellow, pink, gray, and brown—the bleached-out colors of her lost children. There was so much sadness to live through, but it was merely personal, nothing that really mattered to the world at large. When James was buried, Nannie had come home, but she wouldn't stay. She left again, soon. She said, "You won't need me." Nannie alone understood her mother's independence, she thought. And she told Nannie, "I can do for myself. I can't think of anything I need. I raise all my food, and the tobaccer brings in enough to trade with. And I can always take in sewing. Jewell looks after me, makes sure I have coal oil and stovewood. And James left enough to see me through."

Nannie didn't come home often—only every year or two. She made her home up in the North, but she wouldn't take one of Christie's quilts to keep her warm. The tie between them was like a spider's thread that had cut loose and was floating free in the air.

She didn't tell any of this to Margaret Shelburne. Because of her babies, Christie had had the chance to open her mind and drink in the new and strange. But she and James never went anywhere together after that trip in the summer of 1900, except to Dundee for funerals. Now she was out in the world again, dealing with strangers and trains and schedules and appointments and not knowing what might happen next or whether there would be a wreck or a flat tire or if they would find anything to eat. For so long now, it had been her pleasure to think small—to think about whether the clabber was ready for churning, or the tomato plants ready for suckering, or whether the spring rains would be enough to carry them through the summer.

Margaret sang some silly Hit-Parade ditties to fill Christie's silence. She stopped to clean bugs from the windshield. After buying gas, she drove on, past many lakes, blue against the spruce and pine. The squared-off farm fields turned to forest, and they sped along like pioneers in a hurry. The car rode smoothly, stones flying.

In the deepening wilderness, there seemed to be such riches—enough water and sun and soil for any creature to thrive. On the way up to Chicago yesterday, Christie saw crowds of the destitute camped along the fringes of the towns. She saw a breadline snaking along a main street. The train passed by like someone improperly going to the head of the line. At home, tramps stopped, and she gave them all the food she could spare. She grew a larger garden this year. She felt fortunate, for she couldn't lose her land. Her babies had paid for it—the money she and James had owed Wad.

"We're almost there!" Margaret sang out, as they began passing tourist cabins and eating places.

Christie noticed an old depot and two lumber mills that appeared to be shut down. A banner stretched across the road—WELCOME TO CALLANDER. A hand-painted banner in front of a hotel said BLESS OUR BABIES. Here and there she saw laundry hanging—dull, plain colors faded from wear. Then, a steep road led up a hill to the tiny town of Corbeil. She saw unmistakable signs of the town's new fame—numerous roadside souvenir stands and more places to eat. Automobiles clustered like dead bugs around the Q-Inn, a tourist camp.

At an intersection, a man in a dark wool cap directed them with a gnarled finger. "Down the new road," he said, smiling broadly.

Margaret said to Christie as they continued, "Are you tired?"

"No, I'm all right."

"Are you sure?"

"I don't think I'll fall asleep."

"Aren't you excited? I'm simply enthralled."

Christie didn't answer. "The road does look new," she said after a while.

"The quints certainly accomplished a great amount for this area," Margaret said. She was not really anything like Amanda, Christie decided. Margaret possessed an air of authority that Amanda had been denied, and she lacked Amanda's gracefulness.

A man in a red uniform directed them into a parking place at the far end of a large asphalt parking lot.

"Can you walk that far?" Margaret asked Christie anxiously.

"I ain't crippled."

Margaret combed her hair and freshened her lip rouge. "We ask for Madame Dupuy when we go in," she said for about the fifth time that day.

"She might not talk English," said Christie.

"Do you know any French?" Margaret asked.

"Not really." Christie remembered a French gymnast in Boone's scrapbook, a man who climbed up the outside of the Eiffel Tower the year it was built. He was called the Human Fly, *La Mouche humaine.* She remembered the most absurd things. Yet she couldn't remember the color of Boone's eyes, or if he had been right-handed or left-handed.

A steel-mesh double fence surrounded several redwood structures, including a large central building that housed the miracle children. The building, made of redwood logs, was picturesque but simple— nothing like the pretentious Forsythe mansion. The line of people waiting for the gates to open at two o'clock was stirring with anticipation, like the crowd at a picture-show theater, Christie thought. It wasn't gloomy, like the breadline she had seen. A man came by, renting out binoculars.

"You can get a better look through these," he said to Margaret. "They don't let you get right up next to them in the observation building. They keep you far away so you won't disturb the little girls and breathe germs on them."

"I don't think we'll be that far away," said Margaret, nudging Christie significantly. "We're going to meet these little girls," she said gleefully. "I'm sure we will."

"You must know somebody who knows somebody!" a woman behind them said.

The people in line were modestly dressed and clean. Christie picked out two pairs of courting couples; some young people made jumpy and atwitter by their youth, occasionally bursting into laughter; young women in short skirts; girls in school uniforms; even families with their own small children. She recognized the lunch wrappings, the cigarette stubs, the orange peels, the plum seeds scattered around. It had been just the same in 1900. But the surroundings were so different. Here, in this Northern landscape with the evergreen forests close by, she did not see a single horse. There was a smooth, new road and a large, well-built house. Across the road she could see the old farmhouse where the girls were born. It was a faded yellow with a red-shingle roof. It was smaller than the house where Christie's babies were born.

The wait was long and the talk idle. Christie closed her eyes to rest for a moment, but that threw her off balance, so she braced herself against a small souvenir shack, which offered a cornucopia of official quintuplets goods—cups, spoons, postcards, dolls, and the like. She closed her eyes again, but she couldn't escape the voices.

"They were so poor, there wasn't even electricity in the house when they were born."

"They're just like royalty now."

"Do you want to buy a fertility stone?"

"Go away, old lady. That's just a stone from the roadside."

"Those little babies were blue when they were born."

"They were almost too little to live. It's a miracle."

"I heard that Madame Dionne had a vision of the Virgin the day before she gave birth."

The Dionne babies were premature, but Christie's babies weren't. Hers were fully formed, and much heavier than she had read the Dionnes were. Hers could have lived. The anger that had worn away over the years started to swell in her again, like an oak gall bursting and dispersing its acrid brown powder. She tried not to feel envious, but when the gates opened and a guide escorted the crowd into the handsome log building and led them down a corridor that paralleled the playground, Christie had to blink back tears.

The windows along the corridor of a *U*-shaped gallery faced the outdoor playground where the five little girls, dressed identically except for different-colored caps, were playing tag. The windows were designed so that the visitors could see out but the children could not see in. Christie pressed her face against the glass and watched the little girls cavorting and giggling. She could hear their laughter through the closed windows, above the chatter of the crowd. She anchored herself at a spot near the center, and the people restlessly pressed around her, commenting and squealing, as if they were at a circus, watching lions or apes. Outside, the children rushed up to an adult who appeared then. They all went to a door of a small building and hauled out five tricycles. For a while, Christie watched the little girls ride their tricycles up and down a stretch of concrete. One of the girls, in a white cap, suddenly hopped off and ran straight toward the windows, then turned a somerset. Everyone around Christie laughed, saying the child was showing off for the visitors. The child waved and seemed to look straight at Christie.

"It was Emilie," the guide said. She was a girl in a red uniform.

Emily Sue, Christie thought.

"They can't see us, can they?" someone asked.

"Supposedly not, but actually they can make out some of the faces, and they know you're here," the guide said. "It's made them into little exhibitionists, I'm afraid."

The guide identified the children, one by one, and spoke of their history, but Christie barely heard. She studied their hair, their size, their playful races on their tricycles. She imagined sewing their clothes, giving them baths, teaching them to tie their shoes, to roll biscuits, to pick beans. Now the little girls were swinging on their jungle gym. Christie wondered when her children would have learned to top tobacco, or to catch a crawfish. She remembered teaching Nannie to make her first four-patch quilt blocks. She could picture Mollie Lee, blond and serious, learning to use a broom, Emily Sue gathering hickory nuts in her apron. She pictured the boys too. They would be larger than the girls, tagging along at James's heels, just as Clint and Jewell had done. She thought about feeding them solid food—mashed potatoes and beans at first, and graduating later to fried chicken. She imagined them fighting over the pulley bone. She thought about the frazzle of keeping up with five children. Would it have been too much for her? Would they have tired her more than what she had actually gone through? These little girls wore expensive clothes and had their black, straight hair carefully curled each day. They were wearing little overall playsuits and jackets and caps and high ankle boots with laces. They would have looked like little boys if not for their curls peeping out from under their caps. Christie stood there, lost in time, gazing at the girls. The guide talked on, about Ontario's responsibility for the quintuplets' training. She used the word "training" several times.

"I've asked for Madame Dupuy," Margaret said, reappearing at Christie's elbow. "The guard at the exit door told us to wait for her after the crowd has gone."

When the children's playtime was over, the people drifted out the gate, exclaiming over how happy the quints seemed, what lovely children they were, so well behaved.

The red-garbed guide directed Christie and Margaret to a private office, where they waited for Madame Dupuy. Christie examined the charts posted on a bulletin board. There was a noonday meal chart for each girl for the current week. Christie read that Emilie had eaten two servings of dessert every day but Monday and Tuesday and two servings of the first course every day this week and two pieces of bread or biscuits on Monday and Wednesday. The chart said Emilie disliked the food on Tuesday, that she played at the table with Yvonne on Monday and with Marie last Saturday. She didn't finish the biscuits on Monday and Wednesday or the first course on Tuesday. She was allowed no dessert on

Tuesday because she didn't finish the main course. She ate with the right hand every day. Her food was removed as punishment for playing with Yvonne at the table on Monday. Next to the meal chart were some toilet charts. Each trip to the toilet was noted, along with the time of day, the length of time spent, and additional circumstances.

A woman with a clipboard burst in and smiled quickly when she saw Christie reading the toilet charts. "So you're the Hopewell mother," the woman said genially. "I'm so pleased to meet you." She spoke with an accent, which Christie presumed to be French. "No one here had any idea there had been another set of quintuplets in North America! I've spoken with Madame Dionne, who is not here presently. She visits early in the day and sometimes again later. If she comes today, she will be here at four o'clock, and she will be happy to meet with you then between four-fifteen and four-thirty, while the children are having their quiet period, before the dinner hour."

Madame Dupuy paused to check something on her clipboard, marking it with her pencil. "Excuse me, I had forgotten to make an entry about the children's playtime. I'm wondering why Yvonne seemed slightly less active today. She seemed to snap at Annette like a puppy with a hurt paw. Did you notice that one of them seemed a little less energetic than the others?"

Margaret and Christie shook their heads no. All the girls seemed healthy, Christie thought, so full of vigor. And she was ashamed to admit she couldn't tell them apart.

Madame Dupuy scribbled some more. "Do you have any questions I can help you with?"

"Why don't they live with their mama and daddy?" Christie asked.

"The Canadian government, in order to protect them from exploitation, is sponsoring the quintuplets," Madame Dupuy explained. "They are King George's wards. The money that has been raised for their support goes into a trust fund for them. We make sure the quints are given every opportunity for education and training. Providing the proper training of five spirited little girls would be quite a challenge, more than parents with several other children could manage! These little girls require a considerable staff to care for them and to train them. There is so much involved! We keep a strict schedule, and discipline is very strong, although we take care not to exert unusual pressures on them. We use an isolation room for punishments, because the children are very close and so devoted to each other that to deprive one of their little society works as a swift, efficient corrective. We make sure that each little person has her share—whether it's food or toys or a place at table. For example, I think you can see their chairs if you peek through this door into the dining room. Annette's color is red, and she has a maple leaf on her chair. Marie has the blue with the teddy bear. Emilie's color is white, with a tulip. Cecile, with the turkey symbol, is green, while Yvonne has a bluebird on a pink background. Unfortunately, you can't see the bluebird on Yvonne's chair from this angle. The children come out to the playground just after their afternoon naps. We try to regulate everything they do so that no little child feels any less than any of her sisters and no one of them is able to assert power over the others."

"I imagine they have loads of toys," said Margaret. "And five of each one, I suppose!"

"Oh, indeed. Dolls and doll furniture. The tricycles you saw. And of course they have books, a piano and other musical instruments, a gramophone. They spend a great amount of time with building blocks; they have easels for painting. They work with plasticine a great deal. But we don't indulge them. We teach them responsibility. Each one has her own toy box, and she has to keep it in order. Also, they are expected to clear their own dishes from their little tables." Madame Dupuy shifted her clipboard to a nest under her arm and stared inquiringly at Margaret. "And how old are your babies, Madame?"

"Oh, not me," said Margaret, blushing and pointing at Christie.

"They were taken away from me," said Christie abruptly. "I don't reckon a mama and a daddy could have trained five little ones," she said bitterly. "We couldn't get a crop out if we had to fool with all them charts. Why, I hadn't thought of training younguns the way we train our mules at home." She would have gone on in this vein, but suddenly felt it wasn't worth it. "I need to set down," she said.

"Oh, I'm so sorry, I should have shown you a place to sit." Madame Dupuy led them to a small waiting room with some soft chairs. "You may wait here, and I'll come and get you when Madame Dionne arrives. May I offer you some tea?"

Christie shook her head. "Does Mrs. Dionne talk English?" she asked.

"She doesn't speak English, but she can understand some of it. I'm sure you'll manage." Madame Dupuy smiled broadly, revealing a bad tooth. "Two mothers with so much in common!"

Madame Dupuy left, and Christie held her head to stop the throbbing that had invaded her brain. It was like a loose plank vibrating against the side of a house in a fierce wind. What did the sensation remind her of? A dumb-bull at a shivaree. So long ago.

"Do you have a headache?" Margaret asked. "I'll get you some powders."

"No. I don't like to take powders," said Christie. "Thank ye kindly."

A woman in a white coat passed by the door. They heard a man's voice, then some adult laughter. Somewhere a gramophone was playing "These Foolish Things." In her mind, Christie listened again to the children's voices that she had heard through the closed gallery windows while she watched the girls at play. It was the squealing of five small children, all equal but separate and different, the joy of small children who haven't encountered any pain yet except the pain of birth itself. There was nothing more precious on earth than that sound. When the five girls had squealed as they rode their tricycles toward the window, Christie was sure they could see her face pressed against the glass. Emilie, the one in the white ribbon, had waved to her.

Christie stood up, feeling stronger. "I'll be leaving now," she said to Margaret. "I don't need to talk to Mrs. Dionne."

"After we've come all this distance?" cried Margaret. "It's just a half hour yet."

"She don't talk English," said Christie, walking briskly down the corridor. Margaret tagged along, protesting and trying to keep up, for Christie could walk fast on a smooth, flat surface. "I don't want to bother her," said Christie, her eyes straight ahead on the open door, with the steel-mesh fences just beyond.

VII

Birthday

1963

WELL, THEY'VE DRAGGED IT ALL UP AGAIN. SINCE YOU WERE HERE, they're fixing to have Hopewell Quintuplets Day this summer. I thought everybody had forgot about my babies, but somebody at the paper figured out it was my ninetieth birthday. (A little bird told them! Tell me the truth now.) And so they want to ride me around the square at the head of a parade in a Cadillac convertible with the high school band a-playing. Some big dudes come out to see me—the mayor, the newspaper editor, and some others. They seemed just like the same bunch that come out to the house one time back then. This little mayor, he says, "We're trying to get Elvis Presley up here to meet you." He beat his gums a right smart, and I had to laugh. He claims his cousin is married to one of Elvis Presley's daddy's cousin's nephews— or somebody—so he expects to get him here. (He talked mighty big.)

I told those folks I was just an old country woman and wouldn't know how to act in town. But the truth is I've had a more unusual experience than most anybody in town is likely to go through. And I reckon Elvis Presley has probably felt something like that too, even at his young age. He must be so whirligigged by all that's happened to him. From his picture he kindly makes me think of James—that young body, shaped so perfect and a good color from the sun and not much hair on him except on his head. James had a good head of hair. Our first year, I'd just stand back and look at him and be pleased right out of my skin. That's the best year of a marriage—that first glow of love, when your bodies are young and supple—but nobody would believe an old woman would know anything like that or ever even think about it.

When you're old, you feel so wise sometimes, it seems like you've learnt everything you need to know before you die. But it don't stop you from wanting to repeat ever day, from here to eternity. Just the simple pleasures—coffee and bacon-and-eggs in the morning; the sunrise, which I *never* miss; finding a bird feather on the porch step; or hearing a bull bawling to his cows; seeing a pair of kittens tangled up a-playing; seeing roses bloom on the trellis once again, from the same rosebush I started in 1897; finding a fresh egg that's still got a sticky spot. Do you know what I mean?

When Mama got old, she didn't want any kittens or flowers around. She just wanted to dwell on herself. Maybe she was thinking about meeting the Lord—dreading it. She always thought she was so unprepared. But I reckon I'm ready for just about anything. I wouldn't be surprised if there wasn't anybody at the pearly gates to meet me; there might not even be pearly gates, but just those garage doors people have now that open straight up. And the welcoming committee up there might not be angels and saints but some big sprawling family, like the Wheelers, who run the place and won't let you have a minute's peace. It would be just my luck. But I reckon a gang of Wheelers would be better than a pack of preachers that think they've got all the answers.

When you've lived this long and you've survived something terrible, folks want to make something out of it. They want to know how you made out. What's your secret? How'd you live so long? they ask.

Whiskey and squirrel stew, some old coot will say. And a pack a day of cigarettes.

Me, I always took an interest in things. I was always busy a-doing something and trying to find out something that nobody else would think to fool with. Partly, it's just keeping ahold of your real self there inside, the same way you need to save out a little bit of sourdough for the next raising. When you're little, you notice ever bird feather and little worm and pig squeal you run across. But grown folks forget to notice the little things. When you have your own chillern, they're part you and part not-you, and then they get away from you and part of you goes with them. But you have to try to remember that part of you that's you and not them. That way, you can let them go.

I've had to let all my children go, at one time or another. There was one three-year stretch when I didn't even see Nannie's face. She turned her back on me when she went off from here. And the boys didn't know what to make of me for the longest time.

My babies would have lived if we'd knowed back then what they know now. The Dionne girls got all the help they needed—and more. You never saw as many play-pretties as they had. They seemed happy then, but I don't believe they could have turned out happy. There was just too much fuss. The things they done to those little girls wasn't right. I didn't envy them or their mama after I saw the way those little girls in Canada were handled. It made me wonder if James and me done the right thing, leaving our babies up there in Washington to be studied for science. Of course the babies wouldn't know. But even if they had lived, they wouldn't have been treated normal. At least they were spared that burden. I carried that burden for them.

For Hopewell, it was just a load of fun. They loved it back then, and then they forgot about it, and now they're finding out about it all over again. It'll entertain 'em for a while and then they'll be on to something else.

If I've had any bitterness all these years about what went on, it was really because of the truth about people, how they'll just eat you alive. And families can smother you. What I wanted was friends—out there, outside the whole thorny red-haw tree of a family. I needed to find some connections that weren't kin, that weren't threaded into me like quilting stitches. Mandy and me were as close as two people could be without being kin, and yet the trouble was we couldn't be close enough because we had too much kin to tend to all the time. She was lonesome, I feel. I still miss that girl. I couldn't help her because I was too quilted up with these kinfolks-stitches. When James and me went out on that trip, I hated everybody that flocked to see my babies. But underneath, I've come to think, I was looking for something. I wanted the free and unattached generousness of a stranger meeting a stranger, where nothing familiar can cast a shadow of obligation on you, or a mirror reflection. No influences, no judgments. I thought it would be more satisfying, and it wouldn't always break your heart. I wanted to explore the whole world. Others. I wanted to know others. When I was a little girl, I went out behind the church with Finis Burnside, a little boy who was visiting Dundee with his mama. He told me his granddaddy had been killed in the War. I wanted him to tell me all about it. Did his granddaddy wear a uniform? What did he eat? Did they go to the War on horses and have guns? And then Finis and me were caught and switched for being behind the church together, out of sight. His mama told my mama, and I never got to talk to Finis again. When we got old enough for boys to pay attention to girls, he came back to our church once, but he never noticed me and he never knew how I was burning with questions.

And now you want to know everything from me. I ain't sentimental, and I can't cry for those babies no more. Time gives you a different way of looking at things. Looking back on it now—all the people coming to see my babies—I hated it, but I loved it too, in a way. It made me feel like somebody. It gave me something to look forward to. Women didn't get to do things back then like they can now. But I didn't realize what I was feeling half the time, I was so hurt, and the horribleness of so much of it just turned me into a statue—or a pillar of salt, I reckon, like Lot's wife. I lost my babies, and a lot of the time I couldn't register a thought or tear. None of it seemed real. But I did love the recognition, I know now, and we went traipsing around that fall because I wanted more of it. I wanted to get away from the farm and see what was out there in the wide blue world. That desire blinded me so I couldn't separate the babies from what-all else was happening. The way I look at it now—what I went through was hard to believe; everything around me was just purely unbelievable. And I was mad at everybody too, and hurt. I was in shock the whole time, but I didn't know it. For years, I'd have dreams that I was still chasing around after that trunk, through one traveling show after another.

In one of the dreams the trunk got away from us, and we had to go to a carnival to find it. And we'd run through all the sideshows—the fat-lady, the Siamese twins, the snake pit, the wolf-man, the frog-girl— except they'd be all mixed up. The wolf-man would be Siamese twins, and the fat-lady would be all covered up with snakes. I'd always wake up before we found the trunk. The traveling shows were more respectable in some ways back then, for people were starved for entertainment. And we didn't have picture shows, so anything odd would attract attention. But looking back, I reckon one of those midways was kindly like a nightmare. I remember a woman with three breasts. And she let people *look*. But it turned out the extra one was on her stomach, and that's the only one she showed. And there was another woman with a hand coming out of a hump on her back. And one with fish-scale skin.

Sometimes, in broad daylight, I'd suddenly be on that trip again. I'd be peeling peaches or milking a cow and I'd see that trunk opening up and the feather pillers would be coming out by theirselves, and the glass case would appear, raising up all by itself. Once I imagined it broke. I was a-sweeping up a fruit jar that had fell on the hearth and broke. A mess of dirt and bark that had come in with the stovewood was all mixed up with the broken glass, and I thought I was sweeping up that glass casket and the babies had turned to dust.

When James and me got home that fall, Nannie wouldn't know us. And Wad was driving Clint and Jewell hard. Alma started in on me one day when I oughter been getting up grub for the hands. She found me up in the loft cutting pictures out of a magazine. She said I'd lost my senses because I was taking time out for myself. I know they put it to Nannie that I wasn't fit to be her mama, and looking back now I guess they thought about sending me off to Hopkinsville to the asylum. Understand, I wasn't the least bit crazy. But I was so changed I fit in even less than I did before. I felt like I could endure anything after what I'd been through. I felt like I could do anything and that I never had to explain myself. It made me plumb sassy. I reckon that's what got to Wad and Alma.

But after that, there wasn't any time for anybody to go crazy anyway. For several years, till they straightened out the tobaccer prices, all hands had to keep busy to get food on the table. I just kept a-cooking and churning and sewing and working in the fields and the garden, and in the fall I cut dark-fire like always. I never let up. I just put the past behind me and looked to what was at hand. But I held on too hard to my chillern. My apron strings were knotted so tight they popped and the chillern just flew off.

I'm glad your mama sent you down here to me, child. You tell her I don't mind talking about it now, I'm not scared to. You've seen to that, and I'm grateful that you dug it out. But if she does come back for my birthday, I'll think I've already died and gone to Heaven, I'll be so happy. Nannie and me didn't see each other a whole lot over the years, so it was hard to get to know each other like grown-up women-folks, but really we were always loving underneath, I believe. With her always so far away, it seemed like there was something between us, like a hard anvil we couldn't hug through. Law, she's an old woman now too. You look so much like her when she was your age.

I had to stop and thread a new tape into this machine. I'm glad you left this thing because I can't scarcely read my feeble hen-scratch any-more. If I'm using this contraption right, you can hear my voice and stop it any time you want to and repeat it anytime you want to. I fooled with it a right smart while. It would speak, but then it started to jabber. These electric voices are still a mystery to me. But I imagine any coun-try that can invent television can go to the moon, and I reckon we'll go there before the decade is out because that's what the President wants. To tell you the truth, I wouldn't mind going myself, and if I live long enough for them to start up a passenger line, I'll sign up to go. I mean it.

How times has changed. You wanted to know how it was back then, but it wouldn't thrill your heart to know. It was good in some ways, but it was a misery in the heart so much of the time for so many. Of course I could claim it was worse for me 'cause of what happened, but I guess I won't claim that. I used to ask why the Lord made women to suffer so. Alma said women suffered because men wouldn't be able to stand what women go through, but I told her I thought women were able to stand it because they had had the practice.

When you're young you think you're the center of the world, and then later on, when you're old, you do again. I hate that notion and wish I didn't think about myself so much. I promised myself not to get like that. I think about Dove McKendree Wheeler. Now I understand her mind. What happens is you lose your sense of responsibility, and you just don't care anymore. You don't care what anybody thinks, and you realize there's not much you'll do from now on out that will mat-ter—at all, to anybody.

I was thinking again about that Elvis Presley. He's a pretty boy.

He's like us, not stuck-up or citified. He surely does make me think of James, when he come a-courting, all mellow eyes and warm mouth, with a devilment in his grin. You didn't know what dirty thoughts an old woman could have, did you?

I had to stop this a minute 'cause I got tickled.

After you were here, I got to thinking about what-all I didn't tell you about them days. I get rusty in talking to people, and I stopped telling my life tale years ago because I didn't want to push it on people. But I got stirred up about it when you were here and it's weighed on my mind. There's things I never told nobody, of course, and maybe I will now that I'm fixing to die—don't grin and say, Oh, no, of course you're not; I never could abide hypocrites. I could hang on till I'm a hundred and seven, I reckon, but it ain't likely. My breathing's good and I still manage for myself and I ain't had no doctor since 1947 and I feel pretty good. And I still drive and I ain't got a scratch on my license! Still, people don't live forever. Some don't even get a start. But I've hung on a long time. Maybe I had to live long enough for all my lost babies, to live their lives, the lives they didn't get to have. So I think back on it a good deal these days.

When we first come to Wad Wheeler's to live, I kindly got used to all that commotion, so when all the strangers come messing and gauming all over the place, it didn't seem so unusual at first. I remember one day when I was in bed with the babies, a man climbed right through the front winder, just like it was the regular way to get in. Alma got mad at him for letting the waspers in. I never will forget that. It seemed just as natural for a total stranger to barge through the winder as anything, but I remember staring at him, and it didn't come to me till a minute later that there was something wrong—like one of those big complicated pictures with a thousand things going on where you're asked, "What's wrong with this picture?" That man stepping through the winder seems like what you'd pick out.

Everybody wanted something. There was a Mrs. Blankenship that made my skin crawl. She wanted to use the babies to make her feel important. We owed the Blankenships money at the time. If I get to Heaven and see her again, I just might not speak to her. But surely the Lord wouldn't send you to Heaven and let it turn out to be a place where everybody who made you miserable in life shows up to do it all over again. That would be Hell, not Heaven, wouldn't it? I never got it sorted out how two people who made one another miserable in life would both show up in the same place after they die. Dove told me you'd change your feelings in Heaven and you'd turn out to love that person who made you miserable in life. Dove didn't have the slightest doubt about Heaven. She thought it would all work out even. She lived to be eighty-three and then went off to join that soldier-boy husband of hers. I often imagined the pair of them gallivanting around up in Heaven, and it's made me laugh many a time. Just imagine them going to the show together!

It's later. I had to go and feed the chickens. I guess I'll round up a little cabbage and cornbread for myself. I don't eat much of a night. I was thinking about Dove and Heaven, and I have to say this. The truth, child, and God may strike me dead as I say this—if there is a God, and if He's paying attention—the truth is, I don't believe there's a Heaven, and I haven't believed it in many years. I saw that feller climb through that winder right to my bedside, and I could see deep into human nature right there. I saw those little babies die one by one, and I saw a world of people surrounding my bedside from the time my littluns was born, and even more of those people flocking around when we went on the trip, and I lost my faith. I didn't know it at the time, and I never told anybody, not even James. But I believe he lost his faith too, and he never let on to me either. Go back and look at that picture I let you have—the one from the newspaper, with us and the little glass casket. Tell me if that ain't two people that's lost their faith. Look at their eyes.

In the last years—the years since my hair got purely white, I'd say—I've stopped fretting so much. I fretted all my life, always wanting something to be different, always wanting to be somewhere else. Back then, I had to please this one and that one, and Wad Wheeler ruled the roost, and of course you always had to serve the menfolks first, and you were a slave to the weather and the seasons because you had to eat. But I reckon if you live long enough you can learn some peace. It's like I've finally caught up with myself. Missy, I have had quite a life!

Back then families were so big, it was boardinghouse reach, where the younguns got trompled underfoot and a man and wife might sleep on a pallet in the same room with an old man off in the corner a-wheezing and a-wallering on a corn-shuck mattress. People had so many chillern, and the chillern didn't move off the way they do now. But back then the whole town, the country, the people in the newspapers, they come a-running, right into our front room. I believe they just thought the whole nation was one big family. Living that first year at Wad's, I knew how cruel a big family could be. Nowadays people are happier spread out, with just a few to a house. I'm sure everybody breathes easier. The happiest time in my life was when James and Nannie and the little boys and me lived in our own little house and James built the furniture. Up there at Wad's homeplace now, it seems odd that there's just the five of them—my grandson Willie and his wife,

Lucy, and the three boys. She's got a washer and dryer. With her a-working real estate and him a-running his milk route and the boys in school, it's like nobody lives there.

You wanted to know what happened to some of the others. Wad's boys had a hard row to hoe, and they hit bottom during the tobaccer war. They could grow enough to eat, but they were low on stock and didn't have much to trade with. Joseph was down in his back, and Mary Ann had to take care of the stock. When Joseph's and Henry's boys growed up, they moved off. Once they started in dividing up the land, there wasn't enough for everybody. No, Boone didn't die of TB. He lived to a fair old age. There wasn't a thing wrong with him but asthma. He just wanted women to wait on him. Up on that landing he breathed enough dust to keep him wheezing. I read in the paper one time about mold, how you can have mold in your piller and breathe it till you're sick. I believe he was breathing in moldy feathers all that time. Mold—that's probably what caused them feather crowns to form. Did I tell you about those things? Ha!

If you think of me from time to time, or tell your chillern about me, just promise me you'll tell it fair. You don't have to make me out to be something I'm not, but I want you to try to understand the way it was for people back then and not blame them. They was just too busy, and there was a lot that went on 'cause they just didn't know any better. That's no excuse for some things, such as the way everybody treated the colored people, but it was how we were told to think. Oh, that was a terrible crime, what we done to those people. I'm glad they're not going to stand for it anymore.

Missy, don't ever think we lived in the good old days. Back then chillern grew up the best they could, like birds pushed out of the nest and left to flutter through danger till they learnt to fly. Alma claimed you had to be hard with younguns so they'd be tough, but the ones that were tender-hearted, like Dulcie and Hub, suffered. Wad liked to make fun of chillern, and him and his boys was big teases. But the time he whipped Jewell with a tobaccer stick James went against him. I don't believe chillern should be ruled too much. Seeing chillern playing and shouting out and running around free is the greatest joy on this earth. It ain't fair to take that away from them. I reckon that's why, when poor Little Bunch took those fits, everybody pretended it wasn't serious. There wasn't anything you could do about fits.

Anybody who met Mandy would say there was tragedy written all over her face and wouldn't be surprised then at how she turned out. But the family didn't think she had it in her to do what she did. Mandy wasn't really to blame for anything except not thinking better of herself. She didn't run off with Thomas Hunt, like I half expected she would do. It was in the winter of the year after she lost Little Bunch that James found her hanging with the hams and shoulders in the smokehouse. She had looped a rope around her neck and swung off the grain chest. Nobody would have thought she had such courage. It nearly killed Wad. He took on like a lost lamb, and he kept asking, "Why? Why? Why did it happen?" He never had the slightest idea why. She was hanging right between the prettiest-trimmed ham and a slab of bacon. It kills me to recollect her beautiful hands a-hanging.

A man will die doing his work—taking it further, experimenting, going up against some force of nature that turns around and whips him—but if a woman doesn't die in birthing, she may pick her own escape from heartache or neglect. It's the only way she can say "I'm free." That's what Mandy was a-saying when she strung herself up.

Of course James died in the middle of his work. He went so sudden. It was several years after the news about Clint from overseas, and my sorrow just renewed itself. Nannie had gone off by then, but she did come home for the funeral.

When the wreck happened, Jewell went slamming into Alma's house to get somebody to help him lift the tractor off of his papa. It had fell over with James on the creek bank. The bank was real steep, and James was setting up so high. He pitched forwards and it fell on him. By the time Jewell got down there with Henry and Hub and some others, James was dead. He was unconscious from the first, Jewell said, so he didn't have any pain. Jewell had been so determined to farm by the new ways, and he just had to have the first tractor on our road. I've never seen such grief in a man as Jewell felt for his papa. But I told him that what happens happens, and even if you were the one that caused it, you have to go on. It wasn't a crime, it was an accident, so he oughtn't to blame hisself. "You have to blame the way God runs things," I told him.

They're saying they want to bring my babies back here and have them buried proper, do honor to the community. I hope they don't do it. There's no honor at home, child. It's all just flattering talk, airy like a angel-food cake. They'll stir up my soul if they bring them babies back. As far as I can tell, folks have got to be a-tinkering with the way things are. Either they fool with the spirit or they mess around with the body. Well, it ain't just one or t'other, I figure. But then I always did want things both ways.

If they do it, they'll have to wait till I'm gone. It's up to Nannie and Jewell. I can't bear following another trail to join those babies again. I couldn't look at them again. Those babies a-laying there under that glass is burned in my brain forever. That was so unnatural. But then maybe that glass has already broken, and the babies have turned to dust.

Now that my life has come down to a few little things, it's all driven inside me. That's called memory, I guess. I've tried not to live on just memories. I'll tell you something about memory. It's like if you took anxiousness or dread and put it up in front of a mirror. What you'd see would be memory, like it's coming out the other side of an event. An event is always worse before it happens or after it happens. But not at the time it happens. You can get through that, because it carries you along. It's afterward that gets you.

I've buried a heap of Wheelers, but there's new ones all over the place. Wad and Alma's sister, Delphinia, left a bunch, though they didn't carry on the Wheeler name. And Joseph and Henry put out enough to fill up a church. Just from Jewell and Nannie, I've got eight grandchillern and twenty great-grandchillern and five great-great grandchillern, at last count. And if them five babies, and Clint, had all lived, they would have plumb broke the family tree. I'm afraid there's too many people on this planet as it is. Yet the Wheeler graveyard has the lonesomest feel to it, way out in the middle of nowhere in that oak grove. Out there, the Wheelers are probably getting along just about like they always did, since they talked past each other and never said what was in their hearts. Out there, you can almost hear their voices blending with the breeze, and now and then the train whistles off in the distance, making background music.

I'm too tired now to go on, and I better turn this thing off before I talk you clean to death. But if you come down here again next month with Nannie, I'll tell you more about the old-timey days. Tell her the March flowers will be up.

One more thing: When I told you all I did about James, I wasn't certain you understood. I want to get it straight that he was a good man at heart. He never said a harsh word to me after we got home from that trip. I always see him as a young man, with his devilish grin. Imagine him, riding home on a chestnut horse with them two pretty cake-stands I showed you. He was the thoughtfulest man. He worked hard for his chillern. In his heart, he loved those babies, and it hurt him to lose them. He just didn't know how to take what fate handed us. I didn't neither, but I've had longer to stew on it.

But I don't aim to live out my days all hunched up over my memories. I want to watch the sun come up and hear a hen cackle over a new-laid egg and feel a kitten purr. And I want to see a flock of black-birds whirl over the field, making music. Things like that are absolutely new ever time they happen.